FOR BETTER, FOR WORSE

FOR BETTER, FOR WORSE

Elizabeth Jeffrey

This first world edition published 2013
in Great Britain and the USA by
SEVERN HOUSE PUBLISHERS LTD of
19 Cedar Road, Sutton, Surrey, England, SM2 5DA.

British Library Cataloguing in Publication Data

Jeffrey, Elizabeth.
  For better, for worse.
  1. Love stories.
  I. Title
  823.9'14-dc23

ISBN-13: 978-0-7278-8301-8 (cased)

All Severn House titles are printed on acid-free paper.

Severn House Publishers support The Forest Stewardship Council [FSC],
the leading international forest certification organisation. All our titles that
are printed on Greenpeace-approved FSC-certified paper carry the FSC logo.

MIX
Paper from
responsible sources
FSC
www.fsc.org   FSC® C018575

Typeset by Palimpsest Book Production Ltd.,
Falkirk, Stirlingshire, Scotland.
Printed and bound in Great Britain by
MPG Books Ltd., Bodmin, Cornwall

One

Stella Nolan got stiffly down from the train and stood on the platform, her valise in her hand, her body rigid with uncertainty. The other passengers who had alighted at the same time milled round her, ignoring her, too anxious to get out of the biting late-afternoon wind and home to their families to pay any attention to the lonely figure waiting there.

It had been a long, exhausting journey; the trains had been dirty and crowded with all aspects of humanity, from weary and wounded soldiers relieved to be back from the horror of the trenches to excited shoppers laden with parcels, eager to celebrate Christmas. It was the first peaceful Christmas for four years, but the aftermath of war still hung over everything. In the towns that the train had passed through it was apparent that many of the shops and houses needed a coat of paint, and even the excitement of Christmas couldn't mask the air of shabby weariness that prevailed in most of the people. Few families hadn't lost a son, husband or brother in the trenches and the predominance of black mourning, or at the very least black armbands, in the jostling crowd added to the gloom of the winter afternoon.

Stella waited, scanning the platform as the crowd thinned, a tall, rather pale, anxious-looking figure. While she could never have been called pretty in the accepted sense, with her large, dark-lashed hazel eyes and regular features she was, nevertheless, strikingly attractive and she carried herself well. She was wearing a dark-blue ankle-length coat with a fur collar, and a matching fur hat perched on her auburn hair. Like most others, she wore a black mourning band on her sleeve.

She chewed her lip uneasily. She hoped they hadn't forgotten she was coming, she had been told she would be met at the station. Then she relaxed slightly and gave a sigh of relief as she saw a tall young man in gaiters and a flat cap emerging through the smoke from the engine; he was obviously looking for her.

He quickened his step when he saw her. 'Mrs Nolan?' he asked with a slightly nervous smile, snatching off the cap to reveal a shock of black curly hair.

'That's right.' She smiled at him with relief. 'I take it you're Mr Hogg?'

'That's me. Henry Hogg, Major Anderson's man and general handyman at Warren's End.'

'Ah, yes, my . . . Mrs Nolan senior wrote that you would be meeting me.'

'Can I take your bag, Ma'am? The trap's just outside. I'm afraid it'll be a bit of a chilly journey, although I've put out a blanket for you to put round your knees.'

Stella gathered her coat more closely round her against the cold north wind as she handed him her valise. She noticed that he took it in his left hand and that he held his right hand and arm at a slightly odd angle. Since he was young and otherwise the picture of good health she assumed that he was yet another victim of the war that had just ended, but she didn't like to ask.

But as he turned away to lead her to where the pony and trap were waiting she noticed that there was a deformity in his right shoulder.

'No, Ma'am, as you can see, it's not a war wound, I was born with it,' he said without embarrassment. 'It kept me out of the army; they said a hunchback wouldn't be any use in the fighting.' He gave a short, bitter laugh. 'But I tried to do my bit. I went to work in a munitions factory. And that was a hell hole if ever there was one.'

'Well, it's all over now,' Stella said, hugging herself and shivering. 'Bombs and shells won't be needed any more, thank God.'

'Aye, thank God. And with any luck them munitions factories'll be shut down for good. Death traps, they were, I can tell you,' he said savagely as he helped her into the back of the trap and tucked the blanket round her. She noticed that despite his deformity he had no difficulty in using his right hand and arm. He lowered his voice. 'I was real sorry to hear about Master, er, Mr John,' he said quietly. 'To be killed like that, almost on the last day of the war . . .' He shook his head. 'It's a damned wicked, cruel thing, war is – begging your pardon at the language, Ma'am.' Touching his cap, red with embarrassment at his slip of the tongue, he hastily climbed up on to his seat then flicked the reins and the pony set off. 'Make yourself as comfortable as you can. It won't be long before we're there, Ma'am,' he said over his shoulder as they rattled across the river bridge and began the climb up the hill to the town.

Stella didn't reply. In fact, she was in no particular hurry to arrive at her destination, to meet the family of the wonderful man who in the course of less than three months had swept her off her feet, married her and left her a widow.

They had had so little time together. She caught her breath against the tears that still threatened as she remembered . . .

It had been love at first sight, which Stella had always regarded as a figment of cheap romances – until it happened to her. She was a VAD at Hill House, the convalescent home on the south coast where Captain John Nolan had been sent to recuperate after a nasty shoulder wound and battle exhaustion. John was there for eight weeks before he was declared fit for duty again. But those eight weeks had been long enough for them to meet, fall instantly in love and realize without any doubt that when the wretched war was over, which from all the signs wouldn't be long now, they wanted to spend the rest of their lives together.

'But why wait, darling? Why don't we get married before I go back?' he had asked impulsively as they lazed by the river bank, simply delighting in each other's company, on a hot late-August day.

'Oh, yes, please, John!' she had replied without hesitation. Then, some time later, she'd pulled away from him and asked, 'But what about your family? Won't they object?' Her own parents had been killed in a Zeppelin raid two years earlier and she had no other family.

He'd frowned. 'Why on earth should they object? They'll love you, just as I do. Well, not quite as I do . . .' he'd grinned, and pulled her to him again.

'But shouldn't we invite them to our wedding, John?'

'Darling, there simply isn't time,' he'd replied airily, uncaringly, since all his thoughts were for this lovely girl who had just consented to be his wife. 'We'll go and see them afterwards. You'll get on well with my sister, she's good fun.'

She pulled away from him. 'I didn't know you'd got a sister, John.'

'Oh, didn't I tell you? Yes, Rosalie. Her husband's in the army. At least he was until . . .' he stopped and gathered her to him again. 'But we don't want to talk about them now, you'll see them in a week or two. At the moment I've got more important things on my mind.'

So they were married by special licence at eight o'clock one misty morning, on the last day of September, at a little church overlooking the Solent; he in uniform and she in borrowed pale-blue shantung and a floppy hat. They spent a memorable week at a tiny hotel in a nearby village, and had planned a further week dutifully visiting his home so he could introduce her to his family. But before they could do that, he was suddenly recalled to his unit in France and had to go back, carrying a slightly out-of-focus photograph of the two of them outside the church in his breast pocket.

'It won't be for long, darling, I promise you,' he had said as she kissed him a tearful goodbye at the train. 'This wretched war will soon be over and then I'll be back with you. For good.'

But he was wrong. By the time the armistice was signed, five weeks later, he was dead; killed by a sniper's bullet. And Stella was a widow.

His parents wrote to the daughter-in-law they had never met and kindly invited her to stay with them for Christmas, an invitation she had been glad to accept since the other alternative was Christmas alone in her dreary bedsit or offering to do extra shifts at the convalescent home.

'Nearly there, ma'am,' Henry Hogg called over his shoulder.

She looked up, startled. She had been so busy with her thoughts that she had hardly registered that they had driven through the town and were now in a residential area on the outskirts. The houses here were mostly large, detached and standing in their own grounds.

'Ah, here we are, Warren's End.' Even as he spoke Henry turned into a short gravelled driveway and Stella saw the house, looking exactly as John had described it to her, square ivy-covered red brick, double-fronted, with four steps up to a front door with an elaborate fanlight. But what John hadn't told her was that it was an old house, a family house, a house that had nurtured the joys and sorrows of generations; a house whose long windows seemed to wink in welcome in the late-afternoon sunlight. A house with a character all its own.

The front door opened even before the trap had pulled up, and a rather austere-looking maid came forward. She was wearing a black afternoon dress and white frilly apron and a cap with long streamers hanging down behind.

She bobbed a sketchy curtsey.

'Good afternoon, Ma'am. Madam says I'm to take you through to the drawing room straight away – that is, if you're not too tired?' She looked questioningly at Stella. 'The family have waited afternoon tea.'

Stella smiled at her, but the girl's expression remained wooden and faintly disapproving. 'Then I wouldn't want to keep them waiting any longer,' she replied, pulling off her gloves. 'I must say a cup of tea would be very welcome.'

'If you'd like to take off your hat and coat, Ma'am, I'll take them up to your room with your bag when I've shown you to the drawing room.'

'Thank you . . . er?'

'Maisie, Ma'am.'

Swiftly patting her hair into place as she passed the hall mirror, Stella followed the girl – who she judged to be in her early twenties, about her own age – across a large black-and-white-tiled hall cluttered with small tables, hat stands, a large elephant's foot holding umbrellas, and an array of greenery in pots which were dominated by the aspidistra standing by the foot of the stairs in a large green jardinière on a tall stand. She noticed that the wide staircase, where a grandfather clock stood at the angle of the stair, was expensively carpeted in thick red turkey carpet. A telephone had pride of place on a small table opposite the front door, with a chair beside it.

Maisie knocked and pushed open a door opposite the staircase into a large, equally overfurnished room with a predominance of red plush. She bobbed a curtsey and stood aside.

'Thank you, Maisie. You can bring in the tea things now that young Mrs Nolan has arrived.' A rather plump late-middle-aged lady in black lace sitting beside the roaring fire waved the maid away and turned to look at Stella.

'Stella, my dear. At last you've come. We've so longed to meet this wonderful girl our son married in such a hurry,' she said. Her words were welcoming but her tone was cool and her smile didn't reach her eyes, which were a quite startling blue. 'Of course, he wrote and told us all about you, before . . .' She broke off and fished for a black-edged handkerchief.

A man, clearly her husband, who had been sitting in an armchair on the other side of the fire, had got to his feet as Stella entered the room. He was of medium height, with the suspicion of a paunch, grey thinning hair and a thick, well-trimmed moustache. 'Come now, Doreen,' he said briskly. 'Let the young lady get inside the door . . . She must be half-frozen after her journey.' He smiled, a genuinely welcoming smile, at Stella.

'Yes, yes, of course. What am I thinking of? Do come and sit by the fire, Stella.' But her tone was lukewarm.

As Stella approached the fire, she was shocked to see the dark-haired young man who had been sitting on the settee attempting to drag himself to his feet with the aid of two sticks. Had he been able to hold himself upright it was clear he would have been some six feet tall, but once on his feet he stood hunched over his sticks, his handsome, clean-shaven face lined with pain.

'Oh, for goodness' sake, Phil, don't try to stand up,' the young woman, obviously his wife, sitting beside him, said impatiently. 'You'll only draw attention to yourself.' She turned to Stella and looked her up and down, frowning slightly at her long dark-blue skirt and loose white blouse with a floppy blue bow at the neck.

'Our daughter, Rosalie,' Roger Nolan explained, since Rosalie seemed in no hurry to effect introductions. 'And Major Philip Anderson, her husband.'

Philip, propping himself on his sticks, so unable to shake her hand, smiled, gave Stella a friendly nod and murmured a few words of welcome before sinking back into his seat. Rosalie was a sharp-featured woman in her late twenties, her dark hair severely parted in the middle and plaited into two earphones. She was dressed completely in black, although her skirt revealed enough of her legs to announce that she was a 'modern' woman. Her blouse was plain to the point of austerity. Her only concession to femininity was the floppy bow at its neck. She hadn't bothered to stand up, and she frowned as she shook Stella's proffered hand.

'Why aren't you in proper mourning?' she asked rudely. 'John's only been dead a couple of months.'

'Nine weeks and three days, to be exact,' Stella said quietly, slightly taken aback by Rosalie's tone. Then, her voice firm, she added, 'But he insisted that if the worst happened I was not on any account to wear black. He said he didn't like it, and anyway it wouldn't suit me.' She gave a twisted little smile at the memory of his words and at how she had distracted him from speaking further about such a disagreeable subject. A faint flush rose to her cheeks as she recalled that it hadn't been difficult.

She glanced round the room, at the numerous pictures and mirrors all draped in black crêpe, the black ties of the men and the two jet-encrusted black-clad women, and knew how much John would have hated such an ostentatious display of grief. Her own loss was no less keenly felt because she kept it privately in her heart.

'I'm sure Rosalie meant no criticism, Stella. She speaks before she thinks,' Doreen said. 'Although of course it is a little unorthodox for a wife not to go into full mourning for her husband.' Her voice rose a little. 'But I'm sure it's of no consequence.' Her tone implied the complete opposite. She managed to force a smile. 'Well, now, come and sit beside me.' She patted the chair next to her. 'Naturally, we're all delighted that you've been able to come and visit us, my dear. Of course, you understand we shall spend a very quiet Christmas, under the circumstances.' She gave a sad smile, her eyes once again moist with unshed tears.

Rosalie gave a barking laugh. 'Under the circumstances? What on earth do you mean, Ma?' she remarked acidly. 'Our Christmases are never anything other than quiet!'

Her mother looked at her reproachfully. 'That's probably because there are no children here. If we had grandchildren . . .'

'Oh, Mother, for goodness' sake, not that again!' Rosalie raised her eyes to the ceiling.

'You really shouldn't speak to your mother in that tone, Rosalie,' Roger Nolan said mildly, from the depths of his armchair. It was clear he was not used to remonstrating with his daughter.

'No, old girl. Let it rest,' Philip said softly and took his wife's hand. She pulled it away sharply, but said no more because at that moment Maisie came in with the laden tea tray and conversation ceased until she had settled it in front of Mrs Nolan, who busied herself with teacups and making sure everyone had a plate and napkin and a crumpet.

During tea the slightly stilted conversation was inevitably centred on John, what sort of a child he had been, the mad, impetuous escapades of his youth, his ambition to do his bit for England by joining the army. As Stella listened she realized that there was a great deal about John she hadn't known and now would never know, and the enormity of her loss struck her yet again. Surreptitiously, she dabbed the tears from her eyes under pretext of blowing her nose.

'You're looking tired, Stella,' Doreen remarked, choosing to misinterpret the action. 'Was it a very arduous journey?'

'Yes, it was, rather.' Stella nodded and put away her handkerchief so that she could finish the last of the crumpet she had taken only out of politeness and eaten with difficulty. 'I had to change trains several times and they were all very crowded and dirty. Smuts from the engine seem to get everywhere.'

'Then perhaps, when you've finished your tea, you might like to go up to your room and rest until dinner?'

'Thank you. You're very kind. Yes, I think I should like that very much,' Stella said, relieved, even though at the same time she recognized that she was being dismissed. She drained her cup and placed it back on the tray.

'Rosalie, will you ring for Maisie to show Stella to her room?' Doreen said.

'No, it's all right, Ma. I'll take her up myself.' Rosalie got to her feet. 'It's the green room, isn't it?'

'That's right. Make sure she has everything she needs.' Doreen turned to Stella. 'Dinner will be at eight, but Maisie will bring hot water for you to freshen up in plenty of time.'

'Thank you,' Stella said again. Suddenly, she felt drained, both physically and emotionally and she realized what an ordeal it had been, coming face to face with John's family without his comforting presence by her side. She got to her feet, but as she did so she suddenly felt the room start to spin in a most alarming manner. She remembered putting out a hand to steady herself, and then everything went black as she lost consciousness.

The next thing she knew was that she was lying on the settee and Rosalie was holding a smelling bottle under her nose.

'No, lie still, don't try to move.' She recognized Philip's quiet, gentle voice as, embarrassed, she struggled to sit up and she saw that he had somehow managed to move to the end of the settee to make room for her.

'I'm dreadfully sorry,' she said weakly. 'I really don't know what came over me.'

'No doubt it was the strain of having to confront John's entire family at one go,' Rosalie said in a tone of either sympathy or sarcasm, Stella couldn't quite decide which.

'Oh, I'm sure . . .' Stella swallowed. She hoped she wasn't going to be sick. 'Could I have a drink of water, please?'

'I should think a drop of brandy would be more useful.' Roger had been watching the proceedings and now he produced a small flask and handed it over.

The fiery liquid revived her and after a minute she sat up. 'Thank you, I feel much better now.'

'Are you sure, Stella?' Doreen said, peering at her anxiously.

'You don't think you're sickening for this awful Spanish flu that's going about, do you?' Rosalie asked bluntly.

'No, I don't think so.' She managed a wan smile. 'I hope not, at any rate.'

'Well, there's a lot of it about, you know,' Rosalie said.

She gave a sniff. 'Still, you're getting a bit of colour in your cheeks again. So, when you're ready I'll take you up to your room.'

Stella waited a few minutes and then got gingerly to her feet, relieved to find the room was no longer spinning, although she still felt strangely light-headed.

'Are you sure you're all right, Stella?' Philip asked, frowning.

'Yes, really. I'm feeling much better now, thank you.' Slowly she followed Rosalie to the door.

'If you don't feel up to coming down for dinner, I'll have something sent to your room,' Doreen called after her.

But Stella was too busy trying to keep herself upright and to put one foot in front of the other to answer. She struggled up the stairs behind Rosalie, and once inside her room she sank down on to the nearest chair.

Rosalie stood over her. 'How long do you intend to stay?' she asked abruptly.

Stella looked up at her in surprise. 'I'm due back at work on the second of January, but I expect to go back before that.'

'Good.' Rosalie turned away. 'Because you're not wanted here, you know. Ma only invited you to spend Christmas here out of a sense of duty to John, so the sooner you pack your bags and go back to where you've come from the better.'

She didn't wait for Stella's reply, but left the room, closing the door behind her.

Stella sat for several minutes, Rosalie's words spinning round in her head. She couldn't believe what she had just heard. True, Doreen Nolan's welcome had been less than effusive, although both Roger and Philip had been polite and friendly. But if they didn't want her here, why had they invited her? And why for Christmas? A weekend would have been quite sufficient for a 'duty' visit if they felt it was necessary.

She got to her feet with a sigh. Perhaps it would be better if she simply picked up her bag and left. She had no wish to stay if what Rosalie had said was true and she was really not welcome. It probably was true: the atmosphere in the drawing room had been bordering on hostile, to put it mildly. She clutched the back of the chair as a wave of nausea and faintness suddenly swept over her, and she looked longingly at the bed. With its thick green eiderdown and plump pillows, it looked very inviting. Perhaps a half hour's rest would refresh her, clear her mind and give her the strength to decide where to go and what to do, not that there would be many options on Christmas Eve in a strange town. Her mind made up, she went over and slid gratefully under the covers, closing her eyes against the tears of shame that stung them – to think that on top of everything else she had made such an exhibition of herself by fainting.

'Oh, John,' she whispered into the dimly lit room, 'I'm so sorry. I've tried to be polite and pleasant, but I can't stay here. It's plain they don't want me.'

She almost imagined she felt his hand on her hair as she fell asleep.

Two

'Would you believe it! She's curled up under the eiderdown on the bed in the green room, fast asleep,' Maisie announced as she walked into the kitchen with the tea tray.

'Who is?' Emma asked, as she finished filling the kettle and put it back on the stove.

'Why, that young lady. Mr John's wife.'

'Widder,' Emma corrected. 'How do you know?'

Maisie gave an exasperated sigh. 'How d'you think? Because the missus asked me to slip up and see if she was all right before I cleared the tea things.' She put down the tray and picked up the brown kitchen teapot, frowning. 'She don't look very well, I must say. I hope she's not sickening for something.' She lowered her voice. 'From what they were saying when I went in to fetch the tea things, she fainted; so now they're worried she might have that awful Spanish flu that's going about. But I don't reckon it's that; she don't look to me as if she's got a temperature. Not that I know anything about it, of course.' She lifted her eyebrows. 'More tea, either of you?'

'Yes, please, Maise.' Henry Hogg pushed his cup over for a

refill. 'Come to think of it, I thought she looked a bit peaky when I collected her from the station,' he said, 'but I thought she was just tired and perished with cold. It was freezing on that station, that north wind was enough to cut you in half. But I didn't reckon it was my place to say anything.'

'Well, she'd had a long train journey, coming all that way from the south coast. I expect she would be cold. And tired.' The south coast could have been the moon as far as Emma Blatch, the daily help, was concerned; she'd never been on a train. She glanced at the clock on the wall, with its shining brass weights and swinging pendulum. 'I really ought to be going,' she said uncertainly. 'But, yes, I could do with another cup, Maise.' She handed Maisie her cup.

The three of them sat round the scrubbed kitchen table, drinking tea and eating Maisie's home-made biscuits. Emma, at thirty-two, was small and would have been inclined to plumpness if she'd had enough to eat and nothing to worry about. As it was, she bordered on scrawny, with sharp blue eyes that missed nothing, in a face that was lined beyond her years, and hair that was really too frizzy to tame into a bun and kept escaping. In contrast Maisie, who lived in, and therefore considered herself superior to the other two, was a tall, slim woman of twenty-five, pale, with sharp, discontented features, black hair that stayed neatly coiled under her cap and large grey eyes. Even with his crooked back, Henry, at thirty-five, was tall. He was a handsome man, too, with pleasant, open features, a shock of black curly hair, dark twinkling eyes and a rugged complexion. His back often gave him pain, but he never complained and neither asked nor received any consideration on its account.

'So, you've both seen her. What's she like, Mr John's wife – um, widder?' Emma asked eagerly, leaning forward, her elbows on the table.

Henry took a slurp of tea. 'Seemed a pleasant enough young woman to me.' He grinned. 'Pretty girl, too. Easy enough to see why Mr John married her.'

'Henry! You shouldn't say things like that. Looks aren't everything,' Emma admonished him, but she was smiling too.

'She's got lovely hair,' Maisie said thoughtfully. 'Beautiful auburn colour, and all thick and wavy. It had come out of its pins and was spread over the pillow.' She sighed. 'Wish I'd got hair like that.' She picked up her cup and saucer, crooking her little finger daintily, and took a sip of tea before she went on, 'I feel quite sorry for the girl in a way, being pitch-forked in with that lot.' She jerked her head in the direction of the drawing room. 'I don't reckon she'll be made very welcome, even though she is Master John's widow. You mark my words, she'll be sent packing as soon as Christmas is over and they feel they've done their duty; and that'll be the last we shall see of her.' There was the merest hint of satisfaction in her voice. 'Don't you remember,' she went on, 'how furious the missus was when she found out her lovely boy had gone and got himself married without even telling the family? And to some-body they hadn't even met!'

'Well, that's what happens when there's a war on,' Henry said. 'People had to grab what they could while they could, because they never knew what might happen next.'

'Good thing they did get married, with him goin' an' gettin' himself killed like that,' Emma went on sadly. 'On almost the last day of the war, as well. At least they had a bit of happiness together.'

'He didn't get himself killed, Emma, he was shot by a sniper,' Henry corrected her. 'But you're right, you couldn't blame them for grabbing their happiness when they could.'

Emma nodded. 'He was such a nice boy, too, Master John. I always liked him, even though he was a bit of a tearaway. Not like his sister, stuck up little . . .' She glanced at the clock again, then drained her tea and got to her feet in one move-ment. 'But I mustn't sit here gassing. If I'm quick, I've just got time to nip home and look to Ivy before I start on the vegetables for dinner.' She was already shrugging on her coat and tying a scarf round her head as she spoke.

'Well, just you make sure you're not gone long, then,' Maisie said sharply. 'Remember there'll be one extra for dinner tonight.'

'Your little one no better, Emma?' Henry asked, ignoring Maisie.

Emma shook her head, her face creased with worry. 'No, Henry, she's not. That cough hacks her to pieces, but the doctor says there's nothing to be done unless we can send her to a sanatorium. He talked about Switzerland. I ask you! With Arthur still out of work and two other children to feed, there's fat chance of that. It was as much as I could do to rake up the money for the doctor's bill – and that was a waste, if that was all he'd got to say.'

Henry pushed back his chair and stood up. 'Do you want a lift, Emma? I can soon harness the trap again.'

'No, thanks all the same, Henry. I've got my bike.' She smiled at him. 'But you could fetch a bottle of them plums we bottled in the summer down off the shelf for me. Then I can make a plum tart for tonight, if that's all right with you, Maisie.'

'That's what I was going to suggest,' Maisie said. 'So you'd better not be long or you won't have time to make the pastry.'

Emma left and Henry sat down again to finish his tea and another biscuit, which he'd filched off the tray while Maisie wasn't looking. He liked Emma, she was the salt of the earth, and she didn't deserve that pig of a husband. True, it wasn't Arthur's fault he couldn't find permanent work, but he was no different to hundreds of other ex-servicemen and the master was always happy for him to do a spot of gardening to help Jack Govan when he felt up to it – which wasn't often, it seemed. And it would be more to his credit if he didn't tip half Emma's wages down his throat to drown his disappointment.

Half a mile from Warren's End down an unmade side road, Emma leaned her bike against the wall of the little two-up-two-down cottage where she lived and went inside. Arthur was sitting hunched over a meagre fire. The room was sparsely furnished but spotlessly clean, and there was half a loaf of bread and a lump of hard cheese on the table.

'Did you chop them logs Henry dropped off for us?' she asked sharply.

'No, I told Charlie to do it.'

'But he's only eleven, Arthur! You can't expect him . . .'

'Why not? He's a growin' lad. Time he did a bit o' work for 'is keep.'

Emma bit her lip. 'Have you bin to sign on today?'

'Yes. There's nothin'.' Arthur stared into the fire. 'A land fit for heroes, they said we were comin' back to.' He picked up the poker and gave the fire a vindictive poke. 'A land fit for bloody heroes, my arse.'

'Watch your language, Arthur Blatch. Remember, Ivy's just upstairs.' She peered at him. 'Is your head bad again?'

He sniffed and gave a shrug.

She glanced at him again and went upstairs to where seven-year-old Ivy was lying in a little bed by the window in the smaller of the two bedrooms, her face hardly less white than the spotless pillow that was propping her up so that she could see out of the window.

'Look, lovie, I've brought you a drop a milk from the House. It'll help make you strong again. You like milk, don't you, sweetheart?' Emma put her arm round her little daughter's thin shoulders and held the mug to her lips while she took a few sips. 'There, I'll leave the rest of it on the chair here so you can reach it. Is there anything else you want?'

Ivy shook her head. 'No, thanks. Are you stayin' home now, mum?'

'No, lovie, you know I have to go back to the House and cook the dinner. But it won't be long before Mary gets home from school, and I'll be home soon after seven because Maisie likes to dish it up and serve it herself.' She smoothed Ivy's fair hair back from her forehead. 'I might be able to bring you a bit of plum tart. Would you like that?'

Ivy nodded listlessly.

'Well, mind and drink that milk up. I want to see it's all gone when I get home.' Emma dropped a kiss on her forehead and went back downstairs. Arthur was still sitting in the chair with his head back and his eyes closed. She took a rag outside and wetted it under the tap, then she went back and laid it across her husband's forehead.

'There. Is that better?'

'Yes.' With his eyes still closed, Arthur reached for her hand. 'You're a good girl, Emma.'

She stood looking down at him for a minute. She could never tell whether his headaches were from his experiences in the war – which he never, ever talked about – or the previous night's drinking. But she always gave him the benefit of the doubt, even though most of the time all he gave her in return was a black eye.

She got on her bike and pedalled back to Warren's End.

When Stella woke, she realized with a start that she had been asleep for a full two hours. She hadn't heard anyone come in, but she saw there was a jug of hot water on the washstand and fresh towels hanging beside it. She quickly got off the bed, washed her face, changed into a fresh blouse, pale-blue this time, and put her skirt back on. Then she brushed her hair and twisted it back into its soft, thick bun on top of her head. She didn't quite know what to do next, so she sat down in the chair by the fire. Had it been alight when she first came into the room? She'd felt so ill she hadn't even noticed. But she felt much better now after her sleep; so, savouring the quiet warmth, she considered her options. Not that she had many. Having slept for so long, there was now no question of leaving tonight; and tomorrow was Christmas Day, so there would probably be no trains running. That meant she would have to make the best of things and stay until Boxing Day at least. She sighed. Knowing she was an unwelcome guest, it was going to be a difficult few days.

She studied her surroundings, partly out of curiosity and partly to put off having to go and be polite to the people downstairs. The green room she had been given was aptly named, with green flock wallpaper, green curtains, green-velvet chair coverings and light bamboo furniture. It was a very nice, light room, but just as cluttered as the drawing room downstairs, with ornaments and pictures on every available surface, intricately carved ivory palaces and castles, and elephants in various sizes and colours. A brightly coloured silk shawl was draped over the green-velvet *chaise longue* at the foot of the bed. She frowned, searching her memory, and recalled John telling her that his parents had spent a long time in India, where his father had been a colonel in the army and had then become a tea planter or some such. That would account for the ivory and the elephants. According to John, his father had retired from the army quite young and after making his fortune had returned to England, where he'd bought Warren's End, one of the larger houses at the more affluent end of the town. Her reverie was suddenly interrupted by a knock at the door, and Maisie stepped inside.

'Dinner is served, Mrs Nolan, but Madam thought you might like a tray brought up if you're not feeling well.'

Stella got to her feet. 'No, it's perfectly all right, Maisie. I'm feeling much better now I've had a rest, thank you. I don't want to put you to extra trouble, so I'll come down.' She smiled at the maid.

The smile wasn't returned. 'It's no trouble, Mrs Nolan. I have the tray on the table just outside the door, but I just wanted to make sure you were awake before I brought it in.' She whisked out of the door and came back with a tray on which was a plate under a silver cover, salt and pepper, and a crisp white napkin in a silver ring.

'Oh . . .' Stella had no choice but to sit down again.

Deftly, Maisie shook open the napkin and spread it on Stella's lap, then took the cover off the plate to reveal two lamb cutlets with rosemary and mint and a selection of vegetables.

'It looks and smells delicious, Maisie, thank you,' Stella said. She felt vaguely disappointed, uncertain whether to feel ostracized by the family or grateful at not having to face them.

'Would you like plum tart and custard to follow, Ma'am?'

'Thank you, yes, that would be very nice.' Stella suddenly realized she was very hungry.

'Madam said to inform you that she's asked Dr Eaves to call and see you later on this evening. He'll be round after surgery.'

'Oh, I'm sure there's no need . . .'

'Madam said "Better safe than sorry!", Ma'am.'

Stella frowned. 'But I feel perfectly well now that I've had a good sleep. I think I was just tired. Is she still worried I might have Spanish flu?'

'I'm sure I don't know, Ma'am,' Maisie said primly. 'If there's nothing else you want, I'll leave you to eat your dinner before it gets cold. I'll be back with your pudding soon.'

Stella picked up her knife and fork, feeling rather like a child banished to the nursery for disobedience. 'Thank you, Maisie.'

Slowly, she ate the lamb cutlets. They were delicious and she did them full justice, quite relieved that she could savour them without having to make polite conversation with John's family. The plum tart was equally tasty, with pastry that melted in the mouth and rich, creamy custard.

Stella complimented Maisie on the meal when she came back with a cup of coffee for her. 'So I suppose I've just got to stay here until the doctor comes,' she said with a sigh as she accepted it.

Maisie put her head on one side. As far as she could see, the girl looked the picture of health now. 'Yes, Mrs Nolan. Um . . . Mrs Nolan thought it would be best.'

Stella smiled, a smile that transformed her face. 'Why don't you call me Mrs Stella, Maisie. I think that would be less confusing than two Mrs Nolans, don't you?'

Maisie almost returned her smile. 'Yes, it would. Thank you, Mrs Stella.' She cocked her ear. 'Ah, that was the doorbell. It'll be the doctor. I'll bring him straight up.'

'Thank goodness for that,' Stella breathed a sigh of relief as Maisie hurried away.

Dr Eaves was an elderly man, with white hair – at least, what there was of it – and a thick white moustache. His nose showed a marked proclivity towards the whisky bottle.

A little behind him, and looking decidedly reluctant, hovered her mother-in-law.

Stella submitted a little impatiently as the doctor took her temperature and pulse, then looked down her throat and into her eyes.

'No, your fears are quite ungrounded, Mrs Nolan. The young lady shows no sign of Spanish flu,' he said, straightening up and speaking directly to Doreen, which annoyed Stella even further.

'I could have told you that,' Stella said sharply. 'In fact, I don't feel in the least ill now, so I'm sure there was really no need to trouble you. I simply fainted, probably because I was very tired and the room was warm. But I'm feeling perfectly well now that I've had a rest. Thank you, Doctor,' she added belatedly, as she realized her words might have sounded a little rude.

He turned back and looked at her, smiling, his head on one side. He didn't seem to have taken offence at her outburst and she might have liked him if she hadn't been so cross. 'Nevertheless, I would just like to do a further examination, my dear, if you don't mind,' he said mildly. 'Just hop up on the bed and loosen your stays a little, if you please.'

Stella did mind, she minded very much, but Doreen, still hovering near the door, looked so fierce that she submitted with as good a grace as she could muster.

When he had finished poking and prodding her and asking her intimate questions, which were none of his business and made her more and more angry, he nodded and straightened up.

'As I rather suspected, young lady. You're as fit as a flea. Nothing wrong with you at all. Probably the reason you fainted was that you're pregnant. As far as I can tell, you're getting on for three months.' He chuckled and beamed down at her. 'But of course, you must have known that.'

She stared up at him, her eyes wide. Then as the news sank in, she sat up and put her hands to her face, tears of joy running down her cheeks.

'No,' she said, shaking her head in bewilderment. 'I didn't know . . . I'd no idea . . . I thought it was the shock of losing John that had upset . . . that had stopped . . . that was why I hadn't . . .' Even in front of the doctor, who had already asked the question, she couldn't bring herself to speak of her monthly cycle. 'But this must be why I've felt so tired and drained lately. I thought it was the effort of facing life without John.' She put her hand on her stomach and said softly, 'But now I'll have his baby, so I won't feel I've quite lost him after all.'

She looked up at the old doctor, smiling through her tears. 'Oh, thank you, thank you, Dr Eaves. Thank you so much.' Now, instead of being angry with him, she had difficulty in restraining herself from flinging her arms round his neck and kissing him.

Three

Stella was thankful when Doreen left the room with Dr Eaves. She just wanted to be left alone to savour the wonderful and totally unexpected news she had been given. Her mind in a whirl, she tried to think back over the past months; she remembered vaguely realizing that her monthly 'curse' was a bit late, but the shattering news that John had been killed had put all thoughts of such mundane things out of her mind. Her world had been ripped apart; she had hardly been able to think what she had to do from one day to the next, and hadn't much cared. She had felt so sick and ill with grief that she'd hardly had the strength to drag herself to work every morning.

At least she had thought it was grief.

It had never occurred to her that she might be pregnant, although on reflection – she gave a little secret smile at the thought – there was every reason to suppose that she might be.

She laid her hand on her stomach. With her corset still unlaced after the doctor's probing, could she detect a slight rounding? She smiled to herself again, comforted by the knowledge that with his child to care for she would always have a part of John to love. Her only regret was that he had never known the legacy he had left her. She closed her eyes against the tears that were threatening to spill, but the smile was still there.

After another minute she got up from the bed and straightened her clothing, then sat down by the dying fire, still a little bemused.

'There, now! John's baby! Isn't that the most wonderful news?'

She turned quickly, frowning. She hadn't heard the door open, and for a second she resented the intrusion into her moment of privacy. But she managed to force a smile as her mother-in-law came over to her, beaming widely and enfolding her in an embrace of black lace and jet beads.

'I'm so sorry for banishing you up here like this, my dear,' Doreen said; and there seemed to be genuine regret in her voice. 'What must you think of us! But with this dreadful influenza killing so many people, one really can't be too careful, can one? After all, one never knows, does one?'

Stella shook her head, amazed at this sudden transformation in her mother-in-law. 'To tell you the truth, I really hadn't thought about that before you mentioned it. I was simply too embarrassed at fainting like that. It's not anything I've ever done before.'

Doreen went over and sat down in the chair opposite her. 'So you really had no idea you might be expecting a child, my dear?' she asked happily.

'No, you probably think I'm naïve, but I had no idea at all. I thought it was because I was so upset over John being killed that I was feeling so ill and . . .' she bit her lip, tears still not very far from the surface.

'Of course you were. I quite understand.' Doreen put her head on one side. 'But you are pleased, dear, aren't you?' she asked doubtfully.

'Oh, yes,' she replied softly. 'I'm absolutely delighted.'

'And so am I.' Doreen got to her feet and came over and kissed her again. 'Well now, why don't you come downstairs and sit with us for a while? Rosalie and Philip have gone back to their flat across the yard. Well, at least, Philip has; his legs often pain him. He was quite badly injured at Ypres – at least I think that was where it was – as you probably know.'

'No, John didn't . . .'

Doreen ignored the interruption. 'But if I know my daughter, she's probably taken herself off to some meeting or other; so there'll only be the three of us. Do you feel like it, dear, or would you rather rest?'

'No, I feel perfectly well now, thank you.' Stella hesitated. 'But I'll be quite content to stay here in my room if you would prefer it. And then, tomorrow . . .'

Doreen looked at her with a puzzled frown. 'No, no, no. Why on earth would I prefer you to stay in your room, dear?

We want to get to know you a little, not to imprison you. Ah . . .' Her face cleared. 'You're offended that I sent your dinner up to you. I'm sorry about that. But as I told you, one can't be too careful. With this awful influenza . . .'

'No, it's not that at all,' she lied. 'I had a very nice dinner, thank you.'

'Good. Yes, Emma is a very good cook.' She dropped her voice. 'Although between you and me, Maisie likes to take most of the credit.' She held out her hand. 'Now, come along downstairs with me.'

At the door to the drawing room Doreen paused and whispered, 'I won't embarrass you by speaking of your condition to Roger, I'll tell him in private later. I know he'll be very pleased.'

The evening passed very pleasantly, much to Stella's surprise. Neither the Colonel nor his wife gave the slightest indication that she wasn't a very welcome guest. They told her of John's escapades as a child, laughing indulgently at the more outrageous ones, Doreen surreptitiously wiping her eyes now and then. In return, Stella shared her memories with them, smiling a little as she told them of his sudden determination to marry her before he went back to the Front.

'I wanted to wait and invite you all to our wedding, but he said there wasn't time,' she explained. 'And as it happened, there wouldn't have been. If we'd waited we would never have married at all and . . .' She broke off, her hand stealing possessively to her abdomen.

'Oh, that's typical of John. He was always impetuous,' Doreen said, smiling a little at her memories. 'Wasn't he, Roger?'

'Yes, indeed. I remember the time he . . .' And he was off again, reminiscing about the son he had obviously idolized.

When Stella finally retired for the night, it was with a deeper knowledge of the man she had married and conflicting thoughts about his family. Doreen had been so cool and unwelcoming when she first arrived, yet this evening she had gone out of her way to be pleasant and to make her feel included in the family. It was odd.

Then there was Rosalie. She had been quite vindictive, telling her she wasn't welcome at Warren's End, that she had only been invited so that they could see the sort of woman John had married. Was that true, or could it simply be that Rosalie was jealous and she had spoken out of spite? But jealous of what? The more Stella tried to make sense of Rosalie's outburst and Doreen's change of heart, the more perplexed she became; she could make no sense of any of it.

Not that it mattered; she would be gone from Warren's End in a few days and would probably never see any of them again. On that comforting note, she fell asleep.

Christmas Day was spent quietly as befitted a family in mourning.

They all went to church, Henry pushing Philip in a bath chair as far as the church door, although he insisted on walking into the church – a slow and laborious business with two sticks that left him with a sheen of perspiration on his forehead by the time he reached the family pew. Stella was amazed to see an expression of impatient irritation on Rosalie's face in an unguarded moment as she watched her husband's progress up the aisle. Why wasn't she simply thankful that he was alive? If only John . . . She pressed her lips together, determined not to let tears spill over.

But as the service went on, with joyous hymns and carols to celebrate the birth of Jesus, she thought of the baby she was carrying under her heart – John's baby – and she rejoiced and sang to celebrate her own coming child.

Back at Warren's End, Emma and Maisie were putting the finishing touches to Christmas dinner, which was to be eaten in the middle of the day so Emma could spend the rest of the day with her family and Maisie could visit her sister in the next village. Emma had brought thirteen-year-old Mary with her to help with washing the dishes and she was already at the sink, swathed in a voluminous white apron covered with an equally large one made of coarse sacking, washing the pans and basins that had been used in making the sauces and custards.

Henry came in, looking hot from the exertion of pushing Philip home, and took off his coat and hat. 'He never complains, that man,' he said admiringly, 'although I know he's always in pain.'

'Well, here's a little something to keep the cold out,' Maisie said, handing Henry a hot toddy. She gave him a smile that bordered on being arch. 'I always like to keep a drop of whisky in my pantry, in case of emergencies.'

'Very sensible, too,' Henry said, taking several sips. 'Ah, that's a drop o' good. But what about Emma? I reckon she could do with a little drink, too, seein' as it's Christmas.'

With obvious reluctance, Maisie poured a small drink for Emma. 'I thought she was like me and didn't imbibe,' she said disapprovingly.

'I don't as a rule, but seein' as it's Christmas . . .'

'Oh, well, if you put it like that . . .' Maisie poured herself a generous measure.

Henry held up his glass. 'Here's to a merry Christmas for us all.'

'A merry Christmas!' they all replied.

'You'll be coming to us later on, won't you, Henry?' Emma said as she sipped her drink. 'Arthur's expecting you.' Henry lived in the cottage adjoining Emma's and, as well as being neighbours, he frequently helped Arthur home from the Nag's Head on a Friday night.

Mary turned round from the sink. 'Oh, yes, Uncle Henry, please come!' she said eagerly. 'We can play games round the fire after tea and roast chestnuts. We've saved the ones Charlie collected from the woods.'

'You get on with your work, my girl and don't interrupt when your elders are talking,' Emma reprimanded her automatically.

'Let the girl be, Emma. It's Christmas,' Henry said with a smile. 'And thank you kindly, I'll be pleased to come and sit by your fire and roast chestnuts.'

'You can take what's left over from the Family's dinner. My sister always keeps a good table, so there's no call for me to take anything to her,' Maisie said, with a faintly supercilious air.

'Oh, goody! I hope there'll be some plum pudding left,' Mary said into the washing-up suds.

Although she had thought to put it out of her mind, Stella found herself watching carefully throughout the day for any sign that she was not welcome at Warren's End. But she saw nothing. Even Rosalie seemed to have forgotten her outburst of the previous day and was at least polite, if not exactly friendly, towards her. Stella put this down to Rosalie's preoccupation with the unfairness of the voting system. There was to be a general election later in the week at which women would be allowed to vote, but only if they were over thirty.

'It's so unfair! So infuriating that I'm not quite old enough to vote!' she said, thumping the arm of her chair.

'I've never known you to wish yourself older before, darling,' Philip said mildly. 'Women are usually at pains to be thought younger.'

She looked at him scathingly. 'And what would *you* know about how I feel?'

He gave her a lopsided smile. 'Not a lot, these days, I must admit,' he said, 'but I'm not entirely stupid.'

'You're stupid enough to imagine I wish myself older. What I wish is that they'd allowed us to vote at twenty five!'

'Philip, as it's Christmas, would you sing for us?' Doreen broke in. She hated these spats between Rosalie and Philip, because she knew that it was Rosalie who invariably started them.

'Of course, Doreen. If Rosalie will accompany me,' he replied, anticipating her refusal. 'As it's Christmas.' He repeated Doreen's words deliberately.

'No, I don't think so. I don't feel like it,' Rosalie said, picking up her book and starting to read.

Philip turned to his mother-in-law. 'That's it, then. I'm sorry, Doreen, I'm afraid I'm rather rusty, so I need a bit of accompaniment.'

'Well, never mind,' Doreen said, clearly disappointed. 'But you have such a nice voice, I do enjoy hearing you sing.'

Stella cleared her throat. 'Perhaps I could accompany you?' she said tentatively. 'I sometimes play for the men at Hill House, where I work. They like to sing and some of them have very good solo voices.'

'Oh, would you?' Doreen said, clearly pleased. 'That means you'll be able to sing for us after all, Philip.'

Rosalie threw down her book. 'Oh, very well, I'll play for you,' she said quickly. Plainly she was not going to allow Stella to accompany her husband. She went over to the piano and lifted the lid. 'What do you want, then?' She began to riffle through the music in the canterbury.

He struggled over to her. 'These two,' he said, making his choice.

'OK,' she said with a shrug.

Roger caught his breath. He hated to hear Rosalie use slang but realized that now was not the moment to remark on it.

Philip had a very pleasant tenor voice, and he sang well and without self-consciousness. Rosalie's piano playing was competent, although it lacked feeling.

'Oh, that was lovely,' Doreen said when the last strains of 'I Passed by Your Window' had died down. 'You have such a beautiful voice, Philip. And you play very well, Rosalie.'

'So she should, the amount of money I lavished on piano lessons for her,' Roger mumbled quietly into his pipe.

Philip sang two more pieces and then Rosalie got to her feet. 'That's enough,' she said briefly, 'you'll tire yourself if you sing any more.'

It was obvious Rosalie had got tired of accompanying him.

'Then perhaps you'd like to play something for us, dear?' Doreen said, smiling at her daughter.

Rosalie gave a shrug, but sat down at the piano again and rattled impatiently through a Schubert impromptu.

'Thank you, dear,' Doreen said when she had finished and slammed down the lid.

The rest of the day passed pleasantly enough. After supper, which Maisie had left prepared on the trolley and Stella helped Doreen to wheel in, Rosalie fetched the new gramophone that Philip had given her as a Christmas present. She wound it up and as the record revolved she placed the needle carefully in the groove so that they could listen as songs of the day – 'Swanee,' 'Home Sweet Home,' 'I Dreamt I Dwelt in Marble Halls' and several more – sounded tinnily out through the large pink horn that sat on the top.

'Marvellous invention, marvellous invention,' Roger remarked, shaking his head. 'Whatever will they think of next!'

'Wireless. That'll be the next thing, sir,' Philip said. 'I believe an Italian chap called Marconi is already beginning to experiment with sending the human voice over air waves.'

'Why on earth would anyone want to do that?' Doreen asked, raising her eyebrows. 'I never heard such nonsense. Nobody could shout that loud.'

'They wouldn't have to shout, their voices would be carried over the airwaves in some manner that I confess I don't fully understand.' Philip smiled at her as he spoke. 'And as to why. To see if it can be done. It's called progress. And, make no mistake, Doreen, when you hear music that's being played in London coming out of a box in the corner of this room you'll think what a marvellous invention it is.'

She shuddered. 'Oh, I don't think so. It's not natural. In fact, I find the whole idea quite spooky.'

'Well, if you think that's spooky, what about if there was a machine that could show us, here in this room, what is going on hundreds of miles away? I've been reading about that, too.' He shook his head. 'It all sounds incredible, but I don't think it's that far into the future, either.'

'You've been reading too much Jules Verne, my boy,' Roger said with a laugh. 'I don't think any of these things will come to pass in my lifetime.'

'I wouldn't be too sure of that, Pa,' Rosalie said, in one of her rare moments of agreement with her husband. 'These things will happen, I'm sure of it.'

'But this machine thing you're talking about – if we can see them, will they be able to see us?' Doreen asked anxiously. 'I shouldn't like to think of strangers watching what we're doing.'

'No, of course they won't, Ma,' Rosalie laughed.

'No, I don't think you need to worry on that score, Doreen,' Philip said, joining in the laughter. 'And it'll be several years before it happens, I dare say, so you can sleep easily in your bed.'

'Oh, thank goodness for that.' Doreen relaxed visibly.

Later, as Stella climbed the stairs to bed she decided that, all things considered, and in spite of Rosalie's harsh warning, which was always at the back of her mind, it had been a very pleasant day.

★ ★ ★

The next morning when she went down to breakfast Stella found Doreen, in a pale-mauve negligée, sipping coffee and eating toast.

'Ah, good. Come and sit down, my dear,' she said, indicating a chair nearby. 'Did you sleep well?'

'Yes, thank you, but where is everyone?' Stella looked round the empty table as she took her seat and helped herself to coffee. 'Maisie didn't bring my tea until eight o'clock, but I didn't think I was late.'

'No, you're not late, dear, it's only half past eight. I told her not to disturb you before eight. Oh, yes, please, pour me another cup.' Doreen pushed her cup across. 'Thank you. Where is everyone, you ask? Well, Roger always gets up early and takes the dogs out. And Rosalie and Philip take breakfast in their flat – Roger had part of the outhouses overlooking the garden converted for them – but we always eat *en famille* in the evening. You say you slept well?'

'Yes, thank you. I slept very well.' Bemused at being asked a second time, Stella added, as she buttered herself some toast, 'It's a very comfortable bed.'

'Ah, I'm glad you said that,' Doreen gave a satisfied nod.

Stella looked up at her in surprise. 'Why . . .?'

'Well, it's like this,' Doreen leaned her arms on the table, at the same time making a great play of arranging the frills on her negligée. 'I . . . That is we, Roger and I, have a proposition to put to you.'

Stella paused, her toast halfway to her mouth. 'A proposition?' she asked suspiciously.

'More of an invitation, really. And you needn't make up your mind right away. Well, not for a day or two, anyway. Oh dear, I'm not making much sense, am I?'

Stella shook her head, frowning. 'Not really.'

'Roger and I would like you to stay here. To come and live with us.' The words were tumbling out in her eagerness. 'There's plenty of room and you could have your own quarters, just like Rosalie and Philip. I don't know what your plans are with regard to the baby . . .'

'I haven't made any plans yet,' Stella said warily. 'I've hardly had time. In fact, my head's still reeling with the news . . .'

'And you really, honestly, had no idea?' Doreen's eyebrows shot up nearly to her hairline. 'Then it must have come as quite a shock, because you were only married – how long? – before John had to go back to France?'

'Ten days.' Stella flushed and said with a smile, 'It was obviously long enough, though. And it wasn't a shock, Doreen, it was a wonderful surprise; John couldn't have left me a nicer present. But as to plans, I haven't really had time to make any yet.' She frowned thoughtfully. 'I've got a little money invested that my parents left when they were killed, so I'm not quite destitute. And I can still work, I've still got my job . . .' Her voice tailed off as she realized that she wouldn't have that for long, not once they discovered she was pregnant. And a small bedsit – which was probably all she would be able to afford – was hardly the ideal place to bring up a child. But she would cross that bridge when she came to it; looking after John's baby was the important thing.

'Well, perhaps you'd like to give our suggestion some thought, dear.' Doreen took several sips of her coffee, then went on, 'As soon as I told Roger . . .' She laid a hand on Stella's arm. 'And I must tell you, he's as delighted as I am that you're to have John's baby. And equally anxious that we should do all we can for you.' She put her head on one side. 'Of course, the decision is yours, but I do hope you'll agree to our suggestion. It would make us very happy.'

'Thank you. It's very kind of you. I don't know what to say . . .' Stella found she had crumbled the remains of her toast into a buttery mess on her plate. She wiped her fingers on her napkin and smiled at Doreen.

'Oh, don't say anything yet, dear. Think about it while you're here. You're not planning to go back yet, are you?'

'Well, I had thought I should go back tomorrow . . .,' Stella said doubtfully.

'Tomorrow! But, my dear, you've only just got here!' Her eyebrows shot up again.

'Well,' Stella moved uncomfortably in her seat. 'I was rather under the impression that you hadn't really wanted me here in the first place.'

Doreen frowned. 'Whatever gave you that idea? Of course

we wanted to meet the girl John married. Although, naturally,' she hesitated and smiled a little, 'we were a little apprehensive, knowing how impetuous John is . . . was. I'm not quite sure how we would have received a chorus girl in fishnet tights and a feather boa,' she finished dryly.

'Was that likely?' Stella asked, surprised.

'With John one never knew,' Doreen replied vaguely. She leaned over and squeezed Stella's arm. 'But having met you, I don't think he could have chosen better if I'd picked you myself.' She got up from her chair and said briskly, 'Now, do think about what I've said, dear. We really would like you to come to live with us. It would be so fitting for our son's child to be brought up here, wouldn't it?' She dropped a kiss on Stella's forehead and left the room.

Four

That night, after a day in which Doreen's words were never far from her mind, Stella lay in the soft feather bed in her bedroom at Warren's End, the thick velvet curtains drawn to shut out the wild winter night, a hot-water bottle at her feet, and the last glimmering embers of the fire still burning in the grate. She wiggled her toes luxuriously and basked in the contrast between this life and her chilly little room on the top floor of the convalescent home, where a hard single bed, an armchair and a shelf of books were her usual companions when she finished work for the day. Not that she was ever lonely. Nursing at Hill House brought her into contact with people from all walks of life and she could always spend her off-duty hours in the comfortable communal recreation room, playing cards – which she didn't much like – or playing songs on the piano for the convalescing officers to sing, which she enjoyed. Best of all she liked simply talking to them, hearing about their hopes and aspirations and listening to their worries, the uppermost of which was always that their wives or sweethearts would not want them now that they were crippled or maimed.

Or worse, would only stay with them out of pity. She tried to reassure them, knowing she would still love John even if he came back maimed (she always crossed her fingers as she said the words, not that it would do any good) and they often said it had been a help to have someone to talk to, someone who listened.

But she wouldn't be able to stay there. Not now. It was against the rules. Matron would never countenance a pregnant nurse; with all those men around, it wouldn't be right. And it wouldn't be many weeks before she could no longer keep it a secret. So although she enjoyed her job very much and would be sad to leave – not least because it was there she had met John – she knew her time at the convalescent home was limited.

So where would she go? What could she do if she didn't accept Doreen's offer? She turned over and thumped her pillow as she tried to think. She had her parents' legacy. But, though carefully invested, it wasn't bringing in enough to live on even now, let alone with a child to care for. Then there was the problem of finding somewhere to live, and work of some sort to support herself and the coming child. That wouldn't be easy. Now the men were coming back from the war they would take priority in the workplace; and women, let alone pregnant women and women with babies, would no longer be wanted. So that would mean working at home. But at what? Sewing? Addressing envelopes? She'd heard about women trying to make a living like that, exploited and having to work far into the night just to make enough to pay the rent. She shuddered. The middle-class background she came from hadn't fitted her for such a life.

She stared up into the darkness. Doreen's offer was generous and she seemed genuinely anxious that Stella should make her home at Warren's End. So why was she hesitating? Why did this feeling of unease persist? Was it because of Rosalie's words? *You're not wanted here. You were only invited out of a sense of duty to John.* It was puzzling.

It was another two days before Stella finally plucked up the courage to speak to Doreen. By that time, having thought about it endlessly, she had managed to convince herself that

Rosalie had spoken out of either spite or jealousy, so her words could be disregarded. In any case, if she didn't stay here, where would she go? It wasn't so much a choice as a lifeline.

She found Doreen sitting in the morning room, a room that would have been sunny on a less grey day, with bright-yellow walls and gold curtains and a green-and-gold-patterned carpet on the floor. She was writing letters at her desk, dressed in a dark-grey morning dress liberally trimmed with black, a pair of gold-rimmed spectacles perched halfway down her nose. She looked up over the top of them as Stella entered the room.

'Ah, come in, my dear. I was just finishing.' She laid down her pen and blotted the sheet she had just written, then took off her spectacles and turned to Stella with a smile. 'Sit down, dear.'

Stella sat down on the edge of the small ladies' chair Doreen had indicated. 'It's about what you said the other day,' she began uncomfortably, making a conscious effort not to twist her hands in her lap. 'Your invitation . . . Asking me if I would like to come and live here at Warren's End . . .'

'And . . .?' Doreen raised her eyebrows, smiling hopefully.

Stella tried to smile back but her face felt stiff. 'It was very kind of you. I've thought about it a lot, and I think I should like to do that if you're still willing to have me.' She knew she sounded stilted and formal, but she didn't want to have to admit that she had nowhere else to go and nobody else to turn to. 'Please,' she added quickly.

'Oh, my dear, I'm *so* glad.' Beaming, Doreen got up from her chair and came over and embraced her daughter-in-law. 'Roger will be delighted, too. He keeps asking me if you've made up your mind.' She sat down again and it soon became apparent that they had never even considered that Stella might refuse their offer. 'Now, there are four rooms in the annexe at the back, which we've decided will be just right for you,' she said, her voice immediately businesslike. 'I think they were all part of the dairy when Warren's End was a farm, but as the family grew they were incorporated into the main house.' She waved her hand. 'All that, of course, happened before we came here. We didn't need the extra space, so we've never really used them. They weren't convenient for Rosalie and Philip because of the steps down into the garden, which was why Roger had the outhouses converted for them. But they'll be perfect for you; it won't be difficult to have them adapted, with a little kitchen and bathroom added. The sitting room will overlook the garden, and there are two bedrooms, one of which is quite small but eminently suitable for a nursery for our grandson . . .'

'It might be a girl,' Stella said with a smile.

Doreen waved her hand dismissively. 'The kitchen will be small, but big enough to make yourself a cup of tea or the odd snack when you're not with us,' she continued as if Stella hadn't spoken. 'Roger saw the builder yesterday and he's going to start work tomorrow.' She beamed at her daughter-in-law.

Stella didn't smile back. Her head was spinning at the rate things seemed to have moved already. 'But what if I'd said no?' she asked.

Doreen looked at her in surprise. 'Why on earth would you have done that? After all, you'll be among family here – and you yourself said you have no close relatives. No, no, you're a sensible girl; of course we knew you would agree.' She leaned over and patted Stella's knee. 'Now, about your things. Have you any particular furniture you would like to bring to put into your rooms? Something from your old home, perhaps?'

Stella shook her head. 'No, my old home was destroyed by the Zeppelin that killed my parents. I'll just have to go back and clear my room at the convalescent home . . .'

'Oh, my dear, do you think you're up to it? All that long journey there and back? Think of the baby . . .'

'I'll be fine, don't worry.'

'But what about this dreadful Spanish flu? Travelling on the train . . . Going back to the hospital where soldiers are coming back from the Front . . . It's rife there, you know.'

'Yes, I do know. That's where I've been working for the past two years,' Stella said, trying not to sound sarcastic. 'But I haven't caught it.'

Doreen wagged a finger. 'Ah, but you didn't know about the baby then, did you?'

Stella couldn't see that knowing or not knowing that she was pregnant would make any difference to whether or not she caught flu, but knew there was no point in arguing. In any case, if she was honest she really didn't relish the thought of more long journeys in the depth of winter in cold, uncomfortable trains. The journey to Warren's End had been bad enough.

'We'll have your things sent on to you,' Doreen said firmly. 'I'm sure that's the best thing.'

Stella got to her feet. 'Yes. I must admit the long, cold train journey doesn't have much appeal,' she said; adding, with emphasis on the first word, 'I shall have to write to Matron and hand in my notice, and tell her why I'm leaving. I'll also write to Cathy, one of the other nurses; she won't mind packing up my things and sending them on.'

'Sensible girl,' Doreen said approvingly.

'Well, there's a turn up for the book,' Maisie said as she made the cocoa for elevenses. 'Did you hear what Henry just said, Emma?' She nodded towards Henry, sitting at the kitchen table.

'No. What did he say?' Emma had just come in from the garden, where she had been gathering herbs. She put the basket on the table and stood rubbing warmth into her hands and looking from one to the other as she waited to hear.

'He says the young Mrs Nolan – or Mrs Stella, as we're to call her – is . . .' She nodded. 'You know . . .' She nodded again.

Emma frowned and looked at Henry, then back at Maisie. She shook her head. 'No, I don't know,' she said, still looking mystified.

'Mrs Stella is going to have a baby,' Henry said, avoiding her eyes in embarrassment. 'Mr Philip told me this morning.'

'Oh, a grandchild for the master and missus. That'll be nice for them,' Emma said, sitting down and smiling.

'Yes, and they've invited her to come and live here,' Maisie said importantly.

'How long for?'

'Pernamently.' Maisie didn't always get the long words she was fond of using quite right.

'And has she agreed?'

'Be daft not to, wouldn't she?' She dispensed the cocoa and took her own seat.

'She's to have the annexe made ready for her, Mr Philip said. There, Emma, now you know as much as I do.' Henry picked up his cocoa and took a slurp.

'What does Mrs Rosalie have to say about it?' Emma asked.

'Mr Philip didn't say,' Henry answered. He wasn't going to tell the two women what he had overheard when he was tidying Philip's room after his bath that morning.

He had heard Rosalie shout furiously, 'So she's staying! Scheming bitch!'

'That's not fair, dear. Your parents have invited her to stay. I expect it's partly because of the baby.'

'And that's about the last thing we need, a bloody squalling brat about the place.'

'I don't suppose it will affect us much, Rosie,' Philip had spoken in his usual placating manner.

'Don't call me Rosie! My name's Rosalie.'

He'd ignored that, saying thoughtfully, 'It might be nice to have a little one around the place.'

'Oh, don't start *that* again! You're always . . .'

At that point Henry had slipped away, not wanting to listen to yet another of Rosalie's tirades, although the sound of her expletives had followed him across the yard.

'Well, it's got nothing to do with Mrs Rosalie, anyway,' Maisie said, bringing him back to the present.

'Might make her jealous,' Emma said thoughtfully.

'Mrs Rosalie? You must be joking. Can you imagine her with a baby? It'd cramp her style too much,' Maisie said with a mirthless laugh.

Henry drained the last of his cocoa and got to his feet. 'Well, I can't sit here talking all day, the Colonel's asked me if I'd mind doing a bit of distempering in the annexe. A nice duck-egg blue is what the missus has chosen. That'll be a nice cosy little place for Mrs Stella when it's all finished. She'll be all right there, I reckon.' He shrugged on his coat. 'I'll just go and have a word with your Arthur, Emma. Jack Govan told me he'd be coming today to help dig the ground, ready to plant the spuds when it gets a bit warmer.'

'He hasn't come,' Emma said quickly. 'His back's bad today.'

'Ah, I see.' Henry nodded. He smiled sympathetically at Emma. 'Well, let's hope it'll be better tomorrow.' He knew as well as she did that, although Arthur continually complained about not having a job and the Colonel was always willing to employ him in the garden, as soon as there was any work to be done either his back was bad or his head ached. He reflected sadly that the war just ended had more to answer for than broken families and missing limbs.

Any misgiving Stella might have had about coming to live at Warren's End vanished when she saw how the annexe had been transformed for her. In not much more than a week the light, airy room overlooking the garden had been decorated and furnished as a very comfortable sitting room. True the furniture was elderly: a rather old-fashioned Pembroke table and four spindly early-Victorian chairs rescued from the attic and cleaned up, which she immediately fell in love with, and a comfortably saggy sofa upholstered in blue brocade and a matching armchair.

'There'll be a sideboard thing, too, when it comes back from being repaired,' Doreen said, as she and Roger excitedly showed her round.

'It's known as a credenza,' Roger said mildly. 'And the wardrobe from the bedroom has had to go to the cabinet-maker in the village for a bit of attention, too.' He chuckled. 'The thing is, all this stuff has been in the attic for a long time; in fact most of it had been left here when we bought the house.'

'I hope you don't mind, dear,' Doreen said anxiously. 'I wouldn't like you to think we were palming you off with any old rubbish.'

'Nonsense, Doreen,' Roger said. 'All this old rubbish as you call it will be worth quite a lot of money in a few years' time.'

'In any case, I love it,' Stella said, her eyes shining. 'I love it all. Thank you. Thank you both very much.'

'That's good. Glad you like it. And we're having the bed from the green room brought down for you because you said how comfortable it is.' Doreen said with a pleased smile. She looked round, pinching her lip. 'It still looks a bit bare, doesn't it?' She brightened up. 'But when you get your own things unpacked it will look better, won't it?'

Stella thought of the two tea chests delivered that morning, which were sitting in the little second bedroom waiting to be unpacked. Her whole life was there. It didn't amount to much.

Nevertheless, by the time she'd lit the fire and unpacked her books and placed her favourite ornaments around the sitting room the flat suddenly seemed like home; a real home. And when the sepia photograph of John stood in pride of place on the mantelpiece, the feeling was complete.

She sat down in the armchair and looked up at the photograph.

'You don't need to worry, darling, your parents are looking after me.' She put her hand on her abdomen. 'And our baby,' she said softly.

A few minutes later the door burst open and Rosalie came in.

'All settled in?' she asked, flinging herself down on the settee. She looked around. 'They certainly didn't waste any time in getting the place ready so they could banish you to your own quarters, did they?'

Stella frowned at her. 'I must say I hadn't thought of it like that at all,' she said. 'In fact I was just thinking how lucky I am to have this little flat and how kind your parents have been to me.'

Rosalie shrugged. 'Hm. Maybe. But it's all for the sake of the child, of course. They're desperate for grandchildren.'

'I'm surprised you haven't seen fit to oblige them, then.' Stella found she was having difficulty being civil.

'No chance of that,' Rosalie said with a yawn.

'Oh, I'm sorry, Rosalie.' She was immediately contrite.

'You needn't be, I'm not. I'm glad.' She twisted the bangles jangling on her wrist. 'By the way,' she said thoughtfully, without looking up, 'the brat *is* John's, I suppose?'

Stella stared at her, her jaw dropping, completely lost for words.

'It's all right, Stella. I won't say anything. In fact, I think it would be quite a hoot, Ma and Pa making all these elaborate preparations for a child that is nothing to do with them.' She giggled, then looked up and saw Stella's horrified expression and shrugged. 'Just a thought,' she remarked, a trifle uncomfortably.

'Not a very charitable one, if I may say so,' Stella said coldly.

'Maybe not. But you still haven't answered my question,' Rosalie said lightly.

'I don't need to. You should be ashamed of yourself for asking it.' Stella got to her feet. 'I don't know why you feel the need to be so unpleasant to me, Rosalie. First you impress on me that I'm not wanted here – which upset me very much, but is patently not true since your parents have gone out of their way to give me a home. And now you try to imply that your brother may not be the father of my child, which is quite outrageous! What John would say if he could hear you talk I can't begin to imagine.'

Rosalie looked at her fingernails. 'He'd probably laugh. We used to have some great laughs together, John and me.'

'Well, I'm not laughing.' Stella sat down again since Rosalie showed no inclination to go. 'Rosalie, I don't want to quarrel with you.'

'Then don't.'

'I would like to be friends with you, but you make it very difficult.'

Rosalie nodded. 'Yes. I'm pretty choosy about my friends.' She looked up brightly. 'Aren't you going to offer me a cup of tea?'

Stella got up and went to the door.

'Two sugars,' Rosalie said, over her shoulder.

But Stella was holding the door open. 'I believe tea is being served in the drawing room at the moment,' she said quietly. 'I should like to go and join my parents-in-law there, but I'm rather choosy about who I leave in my flat when I'm not here.'

Rosalie got lazily to her feet. 'OK. Point taken. I'm going. I'll see you in the drawing room.'

Stella closed the door behind her and leaned against it, her heart beating uncomfortably. She felt quite unsettled by Rosalie's outburst and could only think there must be some deep-seated reason for the woman's animosity towards her. She wondered what it could be.

Five

It wasn't long before Stella developed a routine that fitted in with the family's. It was a relief that Rosalie and Philip always ate breakfast in their own flat; Rosalie's snide remarks about 'eating for two' would be more than she could stand first thing in the morning. Especially as now she no longer felt sick and was becoming ravenous at breakfast, ready to do full justice to the bacon and eggs and lashings of toast laid out in the dining room.

Doreen rarely came down until a good deal later, but the Colonel was always sitting at the table when Stella arrived. As soon as he saw her, he would smile and put down his newspaper so that he could talk to her, asking after her health and if she had everything she needed and then remarking on the political situation of the day. Stella soon came to realize that he was not comfortable with small talk; he was more of a 'man's man', finding conversation less easy in the company of women. But he seemed genuinely kind and concerned for her welfare; and as time went on, he became more relaxed.

'I've noticed you walking in the garden once or twice lately,' he said one morning in late February. 'It's not at its best, of course, at this time of the year. And the weather hasn't helped, with all the wind and rain we've had. It's played absolute havoc with some of the larger shrubs.'

'No, unfortunately I wasn't able to go out very much because of the weather. But I could see from my window that you've got a beautiful garden, so it's been nice to explore it a little,' Stella said. 'It looks as if there are lots of shady places to sit in summer, too, which will be really nice.'

'Oh, yes, I made sure of that when I designed the garden,' he said, obviously pleased. 'We grow most of our own vegetables, too. Jack Govan does a wonderful job looking after things; he's very knowledgeable, you know. And Mrs Blatch's husband comes when he can.' He dabbed his moustache with his napkin and leaned towards her, dropping his voice a little. 'I try to give him the benefit of the doubt, since he's obviously been badly affected by his experiences in the trenches, but I must say I do sometimes wonder if Arthur Blatch isn't a little work-shy. So many times when there's a job here for him to do there's some reason why he can't come. It's either his back's bad or his chest is bothering him, or his head aches or some such.' He shook his head. 'I guess I shouldn't complain, not after all he's been through – he was on the Somme, you know – but I really don't understand the man. I'm told he's a skilled tradesman: a bricklayer or plasterer, something like that. But if there's no work for him in that line, I'd have thought he'd be only too thankful to find work where he could. It must have been very demoralizing for a good tradesman like him to come back from fighting for his country and find there's no job for him to go to. And the terrible thing is, there are thousands like him. It's happening all over the country.' He sighed and shook his head again. Then, after a pause, he went on, more cheerfully, 'Mind you, when Blatch does manage to turn up he works hard. None better, I'll give him that. I just wish we could rely on him a bit more.'

'Yes, I can imagine there's always plenty of work to be done in a garden the size of this one,' Stella said.

'Indeed, there is.' Roger nodded. He was silent for several minutes, finishing the last of his coffee, then he said, 'It's a great pity the man is not a bit more like his wife. Emma Blatch is totally dependable, a really hard-working woman. She's here every day in spite of the fact that she's got that little consumptive daughter to care for, as well as two older children.'

'Oh, I didn't realize that!' Stella said, surprised.

He dabbed his moustache. 'Yes. From what I remember, Ivy – I think that's her name – is a pretty little thing. In the summer Emma sometimes used to bring her along when she came to work. That was before she got too ill, of course; we haven't seen her for some time now. But even when she did come, she was always pale and delicate-looking; just like a little fairy. But now it seems there's nothing can be done for her. It's all very, very sad.' He was quiet for a moment, obviously moved by the thought, then he pulled himself together and pushed his chair back, smiling at Stella as he got to his feet. 'But I mustn't sit here chatting all day, pleasant though it is to talk to you. If you'll excuse me, my dear, I've got some telephone calls to make.' He went to the door, then turned back. 'It looks as if it's going to be a nice day today, so if you go out in the garden do go and look for the winter honeysuckle. It's at the bottom of the garden in the shrubbery, not far from the gate into the wood. Not much to look at but the scent is wonderful.'

'Thank you, I'll do that,' she said, returning his smile. She poured herself another cup of coffee and thought what a nice man her father-in-law was. And not for the first time she wondered how such a nice man could have a daughter as rude and unpleasant as Rosalie.

A few days later, the kitchen was warm when Emma arrived, and there was a pile of washing-up in the sink.

'Sorry I'm late, Maisie, but I was up all night with Ivy,' she said breathlessly, hanging her coat on the back of the door.

'Oh dear, she's not bad again?' Maisie asked sympathetically, with the teapot in her hand. She always made a pot of tea as soon as Emma arrived.

Emma nodded. 'If you don't mind, I'll do what I've got to do here then I'll go back to her.' Her lip trembled and she bit it hard. 'My little girl's not much longer for this life, Maisie.' She took several sips of tea and closed her eyes. 'Oh, this is lovely. Just what I needed.'

'If Ivy's really bad, I think you should go home as soon as you've drunk your tea, Emma,' Maisie said, her voice unusually gentle. 'Stay with her. Poor mite. She'll be needing her mum.'

Emma gave a worried sigh as she looked round. 'I'd like to, but what about . . .?' She nodded towards the dishes in the sink.

'Don't worry about that, I'll get Elsie to see to them.' Elsie Green was the 'scrubbing woman' who came in twice a week to do the heavier cleaning. 'And as for the rest, what don't get done'll get left,' Maisie said firmly. She lowered her voice. 'Mrs Stella has already told me she don't want us to clean her rooms.'

'Why not?' Emma's eyebrows shot up in surprise. 'Don't she trust us?'

'Oh, it's nothing like that,' Maisie said with a laugh. 'She just said she's never been used to it so she's quite happy to manage for herself. She seems quite anxious not to make extra work for us,' she added thoughtfully. 'But I told her the laundry is always done by two women from the village who come every Monday, so she's quite happy to put her laundry out.' Then her voice hardened. 'She's not a bit like that one over there – her place is always in a mess and she don't care how much work she makes for other people.' She nodded in the direction of Rosalie and Philip's flat.

'Don't I know it! I'd better just nip over and clean it up before I go.' Emma hurriedly drained her tea and got to her feet.

'No, you won't. You get off home right now,' Maisie said firmly. 'Go and see to your little one.' She laid a hand on Emma's arm. 'And don't worry, Em, your jobs will all get done and I'll see to it that you won't lose your wages.'

Emma's eyes filled with unshed tears. 'Thanks, Maise. I would be glad . . .' She left the sentence unfinished as she shrugged her coat on and went to open the door, bumping into Henry as he was coming in.

'Where are you off to, then?' he asked in surprise.

'Home. I've got to go back to Ivy,' she said, hurrying off before the tears spilled over.

Henry came in and closed the door. 'I'm not surprised. I knew the little one was bad,' he said as he sat down and laid his cap on the table in front of him. He accepted the mug of tea Maisie had poured for him. 'Thanks, Maise,' he said absently, then went on, 'I could hear her coughing in the night, poor little mite. That cough racks her to pieces. I know Emma was up most of the night with her. The walls between their cottage and mine are paper thin, so you can't help hearing what goes on.' He took a gulp of tea. 'Sometimes you hear more than you want,' he added enigmatically. He drained his mug and put it down. 'Is Arthur here today?'

'How would I know?'

'I didn't know if Emma had said. I heard him come home

from the pub last night. He was banging about enough to wake the dead, so I reckon he'd had a skinful. I didn't go to the Nag's Head last night, I was too tired. I try and keep him a bit quiet when I do go, because I usually help him home. Do you know, sometimes he's that far gone he'd never find his way back on his own.' He began to laugh. 'One of these days he'll end up in the river, if he's not careful. That'll sober him up.'

'You shouldn't say such things, Henry,' she admonished him. 'Many a true word . . .' She frowned. 'Mind you, it beats me where he gets the money from. According to Emma, he doesn't get a pension because they say he's fit enough to work. They don't take into account the fact that there is no work. And if there was, he wouldn't be able to manage it for more than two days at a stretch.' She filled the kettle and banged it down on the hob. 'It's a scandal the way these men who've fought for their country are treated. Standing on street corners because there's no jobs, or going round selling matches to try and make a few coppers. It's not right in this day and age.'

'No, it's not,' he agreed. Then, more forcefully, 'He gets the money from Emma, of course. He bloody well ought to be shot, taking the money she's earned and tipping it down his throat, the way he does.'

'Henry, you know I won't have such language in my kitchen,' Maisie said sharply. She sat down, her elbows on the table, hands cupped round her second cup of tea. 'You're fond of Emma, aren't you?' she said quietly.

He looked out of the window, a dull flush spreading over his handsome face. 'Aye. She's a good sort,' he said. 'That man doesn't appreciate her. She deserves better.' He got to his feet. 'I must go. I've got work to do.'

After he'd gone, Maisie remained sitting at the table, hardly noticing the winter sunlight slanting through the long window on to the shining copper pans lined up on the dresser shelf. Life wasn't fair, she decided. Emma was married, she had a husband, even if he was a bit too fond of drink and not fond enough of work. But at least she did have a husband, while she, Maisie, had never had a man in her life, never felt the warmth of a man's arms round her, his face close to hers, like they described in the penny romances she was fond of reading. And with all the carnage in the war, the thousands of young men lost, she probably never would have, she thought bitterly. Unless Henry . . . Her expression softened. Henry with his dark curly hair and twinkling eyes would be a catch for any girl, even with his deformed back. He'd been married once, before he came to work at Warren's End, she knew that much, but he never, ever talked about his wife. Although she assumed she'd died, Maisie didn't really know, so it was possible she was still alive and they were living apart. It wasn't something he talked about and you couldn't ask . . . She didn't think even Emma knew, and he'd have told her if he'd told anybody.

Henry was very fond of Emma. Maisie could see that, in a hundred little ways; though oddly enough neither of them seemed aware of it. Perhaps it was as well under the circumstances.

She got up from her chair and took the dirty crockery over to add to the pile in the sink. Then she stood and stared at her reflection in the mirror that hung there. Regular features, neat black hair . . . She sighed. There was no justice. If only Henry would take his eyes off Emma for a moment he might see that here was a woman, still young, not bad-looking, with good teeth, ready and only too willing . . . Even if he had still got a wife somewhere.

Flushing to the roots of her hair, she fetched the kettle from the stove and began the washing-up.

After breakfast, Stella went back to her flat and put on her coat and hat to go and find the winter honeysuckle Roger had told her about. She had hardly got down the steps outside her door when an upstairs window opened and Doreen, still in her diaphanous pale-mauve negligée, called to her.

'It's very cold today, dear. Are you sure you're wrapped up warmly enough? I've got a shawl you can borrow if you want it.'

'I'm quite warm enough, thank you, Doreen.' The name still didn't trip lightly off her tongue, in spite of the fact that Doreen had insisted that 'in this day and age there was no need for old-fashioned mother-in-law, father-in-law formality'.

'Well, if you're quite sure . . . And keep to the paths, dear. The grass will be very wet and we don't want you catching cold and risking our precious bundle, do we?'

Stella turned away without answering. She was becoming just a little irritated that Doreen felt the need to keep reminding her to look after John's baby in such a coy manner. As if she needed reminding! But Roger and Doreen had been kind enough to give her a home and to welcome her into their family, so such a minor irritation was a small price to pay. It was only natural for Doreen to be concerned over the only grandchild she was ever likely to have.

She continued on her way across the paved yard between the house and the stable block, most of which was now Rosalie and Philip's flat, although Roger's hunter and Rosalie's horse, Magpie, were still stabled at the far end along with the pony and trap.

Henry appeared round the corner from the kitchen, whistling cheerfully.

When she had greeted him, she asked, 'It's a lovely day, isn't it, Henry? I thought I might go into the town a bit later on. Is it too far to walk? Or is there a bus?'

He grinned. 'No buses, but the trams run every hour, on the hour, Mrs Stella, and I reckon you've just missed one.' He hesitated, then said diplomatically, 'It's a bit over a mile to the shops, so a bit too far for a lady to walk, I'd say.'

'Oh, I'm quite used to walking. But you're probably right. At the moment, anyway.' She shrugged. 'Well, that's that, then; if I wait for the next tram, I'll be late back for lunch. It's the first really nice day, too.' She turned away.

'Hang on a minute, Mrs Stella. I'll have a word with Mr Philip,' he said, his grin broadening. 'It just so happens I'll be taking him into the town myself . . .'

Stella's face lit up. 'So you'll be able to give me a lift in the trap?'

'Better than that, Ma'am. If Mr Philip agrees, we'll take you in his car. He calls her his Tin Lizzie. That's a Model T Ford, in case you didn't know,' he added.

'I did know that.' She smiled broadly when she saw his surprise. 'I wasn't exactly brought up in the ark, Henry. In fact, I often used to drive an ambulance to ferry the patients about when I worked at the convalescent home.'

'Well, I never. A little thing like you, no bigger than a minute, driving an ambulance,' he said admiringly. Then remembered himself, blushed, and added, 'Begging your pardon, Mrs Stella. I shouldn't have said that.'

She laughed. 'It's all right, Henry. I used to get a lot of comments like that when I was at work.' Suddenly, and for a fleeting moment, she missed the camaraderie of the home.

'If you don't mind waiting a minute, I'll just go and have a word with Mr Philip, although I'm sure he won't mind you coming with us; then I'll fetch the car round to the door.' He shook his head. 'It's a great shame, you know. That car is his pride and joy but now, because of his legs, he can't drive it, so I have to do it for him.' He grinned again. 'Not that I mind, of course.'

'No, I'm sure you don't.' Stella watched him go as she waited in the sunshine and thought what a pleasant, cheery man he was in spite of his crooked back, which she knew often gave him pain.

A moment later, Henry came out and put his thumbs up as he went to fetch the car. She went back to her flat on the pretext of having forgotten something, because she knew from her nursing experience how embarrassed Philip would be if she stood watching while he struggled into the car. When he was settled in the seat beside the driver, she went out again. Tin Lizzie, as Henry had called her, was a smart little car, with a dark-red body and a black hood. She was obviously lovingly cared for, with gleaming bodywork and sparkling brass.

'It's very kind of you to let me come with you today, Philip,' she said carefully getting into the back seat.

'Believe me, the pleasure's all mine,' Philip said gallantly. 'It's not often I get the opportunity to take a lady out, so we're glad to be able to help, aren't we, Henry? We usually go into the town once or twice a week, even if there's no shopping to do, but I need to go to the art shop today for some new paints and I'm running out of paper.'

'So what do you do if there's nothing you need to buy?' Stella asked.

'Oh, we just nip into the town, look in at the gallery, and then go and have a drink at the Goat and Boot. When Henry can spare the time, that is.'

She laughed. 'And is that where I'll find you when I've finished my shopping? In the Goat and Boot?'

'No, Mrs Stella. We'll still be either in the art shop or the gallery, probably the art shop, if I know Mr Philip,' Henry said, laughing with her. 'He takes longer to buy a few sheets of paper than it takes the average woman to buy a new hat. And that's saying something.'

'Well, it's a tricky business, buying paper,' Philip said good-humouredly. 'Water-colour, oils, pastel, pen-and-ink, they all need different kinds. And then there's colour to consider, so you see, it's not like going into the shop and buying a writing pad.'

'And to think I've lived here for the past two months and didn't even know you were an artist,' Stella said in surprise.

'Well, it gives me something to do,' he replied briefly.

Henry stopped the car outside the art shop and Stella left the two men, promising to be back in an hour, and went to explore the little market town. The shops were set around a cobbled market square that had several small streets leading off it and a market cross in the middle. The Goat and Boot pub stood next to the art shop, and there was a small art gallery beside it with a water-colour painting displayed in each window. As she made her leisurely way round the square, she counted two banks, an ironmonger's, a second-hand furniture store, a haberdasher's, a milliner's, a teashop, two dress shops and a men's outfitters as well as a butcher's, a greengrocer's, three grocery stores and a small department store with five windows, each displaying objects from different departments. It was a busy little town, even though it was not market day, with crowds of people hurrying about their business or clogging up the pavement to exchange the latest gossip, and there was a constant clip-clop from the hooves of horses pulling delivery carts and coal wagons, blinkered against the sight of the motor cars and trams rushing noisily past them.

Stella wandered round the square, then went into the dress section of the department store and bought two skirts designed to expand and accommodate her growing figure and three pretty smock-like blouses that would go some way to concealing it.

'I wouldn't want you to think I'm ashamed to be pregnant,' she assured the assistant in the dress shop as she paid for her purchases.

'Indeed, no, Madam, but one prefers not to flaunt one's condition, particularly where there are gentlemen,' the assistant said primly. 'And these skirts and smocks are the very latest designs for what you might call . . . concealment.' She leaned forward. 'We have some very nice perambulators in the children's section, just over there,' she said, nodding towards it.

'Thank you.' Stella went over and found everything that she could possibly need for her coming baby, but she contented herself with buying wool and knitting needles and patterns for baby clothes. She couldn't resist just looking at the perambulators, though, and there was one that she particularly liked, but the price was rather high. She decided she would have to go home and do some careful calculations before she could think of putting down a deposit on it. She glanced at her watch. Philip and Henry would be waiting for her. She hurried across the square and back to the car, but there was no sight of the two men. She wondered where they could be.

Six

Stella looked in at the art shop, but neither Philip nor Henry were inside. Puzzled, she glanced up and down the road but there was no sign of either of them, although the car was still there, parked beside the kerb. Then she remembered Philip speaking about the art gallery, so she went along to the double-fronted Georgian house where the sign HUNTER'S MOON GALLERIES, written in gold on a dark-green background, hung.

To her relief she could see Philip inside, deep in conversation with a man with iron-grey hair and a neatly trimmed beard.

From his slightly flamboyant manner and style of dress – including a brightly coloured rather floppy cravat – Stella assumed this to be Benedict Gerard, the proprietor. Diplomatically, Henry was waiting at a discreet distance, ostensibly examining the pictures hanging on the walls.

She was undecided what to do. There was a cold wind blowing, chilling her, but she felt it would be intrusive to walk into the gallery and interrupt Philip's discussion. While she hesitated, the window display caught her eye. It was a single picture on an easel of a beach scene at low tide. A small boat was lying half on its side on the beach and a man a little distance away was stooping to gather something – cockles perhaps – at the edge of the sea. The sun was setting in a sky streaked with yellow, orange and purple, throwing ripples of light over the water and long shadows on the land. The overall impression was of complete peace. She stared at it for some time, appreciating the tastefully draped black material used as a backdrop, which threw up the muted colours. She leaned forward to see the signature in the corner of the painting. It was Philip Anderson.

As she straightened up, the two men emerged from the gallery.

'I was just . . .' she began, but Philip cut across her words.

'I hope we haven't kept you waiting too long,' he said briskly. 'I expect you're dying for a drink.'

'Yes, but please don't let the fact that I'm here interfere with your usual habits,' she said with a smile. 'I won't scandalize the natives by asking if I might come with you to the Goat and Boot, but there's a little teashop over there on the corner. I'll go and have a cup of tea and wait for you there.'

'Oh, it's quite ridiculous!' Philip said impatiently. 'To think that in this day and age a respectable woman can't go into a pub for a drink without getting a bad name.' Then his face cleared and he grinned. 'But as far as I know, there's no reason why men can't go into a teashop without getting themselves talked about. How about it, Henry? We might even manage to persuade them to make us a sandwich, then we could go for a spin in the countryside before we go home. What do you think, Stella?'

'I think it's a wonderful idea,' Stella answered enthusiastically.

Henry nodded, but with less enthusiasm. 'I'll drive you over and then stay with the car while you're in there, sir,'

'Why, for heaven's sake?' Philip asked, frowning. 'The car will be perfectly safe. We'll be able to see if anyone tries to steal it. Not that that's likely.'

'It's not that, sir. It's just that it wouldn't be right for me to come in with you and Mrs Stella, would it? Me being what you might call working-class . . .'

'Oh, for God's sake,' Philip exploded. 'All these damn silly class things. People should have better things to concern themselves with. You're a friend helping me, if anyone asks.'

'All the same, sir, I think it'd be best if I didn't.' Henry looked down at his cheap suit. 'Perhaps you wouldn't mind if I had a quiet pint in the Goat and Boot while I wait for you?'

'Yes, I damn well would,' Philip was clearly beginning to get annoyed and Stella was wishing she had never come in the first place. 'In any case, don't you think tongues would wag even more if Mrs Stella and I went in without you? We'd be the talk of this mean-minded little town in no time.' He started towards the car, saying over his shoulder, 'You go on ahead and order the tea, Stella. And ask if there's a chance of a sandwich. And cream cakes. A place like that must serve delicious cream cakes. For three,' he added firmly.

Stella walked across the square to the teashop, feeling decidedly guilty at having upset the two men's usual habits. She could understand and respect Henry's reluctance to come with them – clearly he would much rather have had a pint in the bar of the Goat and Boot. But it was equally obvious that despite his mild exterior Philip was not a man to be crossed when his mind was made up.

At the same time, she could well imagine the raised eyebrows if she were to be seen out alone with Philip, even though he was her brother-in-law. She glanced around a little impatiently at the people in the square going about their business, women with shopping baskets, tradesmen in striped aprons, mothers pushing prams. After all she'd seen and done working at Hill House, the prejudices of a small country town seemed petty and insignificant. Anyway, she liked Henry and she agreed with

Philip. There was no reason at all why he shouldn't join them for a cup of tea and a sandwich.

The teashop was not very big and the interior slightly dim, with dark-oak tables and chairs and mock-Tudor panelling. But the blue-checked tablecloths and curtains and the pretty blue-and-white china brightened the atmosphere, and the place was obviously very popular because there was only one empty table. Fortunately it was in the bay window, where they could easily see her. She sat down to wait for the two men. The waitress, a young girl of not more than about fifteen in a black dress and frilly white apron, with a matching frilly cap on her curls, was at first doubtful when Stella asked for sandwiches and cakes for herself and the two friends who would soon be arriving, nodding briefly towards the car, where Henry was helping Philip to alight. But she agreed to go and ask the plump, motherly lady, clearly the owner, who was sitting behind the till, and before long a large plate of ham sandwiches and a pot of tea appeared on the table. And by the time Henry had manoeuvred Philip into his chair, there were three bowls of steaming soup as well.

'This looks good,' Philip said, appreciatively rubbing his hands together. 'Clever of you to think of ordering soup, Stella.'

'I didn't. It just appeared,' she said with a laugh. 'I'm as surprised as you are.'

While they were talking, Henry took Philip's hat and coat and hung them on the hat stand and hung his own cap beside them, then thought better of it and screwed it up and put it in his pocket.

'Where shall I sit, sir?' Henry asked in a whisper when he came back to the table. 'There doesn't seem to be anywhere where I . . .'

Philip looked up in surprise. 'Don't be a damn fool, man. You'll sit here with us, of course.' He didn't raise his voice, but there was no doubt he was issuing a command.

Rather uncomfortably Henry did as he was bidden, keeping his eyes fixed on his plate and saying nothing but watching carefully out of the corner of his eye what the others did, anxious not to do the wrong thing by dipping his bread in his soup or tipping the bowl the wrong way. But by the time the soup and half the sandwiches were gone, he had relaxed and was even beginning to join in the conversation. Talking comfortably with these two men, Stella realized she hadn't enjoyed herself so much since she left the convalescent home over two months ago.

Quite a long time later, when everything, including a second pot of tea and a plate of delicious home-made cream cakes, had been consumed, Philip called for the bill.

'That was all absolutely delicious,' he said appreciatively.

The waitress beamed. She leaned down and said quietly, 'Madam says there's no charge. She says she won't make any charge for men what was wounded fighting for their country. Nor for their nurse and driver.'

Philip blew out his cheeks in surprise. 'Well, that's extremely kind of her but I really couldn't . . .'

By this time the plump lady had left her post and come over. 'I'm only too pleased to have had the privilege of serving you, young man,' she said firmly. 'I feel it's the least I can do after what I know you must have been through. The Somme, was it?'

'Ypres,' he said briefly, then returned to his subject. 'It's extremely kind of you to make the offer,' he repeated. 'But I really couldn't accept. We must have eaten all the day's profit . . .'

'Don't you worry about that, dear.' She leaned over and whispered in his ear. 'I make plenty enough out of ladies, like those over there, who've got nothing better to do than drink tea and gossip all the livelong day.' She smiled, but the smile quickly faded. 'I lost my husband at Passchendaele and I started up this little teashop to try and fill the gap in my life that his death left. It doesn't, of course,' she added sadly, 'but at least it gives me something to get up for every morning.' She brightened again. 'And I hear all the gossip!'

They all laughed. Then Philip said, 'Then we thank you for your kindness and I won't insult you by insisting on paying for what we've had today. On one condition.'

'And what's that, dear?'

'That we're allowed to pay for whatever we have in future when we come here. Because we'll be back, I can assure you of that.'

She smiled and nodded. 'That's fair enough. I'll look forward to seeing you all again before too long.'

When she had gone back to her place behind the counter, Henry got to his feet and helped Philip to his. 'I'll get your coat and go and open up the car, sir.'

'Good man.'

When he had gone, Philip leaned towards Stella, grinning. 'How do you like being called my nurse?'

'I've been called worse things,' she said dryly. 'But come on, let me fulfil the role and help you to the car. Here are your sticks. No, if you hold that one like this you'll find it much easier,' she said demonstrating.

Expertly, Stella helped Philip out of the café and into the car.

'Ah, yes, of course, you used to be a nurse, didn't you?' he said as without embarrassment he allowed her to make him comfortable. 'I'd forgotten that. I must say you've still got the Florence Nightingale touch.'

She laughed and went to open the other door. Then stopped. 'Oh dear, I was so busy being a good nurse that I forgot to pick up my bags. I'll have to go back and fetch them.'

They were just where she had left them, but before she left she went over to the counter and said quietly, 'Thank you, Mrs . . .'

'Greenleaf,' the plump lady said, looking puzzled. 'Is something wrong?'

'No, not at all,' Stella said with a smile. 'But I just wanted to get things straight. Major Anderson is actually my brother-in-law, I'm not his nurse. It's Henry who looks after him.'

'Ah, I see. Thank you for telling me. Now I'll know when you come again.'

'That's why I've told you.' Stella smiled again and hurried back to the car.

Henry gave her a blanket to put round her knees and drove home the long way, out into wintry countryside, where the trees and hedges were still frost-rimed and the fields were striped in straight brown furrows after the autumn ploughing. Here and there the few red berries left by the birds brightened the hedgerows, and there were one or two brave branches of lamb's-tail catkins beginning to show.

'Won't be long now till spring,' Henry observed as he turned the car into the drive. 'You can already see a faint fuzz of green where the leaves are beginning to bud in the trees.'

'You must come with us again, Stella,' Philip said. 'We'll take you for another drive in the country when spring has properly arrived.'

'I'd like that very much,' Stella said warmly. 'And thank you both for a lovely time.' She got out of the car. 'I've really enjoyed . . .'

Her words were cut off as Doreen came hurrying across the yard, calling out as she came. 'Where on earth have you been, Stella? I've been worried out of my mind as to what might have happened to you!' She began wagging her finger as she got closer. 'I thought you said you were only going for a walk in the garden.'

'Yes, that's what I'd intended to do, but Philip and Henry were going into the town and they offered me a lift, so I changed my mind and went with them,' Stella explained coolly.

'But you didn't tell me you were going,' Doreen said accusingly.

'I didn't know I had to.' Stella turned her back and reached inside the car for her parcels.

'Well, I like to . . .' She broke off as Stella emerged with three large bags. 'Oh, you've been shopping. Oh, do come and show me what you've bought!' Doreen eyed the bags greedily.

'Not now, Doreen, if you don't mind. I'm a bit tired, so I'm going to put my feet up and have a rest.'

'Oh, very well. Later, perhaps.' Huffily, Doreen went back into the house. She hadn't even acknowledged her son-in-law.

'Good for you, Stella.' Philip whispered. He caught her hand and surreptitiously squeezed it. 'You have to stand up to her or she'll try to rule you. I know. I've had some.'

Stella smiled at him and carried her bags into her flat,

humming happily to herself because she knew she had found a friend and ally in her brother-in-law.

It didn't occur to her to wonder why she should think she might need an ally.

When Henry finished work for the day he called at the Blatches' cottage, ostensibly with a cabbage from the garden at Warren's End.

'Oh, you are kind, Henry. Thanks.' Emma tried to smile at him, but she looked so pale and anxious that Henry had difficulty in restraining himself from taking her in his arms to comfort her. 'Will you tell Maisie I'll be back as soon as . . . Well, it won't be long before I'm back, I know that,' she said, biting her lip and making it bleed.

'Is there anything I can do, Em?' he asked gently. 'Anything at all?' He looked round the little room. It was spotlessly clean and there was a good fire in the grate, thanks, he knew, to the logs he had provided. There was also the remains of a meal on the table.

She shook her head. 'There's nothing anybody can do, Henry,' she said with a catch in her voice. 'I got the doctor to come and see her again, but all he could say was to keep her comfortable and give her warm drinks, and I already knew that.'

'Well, just knock on the wall if you need me and I'll come.'

'Thanks, Henry.' She put out a hand to him, then took it away quickly, flushing slightly. 'It's always a comfort to know you're there.'

'I'll always be there for you, Em, you know that,' he said quietly. He glanced over to where Arthur was sitting hunched by the fire, tears running down his face. 'Doesn't look as if he's much help,' he remarked.

'He's taking it hard,' Emma said loyally, following his gaze. 'He knows we're going to lose our baby.' Her voice broke. 'Our Ivy's only seven, Henry. This shouldn't happen to a little mite who's only seven years old. She should be going to school and playing with her friends and looking forward to the future, to getting married and having a family of her own. Not lying there coughing up her life's blood. It's not right, is it? It's not how things should be.'

'No, Emma, it isn't how things should be.' He touched her shoulder and turned to leave.

'Henry . . .'

He turned back quickly. 'Yes, Em?'

She lowered her voice. 'You could make sure Arthur doesn't drink too much down at the pub tonight. I don't want him coming home drunk, I've got enough to cope with.'

'But surely he won't . . .'

'Yes, he will. He'll try and drown his sorrows. He can't cope with sickness, he says it's women's work. And Ivy's always been his favourite, so he's taking it hard.' Her mouth twisted. 'To tell the truth, Henry, I'd rather he was in the pub out of the way. I can't be doing with him . . .' She sniffed and gave him a ghost of a smile. 'Well, you know what I mean . . . But my Mary's a good girl, she'll help me do what's needed when the time comes.' She put her hand on his arm and this time she left it there. 'It's better this way, Henry, really it is.'

He put his hand briefly over hers. 'Whatever you say, Em. And I'll keep an eye on Arthur, don't worry.'

Two days later, Doreen was down unusually early to breakfast. She came in with a face like thunder just as Stella was pouring a second cup of coffee for herself and Roger.

'Pour one for me as well, will you?' she asked coldly, sitting down and rearranging the frills on her new peach-coloured negligée.

'Please, Stella,' Roger added as a gentle reprimand, folding his newspaper and putting it on the table beside him.

'Yes, of course.' She looked up and gave Stella a rather frosty smile as she accepted her coffee. 'Thank you, dear.'

'So, to what do we owe the honour of this early morning visit, my dear?' Roger asked. Despite his quizzical tone, Stella got the distinct impression that he resented his wife's intrusion into the quiet breakfast conversation that had become something of a habit between her and her father-in-law.

Doreen glanced up at the carved-ivory clock on the mantelpiece. 'It's not that early, Roger. It's gone half past eight.'

Stella allowed herself a small smile to hear those words from a woman who was rarely seen downstairs before nine thirty in the morning. She covered it by offering Doreen the marmalade for her toast.

'Thank you.' Doreen looked at her closely. 'You're looking rather pale, Stella.' She nodded sagely. 'Ah, yes. As I suspected, you're suffering from the effects of your day out. It takes a couple of days for the effect to show.'

'No, I'm not suffering from anything at all. I'm perfectly well, thank you,' Stella said, trying not to sound cross. 'And I was not out all day on Tuesday, we were only gone for a few hours.'

'Well, it seemed a great deal longer than that to me. And over lunch, as well.' Doreen nodded to herself. 'But of course, I was forgetting, you had quite a substantial meal at Daisy's Tearooms, didn't you? With Philip.' She paused. 'And I understand Henry came too, which I find most inappropriate, I must say.'

Stella frowned. She felt as if she'd been spied on.

'I expect you're wondering how I know.' Doreen smiled her frosty smile again. 'I was at the Ladies' Circle yesterday afternoon and Mrs Cole and Mrs Arbuthnot said they'd seen you at Daisy's Tearooms when they went in for a cup of tea. I could tell they were quite shocked to see you there with two men – one of them a servant, no less, and I really can't say I blame them.' She nibbled daintily at her toast. 'I was so embarrassed when they told me that I didn't know what to say in your defence. Well, in truth there was nothing I *could* say. I was as shocked as they were.' She looked across at her husband for support.

She didn't get it.

'I can't see why you should be,' he said, reaching for the coffee pot. 'After all, Philip is Stella's brother-in-law.'

She turned on him. 'Yes, I know that. But didn't you listen to what I was saying? Henry was with them! They should never have allowed him to sit at the same table! He should have waited for them in the car.'

'That's exactly what he wanted to do, Doreen, but Philip quite rightly wouldn't hear of it. And I agreed with him. After all, Henry needed his lunch as much as we did,' Stella said, keeping her temper with difficulty.

'Nevertheless he should have . . .' Doreen began, but Stella held her ground.

'Well, what do you think your friends would have said if I had gone there alone with Philip?' she asked, innocently adding, 'I suppose they would have thought we were having an affair, which would have shocked them even more.' She took several sips of coffee to let her words sink in, while Doreen turned a delicate shade of pink. But before she could speak Stella went on, 'As it was, the very kind lady who owned the shop thought that I was Philip's nurse and Henry his driver, and she was perfectly happy with the situation. In fact, she said she hoped we would go back another day.'

'Well said, Stella,' Roger said, nodding approvingly and dabbing his moustache.

'Well, I most certainly hope you will not!' Doreen said firmly. She lifted her chin. 'I shall speak to Rosalie and tell her to put a stop to it.'

'You'll do nothing of the kind, Doreen,' Roger said in a tone that brooked no argument. 'If Philip offers to take Stella out for the afternoon and stop for a cup of tea at the tearooms, then I hope your so-called friends will mind their own business and not come tittle-tattling to you about it. And if Henry goes with them, then all to the good. But either way, it's no concern of anybody else.'

'It's of concern to us, Roger,' Doreen said more quietly. 'Remember, we are responsible for Stella's well-being and I really don't think it's wise for her to go out in Philip's car, never mind being seen in teashops, with or without Henry.'

'Good heavens, woman, why ever not?' In spite of his efforts to smooth it, his moustache began to bristle.

'Well, it is rather small and I'm worried that it might be bad for the precious bundle to be shaken about in a vehicle like that.' She folded up her napkin and said, without looking at him, 'Henry could always take Stella in the Daimler if she wants to go anywhere, couldn't he, Roger?'

Roger cleared his throat noisily. 'I don't allow Henry to drive the Daimler, you know that, Doreen.'

'Then it's time you did, because you rarely drive it yourself.' Her voice was sharp. 'In any event, if it's a case of protecting your grandson then I would have thought you might stretch a point. I really don't know why you bought that enormous car in the first place. It hardly ever sees the light of day except when you ask Henry to polish it. You won't even allow me to be driven to my Ladies' Circle in it.' Obviously, this was a continual bone of contention between husband and wife.

'I was very comfortable in Philip's car,' Stella interrupted firmly, 'It's a very nice little car and immaculately kept, thanks to Henry. And I have no wish to be taken in the Daimler for a simple trip into the town.' She got up from the table. 'If Philip offers me a lift again, I shall be quite happy to accept. Otherwise I shall go on the tram.'

'And if I forbid you to risk the life of my grandson?'

Stella sat down again and took several deep breaths before she spoke, determined not to cross swords any further with her mother-in-law. 'I would have thought you would know, Doreen that I would never do anything that might harm my baby,' she said quietly but with unmistakeable emphasis on 'my'. 'But things are not like they were in your day, when women in my condition were hidden away out of sight and treated as semi-invalids. I am a normal healthy woman and I intend to lead a normal, healthy life, going for walks and doing what I have always done. And if I get invited to go for a drive with my brother-in-law, I see no reason to refuse. I'm sure it will do me no harm to get away from the house now and again!'

'Well, I'm only thinking of your own good and the good of the child,' Doreen said, with a huffy shrug. 'And,' she added, 'I wouldn't want you to get yourself talked about.'

'I think Stella is perfectly capable of looking after herself and knowing what's best for the child, Doreen,' Roger said quickly, trying to put an end to the conversation. 'Remember, she was a nurse before she came here.'

'Working in a military convalescent home is hardly the same thing,' Doreen replied icily, determined not to be put in the wrong.

Stella bit her lip and poured herself more coffee. She was finding her mother-in-law increasingly infuriating. And it was still another four months or so before the baby was due to be born.

Seven

Doreen sipped her coffee and made a face because it was cold, but said nothing more. She was obviously torn between chastising her daughter-in-law further and annoying her husband by doing so. Stella drank her coffee quickly, anxious to leave the breakfast table before Doreen could get her second wind and complain further about her behaviour. The Colonel alone seemed at ease, engrossed in the financial columns of *The Times*.

But before Stella could escape, the door opened and Maisie came in looking anxious and slightly flustered. She went over and quietly whispered something in Doreen's ear.

'Thank you, Maisie. Oh dear, that's very sad.' Doreen glanced up at the maid, frowning. 'I take it you'll be able to manage without her for a few days?'

'I think so, Ma'am,' Maisie doubtfully.

'Perhaps one of the scrubbing women will come in for an extra hour now and then, and I'll warn Mrs Anderson that her flat won't be cleaned quite as much for a few days. That should help.' She pinched her lip. 'And perhaps Mrs Stella could do a little light dusting in her flat, too.'

Maisie looked surprised. 'Oh, but Mrs Stella always . . .' she began.

'I'll be very happy to do that, Maisie,' Stella interrupted quickly, giving Maisie a conspiratorial wink.

Doreen glanced up at Maisie and gave a slight shrug. 'I'm not sure there's much else we can do to help you, Maisie. I'm afraid you'll just have to manage as best you can.' It was plain that she was quite prepared to inflict sacrifices on other people but not to be inconvenienced herself. 'Please send the Blatches our condolences,' she said almost as an afterthought. 'Oh, and one more thing,' as Maisie prepared to leave the room, 'could you bring in more toast and coffee?'

'The little Blatch child has died,' she informed them flatly when Maisie had left the room. 'It was not unexpected, of course.'

'No, but it's very, very sad,' Roger said, shaking his head. 'Ivy. That's it, that was her name,' he ruminated thoughtfully. 'She was a pretty little thing, too, from what I remember, although of course I never had very much to do with her. She always seemed a bit afraid of me, I don't know why.' Once again he dabbed his moustache with his napkin.

'I'm not surprised. You probably frightened the wits out of the child, strutting about the place the way you do, shouting orders. You've got a voice like a foghorn at times.' Doreen was exaggerating but was obviously still annoyed that he hadn't supported her in her argument with Stella.

He ignored her. 'I must see Radford, the undertaker. Make sure the poor mite has a decent funeral.' He shook his head sadly. 'Ah, it's a bad business, burying a child. Not the proper order of things. Not the proper order at all.'

'Oh, for goodness' sake! Why should you have anything to do with arranging the funeral, Roger? What's it got to do with us? Emma Blatch is only our cook and general help, when all's said and done,' Doreen said irritably.

'Emma is in my employ and so is her husband – when he chooses to turn up. Therefore, Doreen, it's my duty to ensure that their daughter has something better than a pauper's funeral. Surely, even you wouldn't disagree with that?' He fixed his eye on his wife. She had caused him quite enough trouble for one day.

'No, I suppose not,' she murmured, wilting slightly under his gaze. After nearly thirty years of marriage Doreen knew when she was beaten.

Rosalie came in from her morning ride and threw her hat and riding crop down on the settee. Then she sat down and pulled off her boots and left them where they fell.

Philip was just finishing his breakfast at the table by the window. 'Did you have a good ride?' he asked. 'It's a beautiful morning for it.'

'Yes, it was exhilarating. Magpie went well, too. He'll be in good condition for the hunt tomorrow.' She pushed a pile of papers off the chair and sat down opposite Philip, then lifted the lid of the small food warmer. 'Ugh. Only scrambled eggs and bacon. Aren't there any sausages and tomatoes? Or have you eaten them all, greedy pig?' She grinned at him, good-humoured after her gallop across the fields.

He didn't smile back. 'No, there are no sausage or tomatoes because Maisie is a bit overworked. Mrs Blatch isn't in today. Her little daughter has just died. And I'm afraid we'll have to make our own toast, too.'

'Oh, I expect we can manage that.' Rosalie helped herself, then paused, with the lid of the warmer still in her hand. 'Oh dear, poor little Ivy,' she said quietly. 'She used to love to come with me to give Magpie bits of apple or carrot, and she always insisted on letting him take them from her hand even though she was more than half afraid of him – not that he would ever have hurt her, of course. But he must have seemed enormous to her, she was such a little thing. She always looked as if a puff of wind would blow her away.' She sat down and began to eat her breakfast thoughtfully. 'I'll look and see if I've got a black coat I can give Emma. She won't be able to afford to buy mourning clothes, not on her wages. I might have a hat for her, too. I'll have a look after breakfast.'

'That's a nice thought, Rosie, and I'm sure Emma will appreciate it. But first of all,' Philip reminded her, 'we need to do the washing-up and tidy the flat.'

'Oh Lord, yes, I suppose we can't expect Maisie . . .'

'No, we can't,' he said firmly. 'Maisie will have more than enough to do.'

'Not that you'll be much help,' she said, glancing at him.

'Since most of the mess in here is yours, I don't think I need to feel any guilt over that,' he replied without rancour, gazing round the room, at the magazines strewn on the floor, where she'd pushed them off the chair, and the empty whisky glass making a ring on the little table beside her armchair. There was also a pile of ironed clothes that had been brought over from the house, which she hadn't yet put away. He had no idea where she had been last night – these days he didn't even bother to ask – but the coat she'd been wearing when she came in late was flung carelessly down on the other end of the settee, her handbag beside it, her shoes lying where she had kicked them off.

'I expect your room is quite pristine,' she said, with her mouth full.

'I wouldn't say that, but I try not to make more work for Henry than I have to.'

She looked round, noticing the clutter almost for the first time. 'Do you think Henry might . . .?'

'No, I do not. He's a man's man not a lady's maid.' Philip's tone brooked no argument.

'All right, don't get your dander up. I only asked.'

'It won't hurt you to do it yourself, Rosie. You've only got to make your bed and tidy up a bit, for goodness' sake. It won't kill you.'

She looked at her watch, frowning. 'I'm meeting the gang down at the club at eleven.'

He began to struggle to his feet. 'Then you'd better get your skates on, hadn't you? Especially if you're going to look out the things for Emma.' He hooked one of his sticks round the leg of a chair and half-dragged, half-pushed it across to the sink. 'If you wash up, I can sit here and dry the things.' He looked up and saw her thunderous expression. 'Oh, come on, Rosie, it won't hurt you for once.'

She got up irritably from her chair. 'And don't call me Rosie!' was all she said as she poured water from the kettle into the washing-up bowl.

Stella hummed to herself as she flicked a duster round her flat, in the annexe. There was very little to do, in fact, because she took great pride in keeping her rooms clean and tidy, never having had such a pleasant little flat before. And all to herself, too. Sometimes she had to pinch herself to make sure she was not dreaming.

She sat down in her armchair and gazed thoughtfully out at the uninterrupted view of the garden through the French windows. She hoped she hadn't been too short with Doreen, she really didn't want to antagonize her mother-in-law. She appreciated this flat, knowing how lucky she was to have it, especially since she would never have been able to afford anything remotely like it. And it was a privilege to have the opportunity to live in the house where John had been brought up, to walk where he had walked and to see the things he had grown up with. Nevertheless, she was realistic enough to realize that it had only been provided because she was carrying John's baby – the 'precious bundle', as Doreen so irritatingly and possessively called it. Indeed, if she hadn't been found to be pregnant at such an opportune time she would have been back at the convalescent home by now, at her wits end to know which way to turn, and would probably never have visited Warren's End again. But fate had intervened, and here she was in this comfortable little flat. And for that she was grateful, and prepared to put up with a few minor inconveniences.

Not that 'minor' was a word that could ever be associated with Doreen.

And the rather callous way she had received news of the little girl's death gave Stella pause for thought. The death of any child was sad, and even though she herself had never known the little girl she could well imagine the agony Emma was suffering. But it hadn't appeared to affect Doreen; her only thought had been how far she might be inconvenienced. Stella found it difficult to comprehend how anybody could be so unfeeling. And it didn't end there.

It was just over a week later that Roger said at dinner, 'It was a sad little funeral today.' He gave his moustache its ritual dab with his napkin.

'I can't think why you went to it,' Doreen said petulantly. 'After all, you'll pay the bill. What more do they expect?'

'It wasn't a matter of what they expected, I felt it my duty to go,' he replied shortly.

'I would have thought that was well above and beyond the call of duty,' Doreen persisted. 'After all . . .'

'And it was very well done.' He continued as if she hadn't spoken. 'Radford followed my instructions to the letter and did a good job.' He shook his head. 'Pathetic, though, that little white coffin . . .'

'Oh, for goodness' sake . . .' Doreen said with a shudder.

'Did Emma attend? Or was it a men only funeral?' Rosalie asked, picking at a lamb chop.

'Oh, yes, Emma was there. Wild horses wouldn't have kept her away. I must say she looked very smart in that black coat and hat you gave her, Rosalie. Very dignified, she was, too, although she was obviously broken-hearted and at one point I thought that she was going to faint. But she didn't. She held her head high and never shed a tear.'

'I don't suppose the poor woman had any tears left,' Stella said, thinking of her own grieving.

'It was more than could be said of Arthur, poor devil.' Roger shook his head sadly. 'He looked a bit of a wreck and was shaking like a leaf. Fortunately, Henry was there to keep an eye on him.'

'He *is* a bit of a wreck,' Philip said savagely. 'The damned war wrecked him just as much as if he'd had his legs blown off. And now the poor sod – excuse my language, ladies – not only can't get back the job he was trained for, he can't get a proper job at all. It's not right. He's like hundreds of others who fought for their country and now get no help to get back on their feet. Worse than that, they're virtual outcasts. Standing on street corners, propped on crutches trying to sell matches to get enough money to feed their wives and children. It's an absolute disgrace!' He lowered his head, embarrassed at his outburst. 'Sorry. Pass the potatoes, will you please, Rosie.'

'I don't think that's altogether fair in Arthur's case, Philip,' Roger reproved him mildly. 'He knows there's always work here in the garden for him when he chooses to come – which isn't that often, I'm afraid.' He paused thoughtfully. 'Mind you, when he does come he works like a dervish. I've never seen anyone dig so hard for such a long time. But then, of course, his back plays up and he can't come for weeks on end, which isn't very satisfactory from my point of view.'

'But that's all part of his problem. Don't you see . . .' Philip began, but Rosalie cut him short.

'Anyway, I'm glad the coat and hat fitted,' she said brightly, passing Philip the vegetable dish and putting an end to what she considered a disagreeable topic. 'I thought they would. Emma's much about my size.'

'It was good of you to give them to her, dear,' Doreen said, smiling approvingly at her daughter's largesse. 'She'd only got that old tweed coat she always wears, so she probably wouldn't have been able to go to the funeral if you hadn't provided her with proper mourning.'

Rosalie shrugged. 'Well, it's a long time since I wore them, so they were a bit out of date.' She turned to Stella. 'And talking of clothes, that's a very smart blouse you're wearing, although I'm surprised to see you in something quite so flowery. Shouldn't you be sticking to something a bit more subdued? After all, it's not yet six months since John was killed. Mummy and I haven't even gone into half-mourning yet.'

'John didn't approve of mourning,' Stella said quietly. Rosalie never missed an opportunity for a sly dig, but Stella was getting used to it and refused to rise to the bait. 'He told me so. He hated black. He liked me in bright colours. And the girl in the shop where I bought this blouse said these colours suited me,' she couldn't resist adding with a lift of her chin.

'And so they do, my dear,' Roger said gallantly. 'You're looking very well, if I may say so.'

'They make things very . . . um . . . very suitable these days, don't they?' Doreen mused, half to herself. 'Very concealing.'

'Doesn't look as if she's got all that much to conceal, yet,' Rosalie said with her customary rudeness. She put her head on one side. 'You're sure . . .?'

'Rosalie!' Her mother's voice was like a whiplash.

'Sorry.' She had the grace to blush.

'I should think so.' Doreen turned to Stella. 'More vegetables, dear? Another chop? Remember, you're eating for two,' she added with a touch of coyness. 'No?' Her voice hardened as she turned her attention to her daughter. 'Then would you like to clear the plates, Rosalie? I've given Emma the rest of the week off, so it will help Maisie if you put them on the tray ready for her to take back to the kitchen when she brings in the pudding.'

Rosalie got up with an elaborate sigh and began to collect up the plates and dishes and to pile them on the tray in a rather dangerous-looking heap. 'I must say I'll be glad when Emma's back. I'm beginning to feel like a skivvy, myself,' she remarked.

Stella got to her feet. 'I'll help. I'm quite used to . . .'

Doreen put out her hand. 'No, dear, sit down and don't exert yourself. Rosalie is quite capable of managing.'

Reluctantly, Stella sat down again. She wished Doreen wouldn't treat her like delicate porcelain all the time. But things would be different once the baby was born, she was quite determined about that.

The following morning was bright and blustery, typical of early March. After breakfast Stella put on the grey cape her parents had bought her when she began her VAD training. It had been a waste of their money, because she had been provided with the regulation uniform and a cape had been part of it, but she was glad of it now because her blue coat was becoming a little tight round the waist. She studied herself in the long mirror in her bedroom. It was a good-quality cape, her mother had seen to that; and in a funny, almost superstitious way she felt that when she wore it she and the baby were protected, as if enfolded in her mother's arms. She smiled. It was a silly thought, but comforting, since sadly her parents would never see their grandchild.

She put on her hat, picked up her handbag and the letter she was taking to post, and went through the house and out through the front door.

'Where are you going, dear?' Doreen's tinkly voice reached her from the morning room.

'I'm just going to post a letter to one of my nursing friends,' she replied, trying very hard to sound cheerful and friendly.

'Oh, then perhaps you'd put this in the post for me?' Doreen came to the door, still licking the envelope. 'It's a request for Gamages' catalogue. You know, Gamages? The big London firm?' She raised her eyebrows questioningly.

'No, I've never shopped there,' Stella said.

'Oh, goodness me. Well, they sell practically everything you can think of. I'll let you see the catalogue when it arrives.' She smiled. 'Have a good walk, dear. It's a nice bright morning.'

'Thank you. I will.'

Doreen could be quite charming when she chose. Stella went off, her mind made up to always try and think the best of her mother-in-law.

She turned left at the end of the drive, in the direction of the town, past the field that separated Warren's End from the lane where Emma lived. On impulse she took the lane, it was quite a bit further to walk to the postbox, but she was glad to be out of the house and in the fresh air. She passed the pair of cottages where Emma and Henry lived. There was no sign of life anywhere, but it was quite obvious which one was Henry's: it was neatly dug and planted, mostly with vegetables, although there was a border of violets and primroses and a rose rambled round the door. In contrast, Emma's garden was little more than a dirt patch, although a half-hearted attempt at digging it had been begun and left. The spade was still stuck in the ground.

She walked on until she reached the postbox, then walked home slowly, guiltily glad to be away from Doreen's eagle eye. As she walked she tried to imagine that John was by her side, pointing out the places he'd known and the things he'd done. But it was all in her imagination, and she realized with something of a shock just how little she had known about her husband.

Eight

Emma put the finishing touches to the apple pie and looked round the kitchen. The vegetables were all prepared and the soup was on the stove. There were a few bits of ironing still waiting to be done, but they could wait till the morning.

'I'll be off now, Maisie,' she said, rousing Maisie, who was having a quiet five minutes in the chair by the stove before preparing afternoon tea. 'The pie's ready to put in the oven and I've done all the veg.' She took her coat and hat off the hook behind the door and put them on.

Maisie yawned. 'Oh, I must have dropped off,' she said, blinking in surprise – as if she didn't 'drop off' every afternoon at about this time. She watched Emma straighten her hat in the mirror over the sink. 'I'm surprised you wear that nice coat and hat Miss Rosalie gave you every day, Emma,' she remarked with only the merest hint of envy. 'I'd have thought you'd keep them for best.'

Her hat skewered satisfactorily with its jet-tipped hatpin, Emma turned with a worried frown. 'Tell you the truth, I did wonder if it was the right thing to do, Maisie,' she said seriously. 'I thought p'raps I oughta wear my old tweed for everyday, but that seemed somehow disrespectful to my little Ivy, because mournin's mournin' when all's said an' done; it's all the time, not just for special occasions. Not that there ever is any special occasion in our house,' she added. She picked an imaginary speck off the lapel of the coat. She had never had such a nice coat before; the material was lovely and soft and it was quite stylish. She really enjoyed wearing it, it cheered her up; and, goodness knows, she could do with cheering up now Ivy was gone.

'Are you going to the grave again today?' Maisie got up from her chair and pulled the kettle forward on the hob.

'Yes.' Maisie knew she always took a detour on the way home to visit Ivy's grave. Emma couldn't understand why she always had to ask.

'If you see Henry on your way out, tell him I've got the kettle on so there'll be a cup of tea in five minutes if he wants one.' She said it casually, but Emma knew she would be disappointed if he didn't turn up.

'I'll tell him.'

She went round the side of the house to pick up her bike. Henry was there, he'd just finished pumping up her back tyre.

'Did you know it was flat?' he asked.

She nodded. 'I asked Arthur to look and see if there was a puncture. I expect he forgot.' She always made excuses for her husband.

'I'll have a look at it for you tonight when I get home,' he said straightening up. 'Are you going . . .?'

'Yes,' she said quickly, before he could finish. 'I go every day. You know that.'

'Well, I found a few primroses under the hedge at the bottom of the garden so I picked them for you to take. Look, they're in your bike basket.'

'Oh, and you've put them in a little fish-paste jar, too.' Her face lit up with pleasure and she smiled at him. 'Thanks, Henry.'

'You'll just need to put the water in when you get there,' he said, glad to see her smile – a rare occurrence these days – and even more glad that the smile had been for him.

She began to wheel her bike down the drive.

'Oh, Maisie says she's got the kettle on for a cuppa tea, if you want one,' she called over her shoulder.

'Why don't you stop and have one, too?' he called back.

She shook her head. 'No, I'd best get on or I'll be late home,' she said, feeling for the pedal with her foot and hitching herself up on to the saddle.

Emma rode off down the drive. She knew only too well that Maisie wouldn't welcome her return or she would have asked her to stay for a cup of tea in the first place. It was easy to see which way the wind was blowing as far as Maisie was concerned: the poor girl was desperate to be married and have a home of her own. And Henry was a lovely man. It would be a lucky girl he chose to marry, if he ever did marry again. She wondered what his wife had been like. He'd only ever spoken of her once, when Emma had broached the subject, and that was to say briefly that, yes, she was dead. He'd made it quite clear that she'd overstepped the mark in asking. That was before she'd known him very well, but she'd never risked speaking of it again, even when she knew him better.

She reached the churchyard and propped her bike against the wall. She took the primroses carefully out of the basket and went along the path, past the church, past moss-covered gravestones that had been there for a hundred years or more, to the part where the stones were white and the names were newer and still clearly readable. In the far corner, shaded by a big old yew tree, was the pathetically small mound under which her little daughter was buried. As she reached it she pressed her lips together, determined not to cry. She put water in the fish-paste jar and knelt down and scraped a little hole in the mound to place the jar in, careful to keep it upright so the water didn't spill out. Then she rearranged the primroses a little and sat back on her heels, quietly wiping a tear away.

It was six weeks now since Ivy died, but she missed her as much as ever.

Suddenly she felt a hand on her shoulder, and looked up to see Henry standing there.

'Henry!' she said in surprise. 'I thought you'd gone in for a cuppa with Maisie.'

He shook his head. 'I'd just made one for Mr Philip, so I had one with him.' He squatted down beside her and looked into her face. 'Are you all right, Emma?' he asked quietly.

She nodded. 'Yes, I'm all right, thanks, Henry. Well, as all right as I'll ever be. Coming here helps me feel she isn't too far away.' She gave an apologetic attempt at a smile. 'I talk to her, tell her what's been happening . . . What mischief Charlie's been up to, how Mary's been getting on at school . . . I expect you think I'm daft . . .'

'No, 'course I don't.' He was quiet for a minute.

'Of course you don't. I'm sorry, Henry, I was forgetting, you know what it's like. You've lost somebody, too.'

They were both quiet for several minutes, then he said, 'It must be nice to have somewhere to come. Somewhere you can at least lay a few flowers.'

She looked at him sharply, surprised at the note of bitterness in his tone. 'Haven't you got anywhere? Did your wife die a long way from here?' she asked, risking the question because his expression was so bleak.

'Yes,' he said briefly. 'A very long way.'

'Too far to ever visit her grave?'

He didn't answer for a minute. Then he said, 'My Florrie doesn't have a grave. Not as such.'

She frowned, her own tears forgotten for the moment. 'What do you mean, doesn't have a grave? Everybody has to be buried somewhere when they die.' Her voice dropped and she said gently, 'You never talk about her, Henry. Why is that? I talk about my Ivy all the time. I find it helps. It keeps her close in a funny sort of way.'

'Do you? Well, I don't find it helpful at all.' His tone was clipped and his face stony. Ever since it happened he had managed to keep his feelings tightly in check by never mentioning Florrie and the way she died.

'I'm sorry, Henry. I didn't mean to pry. I shouldn't have asked,' she said quietly and busied herself rearranging the primroses on the little grave, simply to give her hands something to do.

He didn't answer but stayed where he was, crouched beside her, watching thoughtfully. Listening to what Emma had been saying made him wonder if bottling it up inside had been the best way to deal with his grief. Maybe he had made things worse by hanging on to it, letting it fester and fill him with bitterness, instead of letting it slide gently into happy memories of the good times they'd enjoyed.

Suddenly, he got to his feet and pulled Emma to hers a little roughly. 'Maybe you're right, Emma, and I've been wrong. Perhaps I should talk about Florrie and the dreadful thing that happened. Come over to that seat in the sun and I'll tell you,' he said.

She shook her head, pulling away from him. 'No, not if you don't want to, Henry. It's none of my business. I don't want you to think . . .'

'No. It's time. I want to tell you, Em,' he said savagely. 'I want to tell you all about it. It's time I got it out of my system.'

Puzzled at his mood, so unlike the Henry she was used to, Emma followed him over to the seat he had indicated; it was in a sunny, sheltered spot looking towards the old church with its round flint-stone tower.

A little reluctantly, she sat down beside him, not liking to speak in case she said the wrong thing. It was peaceful, sitting there in the spring sunshine, the only sound coming from the cawing rooks busy about the rookery at the top of the tall trees in the corner. She was content to wait till he had lit a cigarette and was ready to speak.

'We hadn't been married long,' he began at last, speaking quietly, leaning forward and putting his elbows on his knees so he didn't have to look at her. 'We were living in a little village a few miles from Leeds. We didn't have much money, but we had great plans for the future when the war ended and things got better. Or at least, Florrie had; I was never the ambitious type. Then one day she came home all excited and said she'd heard there was really good money to be earned at the big munitions factory that had just been built on the outskirts of the city. They were asking for workers, and all the girls from the grocer's shop where she worked had applied for jobs there. I suppose it was only natural that she wanted to do the same.' He traced a pattern in the dirt with his toe. 'I wasn't keen on her going, but I couldn't really object because the job I was in didn't pay very well – it's never been easy to get work with a back like mine. But Florrie had ideas of us having a little shop of our own one day; she'd been talking about it for ages. I thought it was just a pipe dream we'd never be able to afford, so I'd gone along with it; but she reckoned if she took this job it would give us our big chance to save up for it.' He took a last drag on his cigarette and ground it under his foot. 'As I said, I wasn't happy about it. But she was so set on going and so excited about it that I agreed that she should give it a go, on the understanding that if she didn't like it she would give it up right away.' He gave a heavy sigh and shook his head. 'I'd no idea what I was agreeing to.'

'No, them munitions factories weren't very nice places to work in, I've heard,' Emma said, frowning.

He straightened up. 'You can say that again! This one was a hell-hole, just like all the others.' He shook his head. 'Yet Florrie just loved it there. Mind you, so did about sixteen thousand other girls.'

'Sixteen thousand!' Emma's eyes widened. 'It must have been a huge place.'

'Yes, it was big, all right. I suppose it was the friendship, the sense of them all being in it together, that the girls all liked. And, of course, they loved the money they earned. Florrie was on a bonus scheme and she could bring home nearly ten pounds on a good week. Ten pounds! We'd never seen so much money.'

'Goodness, nor have I!' Emma said admiringly. 'I wish I'd been there . . .'

'You don't know what you're saying, Emma.' He turned and looked at her, his face bleak. 'The place was enormous, more like a small town. Where Florrie worked there were a hundred and fifty girls working in one huge room where they filled the shells with high explosives, cordite mostly, ammunition for the soldiers fighting at the Front. Florrie said there were ten of these rooms – that was fifteen hundred girls! It was dangerous work, they all knew that. It made their skin turn yellow, some of them had their teeth fall out. People got to know which girls worked there because of their yellow complexions; they used to be called 'canary girls' or 'Barnbow Lasses'. Florrie told me how they'd faint at the bench because of the stuff they were working with and have to be dragged outside till they revived. But if they stayed outside for too long they'd get their pay cut. So they'd go back and carry on filling till the next one fainted or they fainted again.'

'Oh, my Lord!' Emma put her hand to her mouth. 'I never knew . . .'

'No, 'course you didn't. Nobody knew, except the ones who worked there. My Florrie didn't tell me what it was like at first, but gradually it all came out and she admitted she had to strip down to her underwear when she got to work and put on the special smock and cap they all wore so there was nothing to catch fire. And they all had to have rubber soled shoes so there was no chance of a spark; no cigarettes or matches, of course. I hated her being there and begged her to leave, but she wouldn't. She said it was all right as long as you were careful.'

'Surely, that should have been men's work, not women's!' Emma said, aghast.

'All the able-bodied men were at the Front, weren't they, firing the shells these girls were filling with explosives. I went to work there myself. I thought if Florrie could do it, so could I. I used to have to cart the shells away on great trolleys once they'd been filled, but I didn't last long doing that. My back, again, of course,' he said bitterly.

He was quiet for some time and Emma, horrified at what he was telling her, didn't speak but waited for him to continue.

'There were compensations, of course,' he said at last. 'Of a sort. The girls were encouraged to drink plenty of milk and barley water because they thought it helped counteract the effects of the stuff they were working with. The place even had its own farm to produce the milk for the girls to drink. I was sent there, eventually, to help look after the herd; there were over a hundred cows. That was a cushy little number compared with what my Florrie and the other girls were doing; and as you can imagine, that made me feel worse.' He lit another cigarette and drew on it several times, staring into the distance.

'So what happened?' Emma's voice was barely above a whisper.

'What?' He half turned towards her, clearly dragging his mind back from the past. 'Sorry. Where was I? Oh, yes, well, you have to understand the place never stopped working. The girls all worked eight-hour shifts, day and night. There were special trains to bring the workers right into the place; it even had its own railway station to take stuff in and out. Well, this particular night my Florrie was on the night shift. It was in December 1916 and she was all excited because being on the night shift she reckoned she might earn nearly twelve pounds that week – that was over six times what I was earning.'

He looked up at Emma and said sharply, 'I wouldn't want you to think I was jealous because she was earning so much more than me. I didn't care about that; I just wanted her out of that place. But she wouldn't leave. She loved the crowd of girls she worked with. Called them her mates, said they were a good bunch of lasses and they had some good laughs together as they worked. And of course she liked the money. She told me before she left that night that she was going to buy herself some silk stockings and a new hat and she'd got a surprise lined up for my Christmas present. I said the best Christmas present I could have was for her to get out of that place.'

He finished his cigarette and stubbed it out, then went on, 'Oh, she was in no doubt how much I hated her working there. I hated her working with stuff that turned her skin yellow although I'd got used to it by this time. It wasn't so bad if she drank enough milk, but she didn't like doing that because she said it made her fat.'

He paused and was quiet for a long time. Then Emma moved and pulled her collar up a bit higher against the wind that had sprung up.

'Oh, I'm sorry, Em, you're getting cold,' he said immediately.

'No, I'm all right, Henry. Go on. Please, go on.'

He shrugged. 'Not much more to tell. Well, there is. Everything, really. That night there was an explosion,' he said simply. 'Of all the places where it could have been in that vast place, it had to be in the room where Florrie worked. Thirty-five girls died that night and there were terrible injuries among the others. I wasn't there at the time, of course; I didn't have to be there till milking time at five in the morning, and by that time the dead and injured had all been got out and the place was back at work.'

He looked at Emma, shaking his head. 'Can you imagine? An accident like that, with all those women killed or injured, and the whole site full of explosive material, yet everyone else was back at work; they said production had only been halted long enough for the site to be cleared and made safe. Well, as safe as it ever could be.'

'And Florrie?' Emma said gently.

He hesitated, then said briefly. 'She was one of the dead. They found her identity disc, but not much else.' He leaned forward and put his head in his hands. 'I should never have let her go to work there,' he said, his voice muffled.

Emma put her hand on his back; his deformity was very evident. 'Could you have stopped her?' she asked.

He shook his head. 'No, although God knows I tried. But she was a headstrong girl and dead set on "doing her bit", as she called it.'

'It sounds as if she went off to work happy enough that night,' Emma said, trying to find a crumb of comfort to offer.

'Aye. She did.' He straightened up. 'I suppose you might say she died happy. But that's about all you could say,' he added bitterly.

'At least she had a life. She was lucky enough to have you to fall in love with and marry.' She was quiet for a moment, then realizing how her words might sound, added quickly, 'My little Ivy died before her time. She never knew what it was like to fall in love.' She glanced at him. 'But thank you for telling me, Henry. I won't speak about it again.'

'Maybe I won't mind now,' he said thoughtfully. 'I came to live down here to get away from the memory of it all; but what I hadn't realized is that you don't get away from memories, you take them with you wherever you go.'

They were both silent for a while, watching a blackbird pecking about among the gravestones, then she asked, 'Do you like it here in these parts, Henry?'

He nodded. 'Yes, I do. The air is fresh and clean and there's plenty of space. I wouldn't ever want to go back up north.' He paused, then said again, 'Yes. I'm happy here now. Mr Philip is a good man to work for and I know I'm useful to him. I've got a decent little cottage,' he flashed her a brief smile. 'And good neighbours. What more can a man ask? Under the circumstances, that is.'

'Of course.' She smiled at him. 'That's good. And thank you again for telling me about Florrie, I hope it's helped.'

'Yes, it has.' He touched her hand briefly. 'You're a good friend, Emma.'

'You're a good friend to me, Henry. I don't know how I'd manage without you, especially when Arthur . . .' She put her hand up to her mouth in horror. 'Oh Lord, Arthur'll be shouting for his tea . . .' She looked at him apologetically, reluctant to have been the one to break the tenuous link between them. 'If it's not ready when he thinks it should be . . . I'm sorry, Henry, I'll have to go.' She stood up but made no move to go.

He smiled up at her and took her hand, giving it a little shake. 'It's all right, Emma, lass. I understand,' he said quietly. 'You don't want to risk the rough edge of his tongue.' Or worse, he thought, as he watched her hurry out of the graveyard. Not until she had disappeared from view did he light another cigarette, thinking, not for the first time that Arthur Blatch didn't appreciate what a lovely woman he was married to.

Nine

For some time after Emma had gone, Henry sat there quietly smoking. He was experiencing the strangest sensation: it was as if something inside him that had been held in a tight grip for a long time had been loosened or absorbed, leaving him feeling quietly contented and relaxed. He knew what it was, of course. For years he had held the details of Florrie's death close to his heart, consumed with bitterness and unable to talk about it or to share his thoughts or feelings with anyone else. He had been so obsessed with the unfairness of her dying so young and violently that he had never thought to look back with gratitude on the happy times they had spent together. But this afternoon, as she talked about her own little daughter's tragically short life, Emma had shown him his mistake and helped him understand that the best way to keep Florrie alive in his heart was to talk about her, to tell other people what a lively lass, full of life and hope, she had been. Her life had been short, too short, but they had been happy in the few years they had spent together. Florrie had been ambitious, with her plans for their own little shop; plans that he had never really shared, although he had never spoiled her dreams by telling her this. Instead, he had been happy to bask in her excitement, watching her blue eyes shine as she outlined ever more ambitious and hare-brained schemes that he knew could never come to fruition; knowing, too, that some day he would have to bring her down to earth and tell her so.

But with her untimely death, that day had never come and she had died still dreaming her dreams. That, at least, was something to be thankful for.

He took out his pocket watch and looked at it, dragging himself back to the present. Then, as the hour registered, he quickly got to his feet and ground the remains of his cigarette under his heel. He had been away longer than he'd intended; Mr Philip would be wondering where he'd got to. Pulling back his shoulders as far as the pain would allow, he started off back to Warren's End, whistling cheerfully as he went.

Mrs Stella was just crossing the yard as he arrived. She looked the picture of health in a loose, flowery garment in shades of green and gold that set off her brown eyes and auburn hair. With that smock thing on, you'd never know she'd be having a baby in less than three months, he thought admiringly. She wasn't wearing a hat – obviously the missus hadn't seen her go out or she'd have made her put one on – and was carrying a wicker trug with daffodils in it.

She smiled and waved as soon as she saw him.

'Look, Henry,' she said as soon as she got near. 'I saw these in the border at the end of the garden and Mr Govan . . .' She looked enquiringly at him to make sure she'd got the name right, and when he nodded she went on, 'Mr Govan, who was weeding the borders, said why didn't I pick a bunch to take indoors. So I did.' She held them up for his inspection.

'Very nice they are, too, Mrs Stella,' he said, smiling back at her and thinking what an attractive young lady she was. 'They were my Florrie's favourite flowers. She always said they came just when they were needed most, a bit of brightness after the long winter days.' It was good to be able to talk about Florrie; Emma was right, it helped.

'That's why I love them, too,' Stella said. She frowned a little. 'The only thing is, I seem to have picked rather more than I need. Do you think Mrs Rosalie might like some? There were so many I just kept picking . . . You see, I've never had a garden where I was allowed to pick the flowers, so I rather got carried away and didn't realize how many I'd taken. There are still hundreds left,' she added quickly in case he should think she'd stripped them all.

'Yes, I'm sure there are. That end of the garden is always a picture in the spring. I was just going in to Mr Philip, so why don't you come in with me and ask her if she'd like some?'

He pushed open the door of the flat and she followed him into the small square hallway with doors to left and right. He tapped on the one to the left.

'Anyone home?' he called, opening the door a crack.

'No, she's gone out.' Philip's voice came from somewhere on the other side of the hallway.

Henry put his head round the door opposite. 'I've got Mrs Stella with me, sir. She's come to see Mrs Rosalie.'

'Well, since Rosie's not here she can come and brighten my day. Bring her in, man, don't leave her standing on the doorstep.'

Henry stood to one side and Stella stepped into what was clearly Philip's studio. It was a large room, light and airy, with windows all along the length of the wall looking out on to the garden and a skylight in the roof. The far end of the room was curtained off from floor to ceiling by a blue-velvet curtain. Philip was sitting on a swivel chair at his easel with his back to the windows so that the light fell on his work, and there was a table to his right covered in paints, brushes, palettes, bottles and jars of fixer and brush cleaner, bits of rag, and pencils spilling out of a pencil case. A large box of pastels stood open at the end of the table, and a few canvases were propped against the nearby wall.

He looked up and gave a wide smile as she walked in. 'Ah, a beautiful young lady has come to brighten my day.' He waved his hand. 'Sorry about the mess, Stella. I'd have got Henry to tidy up a bit if I'd known you were coming. But you're very welcome. Can you find a chair? Sorry I can't do the polite thing and get up and fetch it for you. Ah, good man, Henry.'

Stella sat down on the chair Henry had brought forward for her. 'I only came in to offer Rosalie a few of these daffodils. I seem to have picked rather a lot.' She held the basket up. 'They are rather lovely, aren't they?'

'Mm, indeed they are.' He put his head on one side and looked from the daffodils to a small table in front of the blue curtains. 'Would you mind putting them down on that little table over there? That's it, just there where I can see them.' He smiled at her again. 'I'm assuming you've got time for a cuppa while you wait for Rosie? I expect she'll be home before long, although goodness knows where she's gone.'

'I'll put the kettle on, sir,' Henry said vanishing through a door next to the one they had come in by.

'Good man.' Philip spoke absent-mindedly. He had put another sheet of paper on the easel and was busy sketching the basket of daffodils.

Stella felt a bit uncomfortable, not knowing whether to make conversation or whether it would disturb him. She was just beginning to think it would have been better if she hadn't come when he whisked the paper off the easel and handed it to her. It was a quick pencil sketch but the daffodils were all there, even the one with the broken stem that was hanging over the edge of the basket as it stood on the table with the folds of the curtain behind.

'My goodness, that was quick!' she said, astonished.

'It's just a rough sketch to remind me,' he said with a shrug. 'I'll do a proper painting of them later for you, if you like.'

'I'd like that very much,' she answered, her voice warm. 'I was looking at one of your paintings while I waited for you outside the gallery the other day. A beach scene at low tide. It was in the window.' She hesitated. 'I liked it very much. It looked so peaceful with the sun setting over the water and the solitary man gathering . . .'

He grinned. 'Probably digging for bait to go fishing with.' He shrugged. 'Anyway, Ben liked it and thought it would sell. He only took it last week, so I guess he's waiting to take it up to London. An associate of his has a gallery there, and Ben looks out for stuff for him. Ah, here's the tea. And biscuits, too. Good chap, Henry, you're a man after my own heart. Brought a cup for yourself?'

'No, sir. I've left mine in the kitchen, thanks all the same. There's a bit of clearing up to do in there.'

Philip gave an exasperated sigh. 'I'll bet there is. My wife must be the messiest woman in Christendom, but I don't see why you should clear up after her, Henry. I thought that was Mrs Blatch's job.'

'Oh, I don't mind giving a hand, sir.' Especially if it lightens Emma's load a bit, Henry thought to himself as he went back into the little kitchen.

'Of course I knew you painted, but I'd never seen any of your work before,' Stella continued, sipping her tea gratefully.

He offered her a biscuit and took one himself. After a few minutes he said, 'If you're interested there are some water-colours over there, waiting to be taken to be mounted and framed.' He nodded towards two boards leaning against the wall.

She got up and turned them over and put them side by side. Two of them were the same size, about eighteen inches by twelve, but the subjects were very different. One was an early spring scene depicting an avenue of elms either side of a rutted lane, the leaves, just breaking into bud in the fore-ground, gradually blurring into a green fuzz as the lane faded into the distance. A single figure, bent under the weight of the bundle of faggots he was carrying, was making his way home after a long day's work. The figure wasn't clearly defined, yet there was no doubt about the weariness in his step and the weight of the faggots on his back.

The other was a picture of a sailing barge stacked with bales of straw, its red sails set, drifting down river on the ebb tide towards a distant misty estuary. Again, there was a single figure, this time standing at the tiller. A faint wisp of smoke drifted on the evening air from the clay pipe clamped between his jaws.

The only things the two paintings had in common were that they were both evening scenes and both included a solitary figure.

The third picture was bigger, a hunting scene bright with red-coated riders galloping across a field, the hooves of the horses kicking up clods of earth as they thundered towards a low hedge, the riders bent over their necks, urging them on. The whole picture was of speed and excitement. Stella turned away.

'Did they catch the fox?' she asked.

He shrugged. 'Probably. We usually did.'

'Oh, you used to hunt, too?' She didn't know why she should have been surprised.

'Yes. In another life.' His tone was neutral.

Slightly embarrassed, she turned back to the smaller pictures. 'I like these,' she said. 'I like these very much. Better than the one of the horses.' She glanced at him, embarrassed again. 'Oh, I'm sorry, I shouldn't have said that.'

'It's all right. You don't have to apologize,' Philip said. 'I agree with you.'

'I don't. I love horsy pictures.'

Stella turned quickly. She hadn't heard Rosalie come into the room.

'Well, of course, you would.' There was an unmistakable edge to Philip's words. 'You love horses.'

'So did you. Once upon a time,' Rosalie said bitterly. 'Not any more, of course.' She threw down her bag and turned to Stella with a smirk. 'I'll bet he hasn't shown you his special collection, has he? The ones he keeps hidden away.'

Stella shook her head. 'No. I was just looking at these. They're very good, aren't they?'

'Oh, you should see the other ones. You really should.' She walked over to the end of the room where the curtains hung.

'No, Rosalie! No!' Philip shouted. 'You know I don't let . . .' Agitated, he tried to get to his feet, knocking his walking sticks on to the floor as he tried to grab them and spilling the tea he had only half finished, so that it ran among the tubes and pots of paint on the table beside him. Defeated, he sank back on to his chair with a sigh and put his head in his hands while Rosalie pulled back the curtain to reveal a number of canvases stacked several deep against the wall. She obviously knew exactly what she was looking for as she chose painting after painting.

Puzzled, Stella watched, frowning, as Rosalie lined them up, obviously relishing the moment, not with any sense of pride in her husband's achievements, but rather with an expression of cruel triumph at what she was exposing.

The paintings were not big, each one about twenty-four inches by eighteen, and at first sight they all appeared uniformly drab, simply bold streaks of black and all shades of grey, apparently daubed at random, making no sense at all. But then as Stella studied them, the nightmares emerged; scene after scene of carnage, of twisted barbed wire, of mangled and partly dismembered bodies, some flung together in mud-filled holes, some half in, half out of ditches, some lying mutilated in fields; of faces stark with horror or pain, of crippled horses, of broken tanks and guns, of chilling, empty desolation.

Shocked beyond words at the horror, Stella sat down on the nearest chair, her hand over her mouth. The paintings showed a rare, brutal but intensely private talent, and at that moment she hated Rosalie for her insensitivity in so cruelly exposing her husband's deepest feelings. Yet she couldn't take her eyes off them.

There was silence in the room. Then Philip heaved a deep sigh.

'All right, Rosalie, you've had your fun. Now, please, put them back where they were.' He spoke quietly, but his face was ashen and as Stella looked up she saw his hand tremble as he passed it across his forehead.

'You should sell them. As a set.' Rosalie said lightly, either oblivious to or wilfully ignoring the effect they were having on him. She put her head on one side. 'War hero's reminiscences. They'd probably make your fortune, darling. Like that other chap, what's his name? Picasso.'

'Don't talk such bloody rubbish!' he snapped. 'Just put them back where you found them. Please!' He turned his head and looked out of the window while she put the paintings back in their hiding place. 'I'm sorry, Stella,' he said distantly. 'Rosalie shouldn't have done that. It was unforgivable of her.'

'Oh, I'm always doing things I shouldn't,' Rosalie said cheerfully, seemingly unaware of the atmosphere in the room, 'so it's nothing new. Oh, those daffodils are nice. Can I have some?'

'What? Oh, yes, I came to see if you'd like some. Take what you want.' Stella waved her hand, still reeling from the shock of what she had just witnessed.

'Thanks. I'll go and find a vase to put them in.' Having helped herself to more than half the daffodils, Rosalie picked up her bag and left.

'I'm really sorry about that, Stella,' Philip said quietly, turning to look at her. 'I'm embarrassed, too. Those paintings are not meant to be seen. They were done when I was . . . Well, at a difficult time.' He peered at her. 'Stella, are you all right?'

With an effort, Stella pulled herself together and smiled at him through unexpected tears. 'Yes, I'll be fine. It was just . . .'

'I understand.' His voice was gentle. 'I can't think what came over Rosalie. She should never have done that to you, especially in . . .' He hesitated. 'In your condition.'

She blew her nose. 'I knew these things happened, of course I did. But those pictures made it all so . . . so real,' she whispered.

'Oh, it was real, all right,' he said grimly. His voice dropped. 'And so were the nightmares. It was only by painting them out of my head that they gave me any peace and I could sleep at night.'

'You showed the things that really went on, the things

nobody ever talked about,' she said, shaking her head. 'They were horrible, but at the same time they were wonderful in the way you . . .'

'You mustn't dwell on them,' he interrupted harshly. 'Just don't think about them. Forget you ever saw them. They weren't meant to be viewed. Rosalie was an insensitive bloody fool to drag them out like that.'

She shook her head again. 'No, I shan't ever forget them, Philip. It was a privilege to have seen them, even though they were so disturbing.'

They sat in silence for several minutes. In the quietness Stella could feel the baby moving inside her, and she laid her hand protectively on her stomach.

Philip noticed and half smiled. 'You'll have John's baby before long, Stella. That's where the future lies, not in the horrors of the past. That's what's important and that's what you must cling on to.' He held out his hand to her and she got to her feet and placed hers in it. He held it for a fraction longer than necessary, and put it to his lips before he released it.

As she crossed the yard to her flat, she realized that in some indefinable way their relationship had altered and would never be quite the same again.

Ten

Back in her own flat Stella arranged the remaining daffodils in a vase and put them on the table, but her thoughts were still with the scenes she had witnessed over at Philip and Rosalie's flat. She found it hard to believe that Rosalie could have been so cruel as to expose those intensely private paintings of Philip's, executed when he was so traumatized and vulnerable. Yet she was glad to have seen them; she felt privileged to have been shown a side of him that few others were aware of. And when he had taken her hand and kissed it as she left, she knew that he understood this and was neither angry nor embarrassed.

Suddenly weary, she picked up a magazine and sat down and put her feet up on a stool. But the disturbing images Philip had painted were still fresh in her mind. John must have witnessed things like that, as had thousands of others on the battlefield. She tried to imagine what their effect would have been on the carefree, impetuous husband she had known. There had been no hint in his letters and he had rarely spoken about such things in their brief time together. Now she would never know how he had felt.

Sometimes she felt she had hardly known him at all.

She tried to turn her attention to an article on making patchwork cushions but couldn't concentrate, so she was almost relieved when there was a tap at the door – even though she knew it would be Doreen, come to make sure she was having her afternoon rest (or to spy on her, as she regarded it in her less charitable moments).

'Come in,' she called resignedly and was surprised when it was Rosalie, not Doreen who appeared.

'Phil nagged at me to come over to apologize and make sure you're OK,' she said, flopping down in the other armchair. 'So. I'm sorry and are you OK?' She sounded neither sorry nor particularly concerned.

Stella nodded. 'Yes, I'm fine, thanks.' She shifted in her chair. 'Although I must admit it was a bit of a shock, being confronted . . .'

'Yes, I didn't think. I suppose I should have done.' She shrugged. 'But that's me, all over.' She got out her cigarette holder and put a cigarette into it and lit it before she spoke again, more pensively. 'I suppose it's because I've got used to it. Because I was the one who had to be there to comfort him in the way only a wife can when he woke up screaming in terror night after night when they first let him home. Not that I was much help at first; I was as terrified as he was, I couldn't understand what was happening. As you can imagine, I was relieved – and that's an understatement – when he began to paint the nightmares out of his system. I could see they were a form of release. I just thanked God he'd got the talent to paint.'

'Does he still have nightmares?'

She hunched her shoulders briefly. 'No, I don't think so. But he mostly sleeps in his own room now, so he won't disturb me if his legs trouble him. Didn't you notice his bed behind the curtain?'

Stella frowned and shook her head. 'I only saw the paintings.'

'Yes, I daresay.' She flicked ash into an ashtray. 'Anyway, it's better that we have separate rooms,' she added with a shrug. 'At least, that's the way I prefer it.' She stood up and took the photograph of John down from the mantelpiece and studied it. 'Do you miss him much?' she asked bluntly, looking down at Stella.

'Of course I do. I'm having his baby, for God's sake, and he's not here to share it with me,' she replied, her voice sharp.

'But at least you've got unspoilt memories.' She put the photograph back where it belonged.

'What do you mean?'

'You've got unspoilt memories of the man you married.' She sat down in the armchair again and drew several times on her cigarette before stubbing it out. 'The man I felt so lucky to marry was six feet tall, the most handsome man in the county and one of the most athletic. He ran and rowed, and his horsemanship was second to none. He rode to hounds and was always in at the kill, was in all the point-to-points, and loved a good gallop over the countryside. He was always in demand at the hunt ball because he danced like a dream and made every woman feel she was gossamer in his arms. He was charming, funny, always on the go, always the first to try something new.' She paused. 'Like joining the army.' She closed her eyes. 'God, and to think I was so proud that he was one of the first to join up.' Her eyes flew open. 'That was the man I married. But look at him now, an old man with a face lined with pain and hair turning prematurely grey, dragging himself around on crutches or sitting and daubing paint on canvas. You can't imagine how I hate the smell of paint and turpentine,' she said savagely. She looked out of the window. 'Maybe you should think yourself lucky that John died. At least your memories of him will always be of the man you married, not the constant presence like a millstone round your neck of some wreck who came back from the bloody war.'

'Rosalie! That's a truly dreadful thing to say,' Stella said in a low voice.

'Yes, I know. I've never actually put it into words before, but I can't help it if it's the way I feel, can I?'

'What about Philip? It can't be much of a picnic for him, either. How do you think he feels, not being able to do all the things he used to enjoy?' Stella spoke sharply, shocked and furious at Rosalie's callous words.

She shrugged. 'Dunno. He doesn't talk about it and I don't ask. He seems to have developed a kind of stoic patience, and even that drives me mad at times. I just wish that now and again he would rant and roar at the injustice of it all.' She got up restlessly and went over to study her reflection in the mirror over the fireplace. Then she put her hands over her hair, coiled in earphones over her ears, and twisted her head this way and that.

'I think I'll get all this cut off,' she said, changing the subject and talking as much to herself as to Stella. 'When it's loose, it reaches halfway down my back.' She turned. 'Do you think a bob would suit me, Stella? Or a semi-shingle? They're all the rage, you know.'

'What?' Stella dragged her mind back to what Rosalie was saying. 'Oh, yes, so I believe.' She put her head on one side and tried to concentrate. 'I don't know. It would make you look very different. What does Philip say? Would he mind?'

'Phil?' She raised her eyebrows in surprise. 'Why should he mind? What's it got to do with him? It's my hair.' She turned back to the mirror and studied her image again. 'I'll have to think about it.'

She sat down again and put another cigarette into the tortoiseshell holder.

'Let's see . . .' she said when she had lit it and blown out a long column of smoke. 'We were talking about horses back there, weren't we? Which is much more interesting. Do you ride? I could find you a hack . . .' She made a face. 'Ah, no, of course not. Mustn't risk the precious bundle, must we?'

'Don't you start!' Stella said quickly. 'It's bad enough . . .' She flushed. 'Oh, sorry.'

Rosalie laughed. 'Don't worry, I quite sympathize. Ma can

be a bit of a pain. But you see, John was her golden boy – couldn't do any wrong in her eyes – and the thought of having his child . . .'

'She's not having his child, I am!' Stella said hotly.

'Make the most of it, then,' Rosalie said dryly, 'because once it's born you won't get a look in if Ma has her way. She's desperate for grandchildren, you know.'

'Well, she's only getting one. Unless you decide to oblige her,' Stella said. She wished Rosalie would go. She was becoming tired of the way she hopped up and down and skipped from one topic to another. And her cigarette was making her feel slightly sick.

'No chance of that.' Rosalie got to her feet again. 'Well, I'll leave you to rest and look after the precious bundle. Cheerio.'

After she had gone, Stella thought over her sister-in-law's words. *Once it's born you won't get a look in if Ma has her way.*

She closed her eyes and put her arms protectively round her stomach. Things never turned out the way you imagined, she thought philosophically. She had never imagined that she would one day be living in the house of her husband's parents, without John but soon to have his baby and uncertain what the future was likely to hold. She had soon come to realize that she had only been made welcome at Warren's End because of John's child growing inside her. The big question was, would she be as welcome once it was born? Or would Doreen try to take him from her? To give him a better life than she, Stella, could offer? Or would she take a more subtle approach?

Subtle? Stella's mouth set. What had happened over the business of the perambulator – or 'baby carriage', as her mother-in-law insisted on calling it – could hardly have been called subtle.

It had happened, as most things seemed to, over dinner one night.

'The Gamages' catalogue has arrived,' Doreen had said brightly. 'You remember you posted off the application for me, Stella? Well, it came this morning and I've chosen the perambulator I think we should have for the precious bundle.' She had beamed round at everybody for approval. 'I'll show it to you after dinner, Stella, then we can send for it. It will come by rail but don't worry, it will be very carefully packed so there's no danger of it being damaged.'

Stella had licked her lips, her mouth dry, although she despised herself for being so nervous about standing up to her mother-in-law. 'But, Doreen, I've already seen a perambulator that I like in the window of Luckings in the town,' she'd said. 'In fact I've put down a small deposit on it.'

Doreen had frowned, annoyed. 'You never told me,' she'd said accusingly. Then her face had cleared and she'd waved her hand. 'But never mind, we can easily get that back,' she'd said, as if it was of no importance. 'How much was this perambulator?'

'Three guineas.' Stella hadn't added that it was the most she could afford.

Doreen had pursed her lips. Then she'd given what was meant to be a disarming smile, though it looked more like a patronizing one. 'Oh, I think we can do better than that, dear. The one I've chosen is a little more expensive but it has ball-bearing wheels and is very well sprung, so it will be very comfortable for Baby.'

'How much more expensive, Doreen?' Roger had asked wryly, dabbing his moustache with his napkin.

She'd given a little shrug. 'It will cost nine guineas, to be exact. But I know you won't begrudge paying a little extra for your son's child, will you, dear?' It was a statement, not a question, and accompanied by a somewhat steely look that brooked no argument.

A steely look that had cut no ice with Roger. 'No,' he'd said thoughtfully, ignoring it. 'Provided it meets with Stella's approval, that is. Obviously, the choice must be hers and if she has already chosen one she likes . . . After all, it will be for her baby.' There was a tiny but unmistakable emphasis on 'her'.

'And *our* grandchild, Roger.' This time the emphasis was quite emphatic.

Of course, when Doreen had shown her the catalogue after dinner Stella knew she was defeated. The luxury baby carriage that Doreen had chosen was far superior in every way to the one she had chosen in Luckings. But it was with not much more than a flat nod that she acknowledged this as she agreed to Doreen's choice, remembering how excited she had been to hand over the ten-shilling deposit in Luckings.

She'd derived some small comfort from the fact that the more expensive perambulator would be better for the baby. But she couldn't help the feeling, a feeling that had stayed with her, that she was being manipulated by a kind of kid-gloved domination – a bit like being smothered in a thick eiderdown that had a layer of steel in the middle.

She lifted her head and looked up at the photograph of her husband, smiling down at her as if he hadn't a care in the world, and a moment of rage boiled inside her at the unfairness of a fate that had taken him from her at the time when she was going to need him most.

How would he have coped with his domineering mother? Would he have stood up to her or gone along with her wishes? The truth was, she really had not much idea of what John's relationship with his parents had been. In fact, she hadn't really known all that much about him when they married; she had simply fallen head over heels in love with this handsome officer who had swept her off her feet. Oh, she knew a bit about his family: where they lived, the fact that he had a sister, superficial bits of information that in retrospect didn't amount to all that much. But she knew very little about the man himself, what made him tick, what he thought about things, other than that he loved and wanted her. He had left her in no doubt about that. She frowned, trying to recall their time together, what they had done, where they had gone. They had been married in church, but it was she who had insisted on that and he'd gone along with it because it was what she wanted. She wasn't even sure what his beliefs were; if indeed he had any. And now she would never find out, unless it was from his sister, who seemed very keen to point out that she knew him much better than Stella did. Or ever would.

She got to her feet and picked up the photograph.

'You're not here to help me fight my battles, my darling, so I shall have to fight them alone,' she whispered. 'And I shall. Nobody is going to take our baby from me, I promise you that.'

She replaced the photograph and sat down again. They were brave words, but hollow, because where would she go, what would she do, and how would she bring up a child alone in the world, with nowhere to live and little money, if she were to be forced to leave Warren's End?

It was a sobering thought.

Eleven

There were still plenty of daffodils in the garden at Easter, which came late that year, and Mr Govan was instructed to take a large basketful to help decorate the church. Stella had already discovered that the family were not regular churchgoers, but Christmas, Easter and Harvest Thanksgiving were the three occasions on which the entire family was expected to attend. This puzzled her. To her mind either you went to church regularly or you didn't go at all, and most Sundays she went to either the morning or the evening service. As a result, the others – especially Rosalie – thought she was a little odd.

'Surely you don't believe all that stuff?' she said scornfully, meeting Stella on her way to church one Sunday, as she rode back, exhilarated, from her morning ride on Magpie.

'It's peaceful and I enjoy singing the hymns and psalms,' Stella replied, looking up at her and resolutely smiling. This was hardly the time to embark on a discussion about such a deep and complex subject.

'Well, each to his own, I suppose. Me, I'd rather be out in the open air than cooped up in a musty old church. Walk on, Magpie.'

But on Easter Sunday Rosalie was given no choice, and for once she put up no resistance.

It turned out to be quite an occasion. Doreen had decided that as John had now been dead for six months the family could finally come out of mourning, much to Rosalie's relief. To mark the occasion Doreen had chosen a pale-blue-silk ankle-length dress, over which she wore a three-quarter-length coat in darker blue and a matching straw hat with a wide brim, decorated lavishly with pale-blue ribbons and feathers. Rosalie was wearing a rust-coloured costume with a long military-style jacket and a skirt with a hemline raised to match her father's eyebrows when he saw it, although he wisely made no comment. Her close-fitting cloche hat was trimmed to match her cream blouse.

At seven months pregnant, Stella had little choice but to wear what she always wore now that the weather was becoming less cold: a green cloak in a light serge, which she had made herself from the pattern of the heavy winter one her mother had bought for her when she began nursing, and a darker green hat with a small turned-up brim.

Before they all set off, Doreen looked her up and down. 'Yes, I think that's suitably concealing,' she said uncertainly.

'It's what I wear to church every Sunday,' Stella replied cheerfully. 'In fact, it's what I wear every time I go out. Not that I'm ashamed of my condition,' she added quickly.

'No, no, of course not,' Doreen said hurriedly, adding in a low voice, 'But one doesn't wish to flaunt it, especially in front of the men.' She turned away and called loudly, 'Aren't you ready yet, Rosalie? And where's Philip? Your father is just bringing the Daimler round.' She said this with pride: the appearance of the Daimler was almost as rare as the appearance of the family at church.

'He's gone on ahead,' Rosalie said as she sauntered along to join them. 'Henry's driving him in Tin Lizzie. He said there wouldn't be room for all of us in Pa's jalopy.'

'Jalopy, indeed! How disrespectful. And that's nonsense. There would have been plenty of room for all of us. Ah, here's your father now. Come along, both of you.'

Stella couldn't help smiling to herself at the way Doreen was marshalling her and Rosalie as if they were children, and the thought crossed her mind that there would be no need for all this fuss if they all made a habit of going every week. But she wisely kept her own counsel and obediently got into the car, though given the choice she would have preferred to walk, as she did most Sundays.

The church was a riot of colour, with spring flowers and

catkins decorating every ledge and huge arrangements of daffodils and narcissi on pedestals, displaying the skill and artistry of some of the more talented ladies.

'Our daffodils look splendid, don't they?' Doreen whispered to Stella, although how she could have been so sure which ones came from Warren's End was a mystery.

After the service and the ritual shaking of the vicar's hand and comments on his sermon, they strolled through the churchyard, matching their speed to Philip's uneasy progress.

Henry was waiting at the gate for him with Tin Lizzie.

'I'm going for a spin before lunch. Anyone want to come?' Philip asked.

'Not me, thanks,' Rosalie said. 'I prefer the comfort of Pa's jal . . . Of the Daimler.'

'What about you, Stella?'

Stella smiled. 'Yes. I'd like . . .'

'Stella will come with us,' Doreen interrupted quickly. She smiled conspiratorially at her daughter-in-law. 'We mustn't risk harming the precious bundle, must we, dear? Come along, Roger's waiting.' She almost pushed Stella into the Daimler beside Rosalie.

'So *there's* telling you,' Rosalie said under her breath, grinning.

Stella said nothing, but she was seething inside at being treated like a child.

'I really can't think what's got into Philip, wanting to go for a drive before lunch,' Doreen complained over the purr of the engine. 'He knows very well I like the meal to be punctual. I do hope he won't be late, so the roast lamb isn't spoiled.'

But when they arrived back at the house and Rosalie removed her hat, Stella at once understood why Philip had decided to keep out of the way for a bit; and she had to bite her lip to prevent herself from breaking into a grin at the horrified expression on Doreen's face.

'Rosalie! What have you done! What *have* you done? Oh, my heavens, look at you! Your beautiful hair, all gone!' Doreen said, holding her hands up in horror as she stared at her.

'Mm.' Rosalie preened in front of the mirror, trying to look at her short, sleek bob from all angles, thoroughly enjoying the knowledge that she had shocked her mother. 'Don't you like it? Bobbed hair is all the rage, you know, Ma.'

'Like it? Of course I don't like it. I think it looks terrible. It's as straight as a pound of candles and makes you look like . . . like . . . some boy!' It was the worst thing she could think of to say. 'And it will take ages to grow again. Have you thought about that?'

'But I'm not going to let it grow again, Ma. I like it this way.' She patted it lovingly, still gazing at herself in the mirror. 'But you're right, it is a bit straight. I think I might have a Marcel wave later on.'

'A Marcel wave . . .! Rosalie, how could you!' Doreen looked as if she was about to faint with shock.

'I might not. I'll have to think about it.' She put her head on one side, still studying herself in the mirror.

Roger cleared his throat. 'Do you think we might move into the morning room so that Stella can sit down and I can have a Scotch before you continue this argument, ladies?' he said mildly.

'But, Roger, it's dreadful. Can't you see? Rosalie's had all her beautiful hair cut off!' Doreen said in desperation.

'Of course I can see, my dear. I'm not blind,' he replied. 'I think Rosalie always looks very nice,' He smiled at his daughter as he endeavoured to shepherd them all into the morning room. In truth he had never liked Rosalie's hair coiled over her ears in what they called 'earphones' or some such, although he would never have dreamt of saying so. He went over to the sideboard. 'Would you like a sherry, Stella?' he asked, smiling at her over his shoulder.

'No, of course she wouldn't! Remember her condition,' Doreen snapped.

He ignored this and raised his eyebrows questioningly at Stella.

She smiled. 'Yes, I think I should enjoy a sherry, Roger, thank you,' she replied. Not that she cared much for sherry but, still smarting over the way she had been hustled into the Daimler after church, she would have agreed to almost anything at that moment to defy Doreen.

Thwarted, Doreen returned to the attack on Rosalie. 'What

does Philip say about your outrageous hairstyle?' she asked. 'I imagine he's furious.'

'Actually, he says he thinks it suits me,' Rosalie said, adding, over her shoulder, 'And if you're pouring drinks, Pa, I'll have a Scotch.'

Doreen glared at her. 'Scotch! Whatever next! I think you must have got in with a very fast set down at the country club,' she said primly. 'You never used to drink whisky. Nor smoke,' she added as Rosalie scrabbled in her bag for her cigarette lighter.

'Well, I do now.' Rosalie blew a smoke ring. 'It's all the rage.'

'I don't know what this "rage" thing is, but what with hemlines going up to goodness knows where, heads practically shorn and women smoking like chimneys, I do begin to wonder what the world is coming to.' She gave a shudder, then looked up as Philip struggled into the room. 'Can't you control your wife, Philip?' she asked sharply.

He gave a snort. 'Control? I'd like to try! Men don't control their wives these days, Doreen, I thought you of all people would have known that.' His reply was tinged with sarcasm, which was quite lost on Doreen. He reached the settee and lowered himself carefully into it, placing his sticks within easy reach, then patted his pockets. 'Oh, give me one of your fags, Rosie, will you? I must have left mine in the car.'

She passed him the packet of Gold Flake and her lighter.

'But what about her hair, Philip! Why did you allow her to have it all cut off?' Doreen persisted.

'It was her choice,' Philip replied, unperturbed. 'She doesn't ask me what she should or shouldn't do. She's a modern woman, Doreen.'

'I'm also here, in the room, and don't care to be discussed in the third person,' Rosalie remarked pettishly.

'So you are, darling. And looking quite charming and boyish with your shorn locks.' Philip smiled at her.

But all he got in return was a vitriolic 'Don't patronize me!'

Just then, Maisie appeared in the doorway.

Roger looked up with a sigh of relief. 'Ah, Maisie. Lunch served? Good. We'll be right there.' He got to his feet. 'Come along, everybody. Mustn't keep the roast lamb waiting.'

★　★　★

Maisie went back to the kitchen, where Henry had just come in with the log basket.

'Mrs Rosalie has had all her hair cut off! Did you know?' she said, her eyes sparkling with the news.

'What *all* of it?' Emma asked, aghast. She was just taking off her pinafore ready to go home.

'No, silly. Of course not all of it,' Maisie said impatiently. 'But she's had it cut short. You know, bobbed, almost like a boy. You should've seen Madam's face! Her look would've curdled milk! Did you know about it, Henry?'

'Yes. Mr Philip told me she'd had it cut.' He grinned. 'That's why he wanted to go for a spin in the car before lunch. He thought he'd stay out of the way till the dust settled.'

'I don't blame him! Does he like it?'

Henry shrugged. 'Don't think he cares much one way or the other, to tell you the truth. Not that she'd ask his opinion.'

'Funny way of going on, in't it?' Emma said thoughtfully. 'I can just imagine what Arthur would say if I went and had my hair chopped off without asking him first. I'd be black and blue for a week.'

Henry was stacking the logs beside the stove, and nobody noticed the look of pain that crossed his face. He turned. 'You're not thinking of having your hair cut off, Emma, are you?'

She shook her head. 'No, 'course not. It'd be too expensive, for a start.'

'Anyway, it's nice as it is.' He smiled at her.

Maisie went over to the mirror. 'Do you think it would suit me to have short hair?' she asked, putting her head on one side.

'You wouldn't be able to keep your cap on if your hair was short,' Emma said practically.

'What do you think, Henry?'

He shrugged. 'I dunno much about women's hair.' He turned to Emma. 'Are you ready to go, Emma? I've finished here for a few hours, so I'll walk back with you.'

'You can have a bit of dinner with us if you like. I left it in the oven and Mary's keeping an eye on it and seeing to the vegetables. There'll be plenty. I don't know that Arthur'll want much, not after the skinful he had at the pub last night. By the way, thank you for getting him home, Henry.'

'Drunk again, was he? I don't know how you put up with it, Emma, I really don't,' Maisie said, pursing her lips.

'I put up with it because he's my husband, that's why,' Emma replied quietly. 'He wasn't like he is now before he went to the war; he was a good, steady man and a loving father. It's the war that changed him. He drinks to help him forget.'

'Forget what?'

'Oh, use your loaf, Maisie! What do you think?' Henry said with a trace of impatience.

'The things he saw and the things he had to do, of course,' Emma explained. She gave a little shudder. 'When he first came home, he used to have the most terrible choking fits. I used to think he'd choke himself to death. It was the gas, it messed up his lungs. He got gassed at least twice in France. He had nightmares, too, at first. He doesn't often get them now, but when there's a thunderstorm it's nothing unusual to find him hiding under the bed, shaking. That's what war did to him, Maisie, and that's why I don't complain when he comes home drunk. The least I can do is to stick by him, poor devil.'

Henry had been watching her as she spoke, his eyes soft. 'You're a good woman, Emma,' he said. He reached down her coat from its hook on the back of the door and held it for her. 'Come on, let's be going or I'll be due back here for Mr Philip before I've had time to eat that dinner you've promised me.'

Maisie sat down at the kitchen table after they'd gone. Maybe, she thought sadly, remembering Emma's words, there were worse things in the world than being single. But there were times, particularly at night when she couldn't sleep and longed to have a man to cuddle up to, when she couldn't think of many.

Back in her room after a delicious lunch eaten in a decidedly frosty atmosphere, Stella sat in front of her dressing table and unpinned her auburn hair, letting it fall round her shoulders in waves. It would be much more manageable if she had it cut short, she decided thoughtfully, putting her head on one side, although it was too curly to wear in a sleek helmet like Rosalie's. There wouldn't be much time for complicated hairstyles when the baby arrived. Not that her hairstyle was complicated, a quick twist into a loose bun on top of her head didn't take two minutes.

She smiled a little, remembering how John had loved to take the pins out and watch it fall to her shoulders; how he would run it through his fingers or brush it until it hung like a silky auburn curtain. Sometimes he would bury his head in it and muss it all up, and have to start brushing it again. She rested her elbows on the dressing table and cupped her chin in her hands. John had loved her hair; he even loved to spread it all round her on the pillow, not caring that it would be a mass of tangles when they woke in the morning. For that reason, if no other, she could never have it cut off.

She sighed. All that seemed so long ago it was like another life. In truth, it *had* been another life; yet, unbelievably, it had all happened less than a year ago. Last Easter she hadn't even known John. It was not until the summer that he had arrived at the convalescent home to recover from his injuries sustained in battle. In their all too brief time together they had lived in and for the minute; but in such terrible and uncertain times, how could it have been any different? She smiled to herself. They had been so happy and carefree in those few weeks they were together, making extravagant and unlikely plans. Plans, she now realized, that had been born of a kind of desperation, a determination to believe that the nightmare times they were living in would pass and that things would eventually return to normal.

But it was not a normality either of them could ever have envisaged. John was dead and now she was living with his family, awaiting the birth of his child. And wondering, with not a little trepidation, what the future would hold for both of them.

Twelve

Stella loved the garden and walked there every day as the weather became warmer. And as the warmth turned to heat she would go through the little wicket gate in the fence at the end of the garden and into the cool wood beyond, relieved to escape from the hot sun and wander in the shade among the trees, watching the squirrels and listening to the birds. One particularly hot day she caught a glimpse of Philip sitting at his easel in a clearing and altered her direction, not wanting to disturb him; but not before she had seen that he was wearing a pair of shorts that exposed his disfigured legs. She felt a stab of pity, at the same time marvelling that he managed to walk at all with such mangled limbs.

But she was too late, he had obviously seen her. 'You don't need to keep out of my way, I won't eat you. I've had my breakfast,' he called.

She turned back and stepped into the clearing. 'I saw you were engrossed in your painting and didn't want to disturb you,' she answered, noticing that he had quickly pulled a rug over his legs to hide them.

'But you always disturb me. Why should today be any different?' he said without looking up. 'You're looking worried. Want to tell me about it?' He glanced up and saw her suddenly guarded expression. 'It's all right, Stella, I don't want to pry. You don't have to tell me anything; you can just come and sit on a log and discuss the weather if you'd rather. Or, of course, continue with your walk.'

She went over and sat down on the trunk of a fallen tree nearby and began to fan herself with her hat. He continued to concentrate on his painting without speaking again. And it occurred to her that she could sit here for an hour with him in silence without feeling in the least embarrassed or uncomfortable. At the same time she knew she could talk to him and he would listen.

'Do you like living here, at Warren's End, Philip?' she asked after a while.

He leaned back in his seat and blew out his cheeks.

'Well, as you can imagine it was not quite where I had envisaged spending my life,' he replied candidly. 'But then, I hadn't exactly anticipated being trampled by a pair of runaway mules dragging a gun carriage behind them on the battle front. But these things happened and had to be dealt with in the best – or the least worst – way for all concerned.'

She nodded. 'Of course. I can see that. It was a stupid question.'

He went on as if she hadn't spoken, 'Obviously, my first consideration had to be my wife. Suddenly to be saddled with something less than the man she married can't have been easy for her.'

'For better, for worse; in sickness and in health . . .' she murmured.

He snorted. 'Ah, yes, that's an easy enough promise to make in a fairy-tale wedding when you are both young and fit and a golden life lies ahead. Not quite so easy when reality kicks in.'

'No, of course not. I'm sorry . . .'

He took a deep breath. 'However, in answer to your question, when the Colonel very kindly suggested making those outhouses into a flat for us it seemed the right thing to do, particularly as Rosalie was enthusiastic.' He paused, then went on, 'He's a good chap, the Colonel. I get on very well with him. He has never made me feel in any way beholden to him in spite of all the money he's lavished on us; and now my paintings are beginning to sell and I'm able to pay my way a bit, he accepts my need to be at least partially independent.' He looked at her. 'Does that answer your question?'

'What about Doreen? Where does she fit in?' Stella answered his question with two of her own.

'Ah, Doreen. She's something else entirely.' He gave a small shrug. 'In truth, I don't have to see all that much of her. Apart from the nightly family dinner, our paths don't cross all that much. We manage to remain polite, since she's learned not to interfere too much with my . . . our lives.'

She began to pick at the daisies on her hat as it lay in her lap. 'I wish I could say the same,' she said without looking up.

He took a piece of rag and began to clean his paintbrush. 'You're thinking of the business with the perambulator – or should I say "baby carriage" – that was discussed over dinner the other night, of course.' He put the brush and the rag down carefully. 'I know I shouldn't stir things up between you, which, of course, is a preamble to doing exactly that, but in my opinion she behaved very badly towards you, Stella. It was nothing short of blackmail in a velvet glove.'

She looked up, her face anguished. 'But what could I do? She was absolutely right. The pram she had chosen *was* much nicer, and it *will* be better for the baby. Of course, it was much more expensive than the one I was going to buy, but I had picked the best I could afford and I was so excited about it . . .' Her voice trailed off and she looked away so he wouldn't see that her eyes had filled with tears. 'What else could I have done, Philip?'

'Nothing. That's why I said it was blackmail. Moral blackmail.'

'She's so good to me in so many ways. I feel I'm being ungrateful . . . I mean, what would I have done if John's parents hadn't offered me a home here when I found I was pregnant? Where would I have gone? They wouldn't have had me back at my old job, and a pregnant widow would hardly be first in the queue to find a new one.' She paused, then added, 'But . . .'

'But what?' he was watching her intently.

She kicked at a loose stone. 'What's going to happen when my baby's born?'

'Meaning?'

'Philip, you know as well as I do that I'm only here on sufferance,' she said impatiently. 'I'm simply the vessel carrying Doreen's grandchild. That's been made plain to me in a hundred ways.'

He leaned back in his chair. 'That may be true as far as Doreen is concerned,' he replied, 'but Roger has grown very fond of you. You must realize that.'

'Yes, he's always very kind to me.'

'It's more than that, and you know it. He is genuinely fond of you, Stella. You are the kind of daughter he would have loved to have had.' He gave her a quirky smile. 'I know that because he's told me so.'

'But he already has a daughter. Rosalie . . .'

His expression hardened. 'Rosalie is too much like her mother. Roger has learnt to control Doreen, she knows just how far she can go. You see, he holds the purse strings and Doreen loves money and the status she feels it gives her. It's that simple.'

She digested this and realized it was true; Doreen was a snob of the first order. 'And Rosalie?' she asked.

'Rosalie's no longer his responsibility, for which I think he's profoundly glad.' He sighed. 'He thinks she's far too modern and self-opinionated. Haven't you noticed how he looks at her sometimes now she's had her hair cut off? But, unlike her mother, who still goes on about it, he's wise enough not to complain.'

Stella smiled and nodded. She had noticed.

'I know he thinks she's heartless in her manner towards me, too, which is rather hard on her under the circumstances. After all, what have I got to offer her, a crippled shell of a man? How can I complain if she goes her own way and lives her life in the way she enjoys?'

'I think you're being very hard on yourself, Philip,' Stella said quickly. 'Just because you can't walk very well doesn't mean you're no longer a real man. Do you still love her? No, don't answer that,' she added quickly, blushing. 'I should never have asked, it was very rude of me.'

'Nevertheless, I'll answer with another question. Do you still love John?'

She was silent for several minutes. 'I think I may be in love with the memory of a man I hardly knew,' she said slowly. 'Six magic weeks . . . Hardly the stuff of everyday life. And now, being here where he grew up, hearing what other people say about him, I sometimes wonder if I knew him at all . . .' She shrugged. 'Who can tell?'

'You'll have his baby in a couple of months.'

She laid her hand on the mound of her stomach. 'Yes.' She

heaved a deep sigh. 'I just hope I don't have too many fights with Doreen.' Her face broke into a grin. 'I can't see her walking up and down all night with a baby that won't stop crying, though, can you?'

'No, indeed I can't!' He laughed with her, then became serious. 'It'll work out all right, Stella. You'll see,' he said.

She sighed again. 'Yes, I expect you're right.' She stood up to resume her walk, and as she did so her hat slipped off her lap. Before she could stoop to retrieve it Philip bent over and picked it up, wincing a little as he did so.

She thanked him and started to walk away. Then she came back.

'Philip, I know you don't like to talk about it, but I can see your legs pain you. Can nothing be done?' she asked gently.

His mouth closed in a hard line. 'It's too late.' he said. 'From what I've been told, they had neither the time nor the facilities to deal with them properly at the field hospital, and were too busy preventing me from bleeding to death.' He shrugged. 'Not that I remember much about it, of course.'

'Let me see.' She saw the look of alarm that crossed his face and smiled a little. 'Philip, I worked in a convalescent home. Do you imagine I haven't seen mangled limbs before?'

Reluctantly, he moved the rug from his legs and looked away.

She knelt down and studied them briefly, then gently drew the rug back over them. She had seen enough of the purple, scarred, misshapen limbs to realize that he was fortunate not to have lost them altogether.

'At least you've still got them,' she said as she got to her feet. 'And you can still walk . . .'

'After a fashion. Not much strength there, though. I did have somebody who came to work on the muscles after I got home. But he moved away and I didn't try to find anyone else because I felt I'd imposed quite enough on the Colonel's generosity.'

'Did it help?'

'I think it was beginning to.'

'There was a masseur at the convalescent home. As well as massage, she used a system of exercises to strengthen muscles. It was very effective and she was kept so busy that she sometimes got me to help her with the more routine bits. I found it very interesting, learning what to do and why. She said I was a "natural", whatever that meant, and suggested I might think about training to become a qualified masseur. But of course I left . . .' She hesitated. 'I wouldn't presume . . . But Henry could probably do it if I showed him what I'd learned. It might help to get a bit more strength back in your legs. The exercises were quite simple, just a matter of stretching your legs and lifting your feet off the floor to begin with and then lifting increasing weight as the legs get stronger. I'm sure Henry . . .' She paused, waiting for some response from him.

'We could give it a try, I suppose,' he said at last. He spoke without looking at her and she could see that he was uncomfortable with the idea. 'I suspect it's too late to do much good, though.'

'But if it helped to get even a little strength back into your limbs it would be worth it, wouldn't it?'

'I guess so.' He still sounded doubtful.

She put her hat on and tucked a strand of hair up under the brim. 'It was just an idea that I thought might help, Philip. If you're not happy with it, let's say no more about it.' She smiled at him to show there were no hard feelings. 'Now, I'd better continue with my walk or I'll be late for lunch and Doreen will have a search party out looking for me.'

As she walked away, he watched until she was no longer in sight. Then turned to the half-finished painting on the easel, but made no attempt to pick up his brushes.

As she got off her bike and wheeled it up the path, Emma could see Arthur sitting on the rickety old bench under the window, smoking a cigarette.

'How are you feeling today, love?' she asked. He had still been in bed when she left for work.

'So-so. Head's bad.'

There was always something. 'Is Mary home from school?' She tried to sound cheerful as she took out her handkerchief and mopped the perspiration off her face.

'Yes, she's peeling the spuds.' He looked at her for the first time. 'Did you get chops for tea?'

'Don't be daft. You know I've no money for chops till I'm paid at the end of the week, Arthur. Maisie gave me some stew left over from last night.' She propped up her bike and sat down beside him.

'We'd be able to have something better than left-over stew if Mary was to leave school and earn a bit,' he said, getting the last puff out of his cigarette before throwing it on to the patch of garden, where even the weeds struggled to grow.

'And if you were to stop using the garden as an ash tray and start growing a few vegetables, we wouldn't have to rely on other people to feed us.' Emma didn't often retaliate, it wasn't worth it. But she was tired and hot and she'd been at work since seven. 'Look at Henry's garden next door, he's got peas and beans and potatoes . . .'

'Oh, shut up about Henry. To hear you talk, the sun shines out of his . . .'

'That's enough of that talk, Arthur Blatch. Henry works hard, which is more than . . .' She turned her head away and bit her lip. She mustn't quarrel with Arthur, he always turned nasty if he couldn't get the better of an argument.

But he wasn't even listening. He'd pulled his cigarette packet out of his pocket and found it empty. 'Bugger! That's the last of me fags gone.' He raised his voice. 'Charlie, nip down the shop and get me a packet of Woodbines. Charlie! Where are you, you lazy little sod?'

Charlie wandered round the corner of the house, hands in pockets. He looked just like his father, Emma mused. She hoped he hadn't inherited his father's temper. No, that wasn't fair, Arthur wasn't like this before the war . . .

'Didn't you hear me? I want you to nip down the shop . . .'

Charlie took one hand out of his pocket and held it out. 'Gimme the money, then.'

Arthur waved it away. 'Put it on the slate. Tell Mrs Pike she'll get it when your mother gets paid.'

'Mrs Pike said no more slate for cigarettes,' Charlie was still holding out his hand.

Arthur's face grew red. 'You tell Mrs bloody Pike . . .'

Emma fished in her purse. 'Here, Charlie. Here's twopence. For goodness' sake go and get his fags,' she said wearily.

After Charlie had run off and Arthur had slumped down in a sulk, she turned her face to the sun, savouring a few minutes' peace and quiet. Arthur hadn't always been like this, she reminded herself for the hundredth time, it was the war that had changed him. She turned her mind back to their courting days. He had been a handsome boy, with his curly black hair and brown eyes. He was full of fun, too, always teasing the local girls and trying to steal kisses from them. She'd been so proud when he'd chosen her to be his special girl. They used to go in a crowd to the 'tuppenny hops', as they called the dances at the local church hall, but he always chose her for the last waltz and walked her home afterwards. He had ambitions, too. He was a bricklayer and dreamed of having his own building business, talking for hours about what he would do when he'd saved enough money. But then they found Mary was on the way, so they had to get married in a bit of a hurry and the money he'd saved had to go towards furnishing the cottage they'd found to rent. When she arrived, he loved his baby daughter. He was just as proud of the other two when they came along, and he never complained that things hadn't turned out the way he'd planned. She closed her eyes, remembering what a good husband and father he'd been. Even though they never had a lot of money, in those days they'd been happy.

Then the war came.

Like most of his mates, he reckoned it was his duty to join up and do his bit for King and Country. And she, God help her, had encouraged him.

As far as he was concerned, it had seemed a brave and glamorous thing to do, with a smart uniform to wear and a chance to see a bit of the world. There might even be a bit of *ooh-la-la* if they were lucky enough to be sent to France, some of them said; although not Arthur, of course, being a family man.

But it hadn't been like that. She didn't know what it had been like, because Arthur never said, but she knew only too well what it had done to him. How it had turned the eager, fresh-faced young man she'd seen off on the train into the grey-faced, hollow-eyed, trembling shell of a man that had come back.

'Where's that bloody boy? He's taking long enough to fetch my fags.' Emma was pulled back to the present by Arthur's grumbling voice. 'Get a move on, boy!' he called as he caught sight of Charlie sauntering along the road. 'Can't you see I'm gasping for a ciggie?'

Charlie gave him the packet and Arthur took out a cigarette and put it between his lips, then patted his pockets. 'Blast, now I haven't got a lucifer. Go indoors and get me a box of matches, boy. Quick, now.'

Charlie fetched the matches and Arthur lit the cigarette. Two draws on it and he began to cough, a horrible rattling, bubbling cough that went on and on. 'Lifesavers . . . fags . . .' he panted between spasms. 'Help to clear the tubes.'

Emma sniffed. 'Be the death of you, more like,' she remarked, patting him on the back, in a useless effort to help him get his breath, and encountering the bones barely covered with skin.

Thirteen

The weather was still hot and humid when Stella went for her walk in the woods the following afternoon. She had been lucky that so far her pregnancy had been largely trouble-free, although Doreen was continually trying to turn her into an invalid to protect the 'precious bundle'. However, she had to admit that she was very glad to rest on her bed for an hour every afternoon on these hot summer days before taking a gentle walk.

Now, as she wandered beneath the cool canopy of the trees she could see that Philip was once again at his easel in the clearing but, embarrassed by the memory of what she had suggested to him the previous day, she tried to give him a wide berth. She was very much afraid that she might have overstepped the mark and jeopardized their friendship by even referring to his disability, which she should have known he hated; let alone presuming she might be able to help.

'Look, Henry's brought a garden chair for you. We thought it would be more comfortable for you than sitting on that log like you did yesterday,' she heard him call, although he hadn't even looked up from his painting. 'Henry will be along later with a cup of tea for us.'

Surprised, she changed direction and went over to him. 'I didn't think you'd seen me.'

'I've got good ears. I heard you coming. But anyway I was watching out for you,' he said, smiling up at her.

'I nearly didn't come,' she admitted.

He raised his eyebrows. 'Why ever not? This is the coolest spot in the garden. That's why I always choose it.'

'It's not that.' She sat down and made herself comfortable in the chair Henry had brought for her. 'I was afraid I might have offended you yesterday by suggesting . . .'

He waved a hand dismissively. 'Don't be silly. It was a good idea and Henry's all for giving it a try if you're willing to show him how.' He didn't look up from his painting.

'But how do you feel about it?' she insisted.

He shrugged. 'Can't do any harm, I guess. And if the sight of my misshapen limbs doesn't sicken you . . .'

'Now it's your turn not to be silly,' she said impatiently. She frowned. 'But you don't sound very keen, so if you'd rather not . . .'

He sighed. 'No, we'll give it a go,' he said, but without much enthusiasm. He looked up. 'Ah, here comes Henry with the tea. I hope you brought a cup for yourself, Henry.'

'Yes, I did take that liberty, sir.'

'Good. Now, sit down, drink your tea and listen carefully while Nurse Nolan tells you what to do.'

Stella took no notice of the sarcasm. She realized that it was born of embarrassment, so ignoring Philip she began to talk to Henry about the methods of exercising and massage which she had been taught to help strengthen damaged limbs.

Henry nodded eagerly as she talked. 'Yes, I'm sure I can help him with that,' he said several times. 'And as the muscles strengthen with exercise, I can make little weights to hang on his feet to give a bit of extra weight as he lifts them. But I'm not so sure about the massage bit. How would I . . .?'

Carried away by both Henry's enthusiasm and her own, without thinking, she slid off her chair on to her knees and began to show him how to massage some life into the crippled legs. Then, suddenly, realizing what she was doing, she stopped, reddening.

'Oh, I'm sorry . . . I shouldn't have . . .' She sat back on her heels, looking anywhere but at Philip. 'But you can see the idea, Henry, can't you?' She attempted to get to her feet, but her extra bulk made her awkward and she glanced round for something to hold on to. The chair she'd been sitting in was too far away for her to reach; and short of crawling over to it on her hands and knees or hanging on to Philip, there was nothing. 'Oh dear! I'm awfully sorry.' She reddened even further. 'I'm afraid I'm a bit stuck down here. Could somebody help me up, please?'

At this, Philip burst out laughing, releasing the tension. 'Oh, Stella, if only Doreen could see you now!' he said, still chuckling. 'She'd throw a fit at what harm you might be doing to the precious bundle. Perhaps we should call her?' He began to roar with laughter again.

'Please, don't make fun of me, Philip,' she begged, 'Can't you see? I'm completely stuck. I can't get up.' But she couldn't help seeing the funny side of the situation too and began to laugh with him – which made him laugh even more, and getting up even more impossible for her.

Henry soon came to her aid.

'Oh, thank you, Henry,' she said breathlessly as he managed to heave her to her feet and help her back on to her chair. She leaned back, wiping the tears of laughter from her eyes. 'Oh dear, I don't know when I've laughed so much,' she said.

'I think you'd better have another cup of tea to recover,' Philip said, still chuckling. 'In fact I think we all need one, don't we, Henry?'

Stella took the cup Henry handed her and drank a little. 'My trouble is I keep forgetting I'm not as agile as I used to be,' she said ruefully, but she was still smiling. 'But it won't be long now. Only a couple of weeks or so.' She became serious and gave a sigh. 'Then we shall see what will happen.'

'I don't think you need worry, Stella. The Colonel will see that you're looked after,' Philip said, reading her thoughts.

She nodded. 'Yes, I'm sure you're right,' she said. 'The trouble is, I'm not sure that I want to be looked after. I want to look after myself.'

'That won't be easy for a while,' Philip pointed out. 'I think you'll need to exercise a little patience over that, Stella. After all, you won't have only yourself to consider.'

She nodded and automatically laid her hand on her swollen stomach. 'You're right, of course. And I wouldn't like you to think I'm not grateful for what's being done for me. I truly am. Heaven knows where I'd be if it hadn't been for Roger and Doreen. In some hostel for war widows, if there is such a thing, or . . .'

'Don't even think about it. Just count your blessings, like I do. Every day.' Philip smiled at her, a warm smile that immediately made her feel better.

That evening, over dinner Roger and Philip discussed the reluctance of the Germans to sign the Treaty of Versailles. It had been their favourite topic for weeks now.

'They'll never sign it. They're being asked to give up too much,' Philip said.

'I don't see they've any choice,' Roger said. 'Look how long it's taken to draw up the treaty. Although I agree with you it was an unsatisfactory armistice.'

'My fear is that if they're forced to sign it as it stands, it won't be the last we shall hear of it,' Philip said, shaking his head.

'Oh, I don't know. I think the terms are reasonable enough.'

'Do you really, sir? Even Lloyd George, who advocated "squeezing the Germans till the pips squeak", thinks the terms the French are demanding too harsh.'

'Hm. Maybe you're right. We shall see. The whole business needs wrapping up, that's for sure. It's well over seven months now since the war ended.'

Philip nodded. 'That's true. But my fear is if they don't get it right this time, it'll take another war to "wrap it up", as you put it.'

'Oh, Phil, for goodness' sake stop scaremongering,' Rosalie said impatiently. 'It's ridiculous to talk of another war. We haven't got over the last one yet.' She turned to Doreen. 'You need to talk to Maisie, Ma. These potatoes are overcooked.'

'I thought they were very tasty,' Stella said. 'I like them roasted like this.' Rosalie always found something to complain about.

'That's good. I'm glad you've still got a healthy appetite, dear. Did you go for your walk today?' Doreen asked with a patronizing smile. 'It wasn't too hot for you? I hope you didn't venture too far and tire yourself. You did stay in the grounds, didn't you?'

'Yes, I did go for a walk. No, it wasn't too hot. And no, I didn't tire myself.'

The veiled sarcasm was lost on Doreen. She repeated, 'You did stay in the grounds, dear, didn't you? It wouldn't be right to be seen in public, not at this stage. After all . . .'

'I can vouch for the fact that Stella didn't stray anywhere near the public highway,' Roger said, his sarcasm not veiled at all. 'I heard her laughing with Philip when I was talking to Govan in the garden.'

'Laughing!' Doreen looked shocked. She gave Stella a look that bordered on panic-stricken. 'I hope you didn't . . .'

'Didn't what, Doreen?' Philip asked with feigned innocence. 'Stella saw me painting in the wood when she took her afternoon stroll. There was a squirrel playing under the beech tree and we couldn't help laughing at its antics, isn't that so, Stella?' He gave her a conspiratorial wink as he spoke.

Stella nodded, keeping a straight face with difficulty. 'Yes, that's right.'

'But was it wise, my dear?' Doreen was still full of concern. 'You really shouldn't be walking too far at this stage, you need to conserve your strength. And it's important that you shouldn't get yourself too emotional or excited. That would be very bad for Baby. Especially in this heat.'

'So now you know, Stella. The oracle has spoken!' Rosalie said with a smirk, helping herself to a plum. 'She'll be wrapping you in cotton wool next.'

'Don't be silly, dear,' Doreen said absently. She warmed to

her theme. 'It's a good thing I've engaged Nurse Bennett. She's coming next week to live in until after Baby's born. She'll keep a watchful eye on you.'

Stella's jaw dropped and she frowned. 'Who's Nurse Bennett? Why do I need her?' she asked crossly. 'You know I've been seeing Dr Eaves regularly, Doreen, and he says I'm perfectly fit. Why do I need somebody I've never even met to look after me? And why does she need to come next week? The baby's not due for another fortnight.'

Doreen cleared her throat, clearly embarrassed. 'This is hardly a subject for discussion over the dinner table, Stella,' she warned. 'Let's just say Nurse Bennett is happy with the arrangements. She's seen the little bedroom in your flat, and she says it will be quite suitable for her needs and quite convenient in case you need anything.' She smiled at Stella's astonished expression and leaned over and patted her hand. 'It's all right, you don't have to worry, dear, it's all arranged.' She looked round. 'Now, has everybody finished? Good. I'll ring for Maisie to collect the dishes and bring in the pudding.'

Suddenly, Stella pushed back her chair and got to her feet. 'I don't think I want any pudding, thank you. I've got rather a headache, so if you'll excuse me . . .'

'Of course, my dear.' Roger got to his feet, full of concern. 'Is there anything you need?'

'No, thank you.' She managed to smile at him, although she was inwardly seething.

'I hope you're not in a paddy because I've engaged Nurse Bennett?' Doreen said sternly as she left the room. 'It's for your own good, you know.'

'No, she probably just needs a bit of peace and quiet. And who can blame her,' Stella heard Rosalie remark as she closed the door firmly behind her. For once, she was in complete agreement with her sister-in-law.

Crossing the hall on her way back to her flat, Stella met Maisie hurrying in response to Doreen's ring.

'Oh, Maisie, would it be too much trouble to bring me a cup of tea, when you've got a minute?' she asked. 'I'm not feeling very well, so I'm going to lie down.'

'Of course, Mrs Stella. I'll bring it as soon as I've taken the pudding in. Or better still, I'll get Emma to bring it, she hasn't gone home yet.'

'Thank you. I'd be very grateful.'

She carried on to her flat, where she kicked off her shoes and lay down on her bed. Her head ached, her back ached, and she felt generally out of sorts – and angry with Doreen for having arranged for this nurse to come without even telling her. Even showing the woman the flat when she wasn't there! It was as if she, Stella, was of no account at all. It was absolutely infuriating the way Doreen took it upon herself to take control of everything. Once the baby was born, maybe she would have more energy to stand up for herself; but unfortunately that wouldn't be for another two weeks or so.

Maisie pushed open the kitchen door with her elbow and sidled through with the loaded tray of dirty dishes. Emma had a second tray, already laden with clean dishes and a large treacle sponge and custard, ready to replace it.

'I'll just wash the dirties up before I go,' she said with a grin. 'You never know, there might be a bit of that treacle sponge left for me to take home. I made a nice big one.'

'Yes, there might, if you're lucky,' Maisie answered. 'But before you start the washing-up, will you take Mrs Stella a pot of tea? She says she's got a headache and I must say she looks a bit peaky.' She frowned. 'Better get a move on, Em. She must be feeling poorly, she usually makes her own tea.'

Emma didn't need telling twice, she was already warming the teapot. Five minutes later she was knocking on Stella's door.

'Oh, Emma, I've got a headache and an awful backache, too,' Stella confided, not admitting that she was afraid she might have done herself some damage attempting to get up off her knees that afternoon.

Emma poured the tea. 'Is it just your back that aches?' she asked, regarding her closely.

Stella hitched herself up on the bed and winced a little. 'Well, no. To tell you the truth, I'm a bit worried really: I get a sort of stabbing pain in my side now and again. I'm afraid I might have done some damage to myself when I tried to get up off my knees this afternoon.' She put her hand to her mouth. 'Oh, for goodness' sake don't tell my mother-in-law I said that, Emma.'

Emma grinned. 'I wouldn't dream of it. I won't even ask what you were doing down on your knees.' She laid a hand on Stella's forehead, then stood looking down at her. 'How often do these stabbing pains come? Regularly?'

'I don't really know.' Stella frowned, then winced again. 'They do seem to be getting worse, though. Oh, Emma you don't think I could have harmed my baby, do you?'

'I shouldn't think so, not for a minute.' Emma gave her a wide smile. 'But unless I'm much mistaken, you'll soon find out. I think your baby's on its way, Mrs Stella.'

Stella's eyes widened in fear. 'But it can't be! Oh, Emma, what shall I do? It's not due for another fortnight.'

'I wouldn't worry too much about that, dear. Babies often don't have a very good sense of time and doctors don't always get it right,' Emma said calmly. 'I've thought for several days when I've seen you around that it wouldn't be much longer. I've seen enough births to know the signs. Just tell me where you've put everything you'll need, and I'll go and tell Maisie to get hot water ready.'

'Emma? I'm a bit frightened.' She put out her hand. 'Will you stay with me?'

'Of course I will, if you want me to, dearie.' The endearment came quite naturally. 'I'll just have to get a message to Arthur and the children, so they know why I'm not home at the usual time.'

'Emma?' she winced again. 'Do we need to tell . . .' she caught her breath, biting her lip. 'I don't want Doreen . . .'

'I don't think you need worry on that score, dearie. If I know the missus, she won't want to be anywhere near. She's not a great one for the sick room.' Emma was already bustling about preparing the room. She paused and stood pinching her lip. 'Now, I think I'd better just go and ask Maisie to let Dr Eaves know what's happening, just in case he's needed, and they can drop a message in to Arthur on the way.' She disappeared for a few minutes and came back with a cool cloth, which she laid on Stella's forehead. 'There, now, don't you worry about a thing, lovie. Everything's going to be fine. Just relax and let the pain wash over you. That's it. You can cling on to me . . .'

Stella had no idea of time; the pain came and went, then came and stayed, getting worse and worse till she thought she couldn't bear any more. But through it all she could hear Emma's voice, talking to her, soothing and calming. Telling her everything was going to be all right. Once she thought she saw John and called to him to help her; but before he could reach her he changed into Dr Eaves, and she cried out to him to come back to her and tried to take his hand. Then quite clearly, through a sea of pain, she was sure she heard Doreen's voice from a long way away: 'Save the child. If there has to be a choice, save the child.' And she knew she was dying.

Then something was clamped over her face and she smelled something sickly sweet but antiseptic.

That was the last she knew.

Minutes later, or so it seemed, she opened her eyes and was surprised to find she was still in her own bed, in her own room. The dreadful racking pain had gone and she felt comfortably drowsy. She thought she might be dead; if so, it was a very pleasant place to be. She closed her eyes again.

'Ah, you're awake. Would you like a cup of tea, dear? You deserve it, after all that hard work.'

She opened her eyes again and was surprised to see Emma, looking haggard with fatigue but smiling broadly. So she wasn't dead, after all. She licked her parched lips. 'Yes, please, I'm very thirsty.' She managed a weary little smile; then suddenly the memory flooded back and she put her hand on her stomach. It was flabby and sore: and flat. A look of alarm crossed her face. 'My baby! Where's my baby? Is it born? Where is it? Have they taken it away?'

'Of course not, dearie. He's right here, look.' Emma lifted the little shawl-wrapped figure out of the cradle and laid him in the crook of Stella's arm. 'A lovely little boy, and the image of his Pa, if I might say so.'

'Oh, he's gorgeous,' Stella breathed, looking down at the tiny form nestled beside her. 'My little son.'

Emma sniffed, her eyes misty; she wasn't usually given to showing her emotions. 'I'll go and fetch you some tea,' she said briskly. 'And do you want some breakfast?'

'Breakfast?' Stella frowned. 'Why? What's the time? Is it morning?'

'Morning?' Emma laughed. 'It's nearly ten o'clock. You've had a busy night, although you didn't know too much about it.'

Stella looked bemused. 'No wonder I'm starving.'

'I'll fetch your breakfast.' Emma went off, smiling. It had been a good night's work.

The baby was back in his cradle and Stella was tucking in to two boiled eggs and several slices of toast when there was a brief knock at the door and Doreen came in.

Stella noticed with private amusement that she glanced carefully round the room to make sure all the unpleasant signs of recent birth had been removed before she sat down rather gingerly on the chair at the foot of the bed. She appeared quite nervous.

'Well, my dear, you surprised us all,' she said with a tight smile. 'But Dr Eaves assures me that everything was normal and straightforward, considering Baby weighed nearly eight pounds.'

'Oh, nobody told me that. He seemed really tiny when Emma put him in my arms. But he's beautiful. Just perfect.' Stella attacked her second egg, trying not to resent the fact that her mother-in-law already appeared to know more about the baby than she did herself.

'Well, a least there's no question about what to call him. Naturally, he'll be John, after his father,' Doreen said, with more than a trace of smugness.

Stella looked up from her egg and smiled. 'Well, no. I've thought about it a lot and I've decided I'm going to call him Jonathan, not John. I feel it's important that he should be his own person and not continually compared with his father, wonderful though John was. Jonathan Roger Nolan. It has a nice ring, and no doubt it will be shortened to Jonny, which will be nice, don't you think? Especially as he'll have his father's middle name and also be named after his grandfather. Roger will like that, I'm sure.'

'I think you're wrong. Roger will expect him to be named John, after his son and the baby's father.' The atmosphere in the room had grown noticeably cooler.

'Well, I'm sure Roger will understand and like the name I've chosen.' Stella finished her egg and wiped her fingers on her napkin, smiling again. 'Aren't you going to take a look at your new grandson? He's asleep in his cradle, there. Emma says he's just like John. What do you think?'

Doreen got up and leaned over the cradle. For a moment her expression softened as she gazed at her little grandson. 'You're right. He does look very tiny,' she said. Then she straightened up. 'He's got a great deal more hair than John had when he was born. No wonder you suffered from heartburn while you were pregnant.'

And with that, she left.

Fourteen

'Another whisky, Gilbert?' Roger asked, holding up the decanter as they sat together in the morning room. Dr Eaves gave a yawn; he looked weary.

'No thanks, Roger. Remember I've got my rounds to do, even if I have been up half the night,' he said with a smile. He got to his feet and picked up his bag. 'So I'll just congratulate you again on a fine little grandson and be on my way.'

'Well, thanks again for attending our daughter-in-law, Gilbert. We appreciate it.'

Gilbert Eaves waved the thanks away. 'I really didn't have to do a lot. Emma Blatch had everything under control.'

'I'm sorry to have disturbed your night's rest. But Doreen insisted on calling you. Just in case . . .'

'She needn't have worried. Emma's a good woman to have at a birth. I've come across her before. She never panics and knows just what to do. She told me once she would like to have trained as a midwife, but of course her family couldn't afford it.' He shook his head. 'Shame about her husband, too. He was a fine, hard-working man before the war and look at him now, a wreck of a man.' He sighed. 'But he's only one of hundreds – thousands, in fact – ruined by it.' He sighed again. 'So many young lives wasted.'

'At least he came back,' Roger said thoughtfully.

Dr Eaves nodded. 'Yes, for what it's worth, at least he came back. Your John didn't, I know that and I'm sorry, Roger.'

Roger nodded, acknowledging the doctor's words. 'It leaves a great gap,' he said briefly.

'It also means your plucky little daughter-in-law will have to bring up her son without a father.'

'She'll be all right. She's got us,' Roger said. 'We'll look after her and the boy.'

'I'm sure you will.'

The door suddenly crashed open and Doreen marched in, her face a mask of fury.

'She says she's going to call the baby Jonathan, Roger,' she said angrily, ignoring the doctor. 'You must put a stop to it and insist she calls him John, after his father.'

'I shall do nothing of the kind, Doreen, and I'll thank you not to burst in like that when I'm having a drink with Gilbert to "wet the baby's head", as the tradition goes.' Roger didn't raise his voice, but his displeasure was plain.

'I'm sorry, Gilbert,' she muttered ungraciously, barely glancing at him. 'But I feel very strongly that my son's child should bear his name.'

'What a good thing it wasn't a girl, then,' Roger remarked with the ghost of a smile.

'Don't be facetious, Roger. Can't you see how upset I am?' She took out a handkerchief and dabbed her eyes.

'I'll see myself out,' Dr Eaves said, picking up his bag. He wanted no part of this dispute, but hoped privately that the young mother would have the strength of will to withstand her mother-in-law's domination. He didn't envy her; he'd known Doreen for a long time.

'Sit down, Doreen, and calm yourself,' Roger said sternly after the doctor had closed the door. 'That was disgraceful behaviour in front of Gilbert.'

'But I'm upset, Roger. Can't you see?' She began to cry in earnest.

'Oh, yes, I can see.' He gave a sigh, knowing his wife could turn the tap on at will. 'But you've no reason to be upset. You've got a beautiful grandson – at least, so I'm told, I haven't been given the chance to see him yet – so you should be thankful, not come to me complaining you haven't been asked to choose his name. And why should you be? He's not *your* baby.' He laid deliberate emphasis on the word. 'Anyway, I think Jonathan is a very nice name – very like John but not exactly the same. Which I consider extremely sensible. Just be thankful Stella didn't choose a name like Horace. Or Algernon.'

Doreen gave a watery smile. 'Now you're laughing at me.'

'I am indeed.' He smiled back at her. He was fond of his wife, despite some of her irritating ways.

'He's to be called Jonathan Roger,' she said grudgingly. Then added, 'He's got very much the look that John had when he was first born.'

Roger's smile widened. 'How gratifying!' he said, but whether because the boy was to bear his name or resembled his son was not clear.

Doreen had deliberately arranged that Nurse Bennett should be in attendance for at least a week before the birth, in case – as she delicately put it – of unforeseen circumstances. In the event, young Jonathan was over a week old by the date she had been booked to come.

By the time she arrived, full of apologies to Doreen at not having been able to leave her previous case any sooner, she was surprised to find that Emma had established a perfectly adequate routine looking after mother and baby, with the help of Mary, her daughter, who was on the point of leaving school anyway.

'I really don't think I'm needed, Mrs Nolan,' Nurse Bennett told Doreen once she had assessed the situation. 'Everything seems to be running like clockwork. Mother and baby are thriving; Emma clearly knows what she's doing, and her daughter is a delightful girl, very willing and able. Under the circumstances, I think I should quietly leave. Of course, there will be no fee.'

This was not at all what Doreen wanted to hear. She pursed her lips, determined to have her own way 'in case things go wrong,' as she put it.

There was no earthly reason why anything should go wrong, Ada Bennett pointed out, but since Mrs Nolan insisted, she agreed to stay for two weeks; she'd been booked for longer, but this seemed a reasonable compromise.

In the event, it was a very happy two weeks for all concerned. Ada was a jolly soul and kept Maisie, Emma and whoever else might be in the kitchen in fits of laughter with anecdotes of her life as midwife and nursery nurse. She was impressed with Emma's skills and congratulated her on the professional way she was caring for Stella and the baby; and at the same time she took Mary under her wing, giving her helpful tips and advice. She managed all this with tact and no hint of interference.

'My word, I've never been in a situation where I've had less to do. This has been quite a holiday for me,' she said when the fortnight was up and her bag was packed ready to leave. 'I've really enjoyed meself these past two weeks and I've never had so much time to put me feet up!'

'And as for you, young lady,' she turned to Mary, who was standing by the table with the suspicion of a tear in her eye at the thought of the elderly midwife, who she had come to regard as a friend, leaving. 'You're a born nursemaid, and don't let anyone tell you anything different. If I hear of a place going, I'll put your name forward.' She turned to Emma. 'With your mam's permission, of course.'

'Ooh, I'd like that,' Mary said, her eyes shining.

'It's nice of you to say that, Ada, but I reckon she's going to be needed here for another week or two,' Emma warned. 'My Arthur's beginning to feel a bit neglected because I've spent so much time away from home lately, although I've made sure he's had everything he needed, taken him his meals and all that. But after what you've said and all you've taught Mary, I shan't have any worries about leaving her here to look after things. She gets on well with Mrs Stella, too. Mind you, Mrs

Stella likes to do quite a lot for herself. And she's getting stronger every day.'

'Yes, she seems a very capable young lady,' Ada said, nodding. 'These modern mothers like to look after their babies themselves; not like in the old days, when the children lived in the nursery and only saw their parents for half an hour a day. I think it's much better. But do make sure she has a rest every afternoon, won't you? Now, I've left you my address, in case you want to get in touch with me for any reason.' She tapped the side of her nose conspiratorially. 'Strictly on the quiet, of course.'

Henry came in and announced that the trap was ready, so she kissed them all warmly and went off to her next job, leaving them feeling they had found a new friend.

For her part, Stella had spent quite a lot of time in between feeding and tending Jonathan, which she loved to do, doing careful calculations to decide whether she could possibly afford to employ Mary as nursemaid on a permanent basis. The money she received each month from the interest on her inheritance was not much, but she decided that if she was very careful and didn't spend any money on herself she could just about manage to pay Mary a small wage. Looking to the future, she recognized that if she was ever going to be self-sufficient and able to leave Warren's End she would need to find some kind of employment so she could support herself and her baby. A nursemaid would be a necessary expense if she was ever going to be able to do that.

One afternoon she was sitting in the garden on a wickerwork *chaise longue* under the shade of a large old beech tree, her usual choice for her afternoon rest when the weather was warm enough. Jonathan was asleep in his pram beside her, and she was making yet more calculations on her notepad to make absolutely sure she had got her sums right before formally offering Mary work when Roger came along.

'I'll swear this child grows by the minute,' he said, chuckling as he gazed into the pram. 'He looks bigger every time I see him.' He sat down on a bench beside Stella. 'And how are you today, my dear? I must say you look a picture of health.'

'Yes, I'm well, thank you, Roger.' She smiled at him and flipped over the cover of her notepad, but not before Roger had seen the page covered with calculations.

He frowned. 'Forgive me, Stella, but I couldn't help seeing . . . You're not in financial difficulties, are you?' Concerned, he looked into her face.

'No, not exactly,' she answered slowly. She hesitated. 'It's just that, well, Mary is such a lovely girl and such a help to me that I would like to ask her to stay permanently, and I was just making a few calculations to see if I could afford to pay her enough to encourage her to stay on.'

He slapped his knee. 'What a capital idea! Of course you must ask her, my dear.' He beamed at her. 'I don't know why nobody's thought of it before.'

'But I'm not sure . . .'

'What it would cost? Don't you worry your pretty little head over that, Stella. It'll come under staff expenses and be paid with the rest. It's not something for you to concern yourself over.'

She frowned. 'It's very generous of you, Roger,' she said doubtfully, 'but . . .'

'Think no more about it.' He grinned and nodded toward the pram. 'Just consider it a little something for my grandson.' He got up and began to walk away. Then he turned back. 'Put the idea to the young gel today. See what she says. Of course, there'll be back wages to be paid as well, tell her, if she takes the job on.' He winked and went off, humming happily to himself.

Stella watched him go, smiling to herself and thinking what a nice man her father-in-law was. She turned her face to the sun. It was a very pleasant garden to sit in, with several shady corners or sunny spots to take advantage of according to the weather. With something of a shock, she realized that she would miss it if − when − she left. Her thoughts turned to the family. She would miss Roger and his kind wisdom, but not his wife. She had come more and more to understand that Doreen wanted control of her grandson and realized that it would have been quite convenient as far as she was concerned if Stella had died in childbirth. She pursed her lips. But she had not died and had no intention of relinquishing control of her baby to his grandmother.

'Enjoying your afternoon rest? Well, I've come to spoil it.'

Stella hadn't heard Rosalie approach over the lawn and she looked up to see her sister-in-law peering into the pram. 'Does he sleep all the time?' she asked without much curiosity.

'Of course not. But he's a good baby, only cries when he's hungry.'

Rosalie flung herself down on the bench Roger had vacated. She was wearing a diaphanous creation in shades of pale orange and yellow that finished well above her ankles, and a matching bandanna round her head. Her bobbed hair was shining and immaculate and her lipstick was a brilliant slash of bright red. It was evident that she had just come back from a long lunch with friends. She began to rummage in her bag for her cigarettes.

Stella put a hand on her arm. 'I'd rather you didn't smoke near Jonathan, Rosalie,' she said. 'It can't be good for him.'

'Oh, give me strength!' Rosalie said impatiently, but she stopped rummaging and closed her bag up. 'Everything revolves round the bloody baby these days.'

'I don't think it affects you all that much,' Stella said coolly. 'I haven't noticed you showing any particular interest in him.' She stopped and turned to look at Rosalie. 'Oh, I'm sorry, that was insensitive of me.'

'Why?' Rosalie raised her eyebrows. She looked genuinely surprised.

'Well,' Stella was embarrassed at having to spell it out. 'You don't have children, and from what I can gather there's not much likelihood . . .'

'So?'

She ploughed on, wishing she'd never raised the subject. 'Well, with Philip's disabilities . . .'

'Ah, so that's it.' Rosalie's face cleared and she held up her hand. 'Now, before you go any further, let's get things straight. I've never been the motherly type and I've never particularly wanted children, much to my mother's disappointment. But the fact that I'm childless has got nothing to do with Philip's ability to father a child. As far as I know, there's absolutely nothing wrong with him in that direction.'

'Oh.' Conflicting thoughts coursed through Stella's mind.

'I know what you're thinking, and you're wrong again.' Rosalie rummaged for her cigarettes again, then remembered Stella's request and closed her bag with a snap. 'It's my fault, not Philip's. I know without any shadow of a doubt that I shall never have a child.'

'Oh, I'm sorry. But how can you be so sure?'

Now Rosalie succumbed to her need for a cigarette, and Stella bit her lip against protesting. When she had taken the first satisfying drag, she looked appraisingly at her sister-in-law. 'Will you be shocked if I tell you?'

'I don't know what you're going to say, so how can I tell?' Stella said with a trace of impatience.

'True.' She nodded and after another long drag on her cigarette stubbed it out. 'Well, to put it in a nutshell, while Philip was at the Front fighting for King and Country I had a fling with an officer I met in the town and became pregnant. He was furious, of course, because he'd already got a wife; and obviously I didn't want a bloody baby, so he paid for me to go to some posh clinic where they didn't ask questions.' She shrugged. 'Posh clinic or not, they messed up the operation. Nearly killed me and left me incapable of ever conceiving, let alone bearing a living child.' She turned to Stella with a bright smile. 'Did me a good turn really, didn't they, because it's something I no longer have to worry about. I can . . .' She waved an arm. 'Well, whatever.'

She left Stella in no doubt what she meant.

'What on earth did your parents say?' she asked, shocked.

'They never knew. They thought I'd gone to stay with friends because I was missing Philip.' Rosalie laughed. 'Funny really, wasn't it? They thought I was pining for my husband when in reality I was aborting another man's child.'

Stella digested this. It didn't seem in the least bit funny to her. 'But what about your husband?' she asked at last. 'What was his reaction?'

'Oh, grow up, Stella,' Rosalie said scathingly. 'It was hardly likely I'd tell him, was it? He never knew anything about it.' She turned to look at Stella. 'Good grief, woman, you're not naïve enough to imagine Phil lived like a monk while he was away, do you? There was a war on, for God's sake. None of those men knew whether they would live or die, so they took their pleasures while they could. And who could blame them?' She shrugged, and paused.

'And don't for a minute imagine that John didn't behave in exactly the same way,' she went on, with more than a hint of malice. 'Even before he joined up, he used to boast of his conquests. He told me once he'd had pretty well all the girls at the country club, so he'd have to start looking farther afield.' She shook her head at the look of horror on Stella's face. 'Just how well did you know the man you married, my innocent little sister-in-law?' She looked her up and down. 'Not as well as you thought, I guess. And now it's too late. Just as well, perhaps.'

Without waiting for a reply, she got lazily to her feet and walked away.

Stella watched her go with something very close to hatred in her heart. How dare John's sister try to tarnish the memory of the man she had loved so much.

Full of excitement, Mary ran home to tell her mother and father she was to be the baby's nursemaid.

'And I'm to live in the flat with Mrs Stella and . . .'

'Just you hold on, my girl,' Arthur said, frowning. 'Are you bein' paid the goin' rate? And what about all these weeks you've been there, workin' for nuthin'?'

'Yes, I'm to be paid the proper rate and I've been paid for the time I've already been there.' Mary was hopping from one foot to the other in her excitement.

'Goodness me, that's generous of Mrs Stella,' Emma said admiringly as she washed the dishes in a bowl on the kitchen table. 'But instead of hoppin' about like that, you could use your energy in dryin' these dishes while you talk. I'm due back at the House in half an hour.'

Mary grabbed a tea towel off the line stretched across the kitchen. 'No,' she said, 'Mrs Stella said it was the Colonel who would be paying me. I'll be staff, like you, Mum.'

Arthur lit a cigarette, coughed long and hard, then held his hand out. 'Well, where is it, then?'

'What?'

'The wages you've already been paid.'

Mary, alarmed, looked at her mother, who said nothing but jerked her head resignedly in the direction of her husband.

Reluctantly, Mary pulled a shilling out of her pocket and handed it to him.

'Is that all?'

'All! She's a lucky girl to get that much. It's very generous,' Emma said hotly.

'I shall get my keep and a uniform. That was supposed to be money for the extra work when the baby was born,' Mary said sullenly, nodding towards her father's hand, still closed possessively over the precious shilling. 'I shan't always be paid that much.'

'Well, whatever you get you can hand over to your mother to help with the family's keep. I said it was time you earned a livin' to help things along.'

'You'd better give it to her then, hadn't you? Instead of putting it your pocket,' Mary flashed, furious at the injustice.

'Mary . . .' Emma began, shocked at her daughter's outburst.

'You speak to me like that, my girl, and you'll get a clip round the ear,' Arthur shouted before she could say more. He began to cough again, the cough racking his thin frame.

'Now see what you've done!' Emma said, rubbing his back. 'You know this always happens when he gets upset.'

Mary flung down the tea towel. 'I'm not staying here, I'm going back to the House,' she said defiantly. 'That's where I'll be living now.'

Fifteen

Ever since the birth of Jonathan, nearly two months ago, Stella had been taking her meals in her own room. For some reason that she couldn't explain, she was more than happy to live in her own little cocoon with her new baby, feeding and tending him, with only Emma and Mary for help and advice.

Of course, Doreen came to visit her grandson. She arrived every morning in time to see him bathed, making everyone nervous with her anxiety over whether he was being held safely or likely to slip off a lap. She was particularly critical when Mary bathed him – which the girl loved to do – refusing to agree that she was perfectly competent.

'Would you like to bath him, then?' Stella asked one day when Doreen was being particularly annoying.

'No, thank you. I have my best morning dress on. I don't want to get it splashed.'

But when he was all clean and sweet-smelling she always liked to hold him, cooing and clucking over him in what Stella regarded as a ridiculous and childish manner. Provided he was quiet, she would sometimes stay for nearly half an hour, which disrupted the day's routine; but she had little to say to Stella, unless it was to criticize, and never once asked after her health and well-being. It was only when the baby became hungry and began to cry that she would relinquish him for Stella to feed, offering useless advice on what she should or shouldn't eat that might affect the baby's welfare.

Stella found all this more than a little annoying. After all, what did Doreen know about bringing up children? From what she could gather, she hadn't even had much to do with bringing up her own, living in India with an ayah to look after them all the time. And surely, a polite 'How are you today, Stella?' wouldn't hurt occasionally. Or was she just being oversensitive and imagining she was being slighted? She tried not to dwell on it. But she hadn't been able to ignore – or forget – the malice behind Rosalie's conversation with her in the garden the other day. It had left her feeling vulnerable and wounded, and made her even more reluctant to join the family at mealtimes.

What did they know about John that she didn't? Were they all laughing at her naïve innocence at having been taken in by the man Rosalie had described – a man she, Stella, would never have recognized? It seemed unlikely: John could never have done wrong in Doreen's eyes, and Roger was far too kind. All the same it was unsettling.

In the end, it was Roger who persuaded her to take breakfast with him as she used to, saying in his genial but forthright manner, 'I've missed our little chats over toast and marmalade, my dear.' And then at breakfast a few days later, 'It would be nice if you joined us for dinner again, Stella. We all miss you.' She knew he meant it and she was flattered. In any case, with Mary now living in and able to keep an eye on the baby she really had no excuse to stay in her own rooms.

And she missed seeing Philip. This was not something she would ever have put into words, even to herself, but she couldn't deny it was there, under the surface. She had been surprised – and not a little disappointed, if she was honest with herself – that she'd seen so little of him since the baby's birth. He'd paid the usual duty visit of the new uncle when Jonathan was not much more than two weeks old, bringing with him a present of a colourful picture of a woodland scene full of little animals and birds that he had painted. He'd said all the right things and complimented her on looking well, but she'd sensed a discomfort in him. Since then, she'd hardly set eyes on him. She couldn't understand it; she had always valued their conversations together and she had thought, wrongly, it seemed, that he had felt the same. Two or three times while Jonathan was asleep she had been to the place in the wood where he was usually to be found painting, but there was no sign of him, which in view of the lovely summer weather she found strange. Yet she was reluctant to knock on the door of his studio, in case he was using the birth of Jonathan as a good excuse to distance himself from a friendship he was afraid was becoming a little too close. Or perhaps he was tired of listening to her fears and worries. Or simply tired of her.

She resolved to keep her distance in future, realizing that she had perhaps used him too much, if not as a shoulder to cry on, then as someone to burden with her problems.

Nevertheless, she remained puzzled and not a little concerned about him until, by casual questioning, she learned from Emma, who had got it from Henry, that Philip was spending long hours in his studio working on a series of paintings that Benedict Gerard, the proprietor of Hunter's Moon Galleries, had commissioned from him with a view to an exhibition in London.

'Henry says he's workin' much too hard, but it's cheered him up no end.' Emma's voice dropped. 'Well, I reckon he'll stand to earn quite a lot o' money if he has an exhibition.' She nodded her head in satisfaction. 'That'll be one in the eye for milady, won't it! She's never rated Mr Philip's pictures, but I think they're nice.' She always referred to Rosalie as 'milady'; there was little love lost there. Her expression changed to a frown. 'Except for those awful grey-and-black ones he keeps hidden away. I can't make head nor tail of them.' She lowered her voice to just above a whisper. 'I don't think anybody was supposed to see them. I only come on them by accident when I was cleaning his room, so I couldn't ask what they were.' She paused thoughtfully. 'Funny, they made me think of the nightmares Arthur used to have when he first came home from the war, when he used to scream and call out . . . Don't know why.'

Stella didn't answer, but having seen them herself she could quite understand why they should.

She dressed carefully for her first dinner with the family since Jonathan's birth. For the first time since John's death she wore the pale-green dress, with diaphanous sleeves and a skirt shot with all shades of green, through to a creamy yellow, that he had bought her on their honeymoon. She wasn't sure whether she had put it on to give her the feeling that he wasn't far away after all, to boost her own confidence, or because he had said she looked beautiful in it. Whatever the reason, she knew that for her own sake she needed to look her best to boost her confidence; and after she had fed Jonathan and given Mary strict instructions to call her if he cried, she tucked a cream rosebud into her hair from the bowl of roses on the table.

'Don't you worry, Mrs Stella, Jonny will be all right with me,' Mary said, her eyes shining at being left in complete charge, even though it was only at the other end of the house. 'And if I may say so, you look a right bobby-dazzler.'

Stella smiled. 'Thank you for that, Mary, it's made me feel a lot better.' She took a last look in the mirror. 'I know it's only for dinner with the family,' she said, putting her head on one side, 'but it seems such a long time since I could wear anything decent I thought it wouldn't hurt to dress up a bit.'

Unaccountably, she felt quite nervous as she opened the drawing-room door.

'My dear, what a pleasure it is to have you with us again. And how charming you look!' Roger said gallantly, getting to his feet and smiling broadly as she entered the room, which immediately put her at her ease.

'Yes, you're looking very well, Stella,' Doreen said with less enthusiasm, from the depths of her armchair. She glanced up at the clock. 'We're just waiting for Rosalie and Philip. They're late again. As usual.'

Even as she spoke, the door opened and Rosalie came in. Philip was behind her and Stella noticed that, although he still used two sticks, he was walking slightly more easily; struggling a little less to drag one foot in front of the other. She didn't remark on this and the others didn't appear to notice, but she made a mental note to ask Emma if the improvement might be due to Henry's ministrations. She was sure Emma would know.

After the usual greetings — coolly appraising on Rosalie's part, warm and with (did she imagine it?) more than a tinge of admiration on Philip's — they sat down to dinner. The evening was warm and humid; even with the French windows flung wide, there was not a breath of air.

'There'll be a storm, I shouldn't wonder,' Roger said, finishing the last of his cold cucumber soup. 'Will clear the air. It's what's needed.'

Stella stole a glance at Philip and saw his jaw tighten. 'Yes, we can do with the rain,' was all he said.

'Phil doesn't like storms, do you, darling?' Rosalie said, with malicious sweetness.

'I'm not keen on them,' he said briefly. He nodded towards his father-in-law, who was carving a ham joint. 'Thanks, Roger, just two slices.'

'I hope the thunder and lightning won't upset Baby,' Doreen said anxiously, pausing in the act of piling salad on to her plate.

'Don't be daft, Ma. It's not old enough to be scared of storms,' Rosalie said.

'Don't call John — Jonathan "it", Rosalie,' Doreen pleaded. 'He's a little boy.'

Rosalie yawned. 'Ah, yes, so he is. I forgot.'

'How are the paintings going, Philip?' Roger cut across the conversation, irritated at the way Rosalie was behaving. He turned to Stella before Philip could answer. 'Did you know Philip was likely to have an exhibition of his paintings, Stella?'

'Oh, that would be exciting,' she said enthusiastically, careful not to answer his question directly. 'How many paintings will you be putting in, Philip?'

He smiled, meeting her eyes for the first time. 'I'm afraid Benedict is asking for rather more than I've got,' he said.

'That's ridiculous,' Rosalie said impatiently. 'You've got hundreds. Literally hundreds.'

'Obviously, they have to be good enough to put on show.' He spoke to Stella, ignoring his wife. 'I'm working on a new set now that I hope to include.'

'So that's why I haven't seen you in the garden,' Stella smiled back at him. 'You've been too busy.'

''Fraid so. You can come and see what I've been doing, if you like.'

'Thank you. I'd like that. When shall I come?'

'Whenever you can spare the time from young Jonathan. I'd . . .'

What he was saying was cut short by a sudden flash of lightning, followed almost immediately by a deafening crack of thunder, and Stella saw the colour drain from his face. He didn't speak again, but his knuckles showed white as he clutched his knife and fork, trying to act normally, pushing his food round the plate without actually picking it up.

Roger noticed. 'I'll just close the doors and curtains. It's beginning to rain,' he said, standing up.

'Oh, don't do that, Pa, we'll all stifle,' Rosalie protested.

'Don't be silly, dear. This is quite a big room.' Roger closed the doors firmly and pulled the curtains across. 'There, that's better.'

'If you'll excuse me, I think perhaps I should go home.' Philip got awkwardly to his feet and tried to pick up his sticks, but his hands were shaking too violently to hold them.

'No, no, you can't do that, it's already raining too hard. Come and sit over here, old chap.' Roger went over to him and helped him to a chair that faced away from the window, although with the curtains drawn the lightning was less visible. 'What about a little piano music, Rosalie?'

'No, I don't think so, I'm not in the mood,' she replied over her shoulder. 'I'll have a bit more of that lemon meringue, Ma. I'm very partial to lemon meringue.'

There was another terrific crash of thunder and Philip visibly cowered in his chair.

'Goodness, that was close,' Roger said, trying to sound matter-of-fact.

'Would you like me to play something?' Stella said quickly, completely understanding Roger's motive.

Doreen frowned and began to shake her head but he said quickly, 'That would be very nice, Stella.'

She got up and quickly riffled through the music in the canterbury until she found a Chopin polonaise that was suitably loud and martial. It didn't quite drown the sound of the thunder but it helped; and then as the storm receded into the distance she chose a quieter waltz, and then a nocturne. As the last notes died away, she glanced over to where Philip was sitting. He was still very pale, but he was no longer trembling and it looked as if he was asleep.

She stood up and moved away from the piano.

'Thank you,' he murmured without opening his eyes, 'that was beautiful.'

'I must say you play surprisingly well, Stella,' Rosalie remarked patronizingly. 'Where did you learn?'

'I had a very good teacher. He wanted me to take it up professionally, but then the war came and I thought I could be more use as a VAD.'

'How very noble of you.'

Stella wasn't sure whether Rosalie was being sincere or sarcastic. Not that it mattered.

'If you'll excuse me, I think I should go back to Jonathan now,' she said to nobody in particular. 'In case the storm frightened him.'

'Oh dear, must you?' Roger said, smiling at her. 'It's been so nice having you with us again.'

'And thank you for the recital, Stella,' Philip said without opening his eyes. He looked much calmer now and was sitting quite comfortably relaxed in his chair. 'It was better than any doctor's medicine.'

She said goodnight and slipped away back to the nursery, feeling a warm glow from Philip's words. It was all very peaceful; Jonathan was sound asleep and Mary was sitting quietly darning her stockings.

In the kitchen, Emma looked up from washing the dishes in alarm at the first clap of thunder. 'I think I shall have to go home, Maise,' she said. 'Arthur always gets into a state when there's a storm and he's only got young Charlie there. I think the thunder sounds like the gunfire in the trenches to him. I'm afraid it'll scare Charlie if he sees his father under the bed crying, especially being there on his own with him. I mean, it's not the sort of state for a young boy to see his father in.'

Maisie looked out of the window. 'I don't think you'll be going anywhere yet, Emma. Look at that rain lashing the windows.'

'Oh dear. You're right. I can't go till it eases up.' She took off her pinafore and hung it on the back of the door, then went back to look out of the window. 'I'll just go and make sure Mary's all right with the baby before I go,' she said, for something to do.

'Won't Henry keep an eye on Charlie?' Maisie said when she came back.

'He would, but he said his back was playin' up so he was going home to bed.'

'That's not like Henry.' Maisie was annoyed that she hadn't known.

'No, it's not. He never complains as a rule. I told him to rub it with wintergreen. I'd offer to do it for him, but it wouldn't be right. And it's no good asking Arthur.'

Maisie pursed her lips. 'No, it most certainly wouldn't be right for you to do it.'

Emma peered out of the window. It was still quite dark after the storm but the rain had eased a little. 'It's not raining as hard now, so I think I can go.'

'You'll get soaked.'

'No, I won't. I've got me bike, so I'll be home in two minutes.' She took her pinafore down off the hook again. 'I'll put this over my head.'

'Fat lot of good that'll do,' Maisie said with a laugh.

Emma pedalled off down the drive, her pinafore draped over her head like a shawl. The rain hadn't lasted long, but it had been torrential and her stockings and skirt were soon soaked from the spray as she rode through the puddles that had formed; and the pinafore was no help at all.

She propped her bike against the wall of the house and hurried inside. Charlie was there, pretending to read a dog-eared comic. He looked up when he heard the door open.

'Oh, it's you, Mum. Is it still rainin'?' he said without much interest, taking another bite of bread and jam.

'Not so much.' She took off the wet pinafore and shook her skirt. 'I'll have to change this, it's soaked.' She looked up. 'Where's Dad? Is he upstairs?' She tried to sound casual, she didn't want to frighten Charlie.

'No, he went out.' Charlie didn't look up from his comic.

'Went out! When?'

'I dunno.' He shrugged.

'Was it before the storm?'

'What? I dunno. It might have been.' He looked up, frowning. 'Does it matter?'

'No, no, 'course not. I'll just go and change this skirt.' She hurried up the stairs and looked under the beds in both rooms, expecting to find Arthur cowering there; but there was no sign of him, nor in the cupboard in the corner. She put on a dry skirt then went downstairs again and looked in the cupboard under the stairs.

'What you lookin' for, Mum?'

She sat down at the table. 'Well, you know your dad gets in a bit of a state when there's thunder about and I thought he might have – might have hid himself somewhere, that's all.' She drummed her fingers on the table.

'Have you looked under the beds? That's where he usually goes.'

She nodded. Of course, it was stupid of her to think Charlie hadn't realized what his father was like. The sad thing was he didn't remember him any other way.

She bit her lip. 'I wonder where he's got to.'

'If he's not here, he must be down the pub.' Charlie wiped the jam off his mouth with the back of his hand and folded the comic. 'Do you want me to go and dig him out?'

'No, he wouldn't like that.' Emma shook her head. She smiled at her son. 'Thanks all the same, love.'

She got up and went over to the window. 'It's stopped raining now. P'raps I'll just nip down and see if he's there. I needn't go in.'

'I'll come with you, if you like, Mum.'

She shook her head. 'I'll go on me bike.' It would help prop him up to get him home if he was the worse for wear. '*If!*', she thought to herself grimly. When did he ever leave the pub in any other way? And he still had the shilling he'd taken from Mary, poor little lass. She got on her bike and pedalled off to the Nag's Head.

He wasn't there. The landlord admitted that he'd been banned until he made an effort to clear the slate, and suggested trying the Rose and Crown.

She had more luck there. They remembered that he'd been there during the storm, through which he had been drinking steadily – or rather, pretty unsteadily. But nobody seemed to know when he'd left, nor where he was going.

It was the same with all the other pubs she enquired at. He'd been seen, but nobody had much idea of the time he arrived nor how long he stayed. They all remembered he'd been 'the worse for wear'.

Wearily, in the gathering dusk Emma pedalled home, hoping against hope that Arthur had got there before her.

He hadn't.

She made a hot drink for Charlie and herself. And because there was nothing else to be done they went to bed, leaving the door unbolted so that Arthur could get in if he found his way home in the small hours.

She spent a sleepless night imagining him out cold under a hedge somewhere, soaked through to the skin. At the crack of dawn she got up and looked all round outside the house, but there was still no sign of him. She knocked on Henry's door as soon as she heard him moving about and asked him to let Maisie know she would be late.

'Tell her I'll come as soon as I've found Arthur.'

'Anything I can do, Emma?' he asked gently, full of concern for her.

'I don't know, Henry. Tell you the truth I'm all at sixes and sevens. I can't think what to do,' she said, running her hands distractedly through her hair.

He finished buttoning his shirt and pulled up his braces. 'Tell you what, I'll let them know at the House what's happening, then I'll nip down the police station, see if they've got any news,' he said.

'Oh, yes, of course. I hadn't thought of going to the police.' She gave him a tired smile. 'Thanks, Henry. I'd be glad.'

He gave her arm a squeeze. 'You go and make yourself a cuppa, Emma. I'll let you know what I find out.' He smiled at her. 'But I reckon by the time I get back the old rascal will be sitting at your kitchen table nursing a sore head.'

'And I shan't know whether to kiss him or kill him for all the worry he's caused,' she replied with a sigh.

Sixteen

It was nearly ten o'clock before Henry came back. He looked haggard and anxious. Emma's heart lurched. But at first she said nothing, simply nodding towards a chair at the table and pouring him a mug of tea from the freshly made pot.

'I've done nothing but drink tea ever since you left,' she said as she pushed it across the table to him, talking quickly to prevent him telling her the news she could see in his face. 'I've had to send Charlie to the dairy for more milk. Will you have a slice of my cake? It's here in the tin. It was fresh baked yesterday . . .'

'Emma. Sit down.' he broke in gently.

She sank on to a chair opposite to him, nodding. 'I know

what you're going to say. It's bad news, isn't it? I can tell by your face. What was it, a pub brawl? He can get very aggressive when the drink's in him.' She looked across at him. 'He never used to be like that, you know, Henry. He was a cheerful, happy-go-lucky boy when I first knew him . . . It was the war changed him.' She gave an exasperated sigh. 'All right. You can tell me where he is, although I reckon I can guess. At the police station? Have they locked him up? Oh Lord, he won't like that. It'll make him even worse.'

'Emma.' He leaned across and took her hand, such an unusual gesture from him that she looked at him in surprise. 'Emma, it's worse than that. Arthur's dead. He drowned in the river.'

She pulled her hand away as if to distance herself from his words and stared at him, shocked. 'Drowned? My Arthur? In the river?' She shook her head. 'No, no, there must be some mistake. What would he be doing anywhere near the river, for goodness' sake? It's over a mile away.'

'There's no mistake, Emma. They've got his body at the police station,' he said quietly. 'I saw him.' He closed his eyes briefly to blot out the memory, then went on, 'They let me identify him, but you'll have to do it officially, I'm afraid.' He took her hand again. 'Don't worry, I'll come with you, Em. From what they said, he must have fallen in off the quay opposite the Anchor. Apparently, it was a very high tide.'

A puzzled look crossed her face. 'But what was he doing there? As far as I know, he never drank at the Anchor . . .' Her voice tailed off. 'Unless he couldn't get them to put it on the slate anywhere else, of course. I didn't think to go that far to look for him . . .' She frowned. 'What happened? Did he fall in? He wouldn't stand a chance if he did, he can't swim.'

'They didn't tell me much at the police station, so I went along to the Anchor to see what the landlord'd got to say.'

'And . . .?' She looked at him intently.

'Apparently Arthur turned up there in the middle of the storm, soaking wet, white as a sheet and shaking like a leaf. He didn't seem to know where he was or what he was doing there. Anyway, he asked for whisky but just as the landlord handed it to him there was a flash of lightning and an almighty clap of thunder, worse than anything that had gone before –

they discovered this morning it had been caused by a thunderbolt that struck a warehouse just along the quay.'

She closed her eyes. 'Oh, my poor Arthur. That would have been the last straw. He'd have been out of his mind. He couldn't bear . . .' She opened them. 'Go on, Henry.'

'You're right. To use the landlord's words, "The poor b . . . looked half-crazed and didn't seem to know where he was or what he was doing." Apparently he put his arms up over his head and looked for somewhere to hide, but the pub was full and that made him worse. Next thing was, he rushed outside but before anyone could follow him a bloke who'd been taking a leak up against the wall – begging your pardon, Emma, but they were the landlord's words – burst in and said he'd just seen a bloke fall over the quay into the water.'

'Oh, my dear Lord!' Emma breathed. 'Couldn't anyone have saved him?'

'They tried, from all accounts. But bearing in mind it was pitch black down there in the water and the blokes who tried weren't exactly sober themselves, it probably took a lot longer to fish him out than it might have done in daylight.'

'And with his chest being bad from being gassed . . .' Emma shook her head and said bitterly, 'He went off to fight for his country an upright young man, scared of nothing, and he came back an old man, terrified if so much as a log crackled on the fire.' She sniffed. 'He may have drowned in the river, but it was the war killed him as sure as if he'd been blown up by a shell. Oh, my poor Arthur.' Suddenly, her face crumpled and she looked up hopelessly. 'What will I do now, Henry? How much more will I have to bear? That's two of my family gone in less than a year, first my little Ivy and now my husband. I must be very wicked to have all this suffering heaped on me.' She began to cry, huge racking sobs.

Henry stood up and pulled her to her feet, putting his arms round her and gathering her to him in the way he'd often longed to do but never thought could ever happen.

'Of course you're not wicked, Em. You mustn't think like that,' he whispered, holding her close and smoothing her hair, guiltily savouring the moment. 'Although I admit I felt the same when my Florrie was killed, so I know just how you feel. But you were always a good wife to Arthur and a good mother to little Ivy. It's not your fault they've been taken from you any more than it was my fault Florrie died. It's just something we have to accept and bear as best we can.' He went on talking, soothing and comforting her while she wept, clinging to him, grateful for the warmth and comfort of his strong arms.

The following days were chaotic at Warren's End. On hearing the dreadful news, Roger had immediately been to see Emma and given both her and Mary as much time off as they needed to come to terms with Arthur's death. He himself accompanied Emma to the inquest, at which a verdict of accidental death was recorded, and quietly supported her in other ways, both arranging and attending the funeral and making sure she had no financial worries.

Doreen's reaction was very different. It didn't take long for her sympathy to wear thin.

'You've been very good to Emma, Roger, and I'm sure it's right to give her all the time off she needs. It was a truly dreadful thing that's happened, and of course I sympathize with her in her sad loss, we all do. But I do feel that sometimes it's much better to keep working when one is grieving,' she suggested one night over a dinner in which the dumplings were heavy and the custard was lumpy. 'Apart from anything else it really is expecting too much of Maisie. She's now having to do all the cooking as well as her other work. I could have written my name in the dust on the credenza in the drawing room yesterday. And poor Stella looks tired out with Mary not here to help her with Baby.'

'I'm perfectly happy looking after Jonathan myself,' Stella assured her quickly. 'He's really no trouble. It's just that he's been a bit fractious at night lately, so I've had several disturbed nights. Of course Mary needs time at home with her mother, and also with her brother. It must be a very hard thing for a young boy to come to terms with losing his father, especially in such a tragic way. After all, Charlie's not very old, is he?'

Roger frowned thoughtfully. 'I think he's probably twelve, maybe coming up to thirteen. But I'm not sure.'

'Well, surely that's old enough to start making himself useful?' Rosalie said. 'I can put in a word for him down at the club if you think that might be helpful, Pa. He might be able to help out in the stables, mucking out and so forth. It would take his mind off things a bit and earn him a few coppers at the same time.'

Roger nodded. 'That's a good idea. Yes, he might enjoy working with the horses. See what you can do, Rosalie.'

'I'm sure that's very noble of you both, but it doesn't help the situation here, does it?' Doreen interrupted, her tone frosty. 'The fact remains we are short-staffed. There is simply too much for Maisie to manage single-handed.'

'Maybe I could help out a bit?' Stella said uncertainly. For some inexplicable reason she felt that Doreen's words had been directed at her.

'Oh, what a good idea, Stella.' Doreen turned to her with a patronizing smile. 'Thank you for offering. I'd quite forgotten you used to be a working girl.'

Her tone prompted a quick and furious response from Rosalie. 'Oh, Ma, for goodness' sake, don't say "working girl" in such a condescending manner, you make it sound as if Stella had come from heaving coal down a coal mine,' she said with disgust. 'Not that it would be anything to be ashamed of if she had.'

'Now you're being ridiculous, Rosalie,' Doreen said, offended. 'I only said that Stella used to work for her living, which, of course she did.' She turned to Stella again. 'Perhaps you would like to have a word with Maisie, Stella? I'm sure she would be glad of a little assistance in the kitchen.' She dabbed her mouth delicately with her napkin.

Philip was as furious as Rosalie at the way in which Doreen was treating Stella, but he was anxious to avoid a full-scale quarrel between mother and daughter so he cut in before Rosalie could speak again. 'But weren't you just saying Stella looked a little tired, Doreen? Now you're suggesting piling even more work on to her. That's hardly fair.'

Doreen shot him a venomous look and waved her arm, dismissing his words. 'I was mistaken. It must have been a trick of the light. I was thinking only the other day how well Stella was looking. Motherhood obviously suits her.' She turned her attention once more to her daughter-in-law, smiling sweetly. 'Perhaps you wouldn't mind clearing the table, dear, and taking the tray to the kitchen? That will save Maisie a few steps. You can have a word with her while you're there, can't you?' She sat back complacently, her aim to reduce Stella's status achieved.

Although he had said nothing, Roger had been watching and listening carefully to the conversation. He always tried to think the best of his wife, which was sometimes not easy, but he didn't like the manner in which she was treating Stella, belittling her in front of the whole family. But why she should wish to behave in such an unkind way to the wife of her dead son was completely beyond his comprehension.

Trying to mitigate his wife's rudeness, he smiled at Stella. 'Just make sure you don't offer to take on too much, Stella, my dear,' he warned. 'Remember, you are short-staffed, too. Your little nursemaid isn't here, either, to help you with your baby.'

'Oh, I'll be quite happy to mind my grandson while Stella helps out,' Doreen said quickly.

Suddenly, Roger saw exactly what was in his wife's mind and he didn't like it.

For her part, resenting being discussed as if she was deaf, or not there at all, Stella got to her feet and began to gather up the dirty dishes and pile them on to the tray, making an unnecessary clatter as she did so while not missing a word of what was being said. Carrying the tray to the kitchen she, like Roger, also reflected on Doreen's words. Was she being over-sensitive, or was Doreen trying to reduce her to the status of a servant? Was it the beginning of a subtle campaign to take over control of Jonathan? Or was she imagining things because she was so tired? After all, with both Emma and Mary away, things were not normal in the house; it was therefore quite reasonable for Doreen to accept any help she was offered, so maybe she was being oversensitive.

She reached the kitchen and pushed open the door. And stopped short. Instead of the usual order and neatness and the scrubbed table tops and gleaming saucepans, the place was in chaos. The sink was full of pans waiting to be washed and the table was littered with dirty crockery; something had boiled over on the gas stove and the floor badly needed a sweep. In the middle of all the mess and muddle, Stella was amazed to see Maisie sitting in the rocking chair, her hair escaping untidily from her cap, holding Jonathan on her lap, singing to him.

She started up guiltily out of the chair, but relaxed back into it when she saw it was Stella who had come in.

'Oh, you gave me a fright, Mrs Stella. I thought for a minute it was the missus. She'd kill me if she saw the kitchen in this state, but there's only so much I can do.' She looked down at the baby on her lap. 'I hope you don't mind, Mrs Stella, but the little lad was crying his eyes out and I couldn't bear to leave him there all alone so I brought him in here for a cuddle. I don't get much chance to nurse little ones and I do so love to.' She dropped a kiss on his head, then her jaw dropped as she looked up and saw what Stella was carrying. 'Oh, Mrs Stella, whatever are you doing with that tray? You shouldn't be carrying that. Put it down on the dresser if you can find a space. I'll see to it later. I didn't realize you'd all finished eating. Oh dear! I was so taken up with the little one . . .'

'Thank you, Maisie. Of course I don't mind you picking him up because he was crying. And since you ask, I've brought the tray back because Mrs Nolan is afraid you're being over-worked with Emma being away, so she thinks it might be a good idea for me to give you a hand.' She grinned at the other girl. 'I must say it rather looks as if she could be right.' She put the tray down on the dresser, then took the baby from Maisie and began to rock him on her shoulder. He nuzzled into her neck and before long he was asleep.

When she came back from settling him in his cot, Maisie was already at the sink, tackling the washing-up. 'Oh, I don't think it would be a good idea at all for you to be working here in the kitchen, Mrs Stella,' Maisie said, continuing the conversation, a worried frown creasing her brow. 'It wouldn't be right. It wouldn't be right at all. In any case, you've got more than enough to do looking after the little one. It's all very well for the missus to throw her orders about, but has she forgotten Mary's not here, either?'

'Mrs Nolan says she'll be happy to look after him sometimes,' Stella said, deliberately keeping her voice level.

Maisie gave a sarcastic burst of laughter, then guiltily covered her mouth with her hand. 'Oh, I'm sorry, Mrs Stella. I know I shouldn't laugh, but I just can't see Mrs Nolan doing that! I'll bet she never looked after her own babies, let alone someone else's.'

'Well, we shall see, shan't we?' Stella said carefully. She picked up a tea towel and began drying up, wondering if Maisie realized how much of her true feelings towards her employer she had just revealed.

Suddenly, the bell rang from the dining room, making them both start.

'Oh Lord, I quite forgot, they'll be wanting their coffee,' Maisie said, quickly drying her hands. She began to busy herself with cups and coffee pot.

'I'll carry on with the washing-up,' Stella said.

'You'll do nothing of the kind, Mrs Stella,' Maisie said over her shoulder as she went to the door, the heavy tray in her hand. 'You'll come up to the dining room and take coffee with the family. I'm not having them treat you as a servant.'

'All right, Maisie. You can tell them I'll be there in a minute.' She carried on washing up, mulling over Maisie's last words. A servant. Was that really how Doreen would like to see her?

A few minutes later Maisie came back, trying desperately not to smirk. 'It seems Mrs Rosalie didn't want coffee, she's gone off to the club; Mr Philip went home to work on his painting; and the Colonel's gone to his study for a whisky. So it's just Madam and you for coffee, Mrs Stella. She says she'll wait for you to join her.'

'What do you usually have at this time, Maisie?' Stella was still up to her elbows in suds.

'I usually have a cup of tea when I've finished clearing up. Why?'

'Well, I think perhaps I'll stay down here and have a cup with you. But let's get this kitchen cleaned up first. I'm sure Emma would have a fit if she could see it now.'

'But the missus said she'd wait for you, Mrs Stella,' Maisie said anxiously.

'Well, she'll have a long wait, won't she?'

Later, sitting in the pristine kitchen drinking tea with Maisie, Stella allowed herself a secret smile at the thought of Doreen sitting alone in the drawing room waiting to be joined for coffee. It was a small triumph.

Seventeen

After another week, which seemed interminable to Stella and Maisie, both Emma and Mary were back at work. Mary was pale but Emma was positively ashen, her eyes sunken and her face lined far beyond her years. The shock of Arthur's death, particularly the manner of it, had taken its toll on her. With the resilience of youth, Mary spoke little about it; she was just glad to be back to the normality of caring for Jonathan.

But Emma seemed to find comfort in talking, usually over the mid-morning cocoa with Maisie, which Henry usually came in to share.

'It's strange,' she said thoughtfully, 'When I think about Arthur – and naturally enough I do, all the time – I don't see the skeleton of a man you both knew, who drank too much and didn't work, the man who was frightened of his own shadow and had dreadful headaches and a terrible cough.' She shook her head. 'No, I see the young man I married.' She smiled a little and went on, speaking softly, 'He was a lovely young man, my Arthur. With his curly hair and dark eyes, he was so handsome; all the girls liked him. Oh, I was over the moon when he chose me. He worked hard, too, full of energy he was. And when the babies came along, he was a real family man. He loved his children – and me – so much.' She wiped away a tear and looked up at them. 'And that's the man I'm grieving for, the young man who joined up to do his duty and then had his life and his future taken away from him in the trenches, even though the shell of him came back. It was a wicked, wicked shame. And the tragedy of it is there were thousands more like him.' She paused and stared down unseeingly at a mark on the table.

Maisie and Henry exchanged glances, both unwilling to trot out platitudes in the face of Emma's grief. But before either of them could find words of comfort, Emma pulled herself together and blew her nose and gave them both a wintry smile.

'But that's enough of my troubles for now. Thank you both for listening.' She put out her hand to Henry. 'And thank you, Henry. You've been such a help, always there when I needed you. I don't know how I'd have managed without you.'

He took her hand and squeezed it. 'You know I'll always be there for you, Em,' he said, his voice a little thick.

She nodded, took another drink of cocoa, and said with a rather false brightness, 'So, how have you been managing here?' She gave a little laugh. 'Everywhere looks spick and span, so I guess I needn't have worried that you were missing me.'

'That's because I had help,' Maisie said. Her voice was brittle because she was jealous at the exchange she had just witnessed between Emma and Henry. 'Mrs Stella came whenever she could spare time from looking after the baby. She's been a real brick.'

Emma raised her eyebrows. 'Didn't the missus object?'

Maisie shook her head. 'No, in fact it was her idea in the first place.' Her voice dropped. 'Seems to me for some reason she quite liked the idea of treating Mrs Stella as a servant, though it didn't appear to worry Mrs Stella overmuch.' She shrugged. 'Mind you, the missus was willing to help when it suited her; if you could call it help. She'd come down all businesslike and bossy and pick the baby up out of his pram, even if he was asleep, and say she'd take him and look after him for an hour. But as soon as he cried, she'd bring him back and then it would take ages to settle him again. It made Mrs Stella furious, and in the end she had to tell her not to disturb him. She didn't like that.' A smile spread across her face. 'I didn't mind, it meant I got lots of cuddles. I don't often get the chance to nurse babies,' she added sadly.

'How does Charlie like working at the country club?' Henry asked, changing the subject before Maisie could get maudlin.

Emma brightened up immediately. 'He really loves working

with the horses, can't talk about anything else. It was good of Mrs Rosalie to put a word in for him; it's the best thing could have happened.'

'Yes, she's not a bad sort underneath,' Maisie said. 'Not like her mother.'

'You've really got your knife into the missus, haven't you, Maisie?' Henry said with a frown.

'Well, I don't like the way she's been treating Mrs Stella,' Maisie admitted. 'She'd do things like ringing down and saying the drawing room hadn't been dusted for two days, so perhaps Mrs Stella would see to that when she had time because she knew I was too busy. It made Mrs Stella look like some sort of skivvy, and I thought it was all wrong.'

'But you just said Mrs Stella didn't seem to mind,' Emma reminded her.

Maisie shrugged. 'She didn't most of the time. But sometimes I noticed her jaw tighten a bit, though she never actually said anything.'

'Did she have her meals down here with you?'

'Oh, no. But I believe it was the Colonel who insisted that she ate with the family, which was only right, when all's said and done. I don't think he was at all happy with the arrangement. But I reckon he didn't make a fuss because he knew it wasn't pernament.' She didn't notice she hadn't got the word quite right.

'So the missus didn't manage to get her hands on the baby very much?' Emma asked. 'I shouldn't be surprised if that was what she was angling after all the time, making Mrs Stella work down here so she could get her precious grandson to herself.'

'You could be right. But he always started to cry when she took him, specially if it was near his feeding time. That annoyed her. She'd bring him back and say she hoped he wasn't going to be a fractious child – which of course he wasn't, except when she barged in and disturbed his routine. She hasn't got the first idea how to treat a baby. How she ever brought her own children up I'll never know.'

'Well, they were in India, I believe, so she probably had one of those Indian nursemaids . . .'

'An ayah,' Henry put in.

'Oh, is that what they're called? Yes, one of them, so she never had to do anything.' Emma stood up and took the mugs over to the sink. 'Still, Mary's back now and so am I, so things should get back to normal.'

'I hope so,' Maisie said primly. 'I didn't like to see Mrs Stella treated the way she was. It's not right. She is Mr John's widow, when all's said and done, so she's a rightful member of the family and should be treated as such. And she's ever so nice.'

Emma and Henry both nodded in agreement. 'Yes,' Emma said, 'she's ever so nice.'

Stella too was thankful when Emma and Mary came back to work. She had never admitted to anyone how deathly tired she had been helping Maisie on top of looking after the baby. She remained resolutely cheerful and made sure to get to her feet to clear the dishes after each course at dinner before Doreen had the chance to say 'You can clear now, Stella, and bring in the pudding', or the coffee, in the patronizing manner that was become habitual with her.

Often she could see Philip's jaw set or his fists clench when Doreen was being more outrageously rude than usual and she knew she had an ally there, although in practice there was little he could do about it. Unlike Roger, who would get to his feet and awkwardly begin to collect up the dirty plates, only to be told by Doreen to 'Sit down, Roger. You're being more of a hindrance than a help.'

But Stella always made a point of smiling at him and thanking him for his help.

Nevertheless, this subtle shift in her position was worrying. She had always known that as far as Doreen was concerned she had been given a home at Warren's End while she was pregnant because she was the vessel carrying her grandson; but she had the uncomfortable feeling that now he was born she was becoming expendable. More than that, she was something of a nuisance, standing between Doreen and the child, because as his mother she would always have first claim on him.

On the other hand, when she wasn't seething from some disparaging remark Doreen had made, Stella realized that she really had no grounds for complaint. After all, she had nowhere else to go and no means of supporting herself and her child beyond the interest from her small inheritance, which would barely pay the rent, let alone feed and clothe them both. So putting up with Doreen's jibes and helping with a few domestic chores, she told herself firmly when she was feeling particularly irritated, was a small price to pay for a roof over her head.

Things improved considerably once Mary and Emma were back, because there was no longer any reason for Doreen to continually call on her for menial tasks; and Mary was a great help in looking after the baby, taking over all the considerable washing and ironing entailed and a hundred and one other things.

At the first opportunity, she slipped over to the flat to see Philip. He was busy in his studio putting the finishing touches to his latest painting. His face lit up when he saw her.

'Ah,' he said, 'it's good to see you, Stella. But where's the little fellah?'

'Asleep. Mary's keeping an eye on him while she does the ironing.'

'Well, do come and sit down. Yes, that's right, move those frames so you can sit where I can see you.'

'I'm hoping you'll show me the paintings you're getting ready for the exhibition, now I've managed to get over to see them at last.' She smiled as she sat down. 'I haven't had a lot of time to spare lately, I'm afraid.'

'No, I realize that,' he said without returning her smile. 'But you can relax now, Stella. Henry will be here in a few minutes and he'll make us a cup of tea.'

She started to get up. 'Oh, I'll do it . . .'

'You will not.' His voice was sharp. 'Sit down, Stella. You've played the maid for quite long enough and I can see you're tired out. For what it's worth and at the risk of putting the cat among the pigeons, I think Doreen has been treating you atrociously.'

'Do you really, Philip?' she asked, surprised at his outburst. She frowned. 'You see, I'm not sure. Obviously, I don't like it when she orders me about, but at the same time I've tried to look at it from Doreen's point of view. What I mean is,

I'm living here rent-free and have a very nice little flat, so I suppose it doesn't hurt if I help out a bit . . .' Her voice trailed off.

'That's as maybe. And I'm sure you don't mind giving a hand here and there when needed, but that doesn't give her the right to treat you like a skivvy, the way she's been doing. I think she's been behaving very badly towards you, and I know Roger has been very cross with her.'

'She doesn't like me much.' The words came out involuntarily.

'I know. It's because she's jealous of you.' He leaned forward over his painting. 'I wouldn't let it worry you too much, Stella. The rest of us are very fond of you.'

She glanced at him, wanting to ask who exactly he meant by 'the rest of us', but he had flushed a dull red and appeared engrossed in his picture.

'I'd better go. I can see you're busy,' she said when he volunteered nothing more. She felt flat. She'd thought at first he'd been pleased to see her, but she could see now that he was anxious to continue with his painting and she was in the way.

He looked up and smiled apologetically. 'I'm sorry. No, please don't go, you've only just come.' He laid down his brushes. 'It's such a long time since we had a proper conversation. I've missed that, you know.'

She nodded. 'So have I. And there's one thing I've been wanting to ask you, but it didn't seem appropriate over the dinner table. Is Henry keeping up the good work on your legs? It seems to me you're walking a little better, if you don't mind me saying so.'

'Mm. Maybe I am, a bit. But poor old Henry couldn't help for long because it played his back up. He gets a lot of pain from that back of his, although he never complains.'

'Oh, so it had to stop. That's a pity.'

'Yes. But I was finding it beneficial, so I made enquiries and found a man. I'm not sure whether he calls himself a masseur or physiotherapist, bit of both, perhaps. And he's medically qualified. Anyway, I go to him, or rather Henry takes me, and he massages my legs and gives me exercises twice a week. Now my paintings are selling a bit, I can afford to pay him myself and not sponge off Roger, which is much better.' He smiled at her. 'So I've got you to thank for starting it all off. Thank you, Stella, for galvanizing me into finding Dr Marshall. I think he's very good, although he's warned me I'll never be able to walk normally.'

'But if he can alleviate the pain . . . Dr Marshall, did you say? There was a Dr Marshall back at the convalescent home. I used to know him well. He was very good, helped a lot of crippled servicemen.'

'Maybe it's the same man. I'll ask him if he knows you.'

'No, I'm sure it won't be,' she said quickly. 'He wouldn't have left Hill House. But I'm glad this man's helping you.'

'He's not doing me any harm, anyway.' He gave her an odd look, but said no more about it. After a minute he glanced out of the window, rubbing his hands. 'Ah, here's Henry. And I see he's bringing some of Emma's biscuits to have with our tea. That's good.'

While Henry busied himself with the tea things, then excused himself, saying he would be back later, Philip told her a little more about the forthcoming exhibition.

'It's to be at Oscar Hillyard's gallery in London,' he said, adding, 'I believe I told you about Oscar, didn't I? He's Benedict Gerard's associate. Well, the other way round, actually; Ben's very much the junior. But it's a start, and at least it's in the right place.' He smiled at her. 'I do hope you'll be able to come to the opening, Stella. I'll be very disappointed if you can't.'

'Oh, I'd love to come, Philip,' she said warmly. 'That is, provided I can make arrangements for leaving Jonathan.' She bit her lip thoughtfully. 'I wonder, maybe Emma would stay and help Mary with him. I wouldn't like to leave Mary to manage on her own for too long, after all she's still not quite fifteen. And I couldn't possibly ask Doreen. But I expect she'll be at the opening, anyway.'

'Oh, yes, Doreen'll be there, all right,' he said. 'Just try and keep her away! Not that she's in the least interested in paintings, mine or anyone else's for that matter. She'll only be there in the hope of meeting somebody "important", though I've already told her that's not very likely.'

'How many paintings are you exhibiting?' She poured the tea and handed him a cup and one of Emma's biscuits.

'Thanks. Mm, these biscuits are good,' he said, biting into one. 'As many as I can. It's fifteen at the moment. The ones hanging on the walls over there are ready to go, but the rest are still being framed. Then there are a couple I've yet to finish.' He closed one eye to study the perspective of the painting on the easel in front of him. 'But knowing Ben, he'll be round here foraging among the rest of my rubbish to see what else he can find.'

She walked round, looking at the pictures on the wall. One or two she had seen before, but most were new. There were both landscapes – broad, open stretches of poppy fields – and seascapes. One she particularly liked was an evening scene at low tide, with the sun setting over the water and a lone man in the foreground gathering cockles on the shore.

'Oh, I love this one, I saw it when I came over before,' she said enthusiastically. Then, moving on, 'Oh, and here's that basket of daffodils I picked in the spring! Last time I saw this, it was just a quick pencil sketch. Now they look so real you could almost pick one out of the basket – a real breath of springtime.'

'Mm. It'll go into the exhibition, but it won't be for sale.'

She put her head on one side. 'Oh, that's a pity. I might have bought it, if it wasn't too expensive. Now I won't be able to.'

'You won't need to. I'm going to give it to you. Unless you'd rather have that one.' He pointed to the one next to it.

She looked. 'Oh, it's the scene you painted for Jonathan when he was born, only much bigger. I can see now, it's the place where I used to find you painting in the little wood.' She turned and beamed at him, then turned back. 'And you've even put in the tree trunk I sat on.'

He smiled. 'Well, it was there, wasn't it? Couldn't leave it out. We had some enjoyable conversations while you sat on that log.'

She smiled. 'That's true. It seems a long time ago now, although it's only just over three months.'

'Three months.' He gave a sigh. 'A lot has happened in that

time. Your young shaver has been born, poor old Arthur Blatch has gone . . .' He sighed again and shook his head. 'He was a sad case, Arthur.' He was quiet for several minutes, then he said, 'You know sometimes I think there are worse things in life than dying.' He looked up and gave her a crooked smile. 'I'm sorry, that was tactless of me. I guess you're the last person I should say that to, Stella.'

'No, I think you're right, Philip,' she said slowly. 'I've never said this to anyone before, but I have wondered what would have happened if John hadn't been killed in the war.'

He frowned. 'What do you mean?'

'Well, it's just that the John I married, the man I thought I knew, seems to have borne very little resemblance to the John people talk about here. And to be perfectly honest, I'm not sure I would even have liked that person.' She put her hand up to her mouth, a look of horror on her face. 'Oh, I've never admitted that before, even to myself.' She went on slowly, forming the thoughts as she spoke, 'But Heaven help me, I think it's true. And I guess, if I'm honest, he wouldn't have liked me much, either.'

He studied her closely. 'Rosalie's been talking to you,' he said at last.

She nodded.

'Oh, why couldn't that woman keep her mouth shut!' he said, exasperated.

'It's all true, then, what she said? She wasn't just being bitchy?'

'Of course she was being bitchy. And it would have been kinder if she hadn't said anything at all. But Rosalie doesn't lie, that I will say for her, at least not often; so I'm sure what she said was true. John was a good-looking young man with a somewhat devil-may-care attitude that appealed to the ladies and he capitalized on it. That's all I'm saying.'

'Funny, he didn't give me that impression at all. But of course he was still convalescing, so probably not quite himself.'

'And people do change, Stella. Maybe meeting you changed him. You're enough to make any man . . .' he broke off. 'Well, I guess he thought he'd met the love of his life in you.'

'He only knew me for six weeks.' She shook her head sadly.

'We really didn't know each other at all, did we?' She looked
at him. 'Would he have enjoyed being a father, Philip?'

He laughed out loud. 'The John I knew wouldn't, I'm sure.
He'd have loathed anything that cramped his style.' He paused
thoughtfully. 'John and Rosalie were very alike in temperament,' he said after a bit. 'But as I've said, people change.
Maybe the John you knew would have revelled in it. But it's
something we shall never be able to prove, one way or the
other; so my advice to you is to remember the man you
married and discount the rest.'

'Thank you, Philip, for being honest with me.' She didn't
tell him that the words that would stick in her mind were
'John and Rosalie were very alike in temperament'. She knew
it was true. She had seen – but been too much in love to heed
– signs of it in the man she'd married.

Eighteen

Philip's forthcoming exhibition was the main – indeed, almost
the only – topic discussed round the dinner table in the days
leading up to it. Predictably, Doreen and Rosalie's abiding
concern was with what they should wear. Rosalie had seen a
very fetching yellow-and-white striped dress with a matching
yellow coat in one of the latest fashion magazines and was very
tempted by it. But there was also a similar outfit in burnt
orange that she liked, and she couldn't decide which would
suit her best. At the same time, Doreen was very taken with
a pearl-grey costume which, teamed with royal blue, might
look just right for the occasion. Then there was the question
of hats and shoes and handbags. The discussion was endless.

At the other end of the table, Roger, after congratulating
Philip and telling him how delighted he was with his success,
was much more concerned with his son-in-law's well-being.
How was he going to cope with stairs? And standing for long
periods? And the general strain of it all?

'Ben tells me it's all on the ground floor, so I won't have

to worry about stairs, and he assures me there will be a place for me to sit if necessary. As a last resort there's always the bath chair, I suppose, but I'd hate to have to use it. If people buy my pictures, I want it to be because they like them and see some value in them, not because they've been painted by "a poor crippled ex-serviceman". I should loathe that.' He shuddered.

Roger nodded. 'That I can quite understand.' He went on, 'The exhibition is to last how long? Three days? You'll be staying in London, of course. And obviously you'll take Henry with you to look after the nuts and bolts, so to speak.'

'Oh, yes, Henry will be with me, I couldn't manage without him.' He paused, frowning. 'But I hadn't exactly thought of staying for the full three days . . .'

'Nonsense, my boy. Potential buyers always like to see the artist,' Roger said. 'You can stay at my club.' He held up his hand as Philip began to protest. 'No, I insist. And I'm sure Henry can be found a room nearby. I'll get in touch with the steward; he'll arrange everything.'

'What about me, Pa?' Rosalie had caught the tail end of the conversation and pricked up her ears. 'Where am I going to stay? I can't stay at your club; it's men only.'

Roger regarded her over the rim of the spectacles he had taken to wearing sometimes. 'I'm sure you can find yourself a hotel to stay at if you want to remain in London, Rosalie, although surely that won't be necessary? Unlike Philip, it wouldn't be a problem for you to travel up daily if you want to be there all the time. But this is Philip's show, not yours, remember.'

'Yes, but I am his wife. He'll want me by his side.' She turned to Philip and smiled sweetly. 'Won't you, darling?'

He didn't smile back. 'You'll do as you wish, Rosalie,' he replied with a shrug. 'As you usually do.'

'And what about you, Stella?' Roger turned to her, noticing she hadn't taken any part in the discussion. 'You'll be coming to the opening, won't you?'

'Don't be ridiculous, Roger.' Doreen's voice from the other end of the table was sharp. 'Of course Stella can't come. She can't leave Baby.'

'I don't see why not. It's only for a few hours. I wasn't suggesting she should stay away for a week,' Roger said mildly.

'You're only a man. What would you know about it?' she said huffily. 'Of course she won't be able to come. There's the question of his feeds . . .' She waved her hand vaguely.

Roger raised his eyebrows questioningly at Stella, since she hadn't had a chance to answer for herself.

'Yes, I should very much like to come, Roger,' she said quietly. 'Philip told me he was going to invite me, and I've already had a word with Emma. She's very happy to stay on a little later so that Mary doesn't have to manage Jonathan on her own, although she is becoming extremely competent and Jonathan loves her. He smiles and gets quite excited when he sees her. I'll be quite happy to leave him with the two of them, I know he'll be well looked after. And we've already worked out how his feeds can be managed without . . .'

'We don't need to go into that.' Doreen cut her off. She pursed her lips. 'All I would say is I'm appalled that you could contemplate gallivanting off to London, leaving Baby in the care of servants. You must be a very bad mother to even consider such a thing.'

Roger slapped his hand down on the table furiously. 'Doreen, what are you saying? That's a terrible accusation to make,' he snapped, 'and blatantly not true! I think you should apologize to Stella at once.'

Doreen glared at him. 'I was only thinking of our grandson,' she said coldly, 'since nobody else seems to be giving him any consideration.' In order to put an end to the conversation, she rang the bell with unnecessary vigour for Maisie to come and clear.

But Rosalie had the last word. 'It never worried you if you left us to be looked after by servants when we were children, Ma,' she remarked. 'As I recall, John and I were practically brought up by our ayah. We hardly saw you from one day's end to the next.'

Doreen's only recourse after that was to turn her glare on to Rosalie then vent her spleen on poor Maisie, who had just come through the door. Which she did, with a vengeance, causing Maisie to remark to Emma on her return to the kitchen,

'I don't know what's got into the missus tonight, but if she carries on at me like that again I'll spit in her custard!'

Having listened to Doreen and Rosalie discussing clothes, Stella realized she would have to look to her own wardrobe if she was to accompany the family to London. Finding it definitely wanting, she wheeled Jonathan down into the town a few afternoons later to find something suitable to wear that was not too expensive. She had a pleasant afternoon, which included a visit to Mrs Greenleaf at the teashop, and returned home with a daisy-patterned dress and a three-quarter-length coat in green, a colour that she knew suited her. She also splashed out on green shoes – a real extravagance – and a little green-and-white cloche hat. Her black handbag would have to do; her budget wouldn't stretch any further, except to buy small gifts to give Mary and her mother when she returned home.

Stella travelled up on the train with Doreen – who practically ignored her – and Roger, plus a rather disgruntled Rosalie, who was of the opinion that she should have accompanied Philip when he went up with Henry the previous day.

The Oscar Hillyard Gallery was at the end of a small arcade in a side street off Oxford Street. From the outside it was unprepossessing: small double doors painted in dark blue, with a thin line painted in gold round each of the door panels, and one window with an easel holding Philip's painting of a basket of daffodils against a backdrop of draped black satin. Inside, the three rooms were tastefully appointed and quietly elegant, with thick carpets and a few small chairs painted gold and upholstered in dark-blue velvet strategically placed for potential buyers to rest before they reached for their cheque books. The owner of the gallery, Benedict Gerard's colleague Oscar Hillyard, was a small, dapper man of about forty, clean-shaven and with sleeked black hair. He was wearing an immaculate suit and starched white shirt, looking more like a common or garden London businessman than a dealer in fine art. By contrast, Benedict was all crimson trousers, flowing scarves and large hats, although his beard was neatly trimmed for the occasion. But Oscar Hillyard obviously knew what he was doing:

Philip's paintings were carefully hung to show them in the best possible light and to the best possible advantage.

Philip, in his best suit and a new cream shirt and spotted bow tie, was sitting on a chair behind a small table and looking extremely nervous when Stella and the family arrived. There were a number of people drifting from room to room, and after a perfunctory greeting Doreen and Rosalie went off to see if they could find somebody important to impress with their relationship to Philip.

Roger stayed for a few words with Philip, anxious to make sure he had everything he needed and that he was comfortably settled at his club.

'Yes. Everything's absolutely fine, thank you, sir. And Henry has a comfortable room, he tells me. He's gone off to do a bit of sightseeing, but he'll be back before long.' Philip struggled to his feet and tugged at his bow tie to make sure it was straight. 'Oh, it looks as if you got here just in time. Oscar's about to make his speech and then that man beside him – he's quite a famous art collector – has been invited to open the exhibition.' Roger moved away and Philip beckoned to Stella, who was standing a little to one side. 'I'm so glad you've come,' he whispered, smiling at her. 'I feel in need of a little moral support.'

She smiled back. 'From what I can see, there are already red stickers on one or two paintings. Does that mean they're sold?' she whispered back.

He nodded. 'At the preview, last night. But they can't be taken until the exhibition ends.'

They couldn't talk any more because Oscar was speaking about the fresh new talent of Philip Anderson, eulogizing over colours, techniques, brush strokes, subject matter and depth.

'Don't take too much notice of what he's saying,' Philip whispered. 'It's standard waffle and exactly the same as he said last night. He's got his eye on his commission.'

'That's a bit cynical,' Stella whispered back, trying not to giggle.

Oscar finished speaking and introduced the art collector, Sir William Edgecombe, who spoke at length about his love of art and all things beautiful, after which everybody clapped, mainly with relief, drank a toast to the artist in wine provided by Roger, and carried on looking round the gallery at the paintings. Two or three people came over to talk to Philip, so Stella slipped away. She noticed with amusement that Doreen had already buttonholed Sir William, and in the next room the orange-clad figure of Rosalie – she'd chosen the burnt orange, rather than the yellow, as more eye-catching – was in the middle of a small group holding forth on her husband's method of working and how she had so far resisted his desire to paint her . . . At which, Stella moved out of earshot.

'Well, I never! If it isn't the elusive Stella Bantock catapulted back into my life!'

Stella swung round and saw what had once been a familiar figure, a tall man with dark curly hair greying at the temples and a neat moustache. As ever, he was immaculately dressed; today in a well-cut pinstripe suit, a brilliantly white shirt and neatly knotted tie. She felt an odd sense of being confronted with a person from another life, a life from long ago, although it was not yet a year since she had left the convalescent home.

'Dr Marshall! How nice to see you,' she said, with a small, tight smile.

He put his head on one side. 'You don't sound very welcoming. And why the formality? Aren't you pleased to see me, Stella?'

'Surprised, that's all, Ian.' She was also surprised how difficult it was to utter his Christian name after all these months. 'But what are you doing here? Have you added pictures to your mania for collecting things?' Like women, she was tempted to add, but didn't.

'I'm here at the invitation of Major Anderson. He's been visiting my surgery for treatment.'

She frowned, puzzled. 'Your surgery? You've got a surgery? Philip told me he was seeing a Dr Marshall, but I never dreamed it would be you. I thought you were still at Hill House.'

'No, I decided to move on and seek pastures new. I felt I'd spent quite enough time ministering to the war-wounded, so thought I would return to the place where I'd spent much of my youth and set up in private practice. I'm glad I did; it's doing well.' Now it was his turn to frown. 'Philip? How is it

that you are on first-name terms with Major Anderson? Have
you known him long?'

'Major Anderson is my brother-in-law,' she said coolly. 'He
is married to my late husband's sister.'

'Oh, I see.' He nodded, then became serious. 'I was sorry
when I heard your husband had been killed, Stella. Is that why
you left Hill House in such a hurry last Christmas?'

She shook her head. 'No, I left because my parents-in-law
offered me a home with them.'

'That was very kind of them. But was that wise? Giving up
your career like that?'

'I thought so. I was very grateful for their offer.' She didn't
elaborate further, but looked up at the clock on the wall. 'Now,
I'm afraid you'll have to excuse me, Ian. I'd like to look round
the gallery before I have to go and catch my train.'

'Oh, don't go, Stella. We've got a lot of ground to make
up,' he said, obviously disappointed. Then, with sudden inspir-
ation, 'Let me take you out to dinner, and then we can travel
back together.' He smiled disarmingly. 'We're old friends, so it
could hardly be considered improper.'

She shook her head. 'I'm sorry, but I'm afraid I can't do
that, thank you all the same. I must get back to my son. He's
only four months old and I've never left him for as long as
this before, although I know he's in good hands and being
well looked after.'

'You have a son?' His eyebrows shot up in surprise.

'That's right. His name is Jonathan.' She smiled at his obvious
astonishment.

'Ah, then that would explain . . .'

'Yes, that would explain,' she agreed quickly.

'Then of course I mustn't keep you.' He fell into step beside
her. 'But I'm not going to let you go before you agree to
meet me on another day – when it's convenient for you, of
course. Maybe one afternoon for tea? Tuesday week, perhaps?
How would that suit?'

She laughed. 'Oh, Ian, you haven't changed. You don't waste
any time, do you?'

'Not if I can avoid it. But does that mean yes?'

She laughed again. 'Yes, I guess it does.'

'Then I'll look forward to seeing you Tuesday week.'

'I'll say this for you, Ian, you don't believe in letting the grass grow under your feet, do you?' she said, still smiling.

He didn't return her smile. 'Shall we just say I don't intend to let you slip through my fingers a second time,' he replied.

At his words her smile died, and she walked away.

Over tea and cakes in the dining car of the train, after the exhibition had closed for the day, Roger said, 'I'm glad I suggested Philip should stay at my club. He looked absolutely exhausted, poor chap. The excitement of the whole thing has put him under quite a strain, and he's still got two more days to go.'

'Henry will look after him, he knows what to do,' Rosalie said without much interest. She examined her nail varnish, a bright scarlet.

'There weren't as many people there as I'd expected, considering it was the opening day,' Doreen remarked. 'And I would have expected to see a Member of Parliament at the very least. But there was nobody I could recognize, nobody at all. It was hardly worth the trouble I took to attend. It was on the afternoon of my Ladies' Circle, too.' She was obviously quite put out.

Rosalie found this highly amusing. 'Oh, Ma, what did you expect! Phil isn't exactly Sir Joshua Reynolds. It was only a little tinpot show, when all's said and done.'

'I hope you won't say that to Philip, Rosalie,' Roger rebuked her. 'Everyone has to start somewhere, and I think he's done very well to get an exhibition in a West End gallery, even if it is only a small one. You should be proud of your husband, instead of making disparaging remarks.'

Rosalie's only reply was a bored shrug as she fished in her bag for a cigarette.

'I noticed that there were several paintings with red stickers,' Stella said, making an effort to join in the conversation. 'So he's obviously made some sales. And Dr Marshall was very interested in Philip's work. I shouldn't be at all surprised if he buys one.'

Rosalie's interest perked up and she regarded Stella through a haze of cigarette smoke. 'Yes, I saw you talking to him as if you were old friends. That was quick work on your part, but don't you think he's a bit old for you? He must be thirty-five if he's a day.'

'He's not that old, and I wouldn't say we were old friends. I knew him when we were both working at the convalescent home. He recognized me and came over to talk to me, that's all.' Stella refused to fuel Rosalie's speculations by telling her just how well she had known Ian Marshall at Hill House; nor that he had wanted to buy her dinner, or that she had arranged to meet him in less than a fortnight.

'He's quite handsome,' Rosalie said thoughtfully. 'And he looks as if he's quite rich. Has he got a wife?' She directed the question at Stella.

'No, not that I know of,' Stella replied.

'Well, didn't you ask him?'

'Of course I didn't! Why would I?'

'Quite right, too, Stella,' Roger said, nodding approvingly.

Doreen was following the conversation and looking slightly annoyed. 'Who is this Dr Marshall? Is he somebody important? Should I have been introduced to him?'

'He's Philip's masseur, Ma, that's all.' Rosalie waved her cigarette holder dismissively.

'Oh, nobody important. That's all right then.' Doreen relaxed. 'Pour me another cup of tea, Rosalie, please. Train journeys tend to have a drying effect on the palate.'

Nineteen

Henry was away with Philip for four days, and Emma missed him more than she cared to admit. She missed his cheery whistle as he left early each morning to go to Warren's End to help Philip bathe and dress, and missed him popping into the kitchen at odd times during the day for a cup of tea or cocoa with her and Maisie. She also missed the sound of him in the house next door during the evening and, the walls between the cottages being thin, even missed hearing him go up the stairs to bed just after ten o'clock every night.

But most of all she missed his knock on the door, and his concern. 'Is everything all right, Emma? Is there anything you want?' he would say. Or 'I've brought you a few carrots', or strawberries or apples. And she would make him an apple pie or a bacon dumpling in return.

Because that was what being a good neighbour was all about.

Nevertheless, she washed her face and put on a clean dress when she got in from work on the evening she knew he would be coming home from London, and sat by the window with her knitting watching for his return – but only because the light was better there and so she could tell him she had a meat pie in the oven that he was welcome to share.

Henry was weary. It had been a hard few days. In the unfamiliar surroundings and in his anxiety that his paintings should at least be well received, even if nobody bought them, Mr Philip had been on edge and sharp-tempered instead of his usual easy-going self. Even worse, he had hated the enforced journey in the bath chair from the Colonel's club to the gallery, which was unfortunately too far for him to walk but hardly worth calling a taxi for; and he had cursed Henry at every bump or obstruction along the way, even though he'd apologized afterwards.

Henry swapped his bag into his other hand. God, he'd be glad to get home, even though he knew he'd left the place in a bit of a mess because he'd been too busy with Mr Philip's preparations to worry about the state of it. And he hadn't even thought about something to eat. Not that he was hungry: he was too tired and his back ached. He pushed open the gate that served the two houses and walked up the path, with just a brief glance to see if Emma was anywhere around. Disappointed that he couldn't see her, he opened his door – nobody in the neighbourhood ever locked doors – and went in.

To his surprise, the room was immaculate. Everything had been tidied away, the dirty crockery washed, the floor swept, and there was a fire burning in the grate. He smiled to himself; that must have been Emma's work, bless her. He put down his bag and, glad of the excuse, went next door to thank her.

The door opened before he could even knock and she stood there, smiling. 'Ah, you're back. That's good,' she said by way of greeting, as if she hadn't been watching for him for the past half hour.

'Yes. Just got in. Popped round to thank you for tidying up for me. Didn't have time to do it before I left. It was kind of you, Emma.' He turned to go, for some reason feeling a little awkward in her presence. After all, he'd only been away for four days.

'It wasn't any trouble.' She cleared her throat. 'I've got a meat pie in the oven, Henry. You're welcome to come and share it if you haven't already eaten. Goodness knows what time young Charlie will be home. He's up at the stables, spends all his time up there. He'd sleep there if he got the chance.' She knew she was prattling, but couldn't help herself. The man standing on the doorstep looked so tall and handsome in his best suit, even with his deformed back, that it took her breath away.

He gave a sigh of relief. 'Oh, that sounds lovely. And there's me been thinking I'd have to go and get fish and chips. Thanks, Emma, I'd be glad to come and share it with you.'

'Well, don't stand there on the step then. Come on in and sit down.' She looked him in the eye for the first time. 'You look right worn out, Henry,' she said gently. 'Has it been very hard?'

He nodded. 'It has. A bit. I'm glad to be home. I don't much like being away.'

'I'm glad you're back, it's been funny without you here. I've missed you clattering about next door.'

'I don't clatter about.' He pretended to be affronted but he savoured her words.

'No, but I always know when you're there.' She busied herself with plates and when they were both served she sat down opposite him.

'Oh, this is good, Emma,' he said as he took a mouthful. 'I never had anything as tasty as this in London.'

'What's London like, Henry?' she asked, putting her head

on one side. 'They say it's a big place, but I can't imagine it. I've never been further than Colchester. Is it much bigger than that?'

He laughed as he speared a piece of meat. 'About a hundred times bigger, I should think.' He shook his head. 'I don't reckon you'd like it much, Em. You're a quiet, peaceful person and London's so noisy you wouldn't believe it. Men with barrel organs, hawkers all over the place yelling out what they've got to sell; you can buy everything from sheet music to hot pies on the street, and they all try to shout louder than each other to make people buy. Then there's motor cars honking – I've never seen so many motor cars, Em – all mixed up with horses and carts and hansom cabs, I wonder the horses don't bolt with fright. I tell you, Em, the streets were so full of traffic of one sort or another, you took your life in your hands just to cross to the other side. And you had to be careful where you put your feet or you'd be up to your ankles in horse . . . Well, you know.' He shook his head again and continued eating. After a bit he looked up. 'And the people! Posh people all dressed up to the nines getting out of taxis at all hours, people in working clothes rushing about like they hadn't got a minute to live. Everybody seemed to be in a hurry to be somewhere else. I've never seen anything like it! At times it was more than hard work trying to push Mr Philip along in his bath chair because people didn't step aside to let us through, they were in too much of a hurry to get where they were going, pushing and shoving each other out of the way, even though some of the pavements were as wide as our roads.'

'Gracious me, how rude! No, you're right, Henry. If it's like you say, I reckon I'd hate it. Sounds more like Bedlam to me,' Emma said, her eyes wide. 'I can't even imagine it.'

'No, I don't reckon you can.' His voice dropped and he went on sadly, 'And I'd never imagined I'd see quite so many beggars in the streets, either. You certainly wouldn't have liked that, Emma; you wouldn't have liked seeing children of not much more than seven or eight, filthy dirty, with hardly a rag on their backs, fighting over which one would hold someone's horse for a penny, or scavenging in the rubbish in the market for a few scraps of food.' He pushed his empty plate away and

rubbed the back of his neck tiredly. 'The streets of London
aren't all paved with gold, Em. Some parts are stinking awful.'

'Well, you're home now, Henry,' she said gently. 'Come and
sit in the armchair and I'll make us a cup of tea, then you can
go home to bed.'

He moved over to the Windsor chair that was padded with
patchwork cushions that Emma had made when she was first
married. 'Ah, this is lovely,' he said, closing his eyes. 'Fits my
poor old back a treat.'

'It was Arthur's chair,' she said. 'He always reckoned it was
comfortable.'

She poured the tea and sat down on a low stool opposite,
savouring the sight of him sitting on the other side of the
hearth, looking so comfortable and relaxed. So at home. 'It's
nice to see you sitting there,' she added quietly.

She said no more for several moments, happy just to sit
there, watching him and just being there with him in the
warmth and intimacy of her living room. Then, realizing her
thoughts were straying along dangerous paths, she said, 'Tell
me some more about London, Henry, if you're not too tired.'

He opened his eyes and smiled at her. 'No, I'm not too
tired to sit and talk, Em.' He thought for a minute, then
frowned. 'I think the thing that affected me most was seeing
ex-servicemen, proud men who'd had decent jobs before the
war, standing on street corners trying to sell matches, or
bootlaces, or packets of pins, some of them on crutches, some
with only one arm or with a leg missing. Decent men should
never be humiliated like that,' he said savagely. He shook his
head. 'But I think the worst thing I saw was a young girl
– she couldn't have been more than ten years old – in a thin
summer frock, although the wind was quite chill, pulling her
father along on a home-made trolley because he'd got no
legs. He was doing what he could to help her, trying to push
himself along with his hands, and there was a bowl between
his stumps for people to put pennies in. I'll never forget the
shame and despair on that man's face. He'd lost his legs
fighting for his country and that was all the thanks he'd got,
thrown on the scrap heap and having to beg to buy bread
for his family. I gave him a shilling, which was all the money

I'd got on me at the time. When I'd got more, I went back. I'd have willingly given the poor bloke my last ha'penny, but I couldn't find him again. It's a sin and a shame that good men should be treated like that after what they'd been through,' he finished savagely.

'Oh, Henry.' Emma's eyes were full of tears. 'And I thought we had troubles. But at least we were never going to starve, the children had decent clothes on their backs, and Arthur was . . .' She sniffed. 'Well, it could have been a lot worse.'

'Oh, look, now I've upset you.' He got to his feet and stood looking down at her, shaking his head. 'I shouldn't have told you all that, Emma. I'm sorry. But I just can't get the picture of that man and his little girl out of my mind.'

She looked up at him, tears still glistening in her eyes. 'No, it's all right. I'm glad you did, Henry. I'm glad you felt you could share it with me.' She smiled at him as he helped her to her feet. 'You're an old softie, Henry Hogg, you know that?'

'I'm soft over you, Emma Blatch,' he said quietly, still holding her hands. 'But you know that, don't you?'

She nodded and squeezed his hands. 'Yes, I do, and it's a great comfort to me, Henry.' She shook her head. 'But it's too soon . . .' She bit her lip. 'Arthur's only been gone . . .'

'I know. I'm sorry, Emma, I shouldn't have spoken like that, but the truth is I missed you while I was away. And then coming back and being here with you, well, it just sort of came out, I couldn't help myself. But I promise I won't forget myself like that again, so you needn't worry.'

'I'm not worried, Henry,' she said, quietly. 'I'm honoured. And in a little while . . .' She looked up at him, hoping he would understand.

He smiled reassuringly and bent his head to brush her cheek with his lips. 'I can wait, Emma,' he whispered. 'I've waited all this time, so I'll just say this. When you're ready, I'll be here.'

The following evening, over dinner of roast pork and apple sauce followed by jam roly-poly, Roger took the opportunity to ask Philip whether the exhibition had gone well.

'He didn't sell all that many, judging from the number that

arrived back today,' Rosalie put in before Philip could answer. 'Hardly worth all that effort, I'd say.'

Philip waited until she'd finished speaking, then turned towards Roger, ignoring her. 'I think it was quite a useful exercise even though, as my wife was so keen to point out, there weren't all that many sales. I don't know what Rosalie expected, but Ben Gerard assured me that Oscar Hillyard was more than satisfied, which is the important thing. Apparently his commission more than covered his costs in putting on the exhibition, so there must have been enough sold to make it worthwhile.'

'Indeed, and that must mean you made a few pounds too. That's encouraging for you. No doubt it also means he'll be happy to put on another exhibition, so your name will get known in the right circles. All things considered, I'd regard that as a resounding success. Congratulations, my boy.' Roger gave a satisfied nod and helped himself to more duchesse potatoes.

'Does that mean you'll be famous, Philip?' Doreen asked, her interest aroused. 'I can't say I saw any particularly well-known people at your exhibition, but no doubt when you get more widely known they'll flock to see you.' She smiled happily at the prospect as she dabbed her mouth delicately with her napkin.

'I shouldn't think it's very likely, Doreen,' Philip said dryly. 'I'm not expecting to be invited to exhibit at the Royal Academy.'

'Well, as long as you can amuse yourself, that's all that matters.' Completely oblivious that she had insulted her son-in-law, Doreen turned to Stella to discuss more important matters.

'I saw my grandson in his baby carriage in the garden this morning. I thought he looked a little pale, my dear. I think perhaps we should ask Dr Eaves to examine him to make sure he didn't take any harm when you left him in the care of the servants,' she said, with an expression that was supposed to convey friendly anxiety but didn't hide her disapproval. 'It's important not to take any chances with him.'

Stella found she was clenching her fists under the table, but managed to keep her voice level as she answered her mother-in-law. 'Jonathan is perfectly healthy, thank you, Doreen. This morning he was laughing and splashing in his bath so much that Mary had to go and change her pinafore. And as for not leaving him for a few hours with servants, as you put it, I'm quite sure Emma has had more experience with babies and children than any of us, and she's already taught Mary – and me, for that matter – a great deal. I would never hesitate to leave Jonathan with either of them, especially since Mary is now employed as his nursemaid and expects to have care of him. What's more, Jonathan loves both Mary and Emma. His little face lights up when he sees them.' Which is more than it does when he sees you, she thought; but bit her tongue against adding.

'He wasn't smiling this morning. When I looked into the baby carriage and talked to him, he began to cry. I think perhaps he's suffering from colic.'

'No, he isn't suffering from colic. You probably woke him up,' Stella suggested, gritting her teeth. 'He does get cross if he's woken from his nap.'

'Nevertheless, I shall call Dr Eaves,' Doreen insisted. 'One can't be too careful.'

'I'd rather you didn't, Doreen.' Stella was equally insistent. 'If the doctor is called too many times unnecessarily, he'll be reluctant to come in a real emergency. As I said, there's absolutely nothing wrong with Jonathan. And I should know,' she added. 'After all, I am his mother.'

'Has everybody finished?' Tight-lipped, Doreen looked round the table, ignoring Stella's words. 'Then perhaps you would clear the plates, Stella, and I'll ring for Maisie to collect them and bring in the pudding. I do feel it's important not to put too much pressure on the domestic staff, they have quite enough to do without burdening them with extra work.'

'That's not extra work, Ma,' Rosalie remarked, examining her fingernails. 'Clearing the table is part of the job.'

'Rosalie is quite right, Doreen. It's one thing to help out in an emergency, but quite another to expect members of the family to do the work for which the domestic staff are adequately, I might even say generously, paid,' Roger said with a steely look at his wife. He turned to Stella and said more gently, 'Please sit down, Stella. You're our daughter-in-law, I won't have you treated like an unpaid skivvy.'

'Unpaid skivvy, indeed!' Doreen was flushed with fury at being bested yet again. 'She's very well paid, if you ask me. She lives here rent-free, with all found . . .'

'That's enough, Doreen!' Roger banged his fist on the table. 'I'll hear no more of this. Please ring for Maisie and let us have the rest of the meal in peace. After you've apologized to Stella for your quite uncalled-for remarks, that is.'

Defeated, Doreen put her hand to her head. 'Oh, Roger, you know I can't stand you shouting at me. It always brings on one of my heads. Now I shall have to go and lie down. Perhaps you could ask Maisie to bring me a headache powder?' She got to her feet. As she passed Stella, she laid a hand on her shoulder. 'You may be right about Jonathan, my dear. We'll wait and see how he is in the morning before we send for Dr Eaves.' With that, she groped her way theatrically to the door and went up to her room, and Stella realized that it was the nearest thing to an apology she was likely to get.

'You mustn't mind Doreen, Stella, she gets a little over-wrought at times,' Roger said later, pouring oil on troubled waters and custard over his jam roly-poly. 'I'm afraid she tends to worry unnecessarily over the little boy.'

'Hmph. She doesn't like being crossed, either. You did well there, Stella,' Rosalie remarked, winking at her in an unusual show of solidarity. She turned to her husband. 'Did Dr Marshall turn up this afternoon, Phil? You said you were expecting him to come here instead of you going to him.'

'Yes. He apologized for being late, he'd been held up. He's coming again tomorrow.'

'What, two days in a row?'

'Yes. He'll be coming every day for at least the next week or so. Says I need "loosening up", whatever that means, and it'll be easier for me if he comes here to do it.'

'That's probably because you'll have been under quite a lot of nervous tension while the exhibition was on,' Stella said thoughtfully. She looked up. 'Oh, I'm sorry. I spoke without thinking.'

'That's all right. In fact it's exactly what Dr Marshall said,' Philip said with a smile.

'Are you sure it's just you he's coming to see, Phil?' Rosalie asked, her face a picture of innocence.

Philip frowned. 'What do you mean? Of course it is. Who else would it be?'

'Well, maybe he intends to kill two birds with one stone and call on Stella while he's here. They were having quite a conversation at the opening of your exhibition. Apparently they worked together at the convalescent home, so perhaps he thinks it will be a good opportunity to renew their acquaintance.' She shrugged, shamefaced, as she saw her husband's expression. 'Just a thought.'

Before Philip could speak, Stella said quietly, 'I never actually worked with Dr Marshall, although I did know him quite well at Hill House.' She smiled. 'But to tell you the truth, once I met John, the King could have turned up and I wouldn't have noticed.'

'But Dr Marshall obviously noticed you.'

'Oh, for goodness' sake, Rosie, leave it alone,' Philip said irritably.

'He remembered me, anyway,' Stella answered Rosalie, 'and he's asked me to have tea with him Tuesday week. No doubt he'll want to talk about Hill House, which might be a bit difficult for me since that's where John and I . . .' She bit her lip and took a deep breath. 'But I expect I'll manage.'

'I'm sure you will,' Philip said shortly. He dragged himself to his feet. 'Now, if you'll excuse me, I think I'll go back to the flat. I've still got some work to do.'

'My, my, I wonder what's ruffled his feathers?' Rosalie remarked under her breath, watching him struggle out through the door.

Twenty

Maisie carried the coffee up to the dining room and returned with the rest of the dirty dishes. She was always tired at the end of the day and clearing up after the family dinner was the last straw as far as she was concerned. Emma knew this and nearly always stayed behind to help with the washing-up. As she pointed out, it hadn't been so easy in the past, never knowing whether Arthur would be getting drunk at the pub or watching the clock and shouting the odds because she was late; but now he wasn't there it didn't really matter what time she got home. Especially with Mary living in at Warren's End. It often meant she could see her daughter for a few minutes in the evening.

Also, although Emma didn't say this to Maisie, if she timed it right Henry would have finished his work with Mr Philip for the day and they could walk home together, talking over what they had been doing, or just being companionable. It worked out very well, because Henry had told her that Mr Philip preferred to put himself to bed as long as Henry left everything to hand. That way he could stay up till the small hours if he wanted to, which he often did, without inconveniencing anybody. The walk home with Henry in the dark was the best part of the day as far as Emma was concerned – although she never admitted this to anyone, least of all to Henry.

She was thinking along these lines when Maisie came back into the kitchen, balancing the laden tray carefully as she pushed the door closed with her foot.

'You wouldn't think a meal for five people would make so much washing-up, would you?' she said, blowing a wisp of hair out of her eyes.

'Well, there's only them bits to do now. I've done everything else, including all the pots and pans,' Emma said cheerfully.

'Thanks, Em. I'm nearly dead on my feet.' She put the tray on the draining board. 'Don't know what's been going on up there,' she jerked her head in the direction of the dining room, 'but you could cut the air with a knife. I shouldn't be surprised if the missus has been having a go at Mrs Stella again. She's really got her knife into that poor girl.'

Emma nodded, swirling fresh suds into the bowl. Then she paused and leaned her elbows on the sink. 'Do you know what I reckon?'

'No. What do you reckon?'

'I reckon the missus had the idea that once the baby was born Mrs Stella would be glad to hand him over and go off and forget about him. Although where she got that idea from, goodness knows.'

'She must have a screw loose,' Maisie said. 'Anyone could see with half an eye that was never gonna happen, all the little bits the girl knitted and sewed for him while she was expecting.'

'All the same, I reckon the missus thought she'd have first claim because it was her son that was the baby's father. Not that I could ever see her changing dirty nappies!' she added with a laugh as she tackled the rest of the dirty dishes.

Maisie nodded. 'And now she's riled because Mrs Stella's having none of it, so she can't get her own way. Yes, I reckon you're about right, Em.'

'Of course I am. That girl's never going to hand her baby over; she'd live in a field before she'd let go of Master Jonny, any fool can see that. She's got her own ideas about the way he's to be brought up, too, and I don't blame her for that, either.' Emma dried her hands vigorously to prove her point.

'No more do I,' Maisie agreed. 'From what I can see, the missus hasn't got any idea how to treat babies, even though she's had two of her own. Not that I'd know anything about it, of course,' she added hurriedly. 'But it can't be right to go and pick the poor lamb up when he's lying there asleep in his pram, or "baby carriage" as she likes to call it. No wonder he cries when he sees her.'

'Of course, the real trouble will come when Granny and Grandpa – well, Granny, anyway – want to provide him with things his mother would never be able to afford,' Emma said thoughtfully.

'Like what? The "baby carriage"?' Maisie made a good imitation of Doreen's voice. Like most things that went on upstairs, it had been well discussed at the time in the kitchen.

'No, more important than that, although that was bad enough.'

'What then?'

'Well, expensive schooling, for one thing. Mrs Stella's never going to be able to afford to send him to a posh school, is she? But they could. And if Mrs Stella wants what's best for her boy . . .' She paused and looked up at the clock: Henry should be finished at Mr Philip's by now and she didn't want to keep him waiting. Though he would wait for her, she knew that; and the knowledge gave her a warm glow. She gave a quick shrug and went on briskly, 'However, that's well into the future. A lot can happen between now and then, the poor lamb's not a year old yet.' She looked round the kitchen. 'Well, that's all the clearing up done, so I'll be getting along home. I've got some ironing to do before I go to bed tonight.' She reached her coat down from behind the door. 'Goodnight, Maise.'

'Goodnight, Emma. And thanks for staying on.' After she'd gone Maisie glanced round the now immaculate kitchen, then sat down in the armchair by the fire to enjoy an hour with her new book, *The Keeper of the Door*, by her favourite author, Ethel M. Dell.

Back in her flat, Stella's thoughts were running along much the same lines as those that had been discussed in the kitchen. Things had rather come to a head tonight, with Doreen showing her true colours, and it had been quite devastating to hear spelt out in such a vitriolic fashion exactly what her mother-in-law thought of her. She gazed up at the photograph of John on the mantelpiece.

'I had a wonderful six weeks with you, my love, and I don't regret a minute of it, but look at the pickle it's landed me in,' she said to the figure smiling down at her as if he hadn't a care in the world. 'True, I've got our precious baby, and a pleasant little rent-free flat, which is not to be sneezed at, but I've also got a mother-in-law who hates me and wishes me out of the way. How do I cope with that all by myself, John Nolan, since you're no longer here to help me?' Voicing those words, an emotion, something akin to rage, washed over her, surprising her with its intensity, because she knew she was trapped and she could see no way out.

On the other hand, Roger was kindness itself. It was obvious he was trying to compensate for his wife's behaviour without actually being disloyal to her.

'You know that there will always be a home for you and Jonathan here, don't you, my dear?' he said, seeking her out

the next day in the garden. 'Always. For as long as you want it.'
He put his hand on her arm. 'I do understand that it's not always
easy for you, Stella,' he continued, 'but I wouldn't want you
to rush into anything you might later regret because of hasty
words spoken in the heat of the moment.'

Stella knew he was referring to her planned meeting with
Ian Marshall, and appreciated his concern. Though talking over
shared acquaintances at Hill House with a man she had once
been close to but had then rejected was hardly likely to result
in her being tempted to rush into anything at all, apart from
getting back to her beloved son. But before she could speak,
he cleared his throat and continued gruffly, 'You realize, don't
you, Stella, that having you and your little boy living here is
making an old man very happy?' With that, he walked away
before she could answer.

She soon realized that Roger must have had words with
Doreen, too, because she noticed with relief that her
mother-in-law no longer demeaned her in front of the family
by treating her as a servant. Nevertheless, Doreen still managed
to wage her own subtle war by criticizing practically everything
Stella did, under the guise of 'having a quiet word' with her
'in private'. This was wearing and annoying, particularly as
most of the criticisms were petty and totally unjustified.

At times Stella felt ready to scream with frustration, but the
one thing that made it all bearable was that there was someone
she knew she could tell her troubles to and who would understand. Philip was always ready to listen. If things got too difficult,
she would go over to his studio for a cup of tea and a chat
while Jonathan was having his afternoon nap, although ostensibly it was to see how the latest work in progress was coming
along. And indeed she did enjoy watching the paintings emerge
from a few lines on the paper to a fully fledged landscape or
still life, and she marvelled at the intricacy of some of the work
he did.

'You don't paint portraits, do you, Philip?' she asked one
afternoon.

'Not so far, but I'm always ready to give anything a go.' He
leaned forward, concentrating on what he was doing. 'Why?
Would you like me to paint your portrait?' He glanced up at

her with raised eyebrows. 'Do you think Dr Marshall might like it?'

She frowned. 'Good grief, no. Not that I'd ask him.'

He shrugged and said nothing.

'Philip, I've agreed to meet him for tea tomorrow afternoon. As far as I'm concerned, it's to talk over old times at Hill House,' she explained, as if talking to a child. 'Not that we've got much in common to talk about these days,' she added thoughtfully. She shook her head in exasperation. 'In truth, I'm only going out of politeness. I don't know why people seem to think it's such a big thing.'

'Well, isn't it?' He didn't look up from his painting.

'It may have been once, although more on his side than mine. But definitely not any longer.' She watched him for a few moments. 'You ought to know me better than that, Phil,' she said quietly.

He looked up and their eyes met. He smiled in understanding, and the tension between them relaxed. 'So whose portrait would you like me to paint, then?' he asked, his voice gentle now.

'Well, I wondered . . . Could you paint Jonathan?' she asked a little shyly. 'I want to give Roger a picture of his grandson. I know he'd like that.'

He leaned back in his chair and nodded, and she could see he was pleased at the idea. 'Yes, I don't see why not. Bring him over and I'll make some sketches.' He smiled at her again, and the unspoken thought went between them that it would be an added excuse for visits. The moment passed and he said, his eyes twinkling, 'Is this your way of getting back at the Old Trout, trying to make her jealous?' The 'Old Trout' was their private nickname for Doreen.

Stella smiled back. It was such a relief to have someone she could talk to openly about the way Doreen treated her 'That wasn't the original intention, I'm sure Roger would like it. But what do you think?'

'I think I wouldn't blame you if that was your intention. What's her latest barb?'

Stella sighed. 'Her latest? I'm not sure where to begin!'

She was quiet for a moment, then frowned. 'I've an idea

she's working on Mary now, which is very unfair. After all, the girl is only fifteen and this is her first job. If Doreen tries to contradict or even countermand everything I ask Mary to do, the poor girl won't know who's right nor who to take her orders from. For instance, she says things like "Oh, Mary, I'm surprised Mrs Stella has told you to leave my grandson outside in this cold wind. He should be indoors, where it's nice and warm. I'll take him in to my room." It's ridiculous. Everybody knows babies need a certain amount of fresh air every day, and he's always well wrapped up. Of course, Mary daren't disobey Doreen, but she knows it's not what I want. On the other hand, she doesn't want to be accused of telling tales, so she really doesn't know which way to turn.'

She sighed again and looked so worried that Philip said with a laugh, 'I must say you do a very good impression of our mother-in-law, Stella.'

'It's not really funny, Philip,' she replied seriously. 'The thing is, what can I do about it without involving the poor girl too much in my problems?'

'No, of course it isn't funny, Stella, and I shouldn't have laughed.' Then he chuckled again. 'I'll bet you wouldn't dare do that to her face.'

Her face broke into a grin. 'No, I wouldn't. Not that she'd recognize herself if I did, she's got no idea what she sounds like.'

He nodded. 'That's better. At least you haven't lost your sense of humour. But in answer to the serious question . . .' He paused and thought for a minute, then looked up. 'Have you thought of speaking to Emma? She's probably the best person.'

Stella's face cleared. 'Of course! She's the obvious one. Why didn't I think of that?'

'Because you're too close to the problem, that's why.' There was a brief knock on the door and Henry came in. 'Ah, good man, Henry, you've come to make the tea. Did you know Mrs Stella was here?'

'Yes, Mary told me. But I guessed she might be.' He turned to Stella. 'Mary says can she take Jonathan with her to the post office, Mrs Stella?'

'Yes, of course she can,' Stella answered.

'Good. I'll tell her when I go back.' Henry busied himself in the kitchen. After he brought in the tea tray, he left.

'Looks as if Mary might be solving the problem in her own way,' Philip said thoughtfully as he watched Stella pour the tea.

'Yes, she's a bright girl. Perhaps she understands more than I give her credit for.' She handed him his tea and then sipped her own. 'Oh, I wish I could find some way of becoming independent,' she said after a while. 'If only I could earn some money so that I didn't have to depend on Roger's charity.'

'I'm sure he doesn't see it like that,' Philip said. He looked at her over the rim of his cup. 'Roger is very fond of you, Stella.'

She nodded. 'And I'm very fond of Roger,' she replied quietly, returning his gaze.

Suddenly, the door burst open and Rosalie nearly fell in, her cheeks rosy with cold, and her head, surmounted by a little cloche hat, looking too small for her body, which was wrapped in a thick fur coat reaching nearly to her ankles.

'Now, here's somebody who's never likely to worry about finding work,' he said, under his breath.

But Rosalie was too full of her news to even notice his remark. 'What do you think?' she said excitedly. 'It's on all the placards! Oh, is there a cup of tea for me?'

'I expect there's still one in the pot. Get yourself a cup.' Philip was used to these outbursts. 'Then you can tell us what it is on all the placards that's making you so animated.'

'It's Nancy Astor! She's won the Plymouth by-election! She stood for election because her husband's been elevated to the peerage. And she won! She'll be the first woman to sit in Parliament.' She began to dance round the room. 'You'll see, eventually we'll have a woman Prime Minister.'

'Oh, I don't think insanity will prevail that far,' Philip said dryly. 'Now, are you going to get a cup, or are you going to wait till the tea's cold? And for heaven's sake, stop prancing about.' He raised his eyebrows towards Stella as Rosalie went off to the kitchen. She came back with a cup and saucer and put them on the tray in front of Stella.

'Don't you see? It's history in the making. All the work of
the suffragettes is paying off.'

'Oh, were you one of the suffragettes?' Stella asked, looking
up, the teapot in her hand.

Rosalie shuddered. 'Me? Oh, no. I didn't fancy being sent
to prison and being force-fed. But I very much admired them,
and I think it's marvellous what they've achieved for us women,
don't you?' She waited for Stella to pour her tea, then picked
it up.

'I think it had to come,' Stella said thoughtfully. 'The suffragettes were very brave and of course they paved the way, but
I think a lot of the jobs women did during the war influenced
things a great deal. Working on the land, as bus conductresses,
driving ambulances (incidentally, I did that), working in the
munitions factories and in offices . . . Doing so many jobs that
had previously been done only by men, and enjoying the
freedom it gave. It's small wonder women have decided they
want a say in how the country should be run. So, yes, I do
think it's wonderful. And it'll be even better when we don't
have to wait quite so long before we can vote.' She paused.
'But I think there's a long way to go before there are equal
rights for women. It's still very much a man's world.'

Rosalie sat down and began to drink her tea. After a minute
she put her cup down and said thoughtfully, 'You know, you're
not a bad egg, Stella. There's more to you than meets the eye.'

'Thank you very much!' Stella said with more than a hint
of sarcasm.

'And you used to drive an ambulance?'

'Only to ferry the wounded from hospital to the convalescent
home. I wasn't in France like some of the nurses I knew.'

'All the same . . .' Rosalie viewed her sister-in-law with a
new respect. 'I'm quite ashamed to admit I can't drive at all.'

Philip picked up a brush and examined the tip. 'When I
buy a new car I'll pass Tin Lizzie on to you, Rosie, and Henry
can teach you.'

She turned to him, her eyes shining. 'Do you really mean
that, Phil?'

'Yes, but don't get too excited. I said *when* I buy a new car.
It won't be yet, I can't afford one at the moment.'

'But your pictures are selling.'

'Yes. They're beginning to. Slowly and fairly inexpensively.'

'Don't be so modest. You've always sold the odd one, but after your exhibition . . .'

'I seem to remember you called it a "little tinpot affair", so surely you're not now expecting it to suddenly make a fortune, are you?'

'Oh, you are an insufferable man! One minute you promise to buy me a car and the next you say you can't afford it. I wish you'd make up your mind.' She banged her cup and saucer down on the table. 'I'm going down to the club. I probably won't be back in time for dinner.' With that she flounced out of the room, and the door banged as she left the flat.

'Sorry about that,' Philip said, not sounding sorry at all. 'My wife has got flouncing down to a fine art when things don't go her way.'

Stella stood up. 'I'll put the tea things in the kitchen and then I'd better flounce off, too.'

'You never flounce, Stella. You're the most restful person I know,' he said, smiling at her.

'That's because you've never seen me in a rage.' She smiled back at him.

'Ah, now, that would be something,' he remarked enigmatically. 'And what would be likely to prompt it?'

She went to the door. 'If Doreen's been upsetting Mary again, I might come close to it. And also,' she added after a moment's hesitation, 'if people insist on reading too much into my meeting with Ian Marshall. That would really make me see red.'

She closed the door before he could answer.

Twenty-One

Stella dressed carefully for her meeting with Ian Marshall, not because she wanted to impress him; it was rather the reverse, she was anxious that he shouldn't feel she was attaching any particular importance to it. Not that she had a great deal of choice in what she wore, since her wardrobe was limited.

In the end, she chose a plain grey ankle-length skirt and a pink blouse with a beaded collar. Her dark-blue winter coat was still fairly new. She had bought it for her visit to John's parents, never dreaming she would still be with them nearly a year later, and hadn't worn it a great deal because of her pregnancy. But she was only meeting Ian Marshall out of politeness, because they had both worked at Hill House, not to rejuvenate a relationship that, as far as she was concerned, had never really blossomed. She put on her little fur hat and surveyed herself in the mirror. Then, satisfied that she looked reasonably smart without having made too much of an effort, she picked up Jonathan, who was gurgling in his pram, gave him a prolonged hug, and smothered him in kisses.

'Now, be a good boy for Mary while Mummy is out, won't you, my darling,' she said, giving him a final hug before hurrying off to catch the tram.

Ian Marshall was waiting for her in the square. He was a distinguished-looking man, tall and slim, and was wearing a well-cut tweed suit. His first words to her as he doffed his hat were, 'You're looking quite charming today, Stella, my dear.'

She managed a small smile, although she objected to him calling her 'my dear'. But before she could say so he went on, 'I've reserved a table at the little teashop on the corner. It seemed prudent to do that because as far as I could see there aren't any others, and it looks a busy little place. Do you know it?' And as he spoke, he guided her towards Daisy's Tearooms.

'Oh, yes, I know it very well,' she answered briefly, as he stood aside for her to precede him into the familiar dim interior, with its dark-oak linenfold panelling and matching dark-oak tables and chairs, the dimness lightened by crisp blue-checked tablecloths with matching napkins and pretty blue-and-white china.

Mrs Greenleaf herself showed them to their table, staying to chat with Stella and to ask after Jonathan and Major Anderson while waiting for the little waitress to bring their cream tea and cakes.

'You seem to be on very good terms with the proprietor,' Ian Marshall remarked in a faintly disapproving tone when Mrs Greenleaf had gone off to attend to other customers. 'Or is she just as garrulous with all the people who come in?' As he spoke, he helped himself to jam and cream for his scone.

'She's a very friendly person. That's why her teashop is so popular,' Stella said, defending the woman she had come to regard as a friend. 'And yes, I often come here when I'm shopping in the town.' She smiled at him. 'Philip sometimes comes too, so we know Mrs Greenleaf quite well. She makes the most delicious scones and cakes in the town.'

'These scones certainly melt in the mouth.' He took another one from the dish. When he had smothered it liberally in jam and cream, he leaned forward and whispered, 'This may not have been such a happy choice of venue, after all. I didn't realize it would be full of old biddies with nothing better to do with their time.'

'Maybe you should have checked it out more carefully then.' She watched with something not far from disgust as the whole scone disappeared into his mouth and he reached for a third.

She turned her head and saw two of Doreen's Ladies' Circle friends trying not to appear to be watching them.

'Good afternoon, Mrs Arbuthnot, Mrs Beales,' she said brightly, smiling at them.

They both murmured a reply and turned away, annoyed at having been spotted watching her.

'Do you know *everybody* in this place, Stella?' he asked, trying unsuccessfully to sound jocular.

'No, I wouldn't say I *know* them, but I am acquainted with several people who come here quite often, like I do. The ladies I just spoke to are my mother-in-law's friends, not mine. I think they come here most days.'

'Then it's a pity they can't find something more useful to do with their time. I can see I should have taken you some-where where you are less well-known.'

She turned a clear gaze on him. 'Why?'

He spread his hands, slightly embarrassed. 'Well . . .'

'We're only having afternoon tea, Ian. That's not a crime, as far as I'm aware.' She picked up the teapot. 'More tea?'

'Thank you.' He handed her his cup and watched as she refilled it, her movements competent and unhurried. He felt at a sudden disadvantage, as if he'd planned a seedy little assignation and she was rebuffing him, which was quite ridiculous.

'Was Nurse Ives still at Hill House when you left?' she asked. 'I was often on duty with her, so I got to know her quite well.'

He frowned. 'I'm not sure. I don't think I know which one you mean.' He gave a little laugh. 'The nurses all looked the same to me.'

'Really? You always seemed to know which one was me.' Her tone was cool.

'Are you fishing for compliments, Stella? Because if you are . . .' He leaned over and took her hand.

She snatched it away. 'Nothing has changed, Ian. I've come here today to talk over old times, not to rekindle a romance that never was.'

'That was not my fault, Stella, you didn't give me a chance.'

'You never had a chance, Ian, even before I met John. And once he came along . . .' she added more gently.

'John's dead,' he interrupted bluntly. 'And since Fate has been kind enough to throw us together again, you can hardly blame me for trying to take advantage of the fact.'

She stared at him, amazed at his insensitivity. 'Well, all I can say is you're wasting your time. You were last time, and you are now,' she replied, equally bluntly. 'So,' she smiled at him brightly, 'shall we change the subject? Why did you decide to leave Hill House? You were doing such good work there.' She regarded him thoughtfully. 'Didn't you enjoy your work?'

He helped himself to a cream horn before replying, obviously still smarting under her rebuff. 'You of all people should know that "enjoy" is not quite the right word for what I did,' he said stiffly. 'As you know, my job was to try – and it was mostly unsuccessful, I must admit – to patch up broken young lives. You'll remember what we were up against. You saw some of those men: I don't need to describe to you how their lives had been ruined in the trenches. And even worse, there were those that looked perfectly normal but were badly scarred mentally. Most people didn't appreciate what those poor blighters were going through, because they couldn't see the damage.' He pushed his cup over for more tea. 'I really don't want to talk about it.'

'Why not? You're still doing the same work, you're helping Philip – Major Anderson,' she said, picking up the teapot for the third time. 'Privately, of course,' she added with barely concealed sarcasm.

He shrugged, ignoring her tone. 'I took him on as a favour. Not that I can do much for him, he'll never walk properly again.'

'Then you're wasting both your time and his money,' she said, with some asperity. 'Why don't you tell him so and go back to Hill House where you could be doing some good?'

He looked at her in surprise. 'Are you lecturing me, Stella?'

She nodded. 'Yes, I think perhaps I am, Ian.' She finished the last of her chocolate éclair and wiped the corners of her mouth on her napkin. 'For what it's worth, I think it's a pity you're in private practice, for the most part pandering to people with imaginary problems and more money than sense, when you could be doing so much good elsewhere. I believe you were very much valued at Hill House.'

'Well, that's straight from the shoulder,' he said, somewhat taken aback. He regarded her thoughtfully. 'So what would you suggest?'

'I've already told you what I think,' she said with a shrug. 'But you've obviously made your decision and no doubt you had your reasons. I just think it's a pity to waste your talents on people who have comparatively little need of them when there are so many you could really help. That's all.'

'Obviously that didn't apply to you,' he remarked dryly.

She looked surprised. 'What do you mean?'

'Well, clearly you felt no guilt about leaving Hill House.'

'I felt no guilt because I had no choice. I was expecting a child, so I couldn't possibly have stayed.'

He inclined his head. 'No, of course not. I'm sorry, I'd forgotten.' He gave her a somewhat rueful smile. 'And to think I came here today hoping it might be the beginning of . . .' He hesitated. 'Well, hoping we might become good friends, shall we say. Instead of which, you're urging me to give up a lucrative practice where I can work or not as I choose, and go back to hospital work where I could be called on at any time day or night and hardly call my soul my own.'

'True,' she agreed. 'But you'd know you were doing useful, necessary work.'

'That's blackmail. Moral blackmail.' He put his head on one side. 'Would you ever consider going back into nursing, Stella?'

'No. How could I? I have my son to consider.'

'I'm sure there are ways round that,' he said enigmatically.

'And speaking of Jonathan, I should be getting back,' she said as if he hadn't spoken, picking up her handbag and getting to her feet.

As they left the tearooms, Stella couldn't help noticing that Doreen's friends were still sitting there and quite openly looking Ian up and down.

That'll give you something to embroider for Doreen, she thought with some satisfaction as he held open the door for her, knowing that their account of the afternoon would lose nothing in the telling.

She was right. Two afternoons later, Jonathan was lying on a blanket on the hearthrug, kicking his legs and gurgling with happiness, while Stella sat at the table busily stitching a blouse for herself on her sewing machine, at the same time keeping a watchful eye on him. Suddenly, the door opened and Doreen came into the room without knocking.

'Where is Mary?' she demanded.

Stella looked up in surprise. 'Mary? She's in the kitchen, ironing. Did you want her?'

Doreen shook her head. 'No, I don't want her. It's you I wish to speak to. I just wanted to make sure she was out of the way.' She glanced irritably at the baby. 'I don't think it's at all appropriate that you should allow the child to lie on the floor like that, Stella. And with his limbs uncovered, too. He'll catch his death of cold.'

'I don't think there's any danger of that, it's very warm in here.' Stella bit off a length of cotton and sat back on her chair. 'I like to let him exercise his legs every day. It will help strengthen them ready for when he begins to walk. Anyway, I don't believe in stifling babies with too many clothes. I think it's bad for them.' She pushed back her chair and got up. 'Please sit down, Doreen. If you've got something you want to discuss privately with me I'll make us both a cup of tea first. I was just thinking I could do with a cup.' She smiled at her mother-in-law.

Doreen sat down, perching on the edge of the sofa, her back ramrod straight. 'No, thank you, Stella, I don't wish for tea. But if I did, the correct thing to do would be to ring for Maisie to bring it. That's what she's paid for. I think it's time you learned proper etiquette.'

'But I'm sure she's busy. And as I have my own little kitchen, which you were kind enough to provide . . .' Stella made sure to add this. 'I could very quickly put the kettle on.'

'As I said, I don't wish for tea.' She took a deep breath. 'I have come because I have something disagreeable and painful to speak to you about.'

Stella sat down in the armchair. 'Oh dear, Doreen. I'm so sorry. Are you ill? Is there anything I can do for you?' she asked, feigning concern. She knew exactly why Doreen had come and was determined not to make it easy for her.

'No, I am not ill, but thank you for your concern regarding my health, misplaced though it is.' She shifted a little in her seat. 'What I have come to say, and I'll get straight to the point, is that I am appalled that you have shown so little respect for my son's memory, not to mention my personal feelings, by taking your men friends to the places that ladies of my acquaintance frequent.' She glared at Stella. 'Well, what have you got to say for yourself?'

Stella gazed at her levelly, although she was seething inside. 'I haven't anything to say if you're expecting excuses,' she said quietly. 'I don't have "men friends" in the sense you quite obviously mean, which I find extremely insulting. I was simply having tea with someone I used to know at Hill House. Nothing more than that.'

'But you were holding hands!'

'We were *not* holding hands. It's true Dr Marshall took my hand but I immediately removed it – if you want the whole truth, which you clearly didn't get from your spies.' She leaned down and picked up the baby and cradled him in her lap. He immediately fell asleep.

Doreen was watching. She would have liked to snatch the baby from his mother, but was afraid he might crease her new silk dress. 'Spies? I don't know what you're talking about,' she snapped.

'I think you do, Doreen. Because you wouldn't even have known I'd met Dr Marshall if Mrs Beales and Mrs Arbuthnot hadn't been in Daisy's Tearooms at the same time and watched every move we made,' Stella said reasonably. 'And even some we didn't,' she added.

'They were not spying, they simply happened to be there that afternoon and couldn't help seeing what was going on,' Doreen said. 'Occasionally, I join them there, though not, thank heaven, on that particular afternoon.' She laid her hand on her heart. 'I think I would have fainted with shame, had I been there and witnessed some of the things they saw.'

Stella frowned and said through gritted teeth, 'I can't imagine what they must have told you, but I can assure you that they did not witness anything except two people who had worked at the same place having tea together. And in case they missed anything, Ian had three scones, three cups of tea and a cream horn, and I had two scones, two cups of tea and a chocolate éclair. And Ian paid the bill. Then I caught the tram home and he went on his way.'

'Don't be rude.'

'I am not being rude, I am simply telling you exactly what happened.'

'It's not what I heard,' Doreen said, determined not to be bested.

'Then maybe you shouldn't listen to gossip,' Stella said. She had managed to keep her temper up till now but was rapidly losing patience. 'Especially when it's not true.'

'Are you suggesting my friends are gossips?'

'Well, aren't they? They obviously couldn't wait to tell you they'd seen me in Daisy's Tearooms with a man and to report what they imagined they'd seen. What they didn't stop to think of was that if there had been anything in the least bit suspect in our meeting, Daisy's would have been the last place we'd have chosen, knowing it was highly likely that they would be there.' She shrugged. 'But if you don't choose to believe me, why don't you visit the place yourself and ask Mrs Greenleaf, the proprietor, what kind of shady activities she allows to go on at her premises? I'm sure she'll be only too pleased to tell you that she runs a totally respectable establishment.'

'Don't be ridiculous. I would never demean myself by conversing in that way with such a person.'

'Then that's your loss, because Mrs Greenleaf is a delightful lady.'

'I hardly think she can be called a lady if she's in Trade,' Doreen said with a sneer.

'At least she's always polite and well-mannered.' Stella's voice was ominously quiet but the implication was unmistakable. 'And she doesn't gossip.'

Doreen sat up even straighter in her seat and lifted her chin, her face white with rage. 'You've gone too far now, my girl. Just remember where you are. Just remember that my husband and I offered you a home here out of the goodness of our hearts because you were expecting our son's child. We have always treated you as one of the family, but I am beginning to wonder if we were wise to allow you to stay once the child was born.'

Stella frowned. 'What do you mean?'

'I mean you have taken advantage of your position and my husband's generosity and given back nothing in return except a somewhat doubtful reputation, even meeting your men friends in public places.'

Stella's face paled. 'That's an outrageous accusation, Doreen, and you know it. I really don't know what's come over you. You're being quite ridiculous to even think such things, let alone say them. I think you owe me an apology.'

'Never. I blame myself, of course. I realize now that we were remiss in not finding out more about you before offering you a home here out of the generosity of our hearts. John was our only son and naturally he sowed his share of wild oats, like all young men do. But we never imagined he would marry anybody who wasn't completely respectable.' She looked Stella up and down, her rage now turning her face from white to purple and her eyes bulging. 'We never thought he would marry a trollop.'

Stella got to her feet. She was afraid Doreen was about to have some kind of seizure or apoplectic fit, so she said, keeping her voice quiet, 'You've gone too far now, Doreen. I think you must be ill, making all these dreadful accusations that you know perfectly well have no foundation. I really don't know what's come over you. Maybe you should go and lie down and we'll talk again tomorrow, when you are in a more reasonable frame of mind.'

Doreen stood up, too. 'There is nothing wrong with my frame of mind,' she shouted shrilly. 'I know exactly what I'm saying. I've never liked you but I've put up with you for the sake of the child, and if you wish to leave my house and pursue your wicked ways I shall not be sorry to see you go.' She thumped her fist on the table, making the baby cry at the sudden noise. 'But if you think you can take the child with you, you're very much mistaken. He will remain here, with us, his grandparents, and be brought up as befits my son's child. It's all arranged. Mary is perfectly competent to care for him for now, and when he reaches his first birthday his name will be put down to attend the boarding school that his father attended from the age of seven. My husband and I have already discussed this at length.' She glared triumphantly at Stella, not adding that Roger had been adamant that nothing would be done without Stella's consent.

Stella was shocked beyond words. She stared back in horror at Doreen, while the child, sensing that something was wrong in his ordered and loving little life, screamed with fear. Then slowly, deliberately, her eyes still on Doreen, Stella sat down and unbuttoned her blouse and put him to her breast. Immediately, he was quiet.

Doreen stared, a look of disgust on her face. Then, knowing she was defeated, she turned and left the room.

Twenty-Two

After her mother-in-law had gone, Stella sat nursing Jonathan and trying to calm her thumping heart and shaking limbs. Angry tears streamed down her face at Doreen's outrageous and totally unjustified accusations. Why had her mother-in-law's so-called friends found it necessary to embroider the totally innocent facts and pass on such spiteful gossip? And how could Doreen ever have believed them?

She buttoned her blouse and stroked her little son's dark head lovingly. She knew very well that Doreen was jealous because Stella wouldn't allow her to control how the baby was being brought up, but for her to come into the room and spill out such vitriolic, venomous lies was bordering on insanity. It was the only explanation Stella could think of for her behaviour.

She started and looked round fearfully as she heard the door open, clutching Jonathan closely to her, afraid that Doreen had returned with more trumped-up accusations. But it was only Mary, cheerful and fresh-faced as ever, carrying a basket of freshly ironed linen. A look of consternation crossed her face when she saw Stella, and she immediately put the basket down and went over and took the baby from her.

'Goodness me, Mrs Stella, whatever's wrong? You look as if you've seen a ghost!' she said, jiggling him in her arms. 'Look at you! You haven't got a scrap of colour in your face and you're shaking like a leaf. Are you ill? Wait a minute, I'll fetch some smelling salts. That's what you need.'

Stella passed her hand across her forehead. 'No, Mary, what I need more than anything is a nice cup of tea. Be a dear and make one for me, will you?' She looked up and managed a weak smile.

'I'll do better than that. I've just had a cup with Mum and Maisie and I'm sure there's still one left in the pot. I'll be back in a jiffy.' With an anxious glance at Stella, she went off with the baby still on her arm.

A minute later it was Emma who appeared with a cup of strong, sweet tea.

Stella took the tea, her hand shaking so much the cup rattled in its saucer.

'Good heavens, Mrs Stella, Mary said you looked as if you were about ready to faint and she wasn't far wrong. Whatever's the matter? Are you ill?' Emma's face was a mask of concern.

Stella shook her head. 'No, I'm not ill, Emma. But I have had . . . Oh, Emma, it was awful. How could she say such dreadful things?' The tears began to flow again.

Emma frowned. She couldn't imagine what the girl was talking about but something had clearly upset her badly, so she said gently, 'Come on, now, drink your tea, it'll make you feel better. Then if you want to talk about it you can.'

Stella gulped the tea gratefully. 'Thank you, Emma, that was lovely; just what I needed.' She handed the cup and saucer back and put her head in her hands. 'Oh, it was dreadful!' she said again. 'How could she . . .? Oh, it was just awful!'

'What was just awful, dearie? I don't want to pry but sometimes it helps to talk,' Emma said quietly, looking down at her. 'I can see how upset you are, but bottling it all up inside won't do you any good at all.' She laid a hand on Stella's shoulder. 'You need to talk to somebody, dearie. If you tell me what's troubling you it won't go any further, if that's what you're concerned about.'

Stella shook her head. 'I know that. Not that I care . . .' She looked up, her eyes still brimming with tears. 'Sit down, Emma. You're quite right. I do need to tell somebody, if only to try and understand why she should . . .' She waited until the older woman was seated on a hard chair by the table before blurting out, 'Oh, Emma, Mrs Nolan has just been here and made the most terrible accusations . . .'

Emma listened, her jaw tightening, as Stella recounted almost word for word, between hiccupping tears, the altercation she had just had with her mother-in-law. 'So now I know exactly what Doreen thinks of me,' she said finally, wiping the tears from her face with the heel of her hand. 'I know she's never really liked me, but to call me such names!' She looked up. 'I'm not like that, Emma, really I'm not.'

'Of course you're not, dearie. Anyone can see that with half an eye.' Emma smiled reassuringly.

Stella smiled gratefully back. Then she frowned. 'But what I really don't understand is why her friends felt the need to pass on such scurrilous tales about what happened in the tearooms. It wasn't even as if I was having a cosy conversation with Ian Marshall. Heavens, we were almost quarrelling by the time we left. Yet they made out . . .' She shook her head again. 'Why did they make up such dreadful lies, Emma? And how could Doreen have believed them?'

'I suspect it was six of one and half a dozen of the other,' Emma said flatly.

Stella stared at her. 'What do you mean?'

'I reckon they exaggerated what really happened because they always enjoy a bit of gossip and knew that was what Mrs Nolan would want to hear. Then she embroidered it a bit more to suit her own purposes.'

'But there wasn't anything . . .' Stella began.

'Well, put it like this. You said Dr Marshall took your hand but you quickly snatched it away. Maybe they didn't see you do that or forgot to say . . .'

'Or deliberately didn't tell her, more likely.'

'I was trying to be charitable, but you're probably right,' Emma said with a sigh. 'Anyway, whatever it was they told her, Mrs Nolan decided you must have been holding hands and whispering sweet nothings the whole time.'

'Ah, yes. I see what you mean,' Stella nodded thoughtfully. 'And that's the way false rumours are spread.'

'Exactly. Although how Mrs Nolan imagined you could manage to hold hands and gaze into each other's eyes and at the same time eat cream cakes and drink tea is another matter!' Emma said.

Stella suddenly burst out laughing.

'What?' Emma asked. She wondered if the girl was becoming hysterical.

'I just had a vision of two people gazing into each other's eyes, with cream cake all over their faces and tea spilling all over the place,' Stella said, her giggles subsiding.

Emma laughed, too. 'Doesn't make sense, does it?' She

became serious again. 'Stupid woman!' There was a wealth of feeling behind those last two words.

'She's not stupid, she's wicked.' Stella said, equally serious. 'What she wants is to take my baby away from me, I've always known that. She'd like to find some reason to send me away because I'm not a fit mother and leave Jonny here. But to say that she and Roger have decided to put his name down for John's old school . . .' She looked up at Emma anxiously. 'Roger wouldn't do that, would he? Not without consulting me?'

'Of course not, dearie. You ought to know the Colonel better than that.'

Stella shook her head. 'To tell you the truth, I don't know anything any more. Not after the things she said this afternoon.' She pressed her lips together in a straight line. 'Except for one thing, that is. I can't stay here at Warren's End any longer. I'll take my baby and go away, tonight. I'm not going to stay here and risk her trying to poison my son against me, as I know she will as he gets older.'

Emma nodded sagely. 'And where will you go?' she asked.

'Oh, I don't know. Anywhere. It doesn't matter, as long as I'm away from this place.'

'Just you hang on a minute, dearie.' Emma held up her hand. 'I reckon you need to give it a bit more thought. You can't just walk out of here with nowhere to go and no idea how you'll manage, now, can you? You've had a dreadful upset, nobody's denying that, so you need to calm down a bit, then you'll be in a better frame of mind to make a sensible decision.' She was not surprised at the girl's words, but she was anxious she shouldn't rush into things in the heat of the moment.

'Well, I can't stay here, that's certain.' Stella was adamant. 'I never want to see that woman again as long as I live after the dreadful things she said to me.'

'I can understand that.' Emma pinched her lip as she tried to think of a way to prevent Stella rushing into something she might later regret. 'Have you spoken to the Colonel?'

Stella shook her head. 'I haven't spoken to anybody except you, Emma. But how could I tell Roger the awful things his wife called me? He'd think I was making it up.' She shuddered. 'In any case . . .' she shuddered again. 'No, I couldn't possibly speak to him. I couldn't tell anybody else. I simply couldn't. I just want to go away and . . . I just want to get away from that woman.'

'I know, dear,' Emma said. 'But if you'll take my advice, I think you need to sleep on it before you come to any decision. It's not just your life, it's your son's you have to think about, remember.'

'I'm not leaving him here!' Stella said hotly.

'I'm not suggesting you should,' Emma said with a smile. 'I'm only saying you need to wait until you've calmed down a little and given yourself time to work out some kind of a plan, that's all.' She paused. 'And another thing. I know it will take courage, but I think you should go in to dinner tonight just as you always do. See how Doreen behaves. Show her she hasn't intimidated you.' Her mouth twisted wryly. 'She might even apologize.'

'That's not likely. She's more likely to continue to rant at me.'

'That would be good. At least the others would see how despicably she's behaving towards you.' She got to her feet. 'I promise you, things probably won't look quite so bad in the morning,' she said, patting Stella's shoulder.

Stella shook her head. 'I still don't think I can stay here,' she said sadly.

'No, but tonight you'll wash your face, put on a pretty blouse, and go in to dinner and be your usual sweet self to everyone,' Emma said firmly.

'Even Doreen?' Stella made a face.

'Even Doreen.' Emma smiled encouragingly. 'You never know, she might be regretting what she did and be all sweetness and light.'

'I can't see that happening,' Stella made a face. She got up and gave Emma a quick hug. 'But thank you for listening to me. I feel much better for having told you all about it. And you're quite right, I mustn't let her intimidate me. I'll go in to dinner and try and behave as if nothing happened this afternoon.'

'Good girl! Anyway, it might all blow over.'

★   ★   ★

That was not very likely, Stella decided when she presented herself with a thumping heart for the usual sherry before the meal and saw Doreen's face. It was a mask of horrified surprise, hurriedly changed to a tight little smile that didn't reach anywhere near her cold eyes. Obviously, she hadn't expected to see her daughter-in-law.

Stella hoped desperately that she wouldn't make a scene at the table.

In fact, the meal passed as it usually did, with Roger and Philip gently disagreeing over the political situation, while Rosalie interrupted at frequent intervals to badger Philip into spending money on her – this time on a 'simply divine' silver-fox coat she had seen at Bakers, the most exclusive dress shop in the town. Doreen spoke little, played with her food and left, pleading a headache, after demanding coffee in her room.

In spite of Doreen's stony stares in her direction, Stella managed to eat most of her meal, although it nearly choked her. She also managed to smile brightly and answer any remarks directed at her. But it was not until her mother-in-law had left, that she felt she could relax a little over her coffee.

'No, I won't have any, thanks.' Rosalie waved Maisie away as she advanced with the coffee pot. She yawned and got up from the table. 'I think I'll go down to the club for a couple of hours.'

Roger turned to Stella after Rosalie had gone. 'You've been very quiet over dinner tonight, my dear,' he said. 'Are you feeling a little unwell?'

'No, I'm perfectly well, thank you, Roger,' she answered, smiling at him and at the same time wondering what he would have to say if he knew the accusations his wife had thrown at her that afternoon. But perhaps he did know and had chosen not to speak about it, yet. Her face burned at the thought and she looked for a way of escape before he could say anything.

Then her eyes lit on the piano. 'Since Doreen and Rosalie have both left, would you like some music to accompany your political discussions?' she asked with a little smile.

'That would be extremely pleasant,' both men agreed.

She got up from her chair, and as she passed Philip's chair

on her way to the piano he caught her hand. 'Are you all right, Stella?' he asked quietly. 'You're very pale tonight. If there's anything troubling you . . .'

'I'm just a little tired, that's all.' She freed her hand and moved on quickly so that he wouldn't see the quick tears that had sprung into her eyes at the concern in his voice.

As her fingers moved over the keys, her mind seemed to clear. She would have to leave Warren's End, she had already made up her mind to that. But now, in this moment of clarity, she admitted what she had known in her heart for a long time now. It was Philip she would miss: Philip who she could laugh with and tell her troubles to. Well, most of them, anyway; she didn't think she could confide this last episode even to him. It was Philip she had fallen in love with. She had never before allowed herself even to formulate those last words in her mind, but now she admitted to herself that they were true. Which was another reason she had to go; and soon, before he found out. Because Philip already had a wife.

She riffled through the music until she came to Liszt's *Liebestraum* – his 'Dream of Love' – and in an act of total self-indulgence picked it up and played it, putting all her pent-up feelings and emotions into it. Though Philip would never know it was her farewell gift to him, because she was determined that after tonight she must never see him again.

The next afternoon, Stella wheeled her baby down the drive, saying she was going to the shops. She didn't come back.

Twenty-Three

It was Mary's day off, so nobody in the family realized that Stella hadn't come back from the shops until she failed to arrive for dinner that night. Even then no one was concerned; it was assumed that she was eating in her room so as to be near in case Jonathan needed attention. Maisie wasn't even asked; and although she knew very well this was not the case, she had assumed the family knew where Stella was. Emma wasn't there;

she usually left early to spend the evening with Mary on her day off.

In fact, alarm bells only began to ring when Mary returned at eight o'clock the following day and announced in a state of near-hysteria that something dreadful must have happened because neither Master Jonathan's crib nor Mrs Stella's bed had been slept in.

Roger was distraught and immediately summoned the family to the morning room to see if anyone could shed light on Stella's disappearance.

'She's probably gone to stay with friends,' Rosalie said with a yawn. She'd had a late night at the club and was slightly hung over. Anyway, she couldn't see what all the fuss was about. Nobody ordered a family conclave if she spent the night away from home, which, in all honesty, she frequently did, so perhaps it was not surprising.

'I don't think she's made any particular friends here,' Philip snapped. 'She prefers to spend her time with Jonathan.'

'Well, wherever she came from, then.' Rosalie waved a languid arm.

'She's hardly likely to take a baby to a convalescent home full of war-damaged soldiers and ask for shelter.' Philip's voice was heavy with sarcasm.

'All right, don't get your dander up.' Rosalie fished in her bag for her cigarettes.

'Oh, for goodness' sake, I don't know what you're all so concerned about,' Doreen said impatiently. She was annoyed at having to get dressed this early in the morning. She preferred to begin her day in a much more leisurely fashion. 'It's perfectly obvious to me where she's gone.'

Roger frowned. 'If you know where she's gone, why didn't you say so in the first place, Doreen?'

Doreen glared at him. 'Well, of course I don't know *exactly* where she's gone, but I can make an educated guess.'

'Well, then, where, for heaven's sake?' There was something in his wife's manner that he didn't much like and he was becoming irritated.

'Why, she's gone off with her fancy man.' Doreen shrugged smugly.

Philip's jaw tightened, but before he could trust himself to speak Rosalie said incredulously, 'Fancy man! *What* fancy man?'

'Why, that man she met in Daisy's Tearooms the other afternoon, of course. She's probably gone off with him. I expect they were planning it all as they sat there holding hands.'

'And where did you get all this information from, Doreen?' Roger asked, his voice steely.

She gave another shrug, but of discomfort this time. 'One or two of my friends were there and they told me about it,' she muttered.

'I'll bet they did!' Rosalie said with a snort. 'With bells on!'

'There's no need to be rude about my friends,' Doreen said haughtily. 'They simply told me what they'd seen, which was that my daughter-in-law was in Daisy's Tearooms with a man. Holding hands. Of course Stella denied it, but then, she would, wouldn't she?'

'What, she denied she was there?' Roger asked.

'No, of course not. She could hardly deny that. But she denied they were holding hands. In fact, she practically accused my friends of telling lies. She was really quite rude. But then I shouldn't have been surprised, should I? After all, we've no idea where she came from or what her background was.' She sniffed. 'Personally, I don't care if I never see her again. If you ask me, she's no better than she should be, the troll . . .' She stopped, realizing she had gone too far. 'All I care about is getting my grandson back where he belongs. Which is *here*. Because in my opinion she's not a fit person to have charge of him.' She thumped her fist on the arm of her chair.

Rosalie scrabbled in her bag for another cigarette. 'Hang on a minute, Ma. Let me get this straight. If you are so sure that Stella is, as you say, "no better than she should be", which I take to mean some kind of loose woman, to put it politely, how can you be so sure that Jonathan *is* your grandson?' She looked up, smiling innocently. 'From what you're implying, he could be any Tom, Dick or Harry's child and nothing whatever to do with John. In which case he isn't your grandson at all, so it doesn't matter where she's taken him. You can't have it both ways, Ma.' She lit her cigarette and blew a smoke ring while she waited for the bombshell to explode.

'That's enough, Rosalie!' Roger exploded. 'I've never heard such rubbish.' He took a deep breath. 'I think your mother is overwrought and not quite herself,' he went on, more quietly, holding his temper in check with difficulty. 'I'm quite sure she didn't mean to make such outrageous and blatantly false accusations regarding our son's wife.' He turned to Doreen with a steely look. 'Did you, my dear!'

Doreen shook her head slightly and muttered, her face flushed with shame. 'No, of course not. You must have misunderstood me. What I meant was . . .'

'Thank you.' Roger cut her off before she could say any more. 'Now, after that little outburst I think we should get back to the matter in hand. This gentleman your friends saw having tea with Stella. Did they recognize him?'

'From their description I think it must have been that doctor person Stella was talking to at Philip's exhibition.' Doreen didn't raise her eyes as she spoke. She realized she had let her feelings get the better of her. She got to her feet, her hand dramatically to her head. 'I'm sorry, I can't tell you anything more. I must go to my room now, I'm not feeling at all well.' She staggered out of the room. Nobody took much notice, they were all used to her theatricals and glad to see her go.

'Dr Marshall,' Philip said. It was what he had expected.

'Then obviously the first thing we must do is to contact the good doctor and see if Stella is there,' Roger said, relieved that there was something practical that could be done to find the daughter-in-law of whom he had become very fond.

'I'll do that,' Philip said quickly. 'Henry's due to take me into the town . . .' He pulled out his pocket watch and looked at it. 'Very soon, actually, to see Ben Gerard about some of my pictures, so we can call at his consulting rooms.' He struggled to his feet. 'And if Ian Marshall doesn't know anything, I'll call on Mrs Greenleaf at Daisy's. She might know where Stella's gone.'

'That's good.' Roger got to his feet with less difficulty than his son-in-law. 'Well, there's nothing more we can do at the moment, so we'll wait to hear what you find out, my boy.' He pinched his lip. 'Although what we have to remember is that nobody's seen her since she left yesterday afternoon. She could have caught a train and be miles away by now.'

'We'll worry about that when we've combed the local area,' Philip said as he went out.

Henry was already waiting with Tin Lizzie at the front door. He helped Philip into the passenger seat and Philip outlined his plan of action.

'That is, unless you've got any better suggestions, Henry,' he said when he'd finished.

'No, sir, can't say I have,' Henry replied.

'Well, she can't just have vanished into thin air. She must be somewhere. I've got to find her, Henry,' he finished desperately.

They pulled up outside the Hunter's Moon Galleries, and Philip was inside just long enough to collect a substantial cheque for three pictures Oscar Hillyard had sold in London.

'He's desperate for your war drawings, you know,' Ben Gerard reminded him. 'He says they'd fetch a really good price. He even talked about putting them into one of the big art auctions. Just let me know when you're ready to sell.'

'Yes, all right, tell him he can have them,' Philip said without very much interest. 'It's probably time I got rid of them: they've served their purpose, helped me get it all out of my system. I don't need reminding what it was like over there in the trenches. You can come and collect them as soon as you like.' He turned to the subject at the front of his mind. 'I suppose you haven't seen my sister-in-law, Stella, and her baby, have you, Ben?'

He looked surprised. 'Me? No. Should I have?'

Philip shook his head. 'No, of course not. Sorry. It's just that . . . Well, never mind. Collect the paintings whenever you like.'

'Later on today?'

'Yes, that'll be fine. Help yourself if I'm not there, you know where they are.'

Henry helped him back into the car and they went on to Dr Marshall's consulting rooms. They were shown into his study by a puzzled housekeeper, in spite of her insistence that Dr Marshall was extremely busy. They found him somewhat distractedly sorting out books, a cigarette dangling from his lips. Several boxes were already filled and there were piles of papers on the chairs.

'Sorry, old chap, didn't my housekeeper tell you?' Ian Marshall said, looking up in surprise. 'I'm not doing any more consultations.' He frowned. 'You hadn't got one booked, had you? I thought I'd notified all my patients.'

'No, I hadn't got one booked.'

Ian Marshal didn't appear to notice Philip's clipped tone but went on, 'You see, I'm giving up my practice here and moving back to Hill House.' He was wearing flannel trousers that had seen better days and a plaid shirt, open at the neck. He hadn't shaved and his hair looked as if he'd run his fingers through it any number of times.

'And I assume you think you'll be taking my sister-in-law with you?' Philip said coldly.

Ian Marshall looked at him in amazement, then gave a mirthless laugh. 'Fat chance of that!'

'What do you mean? Isn't she here?' Philip looked round as if he expected to see her lurking in a corner.

'No, she isn't,' he said, drawing on his cigarette and tapping the ash on to the floor. 'And she never has been. You've got a bloody nerve barging in here like this!'

'Then where is she?' Philip retorted, a bewildered expression on his face.

'How the hell should I know!' Ian pushed a pile of papers off a chair and slumped down. 'I don't know what all this is about and I don't much care. I've got more important things on my mind. But if it helps, I can tell you this, I've absolutely no idea of Stella's whereabouts and I can't imagine why you should think I might have. We didn't exactly part the best of friends last time I saw her, which was in that little teashop in the square.' He pulled out his cigarette case and lit a cigarette from the one he'd just finished, but didn't offer Philip one. He went on, 'To tell you the truth, I'd hoped we might renew an old friendship. Well, I'd always had a thing for Stella and thought it might have been a bit more than that . . . But all I got was a lecture telling me I had no chance with her and was wasting my time in private practice and should go back to Hill House. Predictably, I suppose, she refused even to consider going back there with me. However, I realized she was right, so as you see . . .' He waved his hand to indicate the piles of books. 'I'm getting ready to do just that, especially as when I contacted Hill House they were only too anxious to persuade me to return. In fact, they want me back as soon as I can get there.'

'She hasn't gone on ahead of you?' Philip asked suspiciously.

'No, she bloody well hasn't. I told you, she refused to even consider it.' He stood up. 'Now, I'm afraid you'll have to excuse me. I've got a lot of sorting out and packing to do. I'm hoping to leave in a couple of weeks.'

'Yes, of course. Thank you for your time.'

'Goodbye.' He held open the door. 'I just hope you have more luck with her than I did!' was his parting shot.

'I don't know what he meant by that,' Philip said as Henry helped him back into the car.

'Don't you, sir?' Henry said enigmatically. He climbed into the driver's seat. 'Where to now, sir?'

'Daisy's. When you come to think of it, it's the obvious place, isn't it? She often goes to see Mrs Greenleaf. We were stupid, we should have gone there first.' He drummed his fingers on the dashboard. 'Well, come on, man, put your foot down.'

Mrs Greenleaf was very concerned, but couldn't help. She hadn't seen Stella since the day she had tea with that other man. Mrs Greenleaf hadn't liked him much, he was too fond of himself. But, she was pleased to say, and smiled at the memory, Mrs Nolan gave him short shrift when he tried to hold her hand. She didn't think they'd parted on very good terms, she said with a satisfied nod.

'But do you know where she could be?' Philip broke in impatiently. 'You see, she's gone from Warren's End. Vanished. Run away.'

'Oh, goodness me, I didn't realize it was that bad!' Mrs Greenleaf put her hand up to her mouth. 'And that poor baby! I never thought she'd leave him.'

'She hasn't left him. She's taken him with her. So you haven't seen her?' He shook his head in some irritation. 'No, of course you haven't, or you'd have known he was with her.'

Back in the car, Philip put his head in his hands and said dejectedly, 'I don't know where to go or what to do now, Henry. I was so sure I'd be able to find her, that I knew where she would be.' He brushed his hand across his eyes. 'There's an old saying, "You never miss the water till the well runs dry." All I can say is, it's bloody true.' He turned to look at Henry. 'I would never say this to anyone else, Henry, and I'll bloody kill you if you repeat it, but I don't know what I'll do if I can't find her. I've never felt about anybody the way I feel about Stella; she really is the love of my life, although of course I can never tell her that.'

'I know how you feel, sir. That's the way I feel about Emma, too. I loved my Florrie, of course I did, but that was a young love, if you take my meaning. What I feel for Emma is deeper, more mature. And when her year of mourning for Arthur is up I'm going to ask her to marry me, and I know she's going to say yes.' He turned and smiled at Philip.

'You're a lucky bastard.'

'I know, sir.' They drove on in silence.

Then Philip said, 'We were a bit daft not to have a cup of coffee at Daisy's when we were with Mrs Greenleaf, weren't we? I've just realized I didn't even have time for a cup of tea before Roger called us all together this morning. Now I'm absolutely parched. And when we get back to Warren's End, we'll have to face a barrage of questions and . . .' He gave a sigh. 'Oh, turn the car round, Henry, let's go and have a quiet cup of Mrs Greenleaf's coffee, then we'll decide what to do next before we go back and face the music.'

Henry glanced at him. 'If you wouldn't think it presumptuous, sir, I could take you to my place and make you some coffee,' he said tentatively. 'We're not far away. It would save us driving back into the town, and would give you a few minutes' peace and quiet. Time to think what to do next, so to speak.'

Philip nodded. 'I believe I might like that, Henry. I don't think I've ever seen where you live.'

Henry laughed. 'Well, it's not all that far from Warren's End, but a bit off the beaten track. Me and Emma live next door to each other, which is nice. Here we are, it's down this little

road, so hold on to your seat, sir, it's a bit of a rough ride.' As
he spoke, he swung the car off the main road and down what
was little more than a cart track.

'No wonder I've never been down here before,' Philip
laughed as the car bumped along. 'And I doubt if I ever will
again. I don't think the springs of the car will stand it.'

'Well, we're here now.' Henry pulled up and went round to
help him out of the car. 'Mind how you go, now. My cottage
is the one on the left.' He handed Philip his sticks.

'Don't you ever lock your door?' Philip asked as Henry
pushed open the door.

'No, no need. Hardly anybody ever comes down this lane.'
He pulled the kettle forward on the stove. 'You sit in that
chair, sir. It's nice and comfortable. Fits my poor old back
a treat when I'm tired.' He went to the pantry and picked
up the milk jug. 'Oh, drat! I forgot I was out of milk. Never
mind, I'll just pop next door. Emma's sure to have some.
She won't mind me helping myself, even though she won't
be there.'

'You two might as well be married, the way you carry on,'
Philip said, smiling.

'Not quite, sir,' Henry replied seriously. 'But I'm a patient
man, I can wait. Won't be a minute, sir.'

He went off and Philip closed his eyes, savouring the peace
and quietness. Then he opened them and looked round the
little room. It was sparsely furnished, but spotlessly clean and
there was an array of blue-and-white china on the dresser
and slightly battered copper saucepans on the shelf beside the
fireplace. On the mantelpiece Staffordshire dogs stood sentinel
at each end, with a few cheap ornaments in between. A
slightly faded wedding snapshot of a young man and girl,
obviously Henry and his young wife, had pride of place in
the centre. On the floor a rag rug covered the tiles, and a
scrubbed table stood in the middle with a blue-checked cloth
covering it.

Philip closed his eyes. 'Homely,' he thought to himself. 'I
like it.'

He heard the door latch, but didn't bother to open his eyes
at first because he didn't want to break the spell of where his

thoughts were leading. 'Did you get the milk, Henry?' he said eventually, looking up.

But it wasn't Henry who stood by the table, holding a pretty flowered jug with a beaded muslin cover on it to protect it from flies. It was Stella.

'Henry said you've been looking for me,' she said, smiling down at him.

'Stella!' He stared at her as if he couldn't believe his eyes. 'Indeed I have.' He shook his head in bewilderment. 'But this is the last place I expected to find you. What on earth are you doing here?' He held out his hand to her.

Twenty-Four

Stella put the jug down on the table and almost shyly went to him. He looked at her for a long moment as if he couldn't believe she was really there, then took her hand and pulled her down on to the footstool beside his chair.

'Oh, Stella, why did you leave like that without telling me?' he whispered, 'Didn't you realize I'd be crazy with worry, not knowing where you'd gone?'

She laid her cheek against his hand. 'I'm sorry, Phil. But it was the only way. I knew I couldn't stay under the same roof as Doreen any longer. I wanted to tell you I was going, but I knew I wouldn't be able to say goodbye to you . . .' She paused, her eyes brimming with tears. 'Well, it would have been difficult.'

'So you played me *Liebestraum* – 'Dream of Love' – instead!' He took her chin and tilted it so he could look into her face. 'Is that what . . .?'

'Yes,' she whispered. 'I knew a dream of love was all I could ever have.'

'No!' he said fiercely. 'Don't you realize the hell I went through when I couldn't find you? When I thought I'd lost you?' He stroked her hair. 'It's no good, I can't let you go, Stella,' he whispered. 'We belong together, you and me.' He bent his head and kissed her, tenderly at first and then with increasing passion.

She clung to him, returning his kisses, then pulled away. 'It's no use, Phil,' she whispered sadly. 'It can't be. What about Rosalie?'

He lifted his head and looked away. 'I'll ask her to divorce me,' he said impatiently. 'I've been thinking about it for some time. It's not as if she'll care. In fact, she'll be glad to be rid of me. She hasn't really had any feelings for me since I came back from the war crippled.' He said the word in disgust as he turned to face her again. 'I can't blame her, Stella, because it's perfectly true. I'm not the man she married and it's never going to be any different. I'm never going to be able to walk without sticks or climb into a bath without help. I'm always going to be just that. Crippled.' His voice was bitter. Then he shook his head and gave a great sigh. 'No, I can't ask you to face that, either, Stella. I should have let you go. It was completely selfish of me to come looking for you. I'm sorry.'

She put a finger over his lips. 'Don't be sorry and don't be silly, Phil. To me, that's just how you are. I've never known you any other way except as a brave man who can't walk very well, accepting a life of pain and difficulty without complaint.' She smiled at him. 'Maybe that's what's made you the man you are and why I fell in love with you in the first place.' She kissed him. 'It's only your legs, Phil. Nothing else. What you've had to suffer has made you more of a man, not less.'

He frowned. 'Do you really think that?'

'Yes, I really do.'

'Thank you, my darling.' He squeezed her hand and looked at her long and hard. Then he said quietly, 'There is another thing. I'll be a divorced man – tainted by the scandal of being dragged through the divorce court. It won't be pretty, what I'll have to do in order to get Rosalie to divorce me, although I promise to keep you well away from it all.'

'I realize all that, Phil,' she said quietly.

'Then, although I'm afraid I can't get down on one knee in the time-honoured way, Stella, my dearest girl, when I'm free, will you marry me?'

'There's Jonathan. I couldn't . . .'

'Oh, Stella, you didn't imagine I'd want to part you from your son, did you? What sort of a monster do you think I am? I'll be proud to be a father to him.'

She smiled through tears of happiness. 'Then the answer's a most emphatic yes. As soon as you're free, I'll be honoured to marry you, Phil.'

He bent his head to kiss her again. Some time later, he raised his head a little. 'Speaking of Jonny, where is the young rascal? Surely, he can't have been asleep all this time?'

'No, he's next door, with Mary. Shall I knock on the wall and tell her to bring him over?'

'Yes, do that.'

'Henry must be wondering what's been going on here,' she said as she resumed her place at his feet.

'He's probably guessed,' Philip said, chuckling, as Mary walked in carrying Jonathan, followed by Emma with a welcome pot of tea and by Henry carrying a plate of Emma's home-made scones. They were all wreathed in smiles.

'But I'm afraid it won't be yet,' Philip warned them when they had been given the not unexpected news and offered delighted congratulations. 'There'll be a squalid divorce to go through first, which won't be pleasant.'

'Will Mrs Rosalie agree to a divorce?' Emma asked anxiously. She called it *di*vorce. As far as she was concerned, to talk of divorce was as alien as speaking of going to the moon.

Philip laughed grimly. 'If I know Rosalie, she'll be glad to be rid of me. But what I want to know, is why on earth did Stella end up here? Well, next door, in your cottage, Emma? And what are you and Mary doing here? Why aren't you up at Warren's End as you usually are at this time of day?'

'First things first,' Emma said, pouring the tea and handing it round, while Mary followed with the scones. 'Mrs Stella is here because she really had nowhere else to go. We knew she couldn't stay at Warren's End, not after all those dreadful things Mrs Nolan had accused her of.'

'I did think of throwing myself on Mrs Greenleaf's mercy,' Stella added. She was sitting at Philip's feet, her head on his knee. 'But as Emma pointed out, it wouldn't have taken long for Doreen's friends to spy out the pram or hear Jonny crying and they'd soon have reported back, so I wouldn't have been able to stay there very long.'

'So I suggested she should come here. Just temporary, you understand, it not being quite the way of life she's used to . . .' Emma looked faintly embarrassed.

'You seem to forget I spent several years in a bare little room at Hill House when I was nursing,' Stella reminded her with a smile. 'Your cottage is luxurious compared with that. In fact it's a dear little cottage: very cosy and homely. I love it.'

'Yes, well.' Emma shrugged, but flushed with pleasure at the compliment. 'Anyway, this seemed a good place for them both to come. It's a bit off the beaten track, and who would think to look for them right under their noses, only half a mile away? At the same time, staying here for a while would give Mrs Stella time to think and decide what to do next.' Emma shook her head in Stella's direction. 'She was so upset yesterday I was worried she'd go and do something she might regret later.'

'Like what?' Philip asked, a scone halfway to his mouth.

Emma shrugged again. 'I dunno. Like going off with that doctor chap, I suppose.'

'Oh, no!' Stella gave a shudder. 'That would have been the very last resort.'

'Good.' Philip gave her shoulder a squeeze. 'I'm glad to hear that.' He turned to Emma again. 'But, Emma, I still don't understand how you managed it without anybody knowing? Mary, for instance. She lives here, but she didn't know. She was nearly hysterical this morning when she found they'd gone.'

'Yes,' Emma said dryly. 'I must say she did that well. I think it fooled everyone. Mind you, she practised for ages how she had to behave when she found the beds hadn't been slept in, didn't you, love?' She laughed ruefully. 'She got so good at it I was afraid she might want to go on the stage one of these days.'

'Yes, she was very convincing,' Stella agreed.

Mary shrugged. 'I just imagined they'd been kidnapped. That was such an awful thought that it wasn't hard to fake a scream. Although I was afraid I might have overdone it a bit,' she admitted. 'Maisie even made me drink some of that horrible sal volatile stuff that the missus swears by to calm me down. It nearly made me sick. I was glad when the missus sent me home. She said I might as well go because there was no point in keeping me if the baby wasn't there. I thought that was a bit unkind. Not that I cared!' She gave a little giggle. 'I knew where Jonny was and I couldn't wait to get back to him. Can I have another scone, Mum?'

'Yes, help yourself and hand them round again.'

'That's typical of Doreen, though,' Stella said, sipping her tea. 'I sometimes wonder if that woman has any real feelings at all.'

'I think she's a bit . . .' Emma touched her forehead. 'But of course, it wouldn't do to say so, would it. And the way she goes on and on about "my grandson", as if nobody else had anything to do with him. It makes me sick.'

Nobody disagreed with her.

Philip's mind was on other things. He was looking at Henry with a puzzled frown. 'How on earth could all this be going on without your knowledge, Henry? These walls aren't that thick. Didn't you hear the baby cry?'

'Oh, yes, I knew all about it.' Henry said. 'I heard the baby cry. And I heard Mary practising her screaming. In fact I fetched some of the things they'd forgotten to bring with them.'

'Then why didn't you say? Why didn't you tell me? You let me go on that frantic wild-goose chase . . .'

'I did feel a bit bad about that, sir, and I wasn't sure, at first, what I ought to do,' Henry admitted. 'But you'd got it all planned out, where you were going and everything; and you were so determined to find her I was afraid your idea was to drag her back to the house, which I knew was the last thing she wanted. So I kept quiet. Then when I realized how you felt about her and what a state you were in because she'd gone and how desperate you were to find her, I knew you'd never do anything against her wishes.' He spread his hands, smiling. 'So I brought you to her, and here we are.'

'I see. So what now? Shall I find you somewhere to stay in the town, darling? It's going to take some time – years, maybe – before the divorce will be finalized.'

'What I would really like is to stay here, with Emma, at

least for the time being, if she'll have me,' Stella said, looking at Emma uncertainly. 'I know she's finding it a bit cramped, with the baby . . .'

'Nonsense,' Emma said briskly. 'My cottage was home to me and Arthur and three children.' Her voice dropped. 'Before him and my little Ivy was taken, that is.' She perked up and smiled at Stella. 'Don't you worry, we'll find room for you and the baby, even with Mary at home, because it doesn't look as if she's going to be wanted back there.' She jerked her thumb in the direction of Warren's End. 'And when Charlie comes home, which he doesn't very often, these days, I know Henry will give him a bed, won't you, Henry?'

'Of course I will, Em.' He smiled at her, the love in his eyes plain.

'That's settled, then.'

'Now, all I have to do is offer my wife a divorce,' Philip said with a smile. 'So the sooner I go back and set the wheels in motion, the sooner I can start a new life with the woman I really love.' He bent his head and kissed the top of Stella's head.

She looked up at him. 'Do you think Rosalie will be difficult, Phil?' she asked anxiously.

'No. Why should she be?' he said with a laugh. 'She's got no feelings for me. She'll probably be glad to see the back of me. It'll be mutual,' he added with great feeling. He struggled to his feet. 'Well, come on, Henry, let's get going. The sooner I get this over, the better.'

When they arrived back at Warren's End Rosalie wasn't at home, which was no surprise. She still hadn't arrived back in time for the evening meal, which again was not unusual, so Philip went over to the house alone. This annoyed him: he would have preferred to get the confrontation with his wife over and done with, instead of which it was going to have to smoulder in his mind until she chose to put in an appearance.

It was an uncomfortable meal, during which Doreen dominated the conversation, alternating between complaining about Stella's ingratitude in running off without telling anybody, anxiety over where her beloved grandson had been taken to, and determination that when Stella returned nothing in this world would persuade her, Doreen, to give the ungrateful hussy houseroom again.

'And I don't care what you say, Roger,' though up to this point Roger hadn't managed to say anything, 'I shall never have that woman under my roof again. But we must find my grandson. Goodness knows what she's doing with him.'

'I've no doubt he's her first concern. He always is,' Roger managed to remark.

'Well then, why doesn't she bring him back here where he belongs?'

'You just said you wouldn't have her back under your roof. *My* roof, I might add . . .'

'Oh, you're insufferable. *Your* roof, then. And I don't want *her* back, it's my grandson I'm thinking of.'

'He's my grandson, too,' Roger remarked mildly, knowing it would only fan the flames.

'Well, then, why don't you go and find him, instead of sitting there making stupid remarks?' She flung her napkin on to the table and got to her feet. 'I'm going to my room. When you have news, please let me know.'

As soon as she was out of the door, Roger turned to Philip. 'Whew! Sometimes I wonder how I stay sane.' He got up and went over to the sideboard. 'I think a large whisky is in order after all that.' He poured two drinks and took them back to the table. 'You've been very quiet all evening, my boy, but your manner makes me think of the cat that stole the cream. So, unless I've read the signs wrongly, you know where Stella and the baby are.'

Philip nodded. He couldn't help smiling. 'Yes, I do, sir.'

'Then we'll drink to that.' They clinked glasses and savoured Roger's best single malt.

'There's something else, sir. Something that might upset you.'

'They're not coming back.' Roger took a deep breath. 'It doesn't surprise me. In truth, I never thought they would, not after Doreen's disgraceful outburst, and I can't blame them. Where are they?'

'Strictly between you and me, they're staying with Emma.'

'Well, I'm damned. Right under our noses.' He shook his

head. 'But no, it doesn't upset me. It doesn't upset me at all. I'm just glad to know they're somewhere safe.'

'I knew you would be.' Philip hesitated. 'But the thing that might upset you . . .' He carefully lined up an unused fork with a place mat, then looked up. 'I really don't know how you'll take this, sir, but feel you should be the first to know. I'm going to ask Rosalie for a divorce. I want to marry Stella.'

Roger blew out his cheeks. Then he took out his pipe, slowly filled it from his tobacco pouch, and tamped down the tobacco. When he had got it going to his satisfaction, he looked at Philip through a haze of smoke and nodded.

'I'm not really surprised. I could see how the land lay between you and Stella quite a while ago.' He sniffed. 'Probably before you realized it yourselves.'

'But there's never been anything improper . . .'

'I'm not suggesting there was. I never thought there would be.' He drew on his pipe and went on, 'I should, of course, curse you for a scoundrel.' He looked up and a smile spread across his face. 'But all I can say is, I wish you well, my boy. My daughter has behaved very badly towards you since you came back from the war. I've told her so repeatedly, but it's made no difference. And Stella is a lovely girl . . .' He chuckled. 'If I was thirty years younger, I might even be tempted to give you a run for your money.' He became serious again. 'It's not going to be easy having our name dragged through the courts. And it'll be in all the papers.' He sighed. 'However, I expect we can survive that. On what grounds do you intend to divorce her? I guess there are plenty to choose from.'

'Oh, I won't divorce her, I'm not such a cad. No, I'll give her grounds to divorce me. Not with Stella, though,' he added quickly. 'I don't want Stella to be involved with it at all. No, it'll have to be a seedy hotel and money changing hands with a photographer, and some woman who's happy to be photographed caught *in flagrante* in bed with a strange man . . .' He shuddered distastefully. 'You probably know the form.'

Roger nodded. 'I've heard that's how it happens. It's time the law was changed, if you ask me.' He regarded Philip thoughtfully. 'You're a decent chap, Philip, to be willing to go through all that to spare my daughter's name. I appreciate it.'

'Thank you, sir.'

'And of course, although it's looking well into the future, you know you won't be able to marry Stella in church. The Church of England will never countenance remarrying divorcees.'

'No, I know it will have to be in a registry office. Unfortunately, Stella in particular will find that hard.' He paused. 'One day the Church will relent, but not soon enough for Stella and me.'

'I'm not sure you're right about that. It certainly won't be in my lifetime.' He puffed on his pipe for a few minutes, then said, 'I'd really like to see Stella and the little chap. Would it be very wrong of me to call on them, Philip? Obviously, without my wife's knowledge.'

Philip nodded. 'I'm sure Stella would be pleased to see you. She's very fond of you, you know.'

Roger gave a pleased smile. 'I'll pop along sometime. I guess there's no immediate hurry. I'd like to set up some kind of a trust for my grandson, with her agreement of course. And I'd like to think we'll be able to keep in touch. But that's all well into the future.' He stood up and shook Philip's hand. 'I wish you well, my boy, especially when you confront my daughter. She can be as bad as her mother when things don't go her way.'

'Oh, I don't think she'll object, sir. In fact, she'll probably be overjoyed to be rid of me.'

But in that he was quite mistaken.

Twenty-Five

They were sitting at the breakfast table the next morning; it was the first opportunity Philip had had to speak to Rosalie as the previous evening she hadn't returned home until late. He regarded her thoughtfully. She was wearing an orange-and-purple housecoat with frills at the neck and cuffs that might have looked attractive on a very young girl but certainly did nothing for a woman approaching thirty. Her hair, still cut in a boyish bob, hadn't seen a brush and stood up in spikes, just as she'd rolled out of bed, and her face still bore liberal traces of last night's make-up. Philip felt a fleeting sense of relief that he was no longer forced to wake up beside her; it was bad enough facing her over the breakfast table.

'God, I feel awful!' she said, propping her head on her hand.

'Yes, you look it.' He pushed the coffee pot over to her.

'There's no need to rub it in.' She shook her head at the coffee pot. 'I've already had two.'

'Well, have another. And make sure it's good and black because I've got something important to say to you.' He paused. 'I'm thinking of buying myself a new car.'

'Oh, yes?' She yawned. 'What am I supposed to do, put the flags out?' Suddenly the implication of his words sank in and she perked up. 'Ooh, goody! Does that mean I can have Tin Lizzie?' She rubbed her hands together. 'My own car! That'll make the girls at the club jealous. When can I have it?'

'As soon as you agree to a divorce.'

'What?' She nearly dropped her coffee cup.

'You heard perfectly well what I said, but I'll say it again. I want you to divorce me. More coffee?'

'No, I don't want more bloody coffee. And you're not going to bribe a divorce out of me with Tin Lizzie, either.'

'Please don't swear, Rosalie. Let's at least talk about this in a civilized manner.'

'I'll swear if I bloody well like. And if you think I'm going to give you a divorce just as you're getting a name for yourself and earning big bucks, you've got another think coming. I'm quite looking forward to swanning around, the long-suffering wife of the eminent artist who was crippled in the war. And don't think I don't know you're selling your horrible war pictures. I was here when that Gerald, or whatever his name is, came yesterday and took them. He told me they were worth a fortune. He took some others, too; said he could sell as many as you could paint. Quite excited, he was.' She laughed, but it held no humour. 'If you think I'm going to miss out on that, you're out of your mind.' She fished in her bag for a cigarette. 'So we'll just forget about divorce, shall we, and continue with our lives of private domestic discord?' She blew smoke across the table into his face.

'I was asking *you* to divorce *me*,' he said quietly, fanning it away with his hand. 'But, God knows, Rosalie, I've got more than enough evidence to divorce you.'

'You've got no proof of any indiscretion on my part,' she said haughtily.

'No? Well, apart from what's going on now with God knows which Tom, Dick or Harry, what about your exploits when I was away fighting for my country? What about your affair with Captain Fox? And what about the abortion he paid for so his wife – never mind your husband – should never know?' He was white with rage and frustration.

She paled, staring at him with her cigarette halfway to her lips. 'How did you know about that? You never told me you knew.' Her voice was barely above a whisper.

'I was waiting for you to tell me, but you never did,' he said with a shrug. 'After a while I ceased to care. In fact, I only found out by the merest chance. Fox was in my platoon. He was badly injured and he told me there was something he needed to ask me. I thought he was dying, so I listened as he told me he'd had a "bit of a fling", as he called it, with a girl he'd met at a dance. And when she told him she was pregnant, he'd paid for her to have an abortion because he was already married. He'd never seen the girl since, didn't even know if the abortion was successful. But he'd been riddled with guilt ever since and asked me if I thought he should confess his infidelity to his wife. He said he only embarked on the affair because he was missing her so much. So I told him to go home and stay faithful to his wife if he loved her and to forget about the girl. He said he did love her, very much. Then he took a snapshot out of his pocket, looked at it for a minute, showed it to me, and then tore it up, saying it had really been nothing more than a stupid fling and he didn't know why he'd bothered to keep the photo.' He spread his hands and went on, with more than a trace of bitterness, 'Of course I never told him he'd torn up a snapshot of my wife. That would have been too cruel. And then he died, just two days later. Understandably, I never forgot it.'

'Well, whether it's true or not – and I'm admitting nothing – the man's dead now, so you can't prove anything,' she said, jabbing her half-smoked cigarette into the ashtray on the table.

He gave another shrug. 'No matter. It's all in the past and not relevant. As I've already said, I'm prepared to let you divorce me, a sordid business though it will have to be.'

'And I've already told you that I won't do that,' she said smugly. 'So we're stuck where we've always been, aren't we, darling?' She wriggled her shoulders and blew him a kiss across the table. 'I'm quite looking forward to being the wife of a famous artist.' Then a sudden thought occurred to her and she frowned. 'But why this sudden urge for a divorce?'

'Because I want to marry Stella,' he replied bluntly.

Her eyebrows shot up. 'Oh, I see. You've obviously run her to ground, then. But does she want to marry you? And does she realize what she'd be taking on if she did?'

'Yes, to both those questions, not that it's any of your business.'

'Well, I'm not going to give her the satisfaction of basking in your reflected glory. That's *my* privilege, and I'm hanging on to it.'

'I'll sue you for divorce, Rosalie, if you won't sue me,' he warned.

'You wouldn't be such a cad. You're too much of a gentleman,' she said confidently, lighting another cigarette. 'In any case, you've no grounds. As I pointed out a minute ago, the only person who could corroborate your story is dead.'

'I'm sure there are men at your club. That's a den of iniquity, if ever there was one.'

'That's only what you think. You'd never be able to prove anything.' She lit another cigarette.

He sighed heavily. 'You're right, I probably couldn't. They'd all clam up like oysters. But I ask you again, Rosalie. I'm pleading with you to divorce me.'

She shook her head, smug in the knowledge that she had the upper hand. 'You're my husband, Phil. For better, for worse; for richer, for poorer. If I remember aright that's what the marriage service says. Well, I've had the worse bit, and I'm damned if I'm going to miss out on the richer.'

'I'll make you an allowance,' he offered. 'A generous one.'

'Nope. I want to be by your side when you're fêted and cosseted. I want to be known as the wife of the famous artist.'

He got up from his chair and reached for his sticks. 'I can see it's no good arguing with you. We'll talk later.'

'Talk as much as you like. I shan't change my mind!' was her parting shot.

Twenty-Six

Henry brought the car round and they drove in silence the short distance to Emma's house. He could see Philip was in a black mood, but he knew better than to ask questions. Instead, he left him at the door, saying he had things to do and would call back in a couple of hours if that suited.

Philip gave him a curt nod and went inside the cottage.

Stella had just finished bathing and feeding Jonathan, and the whole place smelled deliciously of Pears soap and talcum powder. Her face lit up when she saw Philip and she relinquished the baby to Mary, who was waiting to take him for a walk, and got to her feet so that Philip could take her in his arms.

'What's the matter, darling?' she asked, when she had been thoroughly kissed. 'I can tell there's something wrong. What is it? Did you tell Roger about us and did he object?'

'No, Roger's not the problem, in fact he's quite delighted.' He moved away and sat down in Arthur's armchair. 'No, it's Rosalie. She refuses point blank to divorce me.' He looked up. 'I know what you're going to say, Stella, I've got plenty of grounds to divorce her; but I couldn't do it. Anyway, I've got no real proof, nothing that would stand up in court. Nothing that wouldn't be denied by all her so-called friends.' He shook his head. 'She's got me over a barrel. She won't sue me for divorce and I can't sue her. So, I'm sorry – no, that's not strong enough – I'm absolutely devastated, Stella, my darling, I can't marry you.' When he looked at her his eyes were bleak.

She sat down opposite him. Today she hadn't coiled her hair up into its knot on top of her head but had let it hang down to her shoulders, making her look young and vulnerable. The sight of it twisted his heart.

'Maybe I could talk to her,' Stella said thoughtfully. 'She told me something once . . .'

'If it's about the abortion she had, I tried that,' he cut in.

Her eyebrows shot up. 'You knew?'

He nodded. 'Yes, I knew. But the man's dead, so there's no proof, and naturally Rosalie will deny it.'

They were both silent for a long time, then Stella said quietly, 'I talked to Emma for a long time last night about her plans. She told me that she and Henry often talk things over, and when her year of mourning for Arthur is up they'll be married. She told me Henry has managed to save quite a bit, and they hope to move to the south coast and have a little private hotel or boarding house that they can run together. She said that of course they can't do anything until they're married, and that won't be for another six months, maybe longer. And I thought, what a waste of time. Two people who have obviously been in love for years have to wait before they can be married because convention dictates she must have a year of mourning for a husband who ill-treated her. Why? Why should they have to waste precious time they could be spending together because of convention? It seems crazy to me. I think they should marry and to hell with convention.'

'I had plans, too.' Philip said, who had been only half listening. 'I was going to ask Ben Gerard if he or Oscar Hillyard knew of any places we could rent or buy down in the west country. They've got their ear to the ground regarding these things because the light's supposed to be particularly good for painting in Cornwall and painters sometimes go and stay there for a while. There are always empty properties in one or other of the villages; in fact, I believe Oscar owns a place down there. In St Ives, I think.'

'If there's nothing in the west country, what about France? Painters often go to live in France, don't they?' she asked. She slid down to the floor so that she could sit at his feet.

He was quiet for a long time. Then he said, 'Yes, maybe

that's what I should do, go away and live in France. Make a new life for myself, since I can't have the one I want.' He shook his head. 'I don't know, Stella. I don't know whether I could do it.' He stroked her hair. 'I had such plans for us, darling. How can I just go away and never see you again?'

She caught his hand and kissed the palm. 'I wasn't suggesting you should, Phil,' she said, smiling. 'In fact, if you go without me I shall follow you.'

He turned her face up so that he could look at her. 'But I can't marry you, Stella,' he said urgently. 'I've already told you that.'

'I know.' She giggled. 'I'll have to be your . . .'

'No.' Shocked, he put his hand over her mouth before she could say the word. 'Do you know what you're suggesting, Stella? I've just told you Rosalie refuses to divorce me.'

'Mm, I know. Shocking, isn't it?' She giggled again.

He frowned. 'You're saying you're prepared to risk your name . . .' He shook his head. 'I don't think you realize what you're saying, Stella. I don't think I can let you do that.'

'If we don't want to be parted, we don't have a choice, do we, Phil?' she said, becoming serious. 'Look, we can go and live in Cornwall or France, or wherever we choose, as Mr and Mrs Brown, or Smith, or Jones – or whatever we like to call ourselves – with our son, Jonathan. And when Major Philip Anderson needs to be in London or somewhere for an exhibition of his paintings, I'll smarten myself up and come with you as your nurse.'

'People will soon see through that.'

'That's their problem, not ours.'

'What about Rosalie? She's quite determined to play the part of dutiful wife at exhibitions, you know. You might come face to face with her.' He shook his head. 'Oh, my love, I don't think I could put you through all that.'

'Then would you rather I simply went away and never saw you again?' Seeing the stricken look that crossed his face, she got to her feet and handed him his sticks, smiling happily. 'I thought not. And don't worry, I know it won't be easy, but we'll deal with Rosalie when the time comes, which is not yet. So, come on, let's go and see Ben Gerard. Together.' She looked out of the window. 'I can see the car's still there, but if Henry's busy I'll drive.' She giggled. 'That's something else I can do: I can be your chauffeur.'

'You'd do all this? For me?' he asked as he struggled to his feet, as if he still couldn't believe it.

'And more,' she said, giving him a peck on the cheek. 'And it's not just for you, it's for me, too, Phil. I want to have a hand in choosing where we're going to live and bring up our children.' She paused. 'At least, now we don't have to wait for a divorce to come through before we begin our lives together, do we? So you could say Rosalie's doing us a good turn.' She pinched her lip. 'I wonder if we can persuade Mary to come and live with us, once we're settled. We'll need a nursemaid . . .'

'Stella Brown, or Jones, or whatever, you're incorrigible!' he said, giving her a hug. 'But first things first, my darling. Let's go and see Ben.'

CPSIA information can be obtained at www.ICGtesting.com
Printed in the USA
BVOW07*1822091113

335553BV00002B/2/P

SPYING with MAPS

SPYING with MAPS

SURVEILLANCE TECHNOLOGIES AND
THE FUTURE OF PRIVACY

Mark Monmonier

THE UNIVERSITY OF CHICAGO PRESS
CHICAGO AND LONDON

Mark Monmonier is Distinguished Professor of Geography at Syracuse University. He is the author of numerous books, most recently *Air Apparent: How Meteorologists Learned to Map, Predict, and Dramatize Weather* and *Bushmanders and Bullwinkles: How Politicians Manipulate Electronic Maps and Census Data to Win Elections*, both published by the University of Chicago Press.

The University of Chicago Press, Chicago 60637
The University of Chicago Press, Ltd., London
© 2002 by The University of Chicago
All rights reserved. Published 2002
Printed in the United States of America

11 10 09 08 07 06 05 04 03 02   1 2 3 4 5

ISBN: 0-226-53427-8 (cloth)

Library of Congress Cataloging-in-Publication Data

Monmonier, Mark S.
    Spying with maps : surveillance technologies and the future of privacy
/ Mark Monmonier.
        p.   cm.
    Includes bibliographical references and index.
    ISBN 0-226-53427-8 (cloth : alk. paper)
    1. Electronic surveillance.   2. Remote sensing.   3. Privacy, Right of.
I. Title.
TK7882.E2 M65 2002
621.389′28—dc21

                                                    2002018124

♾ The paper used in this publication meets the minimum requirements of
the American National Standard for Information Sciences—Permanence of
Paper for Printed Library Materials, ANSI Z39.48-1992.

For Will and Ruby Miller, geographers extraordinaire

Contents

Acknowledgments

In writing this book, I benefited from the insights of Margot Ackley and Doug van de Kamp, NOAA Forecast Systems Laboratory, Boulder, Colorado; Harry Carlson, Department of Public Works, Syracuse, New York; Jerry Dobson, Oak Ridge National Laboratory, Oak Ridge, Tennessee; Gary Hufford, National Weather Service, Alaska Region, Anchorage, Alaska; David Miller, Texas Department of Transportation, Amarillo District; Paul G. Richards, Mellon Professor of Natural Science, Lamont-Doherty Earth Observatory, Columbia University; and Paul L. Robinson, Oklahoma State Bureau of Narcotics and Dangerous Drugs Control. No less useful was the enthusiastic probing of the students in my fall 2000 seminar: Christian Axsiom, Anna Dolmatch, Tracy Edwards, Lillian Jeng, Hilary McLeod, Rich van Deusen, and Tom Whitfield. For illustrations or data I am also grateful to Nancy Adams, Eastman Kodak Company;

Andrew Etkind, Garmin International; Keith Harries, Department of Geography, University of Maryland, Baltimore County; Jolene Hernon, National Institute of Justice; Amy L. King, Geographic Information Science and Technology Program, Oak Ridge National Laboratory; Eric Lund, Veris Technologies, Salinas, Kansas; Lloyd Novick, Commissioner of Health, Onondaga County, New York; and John R. Schott, Remote Sensing and Imaging Laboratory, Rochester Institute of Technology. A one-semester research leave from Syracuse University's Maxwell School of Citizenship and Public Affairs provided valuable time to read, think, and ask questions. At Syracuse University, Becky Carlson and Joe Stoll assisted with scanning and fonts.

My longstanding relationship with the University of Chicago Press is a priceless asset. Penny Kaiserlian, my longtime editor and now director of the University Press of Virginia, was an early backer of the project, and Christie Henry, my current editor, offered encouragement and insightful suggestions. External readers Marc Armstrong, Harlan Onsrud, and Nancy Obermeyer made helpful comments on the penultimate draft; Jenni Fry dealt diligently with ephemeral URLs and other glitches in the manuscript; and Renate Gokl and Russell Harper guided the book through production. I also value the continuing support of Alice Bennett, Mike Brehm, Paula Duffy, Erin Hogan, and Carol Kasper. And at Waldorf Parkway, there's Marge, whose patience I've yet to exhaust. As country musicians revel in saying: Thank you, all.

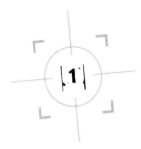

Maps That Watch

Privacy and *mapping* are two words that rarely share the
same sentence. After all, what do most of us have to hide
that anyone would want to map? But toward the end of the
last century, cartographers added privacy to a growing list of
policy issues that includes copyright, liability, and public access. Mapping, it turns out, can reveal quite a bit about what
we do and who we are. I say *mapping,* rather than *maps,* because cartography is not limited to static maps printed on
paper or displayed on computer screens. In the new cartographies of surveillance, the maps one looks at are less important than the spatial data systems that store and integrate
facts about where we live and work. Location is a powerful
key for relating disparate databanks and unearthing information about possessions, spending habits, and an assort-

ment of behaviors and preferences, real or imagined. What's more, these electronic maps are becoming increasingly detailed and timely, if not more reliable. What gets into the system as well as who can use the data and for what purposes makes privacy in mapping a key concern of anyone who fills out surveys, owns a home, or registers a car or firearm.

I could write this book to frighten readers, but I won't. However odious the threat of rampant snooping or a new holocaust, fear founded on mere possibility is less helpful than wariness grounded in understanding. Informed skepticism about cartographic surveillance should encourage the vigorous yet vigilant application of this ambiguous technology that, like the bulldozer and the chemical plant, can—if controlled—do far more good than harm. If this ambiguity is disconcerting, get used to it. A jeremiad that capitulates to gloom and doom would be no better than an equally naïve celebration of trouble-free progress.

A Luddite rant would also ignore some fascinating stories of fortuitous discoveries and unintended consequences. As the following chapters reveal, there are multiple cartographies of surveillance, some concerned primarily with integrating databases, some involving satellite imagery or satellite-based location tracking, and some narrowly focused on specific needs, like growing crops or controlling crime. Although all applications examined here use monitoring to control human behavior—that's the definition of *surveillance* —the behaviors in question range from the predations of war and crime to economic decisions about when to plant and where to spread fertilizer. Big Brother is doing most of the watching, at least for now, but corporations, local governments, and other Little Brothers are quickly getting involved.

If you don't see the danger, think integration. The threat to personal privacy lies mainly in the imminent ease of linking a large number of databases rapidly and reliably in order to track shipments, pollutants, lost children, potential terrorists, campaign contributions, or anyone walking around with a cell phone. An invasive system would not only monitor location in real time but also store the data indefinitely to reconstruct an individual's movements during, for example, the weeks before the attacks on the World Trade Center and the Pentagon. Or on that embarrassing day you

_____. Given your name, a really intelligent surveillance system could even fill in the blank. Much depends, of course, on who's in charge, us or them, and on who "them" is. A police state could exploit geographic technology to round up dissidents—imagine the Nazi SS with a GeoSurveillance Corps. By contrast, a capitalist marketer can exploit locational data by making a cleverly tailored pitch at a time and place when you're most receptive. Control is control whether it's blatant or subtle.

+ + +

Surveillance cartography exploits diverse technologies, the most basic of which is the geographic information system, or GIS, defined as a computerized system (naturally) for storing, retrieving, analyzing, and displaying geographic data. This Spartan definition covers a variety of approaches, including overlay analysis and address matching. Around 1990 the GIS replaced the paper map as the primary medium of map analysis, and government mapping agencies like the U.S. Geological Survey shifted their focus from making maps to compiling electronic data. This change was equally apparent in higher education after GIS replaced traditional cartography as the most popular techniques course for geography majors, and disciplines like forestry and urban planning began to offer their own GIS courses.

Overlay analysis is a straightforward concept, easily visualized as a cartographic sandwich with two or more layers called coverages. As figure 1.1 shows, each coverage represents a separate topic or landscape feature, such as forest cover or soil acidity. Because the layers share a common geographic framework, the user can readily retrieve data for a particular point or define areas with a particular combination of characteristics. Overlay analysis is especially useful in exploring associations between environmental factors and in assessing the suitability of land for development.

A related GIS operation is buffering, described in figure 1.2. Planners wary of adverse effects on nearby residents or wildlife look closely at buffer zones around building sites, proposed landfills, and transportation corridors. Buffering is also helpful to emergency management officials, who need to delineate hazard zones such as those around active faults, toxic waste dumps, chlorine tanks that

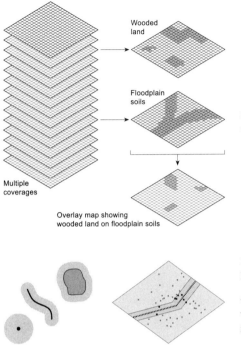

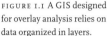

Wooded
land

Floodplain
soils

FIGURE 1.1 A GIS designed
for overlay analysis relies on
data organized in layers.

Multiple
coverages

Overlay map showing
wooded land on floodplain soils

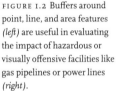

FIGURE 1.2 Buffers around
point, line, and area features
(left) are useful in evaluating
the impact of hazardous or
visually offensive facilities like
gas pipelines or power lines
(right).

might rupture, and railroads and pipelines carrying hazardous materials. To explore the threat of a particularly risky shipment, an analyst defines a hazard zone around the proposed route and overlays this buffer on a detailed population map. A more advanced form of buffering called dispersion modeling can track airborne releases of radiation or lethal gasses and predict the advance of groundwater plumes fed by leaky underground storage tanks.

A more potentially invasive kind of GIS deals with street addresses, road networks, and census data. An application familiar to most Internet users is the Web site that converts an address into a detailed neighborhood map like the example in figure 1.3. The process depends upon a massive database that links addresses like "302 Waldorf Parkway" to the geographic coordinates of intersections at opposite ends of the block. Names of the city and state expedite the search by differentiating this Waldorf Parkway from all the other Waldorf Parkways in the country. The database contains each block's low and high addresses, which the GIS uses to find the specific block. If the even-numbered addresses range from 300 to 312, the lot at 302 is close to the block's low end. Assuming all the lots are equally wide and numbered sequentially, the GIS can easily calculate 302's location between the intersections and plot its position on the correct side of the street. The GIS then fleshes out the map by adding other streets in the vicinity. Knowing where you live is a starting point for probing your environment and interactions.

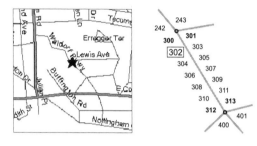

FIGURE 1.3 Online mapping services such as MapsOnUs.com and MapQuest.com plot neighborhood street maps with legible but jaggy labels *(left)* and use address ranges on opposite sides of the street to locate specific homes and businesses *(right)*.

Some address-to-map Web sites also find the shortest route to another address and print out an itinerary. Because the computer knows which streets converge at each intersection, it can keep track of distances, construct and compare trial routings, and compile a list of driving directions like "Go 3.4 miles to State Highway 17, turn left onto Broad Street, and continue 0.6 miles to Main Street." A hybrid itinerary supplements these verbal instructions with small maps of the area around each turning point. Given accurate data, the system can also provide exit numbers for expressways, avoid sending motorists the wrong way down one-way streets, offer a choice between the shortest and the quickest routes, and show motels, gasoline stations, and fast-food restaurants. A particularly rich database can help motorists avoid high-crime neighborhoods and dangerous highways. Some Web sites also offer maps describing recently reported accidents and their effect on traffic—a genre of surveillance cartography I examine in chapter 6.

The prominence of commercial address-to-map Web sites supported by chain restaurants and other advertisers obscures the technology's origin as a tool for tabulating census returns. In the late 1960s, the U.S. Bureau of the Census devised a coding scheme now called TIGER (for topologically integrated geographically encoded referencing) to automatically compile block-level counts for urban areas where households received a mail-back questionnaire. The process is straightforward. An optical scanner converts each completed questionnaire to an electronic record so that a computer can match the address with the corresponding block and add the household's responses to the running tallies for various categories of age, race, and sex. Each block has a unique number as well as separate counters for each category. For example, if a home is in block 517 and its only occupants are a forty-year-old white female and an eight-year-old white male, the computer adds two each to block 517's counters for "all persons" and "white persons," and one each to the counters for "adult white females" and "white males under eighteen." Block counts are essential for congressional redistricting because the federal courts tolerate only small differences in population.

TIGER files also help retailers send catalogs and coupons to receptive homes. Ever wonder why a move to a better neighborhood triggers a different mix of junk mail? It's probably because TIGER-based address matching indicates that you're now in a more affluent census tract with a different demographic profile. Data for census tracts, which contain about four thousand persons and perhaps twenty blocks or more, include a richer variety of socioeconomic indicators than block-level data, based on the "short-form" questions the government asks all households. Age and family structure are equally relevant. If many of your new neighbors are in their fifties or sixties, ads pitching condos in Florida and long-term care insurance will be common. If most area families have young children, expect mailings that tout toys and summer camps. And direct-mail retailers who use geospatial technology to compile their own censuses from sales records can easily send you a catalog when a neighbor places an order.

Illegal aliens as well as citizens worried about privacy have little to fear from the Census Bureau. By law, the bureau cannot divulge information about individuals, even to other government agencies, and must keep their questionnaires confidential for one hundred years, after which a household's responses are of interest only to historians and amateur genealogists ferreting out ancestors. Neighborhoods are a different matter: although block-level data are comparatively innocuous tabulations pigeonholed by age, sex, race, Hispanic origin, home ownership, and residents' relationship to the household, the bureau publishes increasingly rich categorical data for block groups, census tracts, cities and towns, counties, and states. Planners and policymakers depend on these data, as do companies seeking advantageous locations for stores and restaurants. But if an area's population is so small or an individual's circumstances so unique that summary statistics might reveal sensitive information such as the income of a particular person or household, census officials suppress the summary statistics at the tract or town level. And to promote consistency, the Census Bureau has developed software that can scan tabulated data and identify numbers that, if released, would violate the nondisclosure rule. Computer-assisted enforcement of the bureau's privacy restrictions is a wise strategy that saves time and avoids charges of favoritism or malice.

Criminal records are another matter. Some states disclose the addresses of convicted sex offenders, often to the chagrin of individuals who pose little threat to the community. Although fear of rapists and child molesters is understandable, some registries include persons whose only crime is public urination. Notification practices also vary. For example, New York, which used to release information only through a pay-per-inquiry 900-number telephone service, started posting addresses and photographs of high-risk offenders on the Internet in mid-2000. Like Web sites maintained by Arizona, North Carolina, and several other states, the New York State Sex Offender Registry allows searching by name, county, or ZIP code. Intended to warn parents about pedophiles in the neighborhood, sex-offender registries depend upon self-reporting and are often error-ridden and incomplete. In addition to questioning the reliability of databases and the value of community notification, civil liberties advocates reject the posting of maps and addresses as an invasion of privacy and a barbaric form of shaming.

Less controversial are the property-tax assessment registers with which neighbors and real estate agents can find out how much you paid for your house and how many rooms it has. In states that base property taxes on fair market value, the local assessor must disclose recent sale prices and other information useful in challenging as-

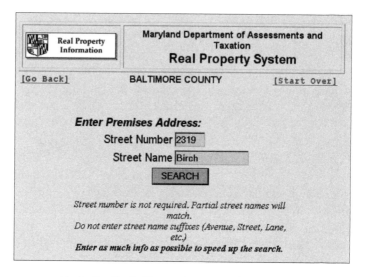

FIGURE 1.4 Maryland's online Real Property System (www.dat.state.md.us/sdatweb/) invites home buyers, sellers, and residents upset about their assessments to search the database by address.

sessments ostensibly out of line with those for neighboring properties. Although publicly available assessment records are not new, a search typically required a visit to the assessor's office, which files its data by lot number, not address. Maryland and several other states now offer assessment data online by street address at a GIS-supported Web site (fig. 1.4). Several years ago, when I sold my dad's house outside Baltimore, the Maryland Department of Assessments and Taxation's online search system was especially helpful in setting an appropriate asking price. An online map showing neighboring properties even told me which property numbers to enter for other lots in the neighborhood. With a sense of selling prices in the area, I was better able to deal with real estate agents and potential buyers.

Address data also warn of explosives and toxic chemicals in your town or neighborhood. Thanks to the Emergency Planning and Community Right-to-Know Act, signed into law two years after the 1984 chemical plant disaster in Bhopal, India, industries must report the storage of dangerous materials to local officials responsible for emergency planning. The act makes this information available to individuals and environmental groups, which have started to map hazards and monitor illness. Like pedophiles, polluters lose privacy when government reveals their location.

+   +   +

When dealing with agriculture, vegetation, and wetlands, geographic information systems typically treat the earth as a grid of tiny picture elements, or pixels, as in figure 1.1. Because grid cells are organized in rows similar to the parallel scan lines, or raster format, of a television screen, grid data are called raster data. By contrast, lists of points representing streets and boundaries (fig. 1.5) are called vector data because mathematicians refer to the short straight-line segments between successive points as vectors. In general, vector data are efficient for representing spot locations, streets, and census-tract boundaries, whereas raster data are tailored to analyzing soil, vegetation, and other phenomena that more or less cover the surface of an area and can be sampled from satellites. Lists of points help the computer draw routes and estimate driving distances, while grid data make it easy to compare layers or check conditions at neighboring cells.

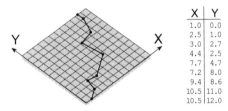

X	Y
1.0	0.0
2.5	1.0
3.0	2.7
4.4	2.5
7.7	4.7
7.2	8.0
9.4	8.6
10.5	11.0
10.5	12.0

FIGURE 1.5 Vector data represent roads, boundaries, and other linear features as lists of point coordinates. The number of points and the precision of the coordinates limit detail.

As the jig-jag streets in figure 1.3 attest, vector data sometimes cut corners quite literally by showing curved features as jaggy lines. This loss of detail is understandable for simple address maps because the substantially larger database required for more aesthetically pleasing plots would be cumbersome to process and costly to maintain. Surveyors and civil engineers find these maps useless, except perhaps for visiting a job site. Highway plans need many more points as well as more precise and reliable coordinates.

Raster data have a similar trade-off: very small pixels result in a relatively large file, and vice versa. Whether improved ground resolution is worthwhile depends on the type of analysis and its computational complexity. Satellite data with pixels 2 meters to a side can be extraordinarily valuable in urban planning and military intelligence, but the same ground resolution would give meteorologists a massive computational headache.

+   +   +

Pixel size is especially important in *remote sensing,* an information technology for taking pictures of the ground from an aircraft or a satellite. Intelligence analysts want the smallest pixel possible in order to track missiles and troop movements as well as monitor more insidious threats like chemical, biological, and nuclear weapons. Spy satellites became a top priority during the Cold War, and Congress generously supported remote sensing. University researchers with government grants carried out basic research, while analysts with security clearances pored over images from the CIA's top-secret Corona satellites at the agency's clandestine National Reconnaissance Office (NRO). Promising but hardly adequate photographs from the first successful Corona mission, launched in 1959, had a ground resolution of 12 meters (40 ft.). Within eight years, a massive research and development effort had refined the pixel down to an impressive 1.5 meters (5 ft.). By contrast, civilian earth scientists had to wait until 1972 for NASA's Landsat-1 and be content with 79-meter imagery. With defense dollars driving development, intelligence satellites have always taken sharper pictures than their civilian counterparts.

The history of remote sensing during the Cold War reads like a Cinderella story in which civilian applications enjoyed the occasional hand-me-down, while only their military stepsisters were invited to the ball. As Corona demonstrated, high-resolution remote sensing was technologically feasible in 1972, but defense officials were reluctant to share classified technology that might provoke an angry Third World reaction to overhead snooping. Although Landsat-4, launched in 1982, impressed scientists with its 30-meter resolution, American civilian remote sensing lost face in 1986, when a French company, Spot Image, began selling 10-meter imagery, and American energy companies, engineering firms, and local governments became eager customers.

Defense restrictions eased markedly in the 1990s. With the Cold War over, Russia's space agency began selling 2-meter imagery on the open market and even engaged a Maryland firm to market its wares in the United States. The firm's pitch apparently impressed the U.S. Air Force, reported in 1994 as pondering a major purchase. According to the trade journal *Aviation Week and Space Technology*, U.S. intelligence imagery was too detailed for Air Force needs, and the Russians offered a better combination of resolution and price than any other source. America recovered its prominence in civilian satellite surveillance in 1999, when Space Imaging, a Colorado company, launched Ikonos-2 and offered to sell or lease 1-meter imagery to all comers, domestic or foreign. Almost all, that is—Washington strongly discourages the sale of high-resolution satellite imagery of Israel, and during the 2001 Middle Eastern campaign, the government thwarted enemy and media hopes by buying exclusive rights to Ikonos imagery of Afghanistan.

If you're a small state surrounded by hostile neighbors, 1-meter satellite imagery doesn't afford much privacy. Iraq and Syria would pay millions to learn where to invade or bomb, or how best to repel an Israeli attack. But as the Ikonos snapshot of the Washington monument in figure 1.6 illustrates, an eye in space records more than targets and fortifications. Roads and buildings are especially obvious, but it's also easy to identify trees, vehicles, and pathways. And the local assessor can readily recognize a new swimming pool in your backyard. Intelligence satellites have even sharper eyes: various estimates suggest that pictures from Corona's most advanced successors have a resolution of roughly 3 inches.

High-resolution snapshots from space are not the only kind of overhead surveillance. Aircraft flying at a few thousand feet capture comparable detail with less sophisticated cameras to the delight of thrifty mapmakers, planners, and civil engineers, who rely largely on conventional aerial photos much like those shot in the 1930s. And airplanes as well as satellites can carry a wide variety of sensors, ranging from optical cameras with photographic film to the sophisticated synthetic aperture radar system with which the space shuttle *Endeavor* mapped most of the world's terrain in little more than a week. As chapters 2 and 3 discuss, electronic imaging systems address a broad and growing array of military and commercial needs.

FIGURE 1.6 Portion of first Ikonos image of Washington, D.C. The Washington Monument is at the lower left, and the longer, darker shape is the monument's shadow. Deciduous trees were still in full foliage when Ikonos-2 took this 1-meter image on September 30, 1999. For additional examples and further details, see the Space Imaging Web site (www.spaceimaging.com). Courtesy of Space Imaging.

A pivotal advance was the infrared scanner, sensitive to light our eyes can't see yet able to distinguish camouflage from natural vegetation as well as pinpoint distressed crops. In the 1970s, thermal scanners extended human vision still further by measuring heat loss and soil moisture. Advances in image processing software help researchers and intelligence analysts classify vegetation and search for suspicious objects or operations, such as missile launchers or indoor marijuana plantations. Change detection, an important aspect of cartographic surveillance, uses the overlay techniques of GIS to compare imagery for different dates.

+   +   +

Remote sensing and GIS rely heavily on a third, much newer electronic technology, the global positioning system, or GPS. Developed by the Defense Department to help troops and missiles find themselves on maps, GPS is an efficient technique for entering new information—field observations as well as remotely sensed data—into a GIS. A classic example of post–Cold War technological trickledown, the military's constellation of GPS satellites now supports a host of civilian applications, including boundary surveys and highway navigation. In archeology, geology, and soil science, for instance, reliable, low-cost GPS receivers have become a standard tool for collecting and mapping field data. And in the consumer electronics market, GPS is a promising enhancement to the personal computer, the personal digital assistant (like the Palm handheld), and the car radio. Once an expensive option for car buyers, the dashboard navigation system will no doubt replicate the success of the FM radio and the CD player and make road maps as we know them as obsolete as 8-track tapes and 45 rpm records.

Equally adept at tracking vehicles, employees, adolescents, and convicted criminals, GPS is very much a surveillance technology, with credible threats to personal privacy. Just ask the former clients of Acme Rent-a-Car, a Connecticut firm that tracked its vehicles by satellite and fined customers for exceeding 79 MPH.

GPS calculates location by comparing time signals from several satellites, each with a direct line of sight to the receiver. Each satellite broadcasts a signal traveling at the speed of light but requiring a measurable time to reach the ground. At a velocity of 186,000 miles per second, the signal takes 0.06774 seconds to reach a GPS receiver directly beneath a satellite at an altitude of 12,600 miles, and a bit longer to cover measurably greater distances to points elsewhere within the satellite's footprint. Although the satellites are moving, the receiver can estimate the satellite's location at the time of transmission. Because the signal encodes the time at which it was broadcast, the receiver can determine the elapsed time from satellite to ground, convert this time to a distance, and compute a circle representing all locations on the surface that far from the satellite. Signals from other satellites yield additional circles, which intersect at the receiver's location (fig. 1.7). And because the triangulation is three-dimensional, the GPS estimates elevation as well as latitude and longitude.

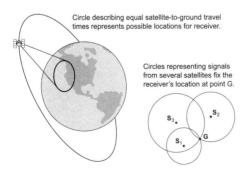

Circle describing equal satellite-to-ground travel times represents possible locations for receiver.

Circles representing signals from several satellites fix the receiver's location at point G.

S_3 S_2

S_1 G

FIGURE 1.7 GPS uses three-dimensional triangulation based on intersecting circles describing travel time from space to ground for signals from several satellites. Each circle describes a range of locations equidistant from one of the satellites, and the circles' point of intersection represents the receiver's location.

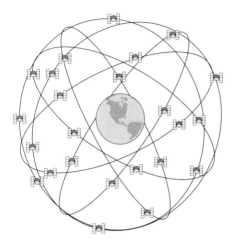

FIGURE I.8 The GPS constellation consists of twenty-four satellites in six orbital planes spaced evenly, 60 degrees apart, and inclined 55 degrees above the plane of the equator. In turn, the four satellites in each plane are evenly spaced in a circular orbit with an altitude of 20,200 kilometers (12,600 stat. mi., or 10,900 naut. mi.). The pattern is easily predictable, with each satellite circling the earth twice a day and tracing the same ground track across the earth below every 11 hours, 58 minutes. Adapted from *NAVSTAR GPS User Equipment Introduction*, public release version (Alexandria, Va.: U.S. Coast Guard Navigation Center, September 1996): p. 1-3, fig. 1-2.

Although GPS receivers can compute location on the fly, accuracy improves when a stationary receiver takes multiple readings, from different positions along each orbit. Because it's also helpful to integrate signals from more than three satellites—more signals mean less uncertainty—the Air Force, which runs the system, maintains a constellation of twenty-four satellites (fig. 1.8), at least four of which should be visible at any time from any place on earth.

Because taxpayers paid over $10 billion to build the GPS system, letting them reap some of its benefits is good politics. And granting equal access to users worldwide creates goodwill as well as an overseas market for American electronics. But goodwill has too high a price, the Defense Department argued, when enemies and allies have equal access. So the White House compromised with a policy of deliberate blurring called Selective Availability (SA). Under a two-tiered system of signals, only military users received all the information needed to estimate location with great precision. And because an enemy might retaliate electronically, the Precise Positioning Service (PPS) gave soldiers and GPS-guided cruise missiles a signal that was less readily jammed than the Standard Positioning Service (SPS), designed for nonmilitary users. Thus, a military receiver could nearly instantly estimate horizontal location to within about 10 meters, while its civilian counterpart might be off by 100 meters or more.

Selective Availability proved a costly and needless inconvenience. During the 1991 Gulf War and the 1994 Haiti campaign, for example, a shortage of the more expensive PPS receivers forced the military to cut down the error injected into the SPS signal. What's more, civilian users willing to wait a bit or link to a precisely located ground station could readily reduce uncertainty to 1 meter, which is sufficiently accurate for drivers and pedestrians with electronic street maps (fig. 1.9). On May 2, 2000, the Defense Department surrendered to pressure from the domestic electronics industry and stopped blurring civilian GPS signals. Dennis Milbert, a top official at the National Geodetic Survey, compared the improvement to a football stadium in which, "with SA activated, you really only know if you are on the field or in the stands [whereas] with SA switched off, you know which yard marker you are standing on." Even so, the Pentagon remains in control. As President Clinton noted in a statement released on May 1, the military can "selectively deny GPS signals on a regional basis when our national security is threatened."

 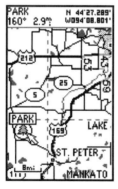

FIGURE 1.9 The ability to zoom in and out allows handheld GPS receivers like the Garmin 12MAP *(left)* to display small but useful maps *(right)*. © Garmin Corporation. Reproduced with permission.

Privacy concerns arise principally with proposals to integrate GPS with other technologies. Connect a portable ground station to a cell phone, for instance, and it becomes an instrument for tracking employees, children, and parolees. Although GPS surveillance can be quite benign—an efficient way to track and dispatch taxis, for example—proposals to clamp a tracking device around a subject's ankle or implant it beneath the skin in a microchip have sinister overtones akin to stalking and branding. Add the possibility of administering pain if a linked GIS observes a child or ex-convict entering forbidden territory, and the scenario is instantly Orwellian.

It's easy to see how punitive electronic tracking might work. The GPS transmits the subject's coordinates to a computer with a detailed geographic database describing no-go areas, diligently delineated with vector data. If the computer detects a first-grader playing near a garbage dump or busy street, the system intervenes with a warning, by pinch or pager. I can see how some child safety experts might approve an auditory warning device IF it's reliable. (My big "if" is deliberate; the computer could be down or its database faulty.) I also see why civil libertarians would object vigorously to remote spanking that could, quite literally, follow a child into adolescence and beyond. But I much prefer my own reasons for never using a child tracker: if parts of the community must be off limits, the parent should teach the child to understand and recognize hazards. If my daughter were too young to appreciate danger, she wouldn't be away from home without adult supervision.

In some circumstances, personal tracking might well be the lesser of several evils. Consider, for example, the alternatives to permanent incarceration of convicted sex offenders. Compared to minimally supervised parole, which could pose a threat to the community, and public outing, likely to inflict emotional stress and undermine rehabilitation, GPS-based monitoring—IF it works— seems a good choice. And consider the senior citizen for whom a tracking device might be—IF it works and monitors relevant vital signs—a suitable substitute to confinement in a nursing home or an adult care center. Even so, both cases admit other solutions as well as circumstances that readily rule out cartographic surveillance. Whatever the ethics and pragmatics of location tracking, the unintended consequences of GPS call for skeptical awareness of our brave new globe and its plausible threats to personal privacy.

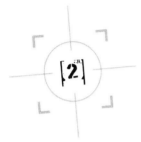

Overhead Assets

Overhead surveillance has three histories: two focusing on
the distinctly different technical challenges of aviation and
photography and a third encompassing the politics and in-
stitutions of a hybrid defense-oriented technology with commercial ambitions. Advances in fluid mechanics, rocket
propellants, and inertial navigation allowed aircraft and artificial satellites to overcome gravity and atmospheric drag,
while cameras and scanners, as extensions of the human
eye and the artist's canvas, have historical roots in optics,
photochemistry, and radar. Although their respective narra-
tives are still evolving, space flight and electronic imaging
have attained impressive plateaus. By contrast, the hybrid
technology's history is less complete but more intriguing.
And as this chapter illustrates, the intelligence commu-

nity's "overhead assets" play a critical yet largely unsung role in national defense and world peace.

+ + +

Like most jargon, "overhead assets" is mildly ambiguous: although aerial reconnaissance is almost always an asset, the observer's eye or camera's lens need not be directly overhead. The French army, which used aerial scouts as early as 1794, tethered their balloons to protect observers and assure timely reports. A mile or more from enemy positions, aeronauts with telescopes could assess an adversary's strength, help artillery officers improve their aim, and direct ground attacks toward weak points along the opponent's line. Because photography would not be invented for several decades, aerial observers made sketches and annotated existing maps, which were conveniently dropped to intelligence officers below. Although the daguerreotype became practical in the late 1850s, long exposure times and cumbersome glass plates limited its military use to anticipatory mapmaking on calm, clear days. The Union army, which deployed a few balloons during the Civil War, discovered another impediment as the war widened: the difficulty of moving aeronauts and their apparatus quickly to new locations.

Airplanes, introduced to battle during World War I, solved the transportation problem and allowed true overhead reconnaissance. As long as a pilot stayed above 18,000 feet, he was generally immune to enemy gunfire. Attack planes designed to overtake bombers and outmaneuver the opponent's fighter aircraft were another matter. Although civilian aerial photography as it evolved in the 1920s and 1930s relied on slow, evenly paced, back-and-forth flying along adjoining, closely spaced flight lines, reconnaissance pilots had to get in and out quickly. Because leisurely flight over enemy terrain was rarely an option, their most informative shots seldom looked directly downward.

Specialized cameras let reconnaissance planes and bombers make the most of their time over hostile territory. During World War II, American engineers devised a rigid frame with three cameras, one pointing directly downward and the others aimed away from the vertical, to the left and right (fig. 2.1). The result was a trio of slightly overlapping pictures: a more detailed vertical shot centered near the nadir point, on the ground directly below the camera, and a pair of oblique views looking outward toward the horizon. Although scale varied widely on these oblique shots, trained photointerpreters could examine a vast area and transfer potential targets to existing maps. Multi-lens cameras were especially efficient for rapid systematic small-scale mapping because the wider nadir swath required fewer flight lines. To assure complete coverage, an electrical or mechanical device snapped all three shutters simultaneously, at a constant interval, while other motors advanced the film automatically. During the mid-1940s, the Army Air Force used three-lens photography to compile a set of small-scale flying charts covering 16 million square miles (41 million km²).

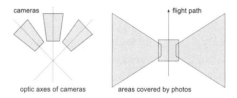

cameras

optic axes of cameras

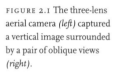

flight path

areas covered by photos

FIGURE 2.1 The three-lens aerial camera *(left)* captured a vertical image surrounded by a pair of oblique views *(right)*.

Oblique viewing helps satellite sensors respond to emergencies with timely images. Commercial satellites like SPOT and Ikonos offer nearly worldwide coverage by orbiting the earth several times a day in a geometric plane that moves steadily westward so that the satellite always crosses the equator at the same time, usually in late morning. As the satellite circles overhead, its scanner examines a narrow ground swath 10 to 200 kilometers wide and doesn't pass directly overhead again for another twenty days or so. Swath width and revisit time reflect the resolution of the satellite's scanner as well as its altitude or orbit. The early Landsats provided 79-meter resolution from an altitude of about 920 kilometers along a swath 185 kilometers wide revisited every eighteen days. By contrast, Ikonos offers 1-meter resolution along a swath only 11 kilometers wide from an altitude of 681 kilometers, but cannot retrace the same nadir track for several months. But by tilting the sensor outward (fig. 2.2, left), Ikonos can advertise revisit times of 2.9 and 1.5 days, respectively, for resolutions of 1.0 and 1.5 meters. Although the larger tilt angle required for a shorter revisit time undermines

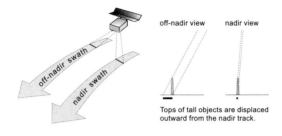

off-nadir view   nadir view

Tops of tall objects are displaced
outward from the nadir track.

FIGURE 2.2 Off-nadir views to the left and right of the nadir swath *(left)* reduce revisit time but displace features outward from the nadir point *(right)*.

resolution, off-nadir viewing is an essential element of high-resolution remote sensing.

Off-nadir images contain distortions common to the periphery of perfectly vertical aerial photographs. When the scanner or camera is not directly overhead, the image shows only the near side of tall structures like the Washington Monument (toward the lower left in fig. 1.6). Similarly, the top of a perfectly vertical obelisk will appear farther from the photo's nadir point than the monument's base (fig. 2.3, left). What's more, the distance between the tops of two obelisks, equal in height but at opposite corners of the photo, will be measurably greater than the distance between their bases. This phenomenon is called relief displacement because higher features, especially near the edges of the photo, are displaced farther outward from the center of the photo than lower features. Because of relief displacement, air photos distort mountains and tall buildings and should not be used to measure horizontal distances, especially in rugged terrain.

Relief displacement proved more an asset than a liability. A pair of overlapping aerial photographs taken from different camera positions (fig. 2.3, right) can be viewed in stereo, with each eye seeing the landscape from a slightly different angle—the same principle employed in the nineteenth-century stereopticon and late-twentieth-century virtual reality. Able to examine land cover in three dimensions, photointerpreters quickly learned to distinguish two-story houses from low-profile chicken coops and identify other features not readily apparent on a single photo. What's more, photogrammetrists devised instruments for measuring relief displacement,

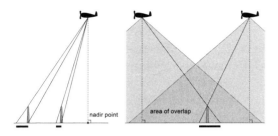

FIGURE 2.3 Because an air photo is a perspective view, the top of a vertical monument is displaced outward from its base *(left)*. On overlapping air photos the joint displacement *(right)* of an object's two images promotes stereovision and provides measurements useful in calculating differences in elevation.

calculating elevations, drawing contour lines, and replotting features in their horizontally correct positions. During the 1930s photogrammetry became the preferred technique for making topographic maps, and three decades later photogrammetrists devised an efficient method for removing relief displacement from aerial photos.

Satellites with dual off-nadir scanners, one aimed forward along the ground swath and the other looking aft (fig. 2.4, left), can mimic the overlapping pairs of air photos used in stereo compilation. A scene captured twice, from different viewing angles, allows stereo viewing and provides joint displacements (fig. 2.4, right) for estimating elevation differences. Imaging software that matches features on the fore and aft views can automatically compile an elevation map, which can be plotted as a three-dimensional terrain diagram, con-

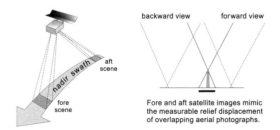

FIGURE 2.4 Fore and aft views *(left)* along a satellite's nadir swath afford joint displacements *(right)* that allow stereo viewing and automatic compilation of elevation maps.

toured like a typical topographic map, or used to filter out all relief displacement. Displacement-free images, called orthophotographs, are also possible when overlapping fore and aft scenes are captured on a neighboring, off-nadir swath.

+   +   +

Like most technologies, remote sensing boils down to a few fundamental trade-offs. Increase altitude, and resolution suffers. Increase resolution with a larger, heavier camera, and you need more fuel, a bigger engine, or a radically different airplane or satellite. In wartime, altitude becomes a conflicted matter of safety and need to know—accurate intelligence is crucial but flying too low can get you shot down. During the Cold War, intercontinental ballistic missiles (ICBMs) and nuclear warheads highlighted another trade-off by vastly increasing the cost of knowing what the enemy was up to as well as the consequences of not knowing and doing nothing. Aware that the Soviet Union now had atomic weapons as well as long-range missiles, the United States needed to monitor its key rival's nuclear activities and missile sites.

So great was the cost of inadequate intelligence that the government launched a crash program of top-secret spy satellites to complement and eventually replace sporadic overflights by U-2 reconnaissance planes, designed for long flights at 70,000 feet, well out of reach of Soviet fighters. First used over Russia in 1956, the one-person spy plane had replaced a less subtle program of unmanned and largely unreliable reconnaissance balloons, which occasionally provoked diplomatic protest. Overflights of the USSR halted abruptly on May 1, 1960, when a surface-to-air missile shot down a U-2 near Sverdlovsk, and the Russians put the pilot on trial as a spy. Fortunately for the CIA, the U-2 was not its only option. On August 18 the first successful Corona satellite, launched as Discoverer-14, photographed more Soviet territory during its single day in orbit than the twenty-four U-2 missions of the previous four years.

Equally impressive was the Air Force's mid-air snagging of the Discoverer-14 recovery capsule carrying 3,000 feet of 70 mm film. Unlike Landsat and its technological cousins, which beam their pictures down to earth electronically, the early Corona satellites were giant disposable cameras. But instead of the entire unit having to be returned to Kodak for processing, the satellite ejected its film in a gold-plated recovery capsule that resembled an oversize kettle-drum. De-orbited by a retro-rocket and dropped over the Pacific Ocean with a parachute, a Discoverer capsule could float for two days—sufficient time for recovery by a Naval team that knew what to look for and where to look. And if the Navy couldn't retrieve it, no one would—a salt plug in the flotation unit would dissolve, and the capsule would fill with water and sink. However clever, water recovery was only a backup: ideally a huge C-119 or C-130 transport plane equipped with a trapeze-like sling would stalk the slowly descending recovery capsule, seize its parachute, and reel the catch into the cargo bay.

Discoverer was a clever double entendre: as a cover name it implied space exploration and biomedical research, but the CIA and Air Force officials running the program focused on discovering airfields, launch pads, and uranium plants. Subterfuge was essential because the powerful two-stage rockets needed to loft a Volkswagen-size satellite into space would surely be noticed by the news media as well as curious residents of Santa Barbara, California, near the launch site at Vandenberg Air Force Base. Although Corona was "deep black"—intelligence community lingo for absolutely top secret—many of the program's goals and operations were openly reported in the trade magazine *Aviation Week*.

A dozen disappointments preceded Discoverer-14's success—rockets failed, satellites spun out of control, and cameras malfunctioned. Launched just one week before Discoverer-14, Discoverer-13 proved a turning point: recovery of the nonphotographic diagnostic mission's reentry capsule, which splashed down 330 nautical miles from Hawaii, marked the first successful retrieval of an object sent into space. But three more failures intervened before the second successful air recovery of film from Discoverer-18, launched on December 7, 1960. It took another year for engineers to work out bugs. Although only six of the sixteen photographic satellites launched in 1961 returned film, seventeen out of twenty Corona missions in 1962 were successful.

Efficient coverage demanded careful coordination of camera and orbit. A slowly rotating near-polar orbit assured multiple ground swaths across the Asian heartland, where the Soviets situated their most secret missile sites and atomic laboratories. The orbit was not a circle but a slightly eccentric ellipse, which varied in altitude from more than 800 kilometers to less than 180 kilometers, to bring the satellite in sufficiently low so that Corona's 5-foot-long camera with a 24-inch-focal-length lens could take pictures that mimicked a resolution of 12 meters. Instead of snapping a shutter, advancing the film, and taking another snapshot a short while later like the cameras used in conventional aerial photography, Corona captured a panoramic view of the scene below on a continuously moving strip of film. As the satellite moved along overhead, the film recorded a ground spot moving perpendicular to the nadir track and reaching outward 35 degrees from the vertical on both sides to capture a swath at least 250 kilometers wide. Continuous exposure avoided gaps and wasteful overlap, and the carefully programmed camera conserved film by turning itself on and off at appropriate points. Although continuous strip panoramic photography was not new, Discoverer-14 set a record by imaging 1,650,000 square miles (4.3 million km²) of Soviet terrain in a single day.

The first Corona camera system was the KH-1, where KH stands for Keyhole, the government's code name for top-secret satellite reconnaissance. Between 1959 and 1962, three new models reflected numerous improvements. KH-2 introduced a more accurate film-advance and scanning mechanism, and refined the resolution to 8 meters. KH-3 introduced a faster lens, which allowed slower, finer-grain film and sharper enlargements. KH-4 extended mission life to six or seven days with additional film and pioneered satellite stereo imaging with two cameras, one aimed 15 degrees forward along the nadir swath and the other pointed 15 degrees aft. Bigger in this case also meant better: according to recently released records, the CIA rated twenty-one of the 9-foot-long camera's twenty-six missions as successful.

Subsequent advances were equally impressive. The KH-4A imaging system, first used in August 1963, added a second recovery capsule, or "bucket," and increased the total film load to 32,000 feet, which allowed missions as long as fifteen days. Other improvements included a resolution of 2 to 3 meters (7 to 10 ft.), depending on altitude, stereo coverage of 18 million square miles (47 million km²) on a typical mission, and a camera malfunction rate of only

4 in 52. The 12-foot-long KH-4B, introduced in September 1967, lengthened mission life to nineteen days, offered greater flexibility in type of film and exposure, and honed routine image resolution down to 6 feet (less than 2 m). In addition to the forward and aft panoramic cameras for stereo imaging, the KH-4B included three types of secondary cameras, which recorded scenes described schematically in figure 2.5. An index camera with a square format captured small-scale terrain images useful for relating and indexing paired sets of panoramic images. Each panoramic camera had its own pair of horizon cameras—one aimed to the left of the nadir swath and the other pointing to the right—to establish altitude and scale. Two stellar cameras, pointing above the horizon to the left and right, recorded the positions of visible stars. Celestial signposts were important to Defense Department mapmakers, who used astronomic observations to calculate latitude and longitude. Clandestine pictures might help the CIA keep tabs on enemy armaments, but if the United States ever needed to retaliate, its guided missiles had to know each target's exact location.

Corona imagery remained sequestered in National Reconnaissance Office vaults until 1995, when President Clinton authorized the release of "scientifically or environmentally useful . . . historical intelligence imagery." Although the official intent was to provide baseline data for assessing environmental change, declassification of more than 800,000 frames of top-secret photography made further denial of American capacity for overhead surveillance pointless, especially when Russian space entrepreneurs were hawking equally sharp imagery to cost-conscious Air Force officials.

Declassification was an opportunity to brag. Engineers who had worked on the rockets, satellites, and cameras could speak openly about their achievements, while intelligence experts praised Corona's accomplishments. By monitoring weapons tests and identifying all Soviet missile sites, defensive and offensive, NRO interpreters had exposed the "missile gap" of the late 1950s as a groundless fear. Satellite intelligence proved especially useful in October 1962 during the Cuban missile crisis, a thirteen-day standoff between Soviet Premier Nikita Khrushchev, who had threatened to bury us, and President John F. Kennedy, who knew the Russians were poorly prepared for a major offensive. In tracking the deployment of

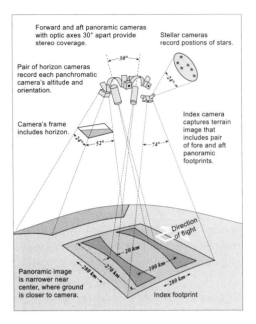

Forward and aft panoramic cameras with optic axes 30° apart provide stereo coverage.

Stellar cameras record postions of stars.

Pair of horizon cameras record each panchromatic camera's altitude and orientation.

Camera's frame includes horizon.

Index camera captures terrain image that includes pair of fore and aft panoramic footprints.

Direction of flight

Panoramic image is narrower near center, where ground is closer to camera.

Index footprint

FIGURE 2.5 The KH-4B imaging system supplemented its fore and aft panoramic cameras, which provided stereo coverage, with an index camera, a pair of stellar cameras, and a pair of horizon cameras for each panoramic camera. Footprints describe areas on the ground covered by images framed for storage and use. This schematic diagram shows only one of the KH-4B's four horizon cameras. Redrawn from figure 8 in National Reconnaissance Office, *The KH-4B Camera System*.

atomic weapons and submarines as well as monitoring Russian assistance to China, Cuba, and its Middle Eastern allies, satellite imagery also demonstrated the feasibility of checking up on rivals and verifying arms-control treaties. Corona not only became the Defense Mapping Agency's key resource for compiling medium-scale maps but also provided basic observations for a long-overdue revision of the worldwide geodetic system, which tells cartographers where to draw meridians and parallels. Less well known is the U.S. Geological Survey's use of classified satellite imagery to revise its 1:250,000, medium-scale topographic maps as well as identify out-of-date 1:24,000 quadrangle maps. Although revision of large-scale maps required conventional aerial photography, straightforward comparison of existing maps with Corona imagery helped USGS focus its efforts on comparatively needy quadrangles.

+   +   +

Corona's final launch in May 1972 provided a convenient cutoff for further official disclosures. But even though the NRO still sequestered post-Corona imagery, journalists specializing in space technology and strategic intelligence offered revealing glimpses of the more sophisticated systems that followed. Foremost among them are John Pike, director of GlobalSecurity.org and formerly the satellite intelligence guru at the Federation of American Scientists, and Jeffrey Richelson, the author of several books on satellite intelligence and the history of electronic spying. Pike, who worked as a science writer and political consultant before joining the FAS, is a respected critic of government space programs and an ardent supporter of arms limitation. Richelson, who holds a Ph.D. in political science, taught government at American University before becoming a full-time author and consultant. Sought out by news reporters whenever breaking stories involve spy satellites, Pike and Richelson were key sources for William E. Burrows, whose 1987 exposé *Deep Black: Space Espionage and National Security* is a surprisingly accurate unofficial history of Corona and Keyhole.

All three authors have relied heavily on technical documents from official sources as well as public testimony before congressional committees looking into arms limitation. The White House had backed test-ban and arms-reduction treaties for over a decade—Richard Nixon helped initiate the Strategic Arms Limitation Treaty (SALT), and President Jimmy Carter called nuclear arms reduction his "most cherished hope"—but skeptics in Congress demanded an effective means of verification, including overhead surveillance. Although the intelligence establishment promised diligent photographic reconnaissance, neither the CIA nor the Defense Department would confirm publicly their use of spy satellites.

The curtain of secrecy remained intact until October 1978, when Carter, speaking to NASA employees at the Kennedy Space Center, pledged that "photoreconnaissance satellites . . . make an immense contribution to the security of all nations [and] we shall continue to develop them." Unofficially of course, Washington knew we had spooks in space. Well-placed but appropriately guarded informants, probably with approval from their superiors, confided in lawmakers and journalists without betraying sensitive details. Added reassurance came from the apparent success of telecommunications and meteorological satellites, Landsat, and the space shuttle, first flown in space in April 1981.

Espionage trials brought further revelations. In 1977, for instance, CIA employee Wilham Kampiles sold a top-secret technical manual to a Russian agent for $3,000. The manual described the operation and limitations of the KH-11 imaging system, employed in a Corona successor. In addition to further confirming Russian knowledge of American spy satellites, Kampiles's November 1978 trial highlighted the conviction a year and a half earlier of Christopher Boyce and Andrew Lee, who had sold secrets about U.S. spy satellites developed by Boyce's employer, the TRW Space Systems Group. In 1980 Boyce further embarrassed the government by escaping from a federal prison and remaining at large for ten months.

According to Pike and Richelson, the Russians clearly knew what the CIA was doing. The two authors testified as defense witnesses at the 1985 trial of Samuel Morison, a former Navy intelligence officer charged with espionage. Morison had sent top-secret satellite photos to *Jane's Defence Weekly*, a prominent British military magazine, which published three of them in an August 1984 issue. The high-resolution images afforded a detailed view of a nuclear-powered aircraft carrier under construction at a Soviet shipyard on the Black Sea. Although motivated by journalistic zeal—he was one of *Jane's* American editors—Morison had broken the rules. Even so, his disclosure was hardly as damaging as prosecutors claimed. The pictures "just didn't really tell me anything that I didn't know," Richelson told the *Washington Post*. "I don't think they provide any new information. Therefore, I don't think it's of any value." Despite evidence that Morison's leak was neither significant nor criminal, a federal court sentenced him to two years in prison.

Unofficial disclosures abound in Richelson's paper "The Keyhole Satellite Program," published in the June 1984 issue of the *Journal of Strategic Studies*. In 1960, the White House set up the super-secret National Reconnaissance Office to manage satellite spying as well as mediate disputes between the CIA and the Air Force. In 1963, the NRO initiated a second generation of space reconnaissance by launching the first satellites with KH-5 and KH-6 systems. The KH-5, a "surveillance" system designed to cover a relatively wide ground swath, carried more film than the KH-4 and extended the typical mission to twenty-three days. By contrast, the KH-6, a "close-look" system intended for sharper pictures of smaller scenes, strengthened resolution to 6 feet (2 m) with an altitude as low as 76 miles (122 km). In 1966, the first KH-7 and KH-8 missions heralded a third generation of surveillance and close-look satellites. According to Richelson, both series operated at generally lower altitudes than their predecessors, and when orbited as low as 82 miles (132 km), the KH-8 could refine its resolution to a remarkable 6 inches (15 cm). A fourth generation emerged in 1971, when the NRO flew the first KH-9 craft, a 30,000-pound, 50-foot-long satellite unofficially known as Big Bird. With an enormous payload, four recovery modules, and missions lasting six months or more, the KH-9 combined conventional film photography for taking sharp, 6-inch-resolution close-ups with a TV-like imaging system able to transmit pictures to earth electronically.

Big Bird's days were numbered. In 1971, the NRO also launched the first KH-11, which replaced film drops with a digital multispectral imaging system similar to but sharper than the scanner orbited a year later on Landsat-1. Not burdened by film or recovery capsules, the KH-11 craft embarked on missions of years, not months. One of Richelson's sources was aerospace journalist Philip Klass, whose 1971 book *Secret Sentries in Space* revealed plans to develop near-real-time satellite reconnaissance. Another was a 1972 news note in *Aviation Week and Space Technology* announcing the imminent selection of TRW to "develop a new generation of reconnaissance satellites [that will] permit real-time photo reconnaissance by means of synchronous data relay satellites." As Richelson explained, when a KH-11 satellite was not within range of a ground station, it would relay imagery to Washington through a telecommunications satellite. What's more, off-nadir cameras allowed coverage anywhere in the world at least once a day, clouds and darkness not withstanding. With a pair of KH-11 satellites in carefully spaced sun-synchronous orbits, NRO intelligence analysts could inspect sensitive areas several times a day. And because the agency usually replaced its satellites before they failed, lack of coverage was rare. From 1977 through 1983, for instance, at least one KH-11 was operating overhead on all but seventeen days.

The KH-11's filmless photography depended on tiny, light-sensitive semiconductors called charged-coupled devices (CCDs). Invented at Bell Laboratories in 1970, the CCDs were arranged in rows and columns to capture the scene below as an array of pixels, each recording the intensity of received light as an electrical charge. The imaging system polled its pixels systematically, row by row, and converted their charges to numbers for virtually error-free transmission. Received in Washington nearly instantaneously, the satellite's digital pictures could be manipulated on a computer to improve contrast and stored electronically for ready comparison with later images.

Impressed with the KH-11's rapid read-out and extraordinary longevity, Richelson says little about its resolution, deemed "greater than the KH-9 [but] inferior to the KH-8." More intriguing was its successor, the KH-12, believed to include thermal imaging for nighttime spying as well as radar imaging to penetrate clouds. First launched in 1986, the KH-12 weighed 14 tons (18 tons in later versions). In addition to a massive camera, similar to the Hubble Space Telescope in its use of large mirrors, the KH-12's satellite carried up to 7 tons of fuel, which powered the rockets used to adjust its orbit. John Pike, who describes the KH-12 as a "space telescope with a rocket," notes the importance of moving closer to interesting areas and evading antisatellite weapons. Pike also highlights the difficulty of keeping salient details secret by calling the much publicized Hubble Space Telescope "an unclassified version of the KH-12."

Although the NRO remains mum about the KH-12's existence, much less its resolution, Pike and other experts accept a conveniently rounded estimate of 10 centimeters (3.9 in.). A calculation by electronics journalist John Adam suggests this number might be conservative. By relating the space telescope's camera to the KH-11's altitude, Adam computed a ground resolution of 7.16 centimeters —a mere 2.8 inches. Although 4-inch resolution seems more likely, not even 3-inch resolution would let an NRO analyst read news paper headlines or license plate numbers, as enthusiastic reporters occasionally claim. In fact, Pike used images of both objects at different resolutions to show that not even 1-centimeter resolution would make normal license plates and headlines readable from space.

Pike has demonstrated that 10-centimeter resolution is quite sufficient for most intelligence needs. Reproduced in figure 2.6, his array of images shows a parking lot viewed from above with ground resolutions of 10, 25, 50, and 100 centimeters. At 10 centimeters, an

FIGURE 2.6 Images of a parking lot viewed with resolutions of 10, 25, 50, and 100 centimeters. Courtesy of John Pike and the Federation of American Scientists.

analyst can describe individual vehicles and even judge drivers' skill in parking between the lines—the large truck at the lower left is too long for its space and partly over the line. At 25 centimeters, the lines are hazy and cars are barely distinct from vans and pickup trucks. At 50 centimeters, identification is difficult at best, although some lines are marginally visible. And at 100 centimeters, the same resolution as the Ikonos image in figure 1.6, size and pattern suggest vehicles in a parking lot, but an analyst would need a wider scene to be certain. It's clear, though, that 10-centimeter intelligence imagery is far more detailed than the 1-meter imagery available from Space Imaging and its competitors.

+   +   +

NRO analysts and their collaborators in the aerospace industry are haunted by a basic question in image intelligence: How fine a ground resolution is sufficient? Because the answer depends on what the analyst is trying to discover, a committee of scientists and intelligence experts developed the National Image Interpretability Rating Scales. Focused on usefulness, NIIRS assigns images and imaging systems an integer rating between 1 and 9, which corresponds to a range of "ground resolved distances," starting with "over 9.0 m" for NIIRS 1 and continuing through "less than 0.10 m" for

NIIRS 9. Each rating includes a list of identifications, descriptions, or differentiations that become possible at that level of resolution.

According to the ratings, Ikonos and KH-12 imagery are radically different. One-meter Ikonos imagery, with the capabilities of NIIRS 5 (ground resolution between 0.75 and 1.2 m), lets users identify specific types of surface-to-surface missiles, distinguish between vehicle-mounted and trailer-mounted radar, differentiate steam and diesel locomotives, and classify rail cars by type (flat cars, tank cars, box cars, gondolas, and so forth). And as with slightly less refined pictures, viewers can count vehicles and detect rail yards, airstrips, helipads, radar installations, and missile silos with their doors open. What Ikonos users can't do is identify the spare tire on a medium-size truck (NIIRS 6, with 0.40–0.75 m resolution) or count individual rail ties (NIIRS 7, with 0.20–0.40 m resolution). By contrast, a trained intelligence analyst with KH-12 imagery, rated NIIRS 8 (0.10–0.20 m), can see a truck's windshield wipers or an airplane's rivet lines. If the analyst knows what to look for, the KH-12's superior ground resolution might mean the difference between merely seeing a truck and identifying its contents.

Because image intelligence focuses on detecting change, 1-meter satellite imagery is often more informative than its NIIRS 5 rating suggests. A new railway spur or clearing, for instance, could signify a new missile site or weapons factory. And a suspicious accumulation of large vehicles might presage an imminent attack. As John Pike observes, "if a picture is worth 1,000 words, two pictures are worth 10,000 words." Look for even bigger word counts once Space Imaging begins marketing the 0.5-meter imagery approved by the National Security Council in late 2000.

However sharp and revealing, visible imagery is nearly useless on a cloudy day. To compensate for clouds as well as darkness, the NRO turned to synthetic aperture radar (SAR), which mimics a flash camera by generating its own energy. Instead of light, an SAR antenna transmits pulses of microwave radio waves, which bounce back to the spacecraft (fig. 2.7). SAR differs from ordinary radar because its antenna is in motion. The distance covered between a pulse's transmission and the return of "backscattered" radiation imitates the much longer antenna needed to recognize revealing variations in terrain and surface objects. Although estimates of

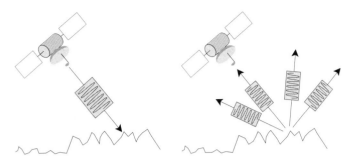

FIGURE 2.7 Radar imaging systems transmit pulses of electromagnetic energy, which are "backscattered" in various directions. Computers on the ground use the relative strength of radar echoes to reconstruct the terrain as well as the position and general shape of surface objects.

ground resolution are vague, space-based SAR imagery is probably no sharper than 1 meter. Resolution varies because the system can cover small areas in greater detail than larger areas. If the imagery meets the wholly plausible NIIRS 6 (1.2–2.5 m) standard for radar, it can detect highway and railway bridges as well as individual vehicles in a known motor pool. And when viewed in pairs or a series, SAR snapshots can help battlefield commanders track the enemy's tanks and trucks.

Real-time radar surveillance is a demanding business both in space and on the ground. For all-weather coverage the United States has relied largely on a pair of radar-imaging Lacrosse satellites, similar in principle to the Magellan space probe sent to map Venus. The space shuttle placed Lacrosse-1 in orbit in 1988, but expendable Titan missiles serviced later missions. Each satellite costs about a billion dollars, weighs roughly 15 tons, and lasts five to ten years. A pair of wing-like solar panels stretching nearly 50 meters from end to end powers a parabolic antenna 10 meters across, which generates 1,500 radar pulses a second. Although a single antenna both sends and receives, the millions of radar echoes it picks up are useless without a high-capacity network of relay satellites and ground stations to deliver the data, and a bank of high-speed computers to reconstruct the terrain.

According to John Pike, *Aviation Week and Space Technology,* and other informed sources, two Lacrosse radar satellites complement two or three KH-12 satellites carrying visible and infrared imaging systems. Although each high-resolution spy satellite can visit trouble spots like Iraq at least twice a day, during the Gulf War images no older than three hours didn't satisfy field commanders, who complained of limited "dwell time." Another gripe was a lack of wide-area coverage. Although money and physics will forever frustrate generals eager to view the entire battle zone in real time all the time, the NRO responded in 1995 with plans for a new 20-ton, $1.5 billion satellite. According to the *Los Angeles Times*, the new satellite would expand coverage of individual scenes from 100 to 800 square miles without any practical loss in resolution. Known as the 8X or the Enhanced Imaging System—the NRO delights in changing code names once the media picks them up—a higher orbit would increase dwell time from five minutes to half an hour. Early in the new millennium the 8X was on duty orbiting the earth 9.7 times a day at an altitude between 2,690 and 3,131 kilometers. As a map on the Heavens-Above Web site confirms, the satellite now known to astronomers as USA 144 had a ground track conveniently close to Iraq and Israel (fig. 2.8).

There's a lot more up there than four or five imaging satellites. Some overhead assets are signals intelligence (SIGINT) satellites, designed to pinpoint defensive radar for the military or monitor communications traffic for the National Security Agency, an NRO cousin with electronic ears in space linked to code-crunching computers outside Washington. Others are measurement and signature intelligence (MASINT) satellites, assigned to track missiles, provide real-time battlefield support, or detect nuclear explosions in space or at the surface. Customized sensors include electro-optical instruments called bhangmeters, which can detect the diagnostic double burst of X rays produced by a nuclear blast, and infrared scanners that can spot and follow a missile's superheated exhaust gasses— missile-interception weaponry like Ronald Reagan's proposed Strategic Defense Initiative, also known as Star Wars and reincarnated as the Bush Missile Shield, rely heavily on thermal tracking.

As with imaging satellites, altitude reflects mission. A low earth orbit (LEO), defined by an altitude typically below 1,000 kilometers, is useful for electronic eavesdropping and thermal detection, whereas a highly elliptical orbit (HEO), in which a satellite's altitude might

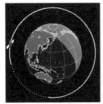

View from above orbital plane

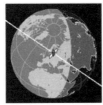

View from above satellite

Ground track

FIGURE 2.8 According to the Heavens-Above Web site, the satellite USA 144, aka the 8X image intelligence satellite and the Enhanced Imaging System, passed over the Persian Gulf shortly after 10 P.M. Greenwich time on May 15, 2000.

vary from a few hundred to more than 20,000 km, can be tailored to wide-area or close-look surveillance. By contrast, a geostationary orbit, in which a satellite hovers above the same spot on the equator at an altitude of 36,000 km (22,300 mi.), is useful for satellite telecommunications as well as continuous wide-area surveillance of weather, enemy communications, missile launches, and nuclear explosions. Because an orbit can serve multiple purposes, dual missions are common, especially when satellites work in carefully choreographed groups called constellations. For example, the Air Force's two dozen Navstar satellites, circling at 11,000 km in medium earth orbits (MEO) to support global positioning system (GPS) navigation, also carry nuclear detonation sensors.

Although all satellites require ground support, terrestrial monitors are a key component of nuclear detection. Aside from suspicious activity at the surface, underground tests easily escape satellite detection. Even so, all but the smallest, most carefully hidden atomic explosions produce seismic waves somewhat similar to the tremors of a small earthquake. These waves travel great distances, beyond the borders of a nation violating its test-ban commitment, to register on the worldwide network of seismographs with which scientists estimate the location, depth, and strength of the thousands of earthquakes that occur each year. Fortunately for world peace, seismologists have learned to distinguish nuclear explosions from natural seismic events.

However sharp our eyes and ears, seeing and hearing are vulnerable to false assumptions. On August 16, 1997, for instance, a small earthquake in the Kara Sea, roughly 100 kilometers from a Russian test site, created diplomatic as well as seismic waves. Although seismologists at Columbia University's Lamont-Doherty Earth Observatory knew otherwise, the CIA promptly claimed that the Soviets had detonated an atomic blast. As the story unfolded, it became clear that the CIA had ignored seismic evidence from Russia and Sweden, gotten the location wrong, and incorrectly linked the seismic shock to the test site. Instead of admitting its error, the agency insisted the temblor was an "ambiguous event," which fostered fears in Congress that test-ban treaties could not be verified.

More worrisome is the accidental bombing of the Chinese embassy in Belgrade in May 1999. Shortly after the incident, which killed three Chinese and triggered anti-American riots in Beijing, an acquaintance far more up on remote sensing than I insisted that the bombing was not an accident at all but a way of showing the Chinese how quickly "we" can retaliate should "they" get out of line. Turns out, we're not so arrogant: in a rush to identify bombing targets, CIA analysts who knew the address of a Yugoslavian weapons depot had assumed that house numbers in Belgrade were as orderly as those in Washington and picked the wrong building. Until Congress figures a way to repeal human error, no surveillance network is foolproof.

+ + +

It's clear that satellite surveillance will play a key role in the diplomatic and military history of the twenty-first century. Less certain is whether overhead assets—ours and others'—will prove a hero, a villain, or a bit of both. Essential for treaty verification, satellite imagery is vulnerable to misinterpretation and clever deception. Valuable for threat assessment, and thus vital to national defense and global stability, high-resolution imagery could also trigger an impulsive invasion or a preemptive first strike. As an instrument for identifying human rights abuses and rallying world opinion behind international peacekeeping missions, satellites can foster the New World Order, or merely encourage ineffectual military meddling in Third World countries. As part of an antimissile system like George W. Bush's Missile Shield, satellite sensors might repel or obviate an ICBM offensive, or help venal politicians waste billions of dollars on naïve electronics easily fooled by a salvo of decoys. Equally plausible is the role of high-tech victim: predictably circling in a celestial shooting gallery, intelligence satellites are eminently vulnerable to anti-satellite missiles or ground-based lasers that could fry their optics.

And that's just for high rollers like the United States, NATO, Russia, and China. Commercial remote sensing beckons still greater ambiguity by suggesting a free market in which high-resolution imagery is readily available to impulsive autocrats, religious zealots, and ethnic purists. Well-intended unilateral efforts to limit access to intelligence-quality photos seem doomed. When sellers outside our borders abound, the "shutter control" favored by the American military merely puts American firms at a competitive disadvantage. International regulation would require that all countries consent to a complex set of rules and sanctions, which is hardly likely according to John Pike, who worries that "every bad guy in the world is going to be buying these pictures."

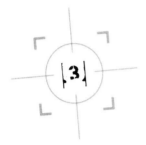

Eyes on the Farm

Agriculture was an early beneficiary of overhead surveillance. During the 1920s and 1930s civil engineers using aerial surveys designed highways, irrigation works, and electric power systems that promoted commercial farming in the semiarid West and brought modern conveniences to rural areas throughout the nation. As an instrument for measuring fields, identifying crops, mapping soils, and monitoring plant growth and pests, air photos also had a direct influence on farming. This role matured rapidly in the 1990s, with the integration of remote sensing, global positioning, and computer modeling. Successful in helping farmers increase production while conserving water and fertilizer, geospatial technology raised privacy concerns when police began using aerial imagery to locate marijuana "grows" and illegally watered lawns.

As independent producers in a free-market system, commercial farmers can be their own worst enemies. The obvious way to increase income is to boost production, but when neighbors harbor similar ambitions, prices can plummet if supply overwhelms demand. This axiom of agricultural economics was seldom more apparent than in the early 1930s, at the onset of the Great Depression, when many farmers found their new tractors more a burden than a blessing. And because falling prices affect all farmers, not just those who mechanize and expand, the Roosevelt administration knew that helping farmers meant stabilizing prices by either buying up the surplus or cutting back production. However implemented, acreage control was crucial: purchasing and storing a year's excess production might avoid excessively high prices if the following year's harvest was poor, but guaranteed prices could easily stimulate further production.

Committed to Secretary of Agriculture Henry Wallace's vision of an "ever-normal granary," New Deal activists took several years to find an effective, constitutionally acceptable way to convince farmers to cut back. The Agricultural Adjustment Act of 1933 focused on production control. Farmers agreed to limit production in exchange for a guaranteed price, partly funded through a tax on processors. To promote "economic democracy" as well as control costs, Wallace turned day-to-day administration of the program over to an innovative hierarchy of state, county, and local committees of farmers.

After the Supreme Court struck down the processing tax in early 1936, emphasis shifted to soil conservation. The Soil Conservation Act of 1936 encouraged soil-building practices and diverted production from soil-depleting crops, which accounted for much of the oversupply. Instead of signing contracts to limit production, farmers applied for payments under whatever programs they were eligible. Production controls returned in 1938, after bumper crops in 1937 proved that conservation incentives alone could not raise farm income. For corn, wheat, cotton, and other critical commercial crops, the Agricultural Adjustment Act of 1938 established national quotas based on past consumption, likely exports, and a reserve for emergencies and prorated these quotas back to the states, counties, and individual farms. Farmers could receive conservation payments only if they accepted voluntary acreage allotments based on the national quota, the local allocation, and their own average yield over the previous ten years.

The need to check compliance and ensure fairness created a measurement crisis. As Howard Tolley, chief of the Agricultural Adjustment Administration (AAA), noted in a 1937 radio interview, "before we can make any payment, we have to find out what each man applying has done to earn it. That means many millions of fields have to be measured." While ground surveys with a surveyor's chain or measuring wheel were slow and costly, air photos promised efficiency and accuracy, especially for irregularly shaped fields. Experiments in a handful of counties in 1935 suggested that a trained worker could approximate ground-survey estimates to within a percent or two by tracing field boundaries on an enlarged print with a carefully calibrated planimeter.

What started as an experimental program quickly became the preferred way to check compliance. In 1937 the AAA planned to map more than 759,000 square miles of farmland in all parts of the country (fig. 3.1). Although existing imagery from commercial firms and other government agencies accounted for slightly over half of the coverage, the remainder was new photography. As AAA technical advisor Harry Tubis told the American Society of Photogrammetry, "the simultaneous photographing of 375,000 square miles of our country, employing 36 photographic crews, is in itself a milestone in the development of aerial mapping."

Coordination and training required a bureaucracy within a bureaucracy. Committees within each of the AAA's five regions prepared guidelines for state and county operations. Each state office had an aerial mapping section that inspected all photos, ordered whatever reflights were needed to plug gaps or correct defects, compiled index maps relating the boundaries of each photo to roads and other local landmarks, and estimated scale from available ground control. In addition, the state sections trained the farm checkers hired by the county committees, spotchecked the checkers' work, and coordinated the ordering of enlarged prints from the Department of Agriculture's new photo labs in Salt Lake City and Washington, D.C. Although the USDA had established a standard scale of 1:20,000 for photo negatives, county offices typically worked with prints enlarged to 1:7,920, the scale at which one inch repre-

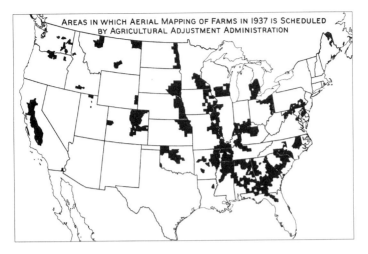

FIGURE 3.1 The AAA's crash program to check compliance focused on the Mississippi Valley, the Southeast, and California's Central Valley. From Harry Tubis, "Aerial Photography Maps Our Farmlands: The Program of the Agricultural Adjustment Administration," *Photogrammetric Engineering* 3 (April-May-June 1937): 22.

sents one-eighth of a mile and a square inch contains ten acres. Enlargement reduced errors likely to arise from imprecise tracing of field boundaries and allowed more detailed annotations for land-use planning.

A potentially important source of error was tilt, the angular deviation of the optic axis of the camera from a plumb line. If tilt is zero, the ground nadir (the point directly below the camera) appears at the exact center of the photo, and if the land is flat and horizontal, scale is constant across the photo. If the photo is tilted, scale generally decreases from the ground nadir toward the photo center and beyond. To correct the problem, engineers in the state office estimated the tilt of each print and supplied "tilt charts" with which planimeter operators in county offices could make an appropriate correction. Although the charts covered tilt as great as 7 degrees, deviations this large were rarely acceptable.

A more troublesome source of error was elevation difference, also called relief. Higher areas in a vertical air photo (typically tableland) appear slightly larger and more detailed than lower areas (bottom-land), which are farther from the camera. To compensate, officials in the state office divided photos with significant relief into two or more zones, marked zone boundaries on the print, and provided a scale or correction factor for each zone. Because a single set of zones would simplify calculations at the county level, the state photogrammetrist usually considered both relief and tilt in delineating zones of equal scale.

Where field and pasture boundaries were well established and easily identified, a set of air photos, zone boundaries, and correction tables could serve for a decade or more. Because the photography was intended for measurement, not crop identification, farm checkers would visit each farm applying for payment under the current year's program. Typical of the AAA's insistence on openness and cooperation was the rule that "in no event should the farm checker proceed in the determination of performance on a farm without the knowledge and consent of the owner or operator." The checker would walk the farm with the operator, identify crops, and verify conservation practices. If a farmer disagreed with an evaluation, his objection was noted in the checker's report.

Checkers took the photographs out to the farm for comparison and annotation. Field procedures called for clipping the photo to a rigid board with a smooth surface, protecting it with a waterproof cover, marking farm and field boundaries with a sharp pencil, and identifying farms with a number in red and fields with a letter in blue. Some counties cared for their photos by tracing permanent field boundaries and other features onto a farm map used for measurement and field checking. Farm maps based on ground surveys (quite crude in the AAA's early years) were used in counties without aerial photography. But the government's program of aerial survey was so effective that when the United States entered World War II in late 1941, the USDA had acquired coverage for over 90 percent of the country's agricultural land.

Thanks to the conservation program and its local committees, aerial photography spurred numerous improvements in drainage, plowing patterns, and pasturing. Overhead images presented dramatic evidence of the need for drainage tiles or contour plowing. And an overview of wells, ponds, and catchment basins of streams often suggested a more efficient allocation of livestock. By the late

1940s, conservation improvements had reconfigured more and more field boundaries, and the USDA was dutifully rephotographing the nation's principal farming areas. To stimulate discussion with local committeemen and conservation experts, the Production and Marketing Administration (the AAA's successor in the 1950s) offered farmers enlarged photographs of their land.

Air photos also provided the cartographic foundation for a national soil survey. As with many of its programs, the USDA maps soils county by county. The soil scientist assigned to a county might spend several years in the field assigning categories and delineating boundaries. A typical soil extends several feet below the surface and consists of a series of layers called horizons. Classification is based largely on the thickness, appearance, and physical properties of these layers, which affect fertility as well as suitability for septic tanks, foundations, and other uses. To see what's below the surface, the soil scientist digs small pits or drills narrow holes with an auger. Air photos expedite fieldwork by suggesting good places to sample, by showing moisture or vegetation differences that mirror soil boundaries, and by providing a convenient base for taking field notes and sketching boundaries, which a cartographic technician in the state office transfers to the finished map. Air photos play an even more valuable role in the published report, for which soil boundaries and category symbols are registered onto a visually subdued aerial photographic base map (fig. 3.2). In addition to saving time and controlling cost, the photos show field boundaries and

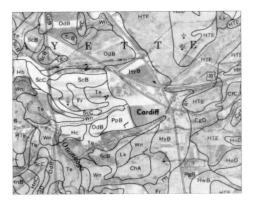

FIGURE 3.2 Portion of a typical soil survey map showing soil boundaries and category abbreviations superimposed on a photomap base. The hamlet is Cardiff, New York, made famous by the Cardiff Giant hoax of 1869. Excerpt from sheet 50 in Frank Z. Hutton, Jr., and C. Erwin Rice, *Soil Survey of Onondaga County, New York* (Washington, D.C.: Soil Conservation Service, 1977).

other features that make the soil information easily accessible to farmers, planners, and civil engineers.

+   +   +

Longstanding links between agricultural cartography and military intelligence fostered a fuller use of aerial imagery in farming. The relationship began in the 1920s, when photointerpreters trained by the army during World War I returned to work at agricultural colleges and the USDA and began using air photos for soil mapping, conservation planning, and forest management. When the United States entered World War II, the USDA provided the military with experienced photogrammetrists as well as the services of its two photo labs. When the war ended, many more imagery-savvy GIs returned to jobs in soil science, agronomy, forestry, and farming. Soils experts and agronomists in particular were eager to experiment with a recent military innovation—infrared imagery, designed to detect camouflage—that was promisingly proficient in delineating moist soils and stressed crops.

Before the advent of camouflage-detection film, the opposing army could hide its tanks and supplies under mottled green tarps and buildings painted green to resemble dense shrubbery from the air. As figure 3.3 shows, live vegetation and camouflage reflect the blue, green, and red light similarly. Both appear green in color to the human eye. But extension of the reflectance curves into the near-infrared (*infrared* meaning "beyond red") portion of the spectrum, where wavelengths are a bit longer and beyond human perception, reveals markedly different spectral signatures. In this part of the spectrum, green canvas or netting reflects much less light than does

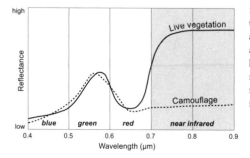

FIGURE 3.3 Spectral signatures of healthy vegetation and camouflage are generally similar for the visible light portion of the electromagnetic spectrum but notably different for near-infrared wavelengths.

leafy vegetation. The vegetation thus produces a much brighter image on the camouflage-detection film, which is sensitive only to infrared light. (Note that near-infrared light, sometimes known as reflected-infrared light, with wavelengths between roughly 0.7 and 1.1 micrometers, is not the same as thermal-infrared (heat) radiation, which has wavelengths between 3 and 20 micrometers.)

In a 1943 magazine ad, Eastman Kodak demonstrated the efficacy of camouflage-detection film with the trio of photographs in figure 3.4. A large factory with a water tower, loading dock, and railway siding can be concealed to look like a wooded area on standard black-and-white film. As the ad explains, infrared film is not so easily fooled. "Natural grass and foliage contain chlorophyll—Nature's coloring matter. Camouflage materials lack this living substance. Chlorophyll reflects invisible infrared light, making the natural areas look light in the picture—almost white. In violent contrast, the 'dead' camouflaged areas show up dark—almost black—in the pictures." Instead of fooling bomber pilots and photointerpreters, ersatz woodland betrayed a promising target.

FIGURE 3.4 With standard black-and-white (panchromatic) film, camouflage netting and artificial trees *(center)* disguise a factory *(left)* that would make an attractive bombing target. Dark, dead-looking tones on an infrared image *(right)* expose the fakery. Reprinted courtesy of Eastman Kodak Company. KODAK is a trademark.

Color-infrared imagery, a related innovation, makes leafy crops and other foliage stand out like the clichéd sore thumb. Conventional color film uses separate emulsions to capture the intensities of reflected blue, green, and red light, and color prints with corresponding dyes produce a realistic composite image. Color-infrared film earns its other name, false-color film, by replacing the blue layer with an emulsion sensitive to infrared radiation and rearranging the bands so that infrared prints as red, red masquerades as green, and green becomes blue. Ignoring the blue band is beneficial:

blue light is readily scattered in the atmosphere and gives normal color air photos their distinctive and disconcerting haze. In color-infrared photos, clear blue water, which absorbs green, red, and infrared light, looks black, and healthy vegetation, which reflects infrared radiation most efficiently, appears bright red.

Intrigued with what air photos might reveal about terrain and hostile forces, military researchers experimented with films and filters. The reflectance characteristics of vegetation and soil were key elements in terrain studies focusing on concealment, enemy food supplies, and the ease with which troops and vehicles could move across open country. Although most of the work was classified, an official from the Navy Photographic Interpretation Center described an agriculturally significant project at the 1953 meeting of the American Society of Photogrammetry. At the request of the National Research Council's Committee on Plant and Crop Ecology, naval researchers had measured reflectance for diseased and healthy cereal crops. A key exhibit compared the spectral signatures of wheat with varying degrees of leaf damage caused by rust spores. As the curves show, severely damaged wheat reflects more reddish radiation and less infrared radiation than less severely affected wheat (fig. 3.5). An accompanying photograph taken with infrared film showed a strong contrast between the dark tones of severely diseased crops and the light tones for fields with relatively little damage.

Overhead imagery would discover a lot more than crop stress. Experiments with photographic and electronic sensing systems led to effective methods for classifying crops, measuring soil moisture, and delineating soils that are chronically dry or chemically deficient.

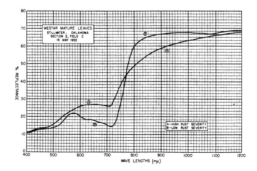

FIGURE 3.5 Military experiment showing different spectral signatures for severely and moderately diseased wheat. From Page E. Truesdell, "Report of Unclassified Military Terrain Studies Section," *Photogrammetric Engineering* 19 (1953): 470.

Multispectral scanners designed to record reflected radiation in comparatively narrow, carefully chosen portions (bands) of the electromagnetic spectrum proved especially useful in identifying fields needing attention. Thermal and microwave radar scanners were equally promising. Although reflected-infrared imagery can point out moisture differences only at the surface, thermal sensors can describe moisture conditions in the soil's upper 10 centimeters. Equally important, synthetic aperture radar (SAR) systems for sensing soil moisture can penetrate the crop canopy as well as provide the all-weather imagery essential for routine, periodic monitoring.

+   +   +

Until very recently commercial satellite imagery has been too coarse for mapping farms at the subfield level, and airplanes and helicopters have carried most of the sensors used in crop management. Color-infrared images from Landsat's multispectral scanners, with resolutions between 79 and 30 meters, provided vivid documentation of changing agricultural land use but did not afford the detail needed to optimize applications of fertilizers, herbicides, and pesticides. The 20-meter resolution of SPOT's multispectral scanner was not noticeably more informative.

Temporal resolution can be more troublesome than spatial resolution. For example, Landsat-7's repeat cycle of sixteen days is much too long for effective crop management even though its scanners were substantially more useful to agriculture than earlier Landsat sensors. The farmer who applies insecticide two weeks late will have already lost the crop.

Even so, medium-resolution satellite imagery has a role in precision agriculture. Research at the USDA's Water Conservation Laboratory in Tucson, Arizona, showed that Landsat-7's Enhanced Thematic Mapper Plus (ETM+) data can be integrated with crop growth models as well as SAR data from current and future earth-imaging satellites. More frequent radar data calibrated to a Landsat vegetation index can partly compensate for the long repeat cycle, and numerical models based on daily meteorological measurements and a detailed soil map can simulate plant growth, soil conditions, and evaporation. Promising developments include expedited processing of Landsat data, growing international interest in radar satellites, improved crop-management models, and inexpensive transmitter-equipped sensors for monitoring conditions in the field. In addition to trouble-shooting maps that highlight areas needing fertilizer, water, or pesticide, process models also generate yield maps and profit maps that help farmers explore diverse planting and harvesting strategies.

The four maps in figure 3.6 demonstrate the scope and scale of subfield analysis. Their focus is a 45-acre field near Salina, Kansas. As the map in the upper left shows, soybean yield in 1999 varied from less than 20 to more than 50 bushels per acre. At the upper right a second map describes the pattern of electrical conductivity (EC), which was measured with a probe-profiler towed behind a tractor. EC, which is negatively correlated with yield, reflects grain size, texture, and other soil properties that affect root development and plant growth. Performance Benchmark Analysis, a software solution that compares yield to the soil's potential productivity, generated the map at the lower left, on which varying shades of gray identify areas performing below their potential. Where the performance level is less than 90 percent, as shown on the map at the lower right, the model estimated the cost of underperformance in dollars per acre. Nitrogen fertilizer and other treatments can significantly increase yield in these areas.

Multiple technologies are typical of precision agriculture, which uses GIS to manage data and support modeling, remote sensing to monitor crops and soil, and GPS to guide sprayers, harvesters, and other machinery. The goal is increased profitability, and the strategy is integration and control. Closely linked sensors and computer models not only advise the farmer but collect data in the field. For example, an automatic variable-rate manure spreader with a GPS, a radio, and its own sensors can send the GIS updated reports on soil conditions and weed density. In addition to directing the application of water and fertilizers, spatial data and process models might eventually control the movement of unmanned agricultural vehicles.

It's clear that "farming soils, not fields," can significantly raise profit margins. Pierre Robert, director of the University of Minnesota's Precision Agriculture Center, compares the increased productivity of information technology to three earlier innovations: the

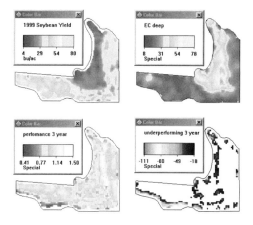

FIGURE 3.6 Subfield maps describing a 45-acre field's 1999 soybean yield *(upper left)*, electrical conductivity *(upper right)*, 1999 performance level *(lower left)*, and the cost of underperformance in dollars per acre *(lower right)*. The original maps are in color. Courtesy of Veris Technologies, a division of GeoProbe Systems.

tractor, agrochemicals, and hybrid crops. Adoption will be slow, he cautions: "It took more than 30 years to see tractors fully utilized." Less clear is the farmer's future role as an independent decision maker and entrepreneur. Crop consultants monitor fields and advise grain farmers on planting, cultivating, and harvesting. In the Midwest, many farmers rely on "custom cutters," who own the combines and hire the crews for efficient, timely harvesting and hauling. As corporate farms grow larger, smaller producers cede greater control to banks, marketing cooperatives, and biotechnology firms hawking genetically engineered seeds. It's hardly surprising that crop consultant Dennis Berglund would wonder whether "the data will [eventually] be worth more than the land."

+   +   +

Adept at monitoring production and controlling weeds, geospatial technology seemed an obvious tool for law enforcement officials eager to find and destroy an outlawed but highly profitable weed, marijuana. But with different goals and ground rules, precision pot busting has yet to replicate the success of precision farming. Effective against greedily indiscreet domestic producers as well as Third World peasants proud of their poppies, remote sensing loses much of its power when savvy cultivators scatter their plants across cornfields and forests. Because cannabis is not markedly different in its spectral signature from most other herbaceous plants, small or sparsely mixed plots are impossible to spot from space and difficult to discern from a plane or helicopter. Even so, authorities are rightly suspicious of cultivated plots in wildlife sanctuaries or on federal land that shouldn't have tended fields with scarecrows.

When imagery won't work, drug enforcement agencies can combine a GIS with an expert system designed to outsmart intrepid growers who circumvent asset forfeiture laws by planting pot in national forests. In the early 1990s geographers Delvin Fung and Roy Welch developed a prototype for Chattahoochee National Forest in northeast Georgia. Intended to predict locations likely to contain pot plantations, their system integrated information about the ecology of cannabis and the behavior of cultivators with data on terrain, roads, streams, and forest cover. Results were impressive: their system not only predicted seventy-five of ninety previously identified marijuana sites but targeted three others for field checking by Forest Service police, who found cannabis planted at all three.

Producers who try to avoid overhead surveillance by moving their plants indoors must be wary of forward-looking infrared (FLIR) sensors, designed originally for nighttime warfare. Windowless hydroponic pot farms replicate natural sunlight with full-spectrum "growlights" that emit both visible and ultraviolet light. In addition to energizing the plants, growlights warm the air, which in turn radiates excess heat through walls and roof. Aimed from ground or air, thermal-infrared imaging systems reveal the excess heat as a bright spot, warmer than its surroundings. That's why thermal imaging is useful for energy-conservation agencies studying heat loss as well as for cops ferreting out clandestine "grow rooms." Because heat from growlights can look a lot like heat from a fireplace or poorly insulated attic (fig. 3.7), thermal infrared alone doesn't justify a search warrant. But when further investigation links an anomalous hot spot to other suspicious activity, few judges will refuse a warrant.

Recent postings to the HempCultivation.Com Security forum reflect growers' concerns about thermal imaging. "James Bong" wondered whether "anyone had detailed information on the use and accuracy of thermal imaging devices on plants of our favour." His query triggered a lengthy reply from "Ganga Warrior," a nongrower (I assume) eager to share experiences and insight.

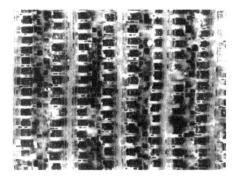

FIGURE 3.7 Thermal-infrared image of a residential neighborhood showing unusual heat loss for a few homes with overly warm interiors or poor insulation. The small bright dots on most roofs pinpoint chimneys. Courtesy of the Rochester Institute of Technology— Center for Imaging Science.

As one of the cops involved in detecting and eradicating dope, I can tell you that thermal imaging is not used much for outdoor grows.

In the early 1990s when peace broke out, the DoD and other agencies with hi-tech equipment that was suddenly under-used came to law enforcement and touted their wares. We tried everything from computer analyzed, false color photography, IR, and thermal imaging. None of them were very effective on outdoor grows.

Thermal imaging is still VERY BIG with indoor grows because of the heat generated by the cultivation.

Infra red (IR) and thermal gear worked best on outdoor grows when used during the heat of the day. The water lines, being cooler than the surrounding terrain and vegetation, show up very well, but there was no way to tell if they were domestic water supply or supporting a grow.

Perhaps the most insidious use of this spy technology was the attempts to use sensitive equipment to detect the minute amounts of radio isotopes in the galvanized chicken wire and the low level electrical impulses put out by batteries in the water timers. These happened at a level much higher than my lowly position so I don't know if they had any success.

Ganga's irreverent remarks are incisive. Drug interdiction is a big business for law enforcement and equipment vendors, and skirmishes over pot are part of the wider war against more potent drugs like cocaine and heroin. Trickle-down from military research encourages integration of diverse monitoring, screening, and tracking technologies, including the unmanned aerial vehicle (UAV) in figure 3.8, equipped with a video camera for "undetected surveil-

FIGURE 3.8 A government grant helped the Pima County, Arizona, Sheriff's Department develop an unmanned aerial vehicle (UAV) equipped with a video camera and transmitter. From Office of National Drug Control Policy, Counterdrug Technology Assessment Center, *Confronting Drug Crime and Abuse with Advanced Technology* (Washington, D.C., 2000), 13.

lance." Even so, police rely mostly on informants, anonymous tips, and the occasional visual survey with a helicopter.

+   +   +

What police consider a clever way to trawl for indoor marijuana farms, civil libertarians see as an assault on the Fourth Amendment, which bans "unreasonable searches and seizures." At issue is a household's expectation of privacy and the extent to which infrared sensors can look through walls and roofs. For the most part, judges have sided with the police. In 1991, for instance, in *United States v. Penny-Feeney,* the Federal District Court in Hawaii held that using a thermal scanner was a reasonable way to check out an anonymous tip and better establish probable cause for a search warrant. Authorized to search Janice Penny-Feeney's home, county police found ten 1,000-watt growlights and 247 marijuana plants. In rejecting Penny-Feeney's petition to suppress the evidence, the court concluded that the sensor sees nothing more than "waste heat"—the legal equivalent of stench from a garbage bag abandoned at the curb for constitutional removal by the sanitation department, snooping neighbors, or enterprising cops. Judges in the Seventh, Eighth, and Eleventh Circuits apparently bought this argument, although additional evidence helped establish probable cause.

Not all jurists agree. In 1998, for instance, in *United States v. Kyllo,* a three-judge panel in the Ninth Circuit Court of Appeals diverged on the obtrusiveness of FLIR scanners. Two of the judges rejected the waste heat excuse and overturned indoor marijuana grower Danny Lee Kyllo's conviction because of a "presumptively unreasonable" warrantless search. Although police had obtained a warrant to search Kyllo's home, their contention of probable cause was based partly on a ground-based FLIR scan. "Even if a thermal imager does not reveal details such as sexual activity in a bedroom," the court's majority declared, "with a basic understanding of the layout of a home, a thermal imager could identify a variety of daily activities conducted in homes across America: use of showers and bathtubs, ovens, washers and dryers, and any other household appliance that emits heat." Not so, their dissenting colleague argued: the scanner merely "measured the heat emanating from and on the outside of a house" and "intruded into nothing." The government requested a rehearing, and sixteen months later the appeals court reversed itself, restored Kyllo's conviction, and pronounced the scanner not "so revealing of intimate details as to raise constitutional concerns."

Kyllo appealed to the Supreme Court, which in mid-2001 ruled in his favor 5 to 4 and sent the case back to the lower court. Writing for the majority, Justice Antonin Scalia declared the search unconstitutional because warrantless use of "sense-enhancing technology . . . not in general public use" violates a citizen's reasonable expectation of privacy. Justice John Paul Stevens, who wrote the dissent, countered that the case involved "nothing more than drawing inferences from off-the-wall surveillance, rather than any 'through-the-wall' surveillance." To bolster his position that the images were not intrusive, Stevens referred to the contested thermal image of a hot spot near the middle of Kyllo's roof, above the growlights (fig. 3.9), and observed that "the device could not . . . and did not . . . enable its user to identify either the lady of the house, the rug on the vestibule floor, or anything else inside the house." The staunchly conservative Scalia was not impressed: "In the home," he maintained, "*all* details are intimate details, because the entire area is held safe from prying government eyes." Civil libertarians were elated at the decision, which one observer called "surprisingly broad." Even so, the ruling neither prohibits police from obtaining a warrant for FLIR surveillance nor addresses the possible proliferation of cheap thermal scanners sold over the Internet or at the local RadioShack.

FLIR image of the
Kyllo home

FLIR image with
interpretative
annotations

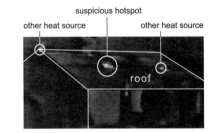

FIGURE 3.9 Thermal image revealing a plausibly incriminating hot spot near center of Danny Lee Kyllo's roof. The unannotated image was a defense (government) exhibit in *Kyllo v. United States.*

Curiously, the *Kyllo* decision diverged from the high court's traditional conservative-liberal split. Justice Scalia's libertarian opinion drew support from not only his equally conservative colleague Clarence Thomas but also the moderately liberal justices Steven Breyer, Ruth Bader Ginsburg, and David Souter. By contrast, Justice Stevens, arguably the court's most liberal member, was joined in his dissent by the conservative Chief Justice William Rehnquist as well as the moderate conservatives Anthony Kennedy and Sandra Day O'Connor. Because views on abortion and school vouchers seem to have little bearing on a justice's attitude toward remote surveillance, it might be difficult without pointed probing to predict a future nominee's stance on surveillance technology.

Equally problematic is the legality of overhead imagery. The last time the high court ruled on aerial photography was 1986, in *Dow Chemical Company v. United States.* Dow had charged the Environmental Protection Agency with committing an unconstitutional warrantless search by hiring an aerial survey firm to inspect its 2,000-acre Midland, Michigan, plant for violations of the Clean Air Act. In ruling in favor of the EPA, the court found that taking pictures of the sprawling plant from navigable air space was perfectly constitutional because the exposed pipes, machinery, and other facilities were more like an "open field" than the "curtilage" (courtyard or fenced-in yard) around a home. Simply put, Dow had no right to expect privacy because "the intimate activities associated with family privacy and the home and its curtilage simply do not reach the outdoor areas or spaces between structures and buildings of a manufacturing plant." Moreover, Congress had authorized the EPA to search for violations.

Although the 1986 court waffled on whether use of "highly sophisticated surveillance equipment not generally available to the public, such as satellite technology, might be constitutionally proscribed absent a warrant," the "open field" argument in *Dow* clearly justifies satellite surveillance like the use of SPOT imagery to ferret out illegal irrigation. But don't expect agreement from ardent privacy advocates. After the *Wall Street Journal* reported the irate protest of a farmer charged with irrigating 39 acres without a permit, libertarians were outraged that the Arizona Department of Water Resources would compare satellite imagery with computer records of irrigation permits. In a Libertarian Party denunciation of "Big Brother" and "spy satellites," national chairman Steve Dasbach complained that "high-tech military equipment ... once used against foreign enemies [was] now being used against American citizens on a routine basis." Arizona was not the only snoop: several states were smoking out pot with thermal scanners, Georgia planned a satellite search for illegal timber cutting, and North Carolina tax assessors were scrutinizing high-resolution satellite imagery for improved properties, soon to be hit with bigger tax bills. I doubt that many libertarians, most of whom abhor taxes, government fees, and government in general, appreciated DWR director Rita Pearson's retort that satellite imagery helped her department cut back its enforcement staff.

If the Supreme Court sets further limits on overhead surveillance, the justices might well draw a line at comparatively obtrusive sensors like active microwave radar. Scanners that generate their own radiation are arguably more menacing than devices that detect waste heat or reflected sunlight. Even so, distinctions between residential and nonresidential buildings seem crucial, as the high court implied in *Dow* and reaffirmed in *Kyllo*. Although the judiciary might distinguish between acceptable government enforcement and excessively intrusive private uses, high-definition satellite imagery will probably pass the "open field" test. Space Imaging no doubt thought so when its house magazine—in an article titled "Sizing Up the Competition: Earth Information Takes Commercial Intelligence to a New Level"—encouraged overhead surveillance of plants, warehouses, and shipping sites by investors and competitors. Increased availability of overhead imagery over the Internet from Space Imaging and at Web sites like terraserver.com defuse much of the high court's unease in *Dow* (and more recently in *Kyllo*) about "highly sophisticated surveillance equipment not generally available to the public."

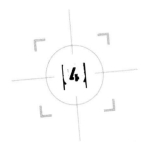

{4}

Tinder, Technology, and Tactics

Wildland fire tops the list of hazards I might have included in my book *Cartographies of Danger* but didn't. It seemed reasonable to omit a hazard so dependent on the current day's weather and the number of years since the last big burn. Besides, I needed to limit the book's scope and length, and no one seemed to be making hazard-zone maps similar to those for tornadoes, floods, and earthquakes. No doubt my oversight also reflects an East Coast bias. Had I lived in Montana or New Mexico, fuel maps and fire atlases would have received the respect accorded groundwater models and toxic plumes.

In June 2000, when I began to plan this chapter, wildland fire was all over the news. That May the Cerro Grande Fire—a "prescribed fire" that got out of control—destroyed more than two hundred homes at Los Alamos, New Mexico, and toward the end of summer, when I started to write, wildfires were on front pages and nightly newscasts almost daily. By then I had a fuller appreciation of the scope and devastation of western fires. For added understanding, a vacation that July included visits to Los Alamos as well as Mesa Verde National Park, in southwest Colorado, where a 1996 fire burned nearly 5,000 acres.

What I saw in Los Alamos spoke of individual tragedy and collective naïveté. Residential development had expanded upslope into scenic woodlands, which rebelled by bringing the fire into backyards and vestibules. Remnant chimneys and burned-out cars testified to the hazards of the "urban-wildland interface"—no less a high-risk zone than a floodplain or shoreline. In some neighborhoods haphazard devastation suggested an evil lottery had targeted one in every four or five homes at random. Chain-link fencing encircled rubble-strewn lots with charred foundations, while life went on next door with few apparent scars. Was it luck, fire-retardant roofs, or successfully deployed lawn sprinklers?

By contrast, Mesa Verde was recovering nicely. Although broad expanses of blackened, leafless trees marked the extent of the 1996 fire, wildflowers and small shrubs had aggressively colonized the recently exposed soil. And in a stroke of serendipity, the fire that burned off the piñon and juniper had uncovered hundreds of Ancestral Puebloan artifacts, eagerly mapped and cataloged by National Park Service archaeologists. But because the spring and early summer had been exceptionally hot and dry, areas that escaped the conflagration four years earlier were now in far greater danger. As my wife, Marge, and I toured the cliff dwellings and agricultural ruins, we saw fire crews busily clearing brush and cutting trees near some of the park's more important sites. Reducing the amount of readily combustible fuel can slow a fire and make it easier to extinguish. We also noticed helicopters carrying huge buckets of water to new fires—small ones, thankfully—started by lightning the night before. Suppressing minor fires while they're still small demands vigilance and luck. Two weeks later the luck ran out: a wildfire triggered by lightning burned a third of the park and sent archaeologists out to the fire lines, to protect previously unknown sites from firefighters' axes.

+ + +

To understand geographic technology's role in coping with wild-land fire requires an appreciation of the factors that influence ignition and spread. Foremost, of course, is fuel. Anything living or dead that will burn, release heat, and feed the fire is considered fuel, whether it's in the ground, on the surface, or in the air. Ground fuel, which includes tree roots, buried wood fragments, and decaying organic matter in the soil, can spread a fire to nearby surface material and is difficult to extinguish when dry. Fire experts distinguish surface fuels like short trees and shrubs, fallen branches and needles, and other surface litter from aerial fuels like the trunks and branches of trees taller than about five feet and their leaves, needles, mosses, and lichens. In this upper layer, a crown fire fed by conifer needles and other fine materials can spread rapidly from tree to tree. Crown fire is less likely with deciduous leaves, which burn readily only when very dry. Even so, dead leaves add to surface fuel, which is more prone than aerial fuel to ignition from a lightning strike or careless camper.

In addition to differentiating among ground, surface, and aerial layers, a fuel inventory must account for the mass, moisture content, and flammability of forest fuels. Compiling a comprehensive fuel inventory can be a complex, costly, and slow process if the forester conscientiously selects sample plots, identifies species, weighs woody material, and carefully estimates its moisture content. Lacking time and budget, forest managers typically delineate boundaries between forest types and assign each zone to a risk category.

During the 1930s, when fuel mapping was relatively new, the U.S. Forest Service focused on identifying intuitively hazardous areas and training field workers to be consistent when using photographic keys to assign categories. Figure 4.1, from a mid-1930s fire control manual, describes the symbols employed in mapping fuels on 15 million acres of federal and privately owned "cooperative" lands. Designed to focus attention on high-risk areas, the map uses contrasting colors to describe the likely rate of spread of a small fire and parallel lines to show the number of firefighters required to put it out. Superposition of what might have been two separate maps recognizes the enhanced hazardousness of areas in which ground cover, steep slope, or other factors would slow construction of a fire control line.

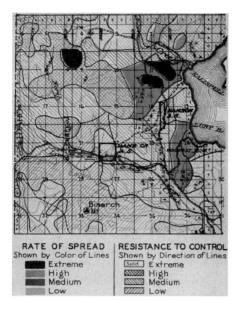

FIGURE 4.1 Portion of 1930s-era field fuel map for Kaniksu National Forest in Idaho. The numbered squares are square-mile Public Land Survey "sections," each of which contains 640 acres. The original map is in color, with black, red, green, and yellow-orange representing extreme, high, medium, and low risk of spread, respectively. From L. G. Hornby, *Forest Fire Control Planning in the Northern Rocky Mountain Region* (n.p.: U.S. Forest Service, Rocky Mountain Forest and Range Experiment Station, 1936), 51.

Contemporary fuel maps reflect wildfire-specific vegetation categories based on carefully controlled laboratory "burns." Experimental measurements of the temperatures attained and amounts of heat released by various kinds of plant matter, alive or dead, provide a foundation for numerical "fuel models" that encompass an array of flammability factors, including the presence of oils, resins, and other highly volatile compounds and the effect of diameter on the rate of drying. Grasses, dry needles, and lichens, for example, can gain or lose most of their moisture in little more than an hour, whereas logs over three inches in diameter might take more than a month to respond to exceptionally wet or dry conditions. Fuel models also consider the amount of time (sometimes measured in centuries) over which surface fuels have accumulated as well as the spacing of burnable material, which might be packed too tightly to produce flames that could spread the fire to nearby litter.

Besides helping the Forest Service prioritize brush removal and other fuel reduction efforts, fuel models are used to assess current fire danger and predict the behavior of actual fires. The National Fire Danger Rating System integrates mid-afternoon weather data with a set of twenty fuel models and calculates a series of indexes representing the potential for surface fires over large areas for a twenty-four-hour period. Each fuel model is named for a type of vegetation; examples include mature chaparral, heavy logging slash, and "closed short-needle conifer (heavily dead)." Depending on the values of the Burning Index, the Spread Component, and the Energy Release Component, officials make an educated guess about whether the next twenty-four-hour period will be a normal day, a fire day, a large-fire day, or a multiple-fire day—categories that reflect demands on personnel and equipment. (As interpreted verbally for campers and passing motorists, a simpler system rates fire danger as low, moderate, high, very high, or extreme.) To predict the behavior of an observed wildfire, the Forest Service relies on a set of thirteen fuel models, which provide coefficients for mathematic equations describing a wildland fire's intensity, flame height, and rate of spread.

Fire-spread models must also consider wind and slope. On a flat, uniform plane a fire expands outward in a circular pattern, as hot gasses from the burning material and thermal radiation from the flames dry out and ignite areas just beyond the flames. Add a steady wind and the circle becomes an ellipse. As figure 4.2 illustrates, even a light, 1-mile-per-hour wind produces a noticeably elongated fire perimeter, and higher wind speeds yield more pronounced elongations.

Not all fires behave like a simple contagious process. As the left-hand diagram in figure 4.3 illustrates, a fire advances more readily in the direction of a steady wind, which pushes superheated gasses forward near the surface, tilts the flames outward over the fuelbed

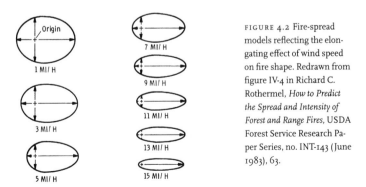

FIGURE 4.2 Fire-spread models reflecting the elongating effect of wind speed on fire shape. Redrawn from figure IV-4 in Richard C. Rothermel, *How to Predict the Spread and Intensity of Forest and Range Fires*, USDA Forest Service Research Paper Series, no. INT-143 (June 1983), 63.

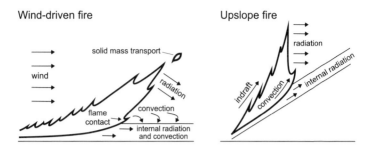

Wind-driven fire

Upslope fire

FIGURE 4.3 Factors in the spread of wind-driven and upslope fires. Redrawn from figures 2 and 3 in Richard C. Rothermel, *A Mathematical Model for Predicting Fire Spread in Wildland Fuels*, USDA Forest Service Research Paper Series, no. INT-115 (January 1972), 5.

directly downwind, and carries airborne ashes, embers, and other "firebrands" well beyond the flame front. Because fires can reinforce the wind by creating turbulent vortexes called fire swirls, shaggy fragments of burning bark can stay lit and aloft long enough to "spot" a new fire more than a mile away. Ellipse-based models designed to represent surface fires cannot predict the growth of large fires, which typically expand by spotting and "breakouts." Richard Rothermel, the Forest Service engineer who pioneered fire-spread models, was well aware of their limitations. In describing the hazards of fighting large fires in very dry conditions, he observed that "the fires literally make their own weather, mostly rain and winds called downbursts. That's how they suddenly blow up."

Terrain further distorts the fire perimeter. As the right-hand diagram in figure 4.3 shows, a fire will advance more rapidly upslope as radiation from its flames attacks the full height of trees and shrubs immediately ahead. Because an upslope fire can "explode" and outrun a firefighter, few places are as dangerous as a ridge crest directly ahead of an advancing wildfire. Narrow canyons are equally hazardous because radiation and embers from one side of the corridor will expedite the fire's advance along the other side and vice versa. And a gully aligned with a strong upslope wind is akin to a flamethrower pointed at anyone on the ridge above.

Given a fuel model, a wind velocity, and a uniform slope, a fire-spread model can calculate the likely perimeter of a small fire several hours after ignition. Because the fire perimeter becomes less regular as the fire grows and conditions change, later estimates are usually based on two or more "projection points" (numbered 1 and 2 in fig. 4.4) representing the forward advance of the fire front. The strongest wind seldom coincides with the steepest slope, so fire control officers treat these effects as vectors and use their resultant to project the fire perimeter forward.

In the 1970s, when fire-spread models were still largely experimental, fire officials typically estimated the expected rate of advance for different areas with graphs or a computer program and transferred the results by hand to a topographic map. Predictions were handicapped by coarse boundaries between fuel types and irregular terrain. As Rothermel cautioned, accuracy depends "upon the skill and knowledge of the user and the degree of uniformity or lack of uniformity of the fuels and environmental conditions." Even so, the fire-spread model is a useful tool for making an educated guess about the most effective way to suppress the fire and protect firefighters.

+   +   +

Computers handle most of the map work nowadays. Although fire-spread models are still valuable in suggesting worst-case scenarios and planning the prescribed fires used to reduce the fuel hazard, emphasis is on real-time management, which includes tracking the

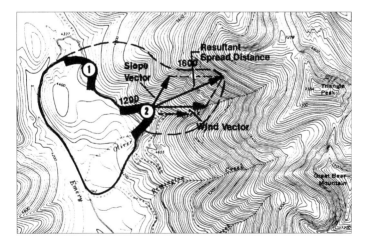

FIGURE 4.4 Projected advance of a fire perimeter based on projection points (1 and 2) and separate distance vectors for slope and wind. Compiled from figures IV-7 and IV-9 in Rothermel, *How to Predict the Spread and Intensity of Forest and Range Fires*, 78–79.

fire front and monitoring the current positions of fire crews and fire engines. Geographic information systems excel at integrating information from such diverse sources as weather maps, satellite imagery of vegetation, maps of fire trails and other local roads, and digital terrain models, which describe accessibility and provide slope data for fire-spread models. Heavily dependent upon telecommunications, modern fire fighting is much like modern warfare as fire crews with two-way radios and handheld GPS receivers update their map coordinates, a helicopter pilot with a GPS unit traces the fire perimeter, and the "fire boss" coordinates communications with community fire departments.

Because GIS software is not nearly as user-friendly as its vendors would have us believe, each of California's twelve Interagency Incident Management Teams includes a GIS specialist. For small fires, a notebook computer with a portable printer and plotter are usually adequate. For larger fires, the team's technical specialist will request a mobile GIS unit and additional "tech specs" to operate the multiple workstations and large-format plotter. California's pyro-cartographers depend on a variety of data, including satellite images, digital elevation models (DEMs) used in fire-spread modeling, "fire-ground intelligence" based on GPS readings, thermal-infrared imagery from Forest Service aircraft, and a set of nine CDs containing topographic data for the entire state. Terrain maps extracted from the CDs form the basis for an Incident Action Plan and illustrate the morning and evening briefings at which fire officials evaluate the situation and assign personnel.

Keeping track of who's where and doing what is especially challenging for large fires like the October 1995 Vision Wildfire, which consumed 11,410 acres at Point Reyes National Seashore in northern California. The fire burned for twelve days, and at its height engaged 196 fire engines, 27 bulldozers, 7 helicopters, 7 tanker aircraft, and 2,146 personnel, including 74 fire crews. Emergency officials assembled a team of four GIS specialists within twelve hours of the fire's ignition. A day and a half later they had set up a fully equipped GIS lab—quite an accomplishment in 1995, when mobile labs were just a cool idea—and were busy plotting updated maps of the fire perimeter and damaged structures. When the fire was out and most firefighters had returned home, GIS experts were busy mapping the impact on wildlife and rare plants and assessing the fire's response to fuel type, slope, and wind. Retrospective modeling is useful for training firefighters as well as making residents and local officials aware of the dangers of living in the urban-wildland interface. According to Sarah Allen, the "tech spec" who directed the effort, GIS maps are "great tools for public relations" as well as priceless data for local communities eagerly seeking federal disaster relief funds.

+   +   +

Because large fires are difficult to manage, much less model, efficient suppression depends on early detection. The principal line of defense used to be a network of fire towers and other fixed, ground-based lookouts staffed by observers who scanned the horizon with binoculars for plumes of smoke and reported in by telephone or shortwave radio. Back in the 1980s GIS helped fire officials reconfigure lookout networks to provide maximal coverage with a minimal number of conveniently accessible observation posts. Nowadays geographic technology provides additional sets of eyes, watching from space and often able to see at night and through clouds or smoke. Detecting forest fires is another role for weather and earth observation satellites already in orbit for other purposes.

A satellite's ability to detect fire depends on its orbit and sensors. Two complementary orbits seem especially appropriate. As configured for the National Oceanic and Atmospheric Administration's Polar-orbiting Operational Environmental Satellites (POES), a low-altitude near-polar orbit provides comparatively detailed, moderately frequent worldwide coverage. As shown schematically in figure 4.5, an orbital plane inclined slightly to the earth's axis moves steadily westward as the satellite circles the globe fourteen times a day in a mildly elliptical orbit. A sensor scanning a ground swath 1,700 miles (2,800 km) wide from an altitude of approximately 520 miles (840 km) provides twice-a-day coverage for mid-latitude locations, and a pair of satellites in orbital planes 90 degrees apart reduces the revisit time to six hours. By contrast, one of NOAA's Geostationary Environmental Observations Satellites (GOES), parked 22,300 miles (35,900 km) above a fixed point on the equator, stares downward at slightly less than half the globe but reports in with a new image every fifteen minutes. This markedly higher orbit limits GOES imagery to a resolution of 2.5 miles (4.0 km) directly over the equator, with progressively larger pixels and fuzzier images with increased distance from the nadir point. The comparatively lower POES orbit compensates for less frequent coverage with sharper images based on 0.7-mile (1.1 km) pixels along the nadir track.

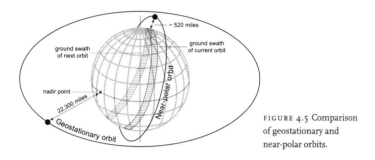

FIGURE 4.5 Comparison of geostationary and near-polar orbits.

POES's prowess as a fire lookout depends on thermal-infrared imagery from its AVHRR (Advanced Very High Resolution Radiometer) scanner. Designed for meteorological, oceanographic, and hydrologic studies, the AVHRR is a multispectral scanner similar in principle to the Landsat and SPOT sensors (see chapter 2), which capture separate images for carefully selected portions of the electromagnetic spectrum. Among the AVHRR sensor's five bands sampling visible, near-infrared, and thermal energy, band 3 (3.55–3.93 μm) is especially suited for detecting wildland fires, in which temperatures range from 500 to 1,000 kelvins (400–1,300°F). Although insensitive to temperature differences within a large fire—pixels reach their maximum brilliance at a "saturation temperature" of only 320 kelvins (120°F)—the band-3 sensor is ideal for detecting hot spots as small as an acre and thus valuable for recognizing fires shortly after ignition, when suppression is most effective.

Imagery and maps for the June 1996 Millers Reach, Alaska, wildfire demonstrate the accuracy and feasibility of near-real-time monitoring. Like most high-latitude locations, Alaska enjoys comparatively frequent AVHRR coverage because POES orbits converge near the poles such that ground swaths often overlap. In reconstructing the fire's evolution, NOAA researchers further reduced the six-hour revisit time by integrating band-3 AVHRR imagery with data from ground-based Doppler radar, the GOES Imager, and polar-orbiting Defense Meteorological Space Program satellites. Despite the geostationary satellite's comparatively coarse resolution (8 km at 60°N), the fire's approximate location was readily apparent shortly after ignition on a GOES thermal-infrared image similar in sensitivity to AVHRR band 3. GIS analysts now knew where to look for further growth and were able to track the expanding burn zone by superimposing various images onto a map with a 1-kilometer grid (fig. 4.6). By 0533 LST (local sun time) on the morning of June 5, the fire was centered on three large hot spots surrounding Big Lake. Arrows on the map show where strong winds carried the fire to the west and south over the next eight hours and more than doubled the number of pixels and acres affected. In addition to successfully tracking a fire from space, imagery used in the study was available within forty minutes after ground stations received the data.

Geostationary satellites offer a promising platform for detecting and monitoring wildfire in real time. Although a GIS can enhance reliability by integrating imagery from complementary sources, noth-

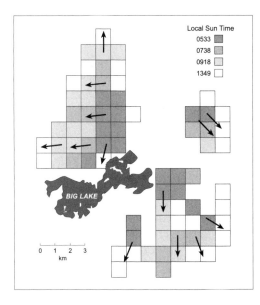

FIGURE 4.6 Fire-affected pixels identified on imagery from NOAA and Defense Department meteorological satellites describe the advance of the Millers Reach fire, in south-central Alaska, over an eight-hour period on June 5, 1996. Movement of the fire front can be tracked outward from the darker pixels, which burned earlier than the lighter pixels. Redrawn from figure 12 in Gary L. Hufford and others, "Use of Real-time Multisatellite and Radar Data to Support Forest Fire Management," *Weather and Forecasting* 13 (1998): 603.

ing beats the timeliness of a fresh snapshot every fifteen minutes. Sharpen its spatial resolution with a specially designed sensor, and a GOES successor might even pinpoint small fires. That substantial improvements are possible is implied by an international commission's call for "an ultimate detection time of 5 minutes, a repeat time of 15 minutes, spatial resolution of 250 meters, and real time transmission to local ground stations." Although this commission, the Committee on Earth Observation Satellites (CEOS), touts the advantages of a sharper, more timely God's-eye view, cloud cover would still be troublesome because thermal signals cannot penetrate thick clouds.

Equally intriguing is the Langley Research Center's proposal for FireSat, a research satellite that would monitor biomass burning worldwide. Proposed in the mid-1990s as a five-year scientific mission but still on NASA drawing boards a half-decade later, FireSat could customize satellite sensors for mapping forest and grassland fires as part of a larger concern with the effect of wildland fire on global climate. A comparatively inexpensive "small sat" would carry a 23-kilogram (50 lb.) scanner in a circular near-polar orbit at an altitude of 520 miles (830 km) and provide four daily passes over northern forests, once-a-day surveillance of middle latitudes, and every-other-day coverage of the tropics. The scanner's seven bands would be optimized for detecting smoke and particulate matter; mapping active fires and recently burned areas; detecting cirrus clouds, vegetation moisture, and fire scars; and measuring surface temperature. Other significant departures from the AVHRR and GOES Imager sensors would include 263-meter (860 ft.) resolution along the nadir track and a saturation temperature of 1,000 kelvins (1,300°F), about the maximum temperature found in wildland fires.

Exceptionally sharp imagery and a high saturation temperature are essential for accurate maps of fire intensity. Although a 500 × 500-meter (1,600 × 1,600 ft) pixel would provide valuable portraits of burn scars and fire fronts, a markedly sharper image, with smaller pixels, is needed because hot air and turbulence would surely blur the picture. According to research on the uncertainty of pixel measurements for active fires, half the radiation measured for a 263-meter pixel might originate outside its nominal ground spot. FireSat compensates with comparatively fine resolution from which deblurring software could recover acceptably sharp images. Even so, this extraordinary spatial detail would be wasted if the sensor allowed the pixels to saturate well below the fire's maximum intensity.

FireSat's originator and most persistent advocate is Joel Levine, a senior research scientist in Langley's atmospheric sciences division and a key collaborator in national and international studies of climate change. Levine's chief concern is the contribution of fires—both deliberate and natural—to increased amounts of carbon dioxide and particulate matter as well as the threats of higher temperatures, deforestation, and ozone depletion. FireSat is partly an effort to document the extent of burning, which affects about 1 percent of the earth's surface in a typical year and is much more widespread than once believed. Humans set most of the fires, principally to clear land for agriculture.

A contributor to the CEOS proposal, Levine is skeptical of the commission's call for a fifteen-minute repeat time, which, he notes, would require "a constellation of sixty satellites." Nevertheless, an image frequency of "an hour or less" seems both feasible and essential, especially if NASA needs support from the Forest Service and the Federal Emergency Management Agency (FEMA), which see fire suppression and timely evacuation as more compelling than scientific studies of global warming. To win their backing, Levine's team would place a second FireSat instrument on a geostationary satellite.

For now, FireSat is only a feasibility study, not an authorized mission. NASA management wants to be sure the mission can deliver everything that its champions claim. To address these concerns, Langley researchers have been busy calibrating existing satellite imagery with temperatures measured on the ground in prescribed fires and working with aerospace-electronics firms to develop a lightweight, long-lived thermal sensor. Levine is philosophical about the delay: if FireSat becomes the world's first dedicated fire-monitoring satellite, it must rely heavily on new, innovative technology designed by the space agency's commercial partners.

+   +   +

Useful in detecting wildland fires, satellite imagery can also identify areas requiring intensified brush cutting as well as additional fire-fighters and equipment. AVHRR imagery is one of several ingredients in the national fire potential index (FPI) map developed by fire researchers at the Forest Service in collaboration with remote sensing experts at the U.S. Geological Survey. Another element is GOES, which helps update the map by relaying data from remote automatic weather stations. The FPI map treats the country as a system of one-square-kilometer pixels and integrates twenty-four fuel models with detailed maps of land cover and vegetation. Each cell's fire potential index is updated daily by moisture data from nearby weather stations and a "relative greenness" index, which relates the cell's current vegetative vigor to its recorded highest and lowest values. As in camouflage detection and precision agriculture, near-infrared energy trumps visible green as a decisive indicator of vegetative greenness.

No state has exploited relative greenness and other FPI concepts more effectively than Oklahoma, which integrates satellite imagery with a state-of-art, real-time weather data network, the Oklahoma Mesonet. Intended for state and local fire officials, the Oklahoma Fire Danger Model produces five separate maps eleven times a day. Figure 4.7 illustrates two of them: the spread component map, which estimates the advance in feet per minute of a wind-driven fire front, and the ignition component map, which estimates the likelihood that firebrands will cause a fire requiring suppression. The model produced these maps for 2 P.M., April 8, 1999, when a prairie fire might have moved more than 120 feet a minute across the state's Panhandle and moderate winds increased the threat of firebrands. Red and orange symbols (dark areas on my black-and-white version) underscore the danger toward the southeast of wildland fire to semiarid grasslands, which can dry out and burn much more rapidly than woodlands.

If you're curious about fire potential or active fires in your area or a favorite vacation spot, visit GeoMAC Wildland Fire Support Web site (geomac.cr.usgs.gov). In cooperation with the Forest Service, NOAA, the National Interagency Fire Center, and several other federal agencies, the Geological Survey provides a cartographic overview of active fires and generalized fire perimeters as well as detailed

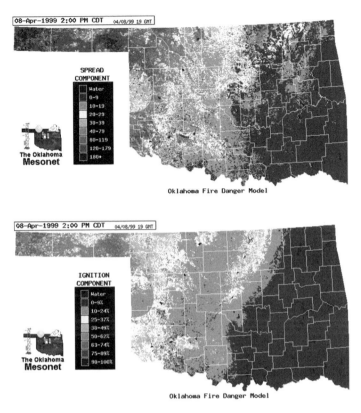

FIGURE 4.7 Spread component *(top)* and ignition component *(bottom)* maps from the Oklahoma Fire Danger Model for 2 P.M., April 8, 1999. From the Oklahoma State University, *AgWeather,* http://agweather.mesonet.ou.edu/models/fire/.

maps of individual fires based on imagery from space, fixed-wing aircraft, and ground locations. The Web is a convenient medium for distributing maps and other data to fire managers and field personnel, and there's no reason to restrict public access. We're paying for the information, after all, and it might make some of us more wary of the hazards of the urban-wildland interface.

+   +   +

Although satellite imagery and geographic information systems are immensely useful for detecting and suppressing wildland fire, a focus on putting out forest fires would be myopic. In the American

West and other dry areas, accumulated biomass that is not removed by prescribed fire or brush clearance will eventually burn—this year, next year, or maybe not for a hundred years. And fuel spared this year can support a bigger fire next year. Clear-cutting is an even worse solution: the tall trees removed for lumber are far more resistant to fire than the shrubs that follow or the litter left behind. And the more environmentally correct but costly practice of clearing brush by hand is practicable only for maintaining firebreaks or protecting specific structures. Equally inefficient are grazing animals—don't look for Smokey Goat to displace Smokey Bear as a fire-prevention icon. At the end of the day, the most dependable strategy is prescribed fire.

As a national policy, fighting fire with fire opens broader roles for GIS and FireSat. Improved modeling will help fire managers plan and control prescribed fires, while enhanced monitoring affords more timely warnings and evacuations as well as more reliable decisions about when and where to let a natural fire burn. Equally important are the roles of geographic surveillance in promoting awareness of urban-wildland hazards, in establishing and enforcing realistic zoning regulations and building codes, and in setting insurance rates that allow for occasional miscalculations like the Cerro Grande Fire. Ultimately unavoidable, wildland fire is less dangerous when fewer people live in the woods.

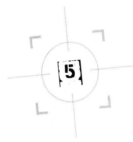

[5]

Weather Eyes

More pervasive than wildfire, destructive storms demand
vigilant surveillance by a vast network of probes and sensors. Networking is crucial: although each measurement of
temperature, pressure, wind, and humidity could contain
an important clue to the atmosphere's next assault, individual numbers mean little without a cartographic framework
that reveals meaningful patterns and ominous trends. In
much the same way that weather maps helped nineteenth-
century scientists unravel the nature of storms, computer
models and satellite images are the mind and eyes of modern forecasting.

Geographic surveillance must accommodate a variety of
meteorological scales, from hurricanes to lightning strikes.
Large rotating storms known as hurricanes or northeasters

were hard to predict when the forecaster's only eyes were land-based instruments. Still not fully understood, big storms are easy to spot from space, and surveillance technologies save thousands of lives by giving local officials ample warning of when and where evacuation is warranted. Less predictable are smaller, more localized phenomena like tornadoes and wind shear, for which the foreseeable future is a matter of minutes, not days. Lightning strikes are too small for exact forecasting, but precise after-the-fact maps warn of possible wildfires and identify substandard power lines.

+   +   +

In *Isaac's Storm,* Erik Larson recounts the tragedy of Galveston, Texas, where more than six thousand people died in September 1900, when an unanticipated hurricane of exceptional strength surged in from the Gulf of Mexico. Larson's hero is Isaac Cline, head of the local U.S. Weather Bureau office. Personal diaries and agency archives tell a tale of foolish pride and bureaucratic paralysis. Forecasters in Washington controlled weather data for the entire country and issued all warnings of serious storms. Although pressure and wind data cabled from Cuba suggested an enormous low-pressure system had entered the Gulf, the Central Office questioned the competence of Cuban meteorologists and ignored their observations. Although wary of rising seas along the Galveston waterfront, a dutiful Isaac Cline echoed the bureau's denials and discouraged evacuation until disaster was imminent. Cline lost his wife, his house, and his trust in Chief Willis Moore, who in the investigation that followed flagrantly distorted the Weather Bureau's actions.

However inexcusable, Washington's incompetence reflects a fatal mix of feeble theory and sparse data. Reconstructing an offshore storm from coastal observations is tricky when forecasters must infer the presence of a low-pressure center from a handful of barometric readings along its periphery. Washington officials knew that a tropical storm had passed over Cuba but assumed it was headed north across Florida like previous hurricanes. Turn-of-the-century forecasters believed that a storm center would tend to follow the generalized path of similar storms traversing the same area in the same direction at the same time of year. Dismissing wind and waves along Florida's west coast as mere "offshoots" of a hurricane more likely to threaten the Carolinas, Weather Bureau officials had no idea that Isaac's storm had slipped into the Gulf of Mexico's warm waters, where it gathered strength for a fatal assault on Galveston. According to their maps, hurricanes that crossed Cuba didn't track northwestward into the Gulf.

Another recent bestseller paints a radically different portrait of meteorological monitoring. The antagonist in Sebastian Junger's *The Perfect Storm* is an intense, well-developed "nor'easter" that formed in the North Atlantic in late October 1991. Its victims were the six crewmembers of the *Andrea Gail,* a commercial fishing boat based in Gloucester, Massachusetts. This time the National Weather Service (so renamed in 1967 and now a part of NOAA) got it right. Satellite imagery had tracked a severe cold front that moved off the northeast coast of the United States. Forecasters knew rogue waves were likely when an enormous, near-record high-pressure system behind the front led to an intense extratropical cyclone along the front, east of Nova Scotia.

Extratropical cyclones are large circular storms that, unlike hurricanes, form outside the Tropics. This one, later named the Halloween Storm of 1991, expanded rapidly and even absorbed Hurricane Grace, which had recently crossed the Atlantic from the west coast of Africa, where most hurricanes originate. On October 27, forecasters chose the rarely used, deliberately ominous adjective *perfect* to warn mariners that a "dangerous storm" would form over the North Atlantic within thirty-six hours. Rather than ride out the tempest on the Grand Banks with its sister vessel, the *Hannah Borden,* the *Andrea Gail* headed back to Gloucester with its catch. The following evening the ship lost radio contact after reporting 30-foot waves and 80-knot winds 180 miles east of Canada's Sable Island, near the center of the intensifying storm.

The story doesn't stop there. On October 29, the system moved southward and westward to flood homes and devastate beaches from Canada to North Carolina. Although the storm's lingering presence caused hundreds of millions of dollars of damage along the East Coast, low-lying areas were evacuated and fewer than a half-dozen coastal residents drowned. As the satellite image in figure 5.1 demonstrates, the storm's size sent a stern warning to anyone tempted to stay behind.

FIGURE 5.1 GOES-7 visible image for 1 P.M. EST, November 1, 1991, showing the extent of the Halloween Storm with an unnamed hurricane at its center. From NOAA's satellite art gallery, NOAA Climatic Data Center, http://www.ncdc.noaa.gov/ol/satellite/satelliteseye/.

This November 1 satellite photo also captured the meteorological oddity of a storm within a storm. A huge counterclockwise swirl describes a vast but dying storm still raining on the Northeast. At its center is a much smaller system with a clearly marked eye. At 6 P.M. New York time, when this snapshot was taken, the storm entered the record books as the Unnamed Hurricane of 1991 after winds near its center reached 65 knots—just above the official threshold of 64 knots (74 MPH). American and Canadian forecast officials agreed not to name the hurricane because the storm had already inflicted its greatest damage and would soon break up. Naming it, they figured, would create needless confusion about storm forecasts and evacuation warnings.

Hurricane Andrew, which rampaged across south Florida the following August, underscores the importance of timely evacuation. As hurricanes go, Andrew was not huge, but it was intense, with sustained winds up to 145 miles per hour. Meteorologists at the National Hurricane Center in Miami had tracked the storm's development since August 14, when satellite imagery revealed an anomaly in the trade winds west of Africa. Andrew reached hurricane strength on August 22 and collided with the Florida coast two days later. As the satellite image in figure 5.2 confirms, NOAA forecasters had ample time to initiate a timely evacuation of more than a million people in Dade, Broward, and Palm Beach Counties. Although the storm caused $25 billion in damage and entered the record books as the nation's costliest natural disaster, only sixty-five people perished, directly or indirectly. Had Andrew taken Floridians by surprise, it would have eclipsed the 1900 Galveston storm as the country's deadliest natural disaster.

According to Louis Uccellini, who directs NOAA's National Centers for Environmental Prediction, "though our forecasts were quite good for [the 1991 Halloween storm], we can do even better today." Participating in a June 2000 roundtable discussion of the Perfect Storm—the movie version of Junger's book was setting box-office records at the time—Uccellini cited marked improvements in storm prediction, which can look ahead as far as ninety-six hours. Although computers run the forecast models, he noted, satellites provide 85 percent of the data. What's more, by signaling the earli-

FIGURE 5.2 NOAA-12 satellite image showing Hurricane Andrew approaching the Florida coast on August 23, 1992. Original color image from NOAA's Historical Significant Events Imagery database, NOAA Climatic Data Center, http://www.ncdc.noaa.gov/pub/data/images/hurr-andrew-19920823-n12rgb.jpg.

est appearance of a tropical disturbance, satellite imagery helps weather officials plan aircraft reconnaissance missions, which yield valuable supplementary data.

NOAA relies on two types of weather satellites: geostationary platforms like GOES-7, which captured the black-and-white snapshot of the Perfect Storm in figure 5.1, and polar-orbiting satellites (POES) like NOAA-12, which caught Hurricane Andrew advancing on Miami in figure 5.2. Although a POES platform circling the globe at an altitude of only 520 miles can take sharper pictures, its GOES counterpart 22,300 miles above the equator allows almost constant coverage of a far broader area and more vigilant surveillance of a storm's position, size, and intensity. Robert Sheets, who directed the National Hurricane Center (now the Tropical Prediction Center) in the late 1980s, was a strong advocate of the GOES gaze. In a recapitulation of the NHC's trials and triumphs, Sheets opined that "if there was a choice of only one observing tool for use in meeting [the center's responsibilities, I] would clearly choose the geostationary satellite."

NOAA's strategy calls for a minimum of two active satellites, a GOES-East mission covering eastern North America, the North Atlantic, and Latin America, and a GOES-West mission for the western United States and the central and eastern Pacific. Although GOES satellites have a design life of five years, contingency plans now include a standby satellite that can be repositioned if one of the assigned satellites fails. Relocation is possible because of tiny rockets called thrusters, also used to fine-tune the orbits of geostationary satellites. When the GOES-West satellite died in 1989, thrusters moved its eastern counterpart westward to a temporary GOES-Prime position covering the continental United States. After NOAA borrowed and repositioned a spare European satellite to cover the North Atlantic, thrusters moved the remaining GOES platform farther westward for fuller surveillance of the Pacific. International cooperation is well established in meteorology, and United States geostationary satellites fill two of five niches in a worldwide weather surveillance system that includes satellites maintained by India, Japan, and a consortium of European weather services.

Think of GOES as a platform, not a camera. The more recent GOES vehicles—GOES-12, launched in July 2001, is similar in design to GOES-8, placed in orbit in 1995—carry a variety of sensors as well as transponders for relaying measurements from a network of buoys and other surface stations. The most prominent sensor is the GOES Imager, with resolutions between 1 and 8 kilometers at ground nadir. Designed for frequent wide-area monitoring of atmospheric moisture, including cloud movement that reflects wind currents, the Imager can be reprogrammed to provide timely snapshots of small areas threatened by severe weather. Complementing the Imager is the independently programmed GOES Sounder, which uses a single visible band and eighteen thermal-infrared channels to monitor water vapor, temperature, cloud height, and other atmospheric conditions. Soundings taken hourly inform numerical forecast models about the current state of atmospheric moisture.

Three imaging schedules provide focused coverage of severe weather as well as preferential treatment of American territory. In routine operation, the GOES-East Imager produces CONUS (conterminous United States) and southern-hemisphere portraits at a half-hour interval and full-disk images (fig. 5.3) at a three-hour interval. Fifteen minutes after each CONUS portrait, a wider shot of the northern hemisphere reduces the interval for the forty-eight contiguous states to a quarter-hour. When unstable air within the focal region calls for more frequent monitoring, the Imager's "rapid-

FIGURE 5.3 Full-disk image from GOES-7 showing Hurricane Andrew advancing on the Louisiana coast at 2 P.M. CDT, August 25, 1992. Original color image from NASA Goddard Space Flight Center, Hurricane Andrew photo gallery, http://rsd. gsfc.nasa .gov/rsd/images/andrew .html.

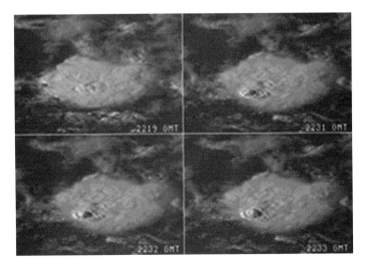

FIGURE 5.4 GOES-8 captured the "explosive" development of a thunderstorm over Tulsa, Oklahoma, during a twelve-minute period on July 20, 1994. The final three of these super-rapid-scan images are only a minute apart. From NOAA National Weather Service, Southern Region Headquarters, NOAA Satellite Tutor, http://www.srh.noaa.gov/maf/SatTutor/cira_rscan.gif.

scan" mode can reduce the CONUS interval to 7.5 minutes on average at the expense of southern-hemisphere coverage, which is cut back to only once an hour. Even more timely monitoring is possible with the Imager's "super-rapid-scan" mode, which abandons the southern hemisphere entirely, except for the three-hour full-disk image, in order to cut delivery time to five minutes or less for a specially designated SRSO sector. Able to scan a 1,000 kilometer by 1,000 kilometer sector at a one-minute interval, SRSO mode can capture volatile phenomena like the upwardly protruding thunderstorm in figure 5.4.

Under a similar plan, the GOES-West satellite provides routine quarter-hour coverage of Alaska, Hawaii, and the western states with alternating northern-hemisphere and PACUS (Pacific United States) scenes a half-hour apart. And like its eastern counterpart, the west-coast Imager produces southern-hemisphere and full-disk portraits at half-hour and three-hour intervals, respectively, in routine mode and reduces its southern-hemisphere coverage during rapid-scan and super-rapid-scan operation. By contrast, the east and west GOES Sounders each have only a single operation plan, which supplements hourly CONUS scenes with less frequent oceanic views and focused soundings of smaller areas such as the Gulf of Mexico and the eastern Caribbean Sea.

The success of satellite-assisted hurricane forecasting lies partly in the storms' size and slow movement, and partly in the sophisticated computer models used to predict storm position. According to a Tropical Prediction Center study of cyclone tracking in the Atlantic Basin between 1970 and 1998, errors for twenty-four-hour forecasts declined by 1.0 percent per year. Marginally more impressive are decreases of 1.7 and 1.9 percent per year, respectively, for forty-eight- and seventy-two-hour forecasts. After adjusting for erratic storm behavior, which increases the difficulty of making reliable predictions, NOAA researchers observed distinctly higher rates of improvement—2.1, 3.1, and 3.5 percent per year—for the period 1994 to 1998. Even so, average errors of 84, 151, and 221 nautical miles impede efforts to forecast a storm's position one, two, or three days hence.

Officials of NOAA and the Federal Emergency Management Agency (FEMA) find this uncertainty troubling, and because many places cannot be evacuated in twenty-four hours, they "overwarn" just to be safe. As a result, hurricane warnings issued a day ahead of landfall typically affect 400 nautical miles of coastline even though a tropical hurricane might leave a trail of destruction only a hundred miles wide. Until track forecasts as well as predictions of storm size and intensity are more precise and reliable, overwarning is preferable to underwarning, even though public confidence might slip when a storm dies or goes elsewhere after triggering a massive evacuation.

+   +   +

To further improve prediction, hurricane forecasters are using radar to probe the internal structure of storms. Unlike passive sensors, which depend on reflected sunlight or thermal radiation, radar is an active sensor, which measures the reflectance of its own electromagnetic pulses and can penetrate clouds as well as operate at night. Especially revealing are three-dimensional radar images from the Tropical Rainfall Measuring Mission (TRMM), a research satellite launched in November 1997 by NASA and its Japanese counterpart. In a circular orbit inclined 35 degrees to the plane of the equator, the TRMM meanders across the tropics at an altitude of 215 miles (350 km). Among the TRMM Observatory's five principal instruments is the world's first space-borne precipitation radar, which supplied revealing views of hurricanes Bonnie, Irene, and Floyd well before they were within range of land-based radar. In addition to describing a storm's horizontal extent, imagery like the overhead snapshot of Hurricane Floyd in figure 5.5 affords a revealing three-dimensional view of vertical variations in precipitation. Moisture profiles akin to those in the upper- and lower-right of this NASA publicity photo allow more reliable estimates of the amount and intensity of precipitation as well as a more accurate picture of the center of circulation within a storm. Rainfall within a hurricane is not uniform, and a sense of where precipitation is likely to be most intense can be useful in last-minute emergency preparations.

Land-based radar is also helpful in tracking hurricanes and warning residents of locally intense rain and tornado-force winds. During Hurricane Andrew in 1992, officials at the National Hurricane Center gained a firsthand appreciation of weather radar when the storm center passed just south of their building. The radar map (fig. 5.6) shows a donut-shaped zone of intense precipitation and turbulence a few miles southeast of the NHC. Although damage is usually more pronounced in coastal locations subject to flooding, Andrew's winds caused considerable destruction inland, thanks to a disastrous combination of inadequate building codes, lower land values, and cheap construction. As indicated by a circular band of high winds just outside the storm's eye, devastation was well underway south of Miami. This map gained a prominent place in weather lore when, minutes later, winds gusting to 164 miles per hour swept the radar antenna off the hurricane center's roof.

The following April, Miami received a newer, more efficient weather radar system, NEXRAD (*Next* Generation *Rad*ar). A cornerstone of the National Weather Service's modernization plan, NEXRAD replaced radar systems implemented in 1957 and 1974. The new system employed Doppler radar, able to measure the direction and speed of wind as well as differentiate among dust, rain, sleet, snow, and hail. Under a program started in 1988, the weather

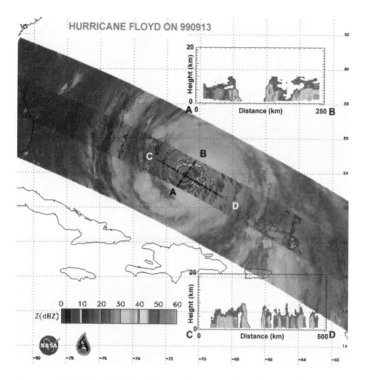

FIGURE 5.5 TRMM precipitation radar provides cross-sectional views (profiles A-B and C-D) showing horizontal and vertical variations in precipitable moisture. This NASA publicity image captures Hurricane Floyd approximately 500 miles east-southeast of Florida on September 13, 1999. Original color image from NASA's TRMM Web site, http://trmm.gsfc.nasa.gov/data/2000_data/HurrFloyd1_md.gif.

service had begun replacing older radars with NEXRAD and reducing the number of forecast offices. Because of the new radar's greater range, NOAA reasoned, fewer offices were required. Cities that lost forecast offices complained, but overall NOAA's new radar network is a marked improvement over its predecessor. NEXRAD is credited with increasing the average warning time for tornadoes from five to twelve minutes, which can be especially significant if trailer parks have shelters, homes have basements or "saferooms," and residents receive timely warnings through NOAA's Weather Radio network, a local broadcaster, or a community siren system. Early detection is useless when likely victims can't take shelter.

Although NEXRAD is a clear success, estimates of the average

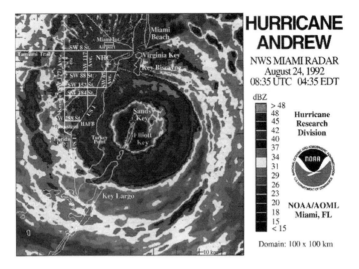

FIGURE 5.6 Radar image of Hurricane Andrew showing a ring of high winds and intense precipitation a few miles away from the National Hurricane Center (marked with a plus-sign labeled "NHC"). Minutes later, winds toppled the center's radar antenna. Original color image from NOAA Office of Public and Constituent Affairs, image gallery, http://www.publicaffairs.noaa.gov/photos/1992andy.JPG.

lead time for tornado warnings vary widely. For example, a 1996 cover story in *Time* magazine reported a NEXRAD-induced improvement from three to eight minutes, while a 1999 proposal by a subcommittee of the National Science and Technology Council (a consortium of federal agencies) claimed an end-of-decade average between fifteen and twenty minutes. By contrast, a NOAA case study published on the Internet by the National Partnership for Reinventing Government (another interagency collaboration) described a steady advance in lead times from nine minutes in 1995, to ten, eleven, and twelve minutes in 1996, 1997, and 1998, while an August 2000 NOAA "goals statement" reported an eleven-minute average—"nearly triple the three minute lead time of 1977"—and suggested that a fifteen-minute average is possible by 2005. These and other claims accord with the Knight Ridder Tribune newspaper syndicate's WeatherQuiz, which credits NEXRAD with extending the run-and-hide time from five to twelve minutes.

Despite the confusion, lead time improved significantly during the late 1990s, when computers learned to interpret radar maps more vigilantly and reliably than the best human forecasters. Because radar maps are visually complex, timely warnings depend upon computer algorithms that recognize suspicious signatures like the "hook echoes" of precipitation being drawn into a rotating storm. Developed, tested, and fine-tuned by teams of forecasters and research meteorologists, computer-assisted surveillance also contributed to an impressive increase in the lead time for flash-flood warnings—up from eight minutes in 1987 to fifty-one minutes in 2000.

Averages hide a fascinating diversity in the storms that generate tornadoes and the protection afforded by weather radar. At a June 1999 hearing before the House Committee on Science, Dennis McCarthy, head meteorologist at the National Weather Service Office in Norman, Oklahoma, described the carnage of May 3, six weeks previous, when more than seventy tornadoes ravaged Tornado Alley and killed forty-two people in Oklahoma alone. Without NEXRAD, the death toll would have been much higher. McCarthy and his colleagues sent out 116 county-level warnings for tornadoes and severe thunderstorms, and "false alarm rates were much lower than average." Lead times for these tornado warnings averaged eighteen minutes—a bit better than the Norman office's average of fifteen minutes, which in turn is higher than the national average of eleven minutes. Still more impressive is the thirty-two-minute lead time for warnings issued for southern Oklahoma City and nearby Moore. McCarty attributed the accuracy and timeliness of these predictions to NEXRAD: "Doppler radars are like CAT scans of the atmosphere enabling forecasters to see wind fields within thunderstorms. These thunderstorm wind fields are precursors to tornadoes."

How thoroughly NEXRAD can scrutinize a thunderstorm depends partly on the storm's size and proximity. Most of Oklahoma's May 3 twisters were byproducts of tall, wide, and relatively long-lived thunderstorms called supercells, which NEXRAD can detect as far as 180 kilometers (112 mi.) away. Proximity is important because the earth's surface curves away from the straight-line radar beam, which at some distance becomes simply too high to detect low-altitude phenomena like tornadoes. Increased distance from the antenna also widens the radar beam, which lowers resolution, an important ingredient of weather radar's CAT-scan effect.

NEXRAD is thus less likely to pick up an offshoot tornado's distinctive low-altitude hook echo beyond about 100 kilometers (62mi.). With a generous thirty-two minutes of lead time, residents of Moore and southern Oklahoma City were no doubt fortunate that Norman's NEXRAD site and highly experienced team of tornado forecasters were less than 10 miles away.

Hall County, Georgia, a rural area about 40 miles northeast of Atlanta, was not so lucky. Around 6:25 A.M. on March 20, 1998, a tornado struck without warning and killed eleven people. According to Don Burgess, who trains forecasters in the use of NEXRAD, the thunderstorm that spawned the March 20 tornado was a mini-supercell, so named because of its narrower diameter and lower top. Harder to detect than its bigger relatives, a mini-supercell is "a challenging event for a forecaster." Hall County had an added disadvantage: the nearest NEXRAD station was more than 80 miles away, in Peachtree City. According to a 1995 National Research Council study, NEXRAD cannot detect mini-supercells more than about 100 kilometers (62 mi.) away, and cannot reliably discern related hook echoes beyond 70 kilometers (43 mi.).

Sensitivity to storm size and height account for minor cracks in the NEXRAD safety net. According to the National Research Council, NOAA's new radar provides much better surveillance for supercells than for mini-supercells. Moreover, the 15 percent of the contiguous states that is either hidden by terrain or outside the maximum detection range of at least one antenna lies largely in remote, sparsely populated parts of the mountainous West. By contrast, the map of mini-supercell detection (fig. 5.7) reveals substantial gaps in the East and Midwest. NRC calculations suggest that 68 percent of the contiguous territory is comparatively vulnerable to this less common and (fortunately) less destructive brand of severe weather. Even so, a small storm cell can be tracked once it's detected, and NOAA encourages forecasters to examine images from neighboring radars as well as consult with neighboring forecasters and officials at the Storm Prediction Center, in Norman, Oklahoma. Because NEXRAD is truly a network, telecommunications can stitch together the islands of surveillance on its mini-supercell coverage map.

+   +   +

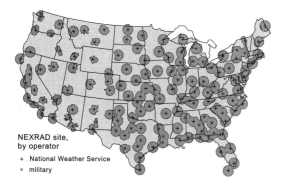

NEXRAD site,
by operator
+ National Weather Service
× military

FIGURE 5.7 Areas of mini-supercell detection by NOAA's NEXRAD network. Compiled from figure 2-4a in NEXRAD Panel, National Weather Service Modernization Committee, Commission on Engineering and Technical Systems, National Research Council, *Toward a New National Weather Service: Assessment of NEXRAD Coverage and Associated Weather Services* (Washington, D.C.: National Academy Press, 1995), 23.

A comparatively sparse network monitors vertical variation in wind currents. At thirty locations in sixteen states, largely in the Central Plains, experimental Doppler radars called Wind Profilers gaze upward past the top of the troposphere to sample wind speed and direction every six minutes. To provide a vertically dense sample, the profilers alternate between two slightly overlapping altitude ranges: "low mode" takes readings every 250 meters (820 ft.) between 500 and 9,250 meters above the ground, while "high mode" provides similar scrutiny between altitudes of 7,500 and 16,250 meters—that's 10 miles up, well beyond the ceiling for most commercial aircraft.

For each profiler location, a time-section chart such as in figure 5.8 describes temporal variation in wind velocity. The vertical axis of the chart shows elevation above sea level and the horizontal axis represents time, with the most recent readings on the left and the oldest on the right. For each height and time a thin, arrow-like staff portrays wind direction and its barbs signify wind speed, with each full barb representing 10 meters per second and a short barb indicating 5 meters per second. Thus, a line with two full barbs and one short barb represents a wind speed of 25 meters per second. Orientation is shown relative to north (toward the top) and east (to the right), as on a map, and by convention wind staffs point downwind.

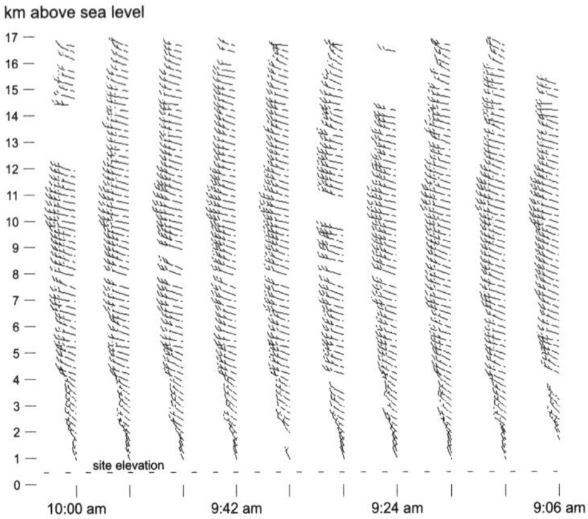

km above sea level

FIGURE 5.8 Time-section chart describing winds above Fairbury, Nebraska, at 9:06 to 10:00 A.M. CT on November 27, 2000. The dashed line represents Wind Profiler site's elevation of 0.43 kilometers above sea level. Redrawn from an illustration published on the NOAA Profiler Network Web site, http://www.profiler.noaa.gov/jsp/index.jsp.

Thus at 10 A.M. the wind at 12 kilometers above sea level was flowing from slightly north of west at approximately 30 meters per second, while at elevations below 2 kilometers air was moving much more slowly from the north-northwest. Missing data vectors indicate measurements rejected by the Wind Profiler's quality control processor because of weak signals or radio interference.

Time-section charts offer a variety of insights. Strong, consistent, high-altitude winds like those between elevations of 10 and 11 kilometers in figure 5.4 suggest the presence of the jet stream—a fact readily confirmed by making a high-altitude winds map from available profiler reports. Winds maps are important to forecasters because upper-air currents can steer storms and deliver precipitation. In addition, radical differences in wind direction within a row or column might indicate turbulence or wind shear, which pilots try to avoid. Wind Profiler data also provide a reality check on numerical models. This complementarity was especially valuable in the hours preceding the May 3, 1999, tornado outbreak, for which NEXRAD provided valuable local warnings once a profiler in Tucumcari, New Mexico, alerted forecasters to the likelihood of severe storms. According to Jim Johnson, chief of the Dodge City, Kansas, forecast office, "the computer models failed miserably with this event [while] data from the profilers . . . tipped the scales toward a successful forecast. What had begun as a fairly low risk for severe storms escalated to an extremely dangerous situation. Fortunately, staff at the Storm Prediction Center . . . used the profiler data early in the analysis cycle and realized the gravity of the situation. If they had trusted model forecasts they would have badly under-forecast a major tornado outbreak with possibly much greater loss of life." Although the Wind Profilers are still an "experimental" program, National Weather Service forecasters consider them indispensable.

+ + +

Completeness demands at least passing mention of a "nowcasting" tool prized by power company engineers and wildland fire officials as well as weather forecasters. Lightning detection networks can discover flaws in transmission systems, pinpoint likely locations of forest fires, and identify severe thunderstorms fifteen minutes ahead of radar. A direct threat to power lines and parched woodlands, lightning strokes yield dramatic images that can signal a storm's development, reveal its trajectory, and herald its decline. Among forecasters worried about sluggish response by a overwarned public, knowing when a warning is unnecessary is nearly as important as knowing when to broadcast an alarm.

Unlike other monitoring methods examined in this chapter, ground-based lightning detection systems estimate a lightning flash's position by comparing measurements for multiple locations. Cloud-to-ground lightning generates a magnetic wave that propagates outward at the same rate in all directions. One approach, called direction finding, estimates the ground-strike location from the angles at which the magnetic wave arrives at two or more sensors (fig. 5.9, left). Although triangulation principles would have two lines of arrival intersect at the strike point, a band of uncertainty of roughly 1 degree surrounds each azimuth. An alternative method calculates the strike location by comparing times at which the magnetic wave arrives at three or more sensors (fig. 5.9, right). For each pair of sensors, arrival times define a parabola of possible strike locations, and a third station defines two additional parabolas, which in principle should intersect at the exact strike location. Although accuracy depends on network density and the number of sensors contributing to the average estimate, time-of-arrival detection is generally more precise than directional triangulation.

The National Lightning Detection Network, initiated in the early 1980s by a consortium of electrical utilities, uses a mixture of direc-

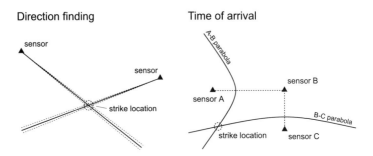

FIGURE 5.9 Lightning detection systems estimate ground-strike location from the estimated azimuths of magnetic waves *(left)* or from time-of-arrival parabolas calculated for pairs of detector sites *(right)*.

tion-finding and time-of-arrival sensors. Linking more than one hundred sensor sites scattered across forty-eight states, the network estimates stroke locations to within roughly 500 meters. Although lightning is sudden—a typical flash consists of four strokes each lasting approximately 30 microseconds—stroke data are usually displayed in one-minute chunks or aggregated into more visually stable images covering periods ranging from five minutes to an hour. To get a sharper picture of a storm's location and intensity a National Weather Service forecaster might overlay fifteen-minute lightning-stroke data on an infrared satellite image showing precipitable moisture or cloud height.

+ + +

Meteorological surveillance systems complement one another in myriad ways. Doppler radar affords more locally detailed pictures than geostationary satellites, which in turn provide continuous coverage of large storms over land and water. Similarly, Wind Profilers offer a closer, bottom-up view of air flow at different levels and furnish valuable guidance to computer models (to which GOES sensors also contribute), while ground-based lightning detection systems monitor electrical storms and tell wildfire officials where to look for future forest fires—a day later, perhaps, after smoldering tree roots ignite surface litter. What's more, systems for watching weather contribute to other surveillance efforts, such as monitoring world agriculture, pinpointing downed aircraft and foundering ships, and understanding global climate. This complementarity includes GPS satellites: because the GPS time signal is measurably retarded by atmospheric moisture, a ground station that knows the right time can estimate the amount of intervening water vapor.

Given this diverse array of relevant sensors and imagers, it's hardly surprising that the most promising—and for a time the most troublesome—part of the National Weather Service's modernization program is the Advanced Weather Interactive Processing System (AWIPS), an intelligent graphics console designed to help forecasters overlay images, explore data, and compare models. Because diverse views of the atmosphere are the key to accurate prediction, the power of meteorological surveillance depends on the forecaster's ability to integrate information.

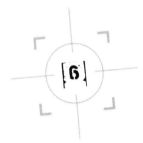

[6]

Wire Loops and Traffic Cams

Traffic signals can be maddening, particularly on lightly traveled roads when the light turns red as you approach. Had
the signal stayed green a second or two longer, there'd be no
need to stop, watch a handful of cars clear the intersection,
and wait that decade-long half-minute for the green light.
Equally frustrating is the certainty that a traffic cop (if we
could afford to replace machines with people) would have already let the waiting cars cross or turn left so that no one,
neither you nor they, need stop and wait. If we can send men
to the moon, why can't we make a smart stoplight?

The answer is that we can. Intelligent traffic signals are
expediting traffic through congested inner cities and allevi-
ating aggravation in the suburbs. In addition to Advanced
Traffic Management Systems (ATMS), which include more

attentive stoplights, Intelligent Vehicle/Highway Systems (IVHS) technologies promise to increase traffic flow by making driving more automatic. Updating that damned traffic signal out on Route 32 is only a question of time and money.

There's more to the story than smart stoplights. Traffic control systems need to know where the cars and trucks are, how swiftly they're moving, and where accidents and breakdowns are disrupting the flow. And because successful modeling depends on predictable behavior, control systems need to know who's undermining the computer model by running red lights or driving aggressively. As motorists in several states are well aware, video cameras can photograph drivers and license plates, electronic character recognition systems can match plate numbers with registration data, and violations tracking systems can send out bills with a picture of the driver caught in the act. What's more, automatic toll collection, a form of electronic surveillance that reduces congestion at toll plazas, might eventually allow authorities to finger dangerous drivers as well as decrease traffic and raise revenue by charging motorists for using city streets during rush hour. An added cost of this automotive utopia is the privacy lost when computers know who we are and where we've been.

+   +   +

At their most rudimentary level, traffic lights have two options: preset timing and traffic-activated interruption. A simple traffic-activated signal would favor the more heavily traveled "major" street with a steady green light except when a motorist approaching along the intersecting "minor" street activates a detector, which changes the signal long enough for a plausible number of waiting vehicles to cross or turn. Used mainly at mid-block pedestrian crossings and entrances to factory parking lots, traffic-activated interruption is the electronic equivalent of a near-sighted traffic cop. More widespread is the clock-driven signal with a programmed green-yellow-red cycle favoring the major street's larger volume with a proportionately greater "split" (longer green light). Although time-of-day adjustments can expedite rush-hour traffic and a more intricate cycle can accommodate left turns and pedestrians, the noninteractive pretimed signal is similar in concept to the light timers used to discourage burglars when we're away.

The effectiveness of a pretimed stoplight depends on predictable traffic and accurate vehicle counts. Before installing a new signal, traffic engineers collect data for several days with portable clock-driven counters housed in kid-proof boxes chained to telephone poles or trees along approaches to the intersection. A flexible pneumatic tube less than an inch in diameter extends outward into the road perpendicular to the curb line. Whenever a wheel rides over the tube, the counter senses increased pressure and records another axle. Anchored to the pavement with large staples, the tube stops short of the yellow dividing line so that the counter registers axles traveling only one way. Although unable to distinguish cars from other vehicles, pneumatic counters are generally more reliable and less expensive than human counters, who become bored or need to pee.

Differential counts provide a rational basis for offering one street a bigger split or adjusting the timing for rush-hour traffic. If turning vehicles require special attention, traffic engineers can place additional counters downstream from the intersection or, in the case of a dedicated left-turn lane, use two upstream counters, one with a shorter tube to capture only vehicles going straight or turning right. The number of vehicles turning left can then be estimated by subtracting the short-tube count from the long-tube count.

Along a heavily traveled rush-hour route, synchronization obviates the need to count vehicles at every intersection. The "time-space diagram" in figure 6.1 describes a typical scheme for coordinating signals so that northbound traffic along a hypothetical Main Street encounters few if any red lights. The vertical axis shows distance, the horizontal axis represents time, and the straight lines sloping upward describe a constant speed of 27.3 miles per hour—the speed at which a vehicle covers the 800 feet between intersections in exactly 20 seconds. The plan shown here calls for a green-yellow-red cycle of 60 seconds. For each signal-controlled intersection a segmented horizontal bar describes the cycle's division into 30 seconds of green (shown in white) followed by 3 seconds of yellow (in gray) and 27 seconds of red (in black). Especially important is the "offset" of the green phase from the green light at 1st Street: synchronized offsets provide a succession of 30-second-wide "through bands" (the white diagonal stripes in fig. 6.1) allowing unimpeded passage for vehicles traveling at 27.3 miles per hour.

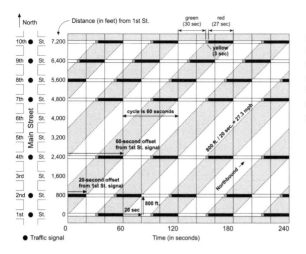

FIGURE 6.1 Time-space diagram for synchronized traffic signals along a hypothetical one-way street with evenly spaced intersections.

In figure 6.1, each white stripe's leading, right-hand edge represents a "green wave" that advances northward as signals change from red to green. Drivers who adjust their speed to the green wave will average 27.3 miles an hour and not need to stop or slow down. When everyone cooperates, synchronization can move many vehicles along an otherwise congested arterial. If Main Street is one-way and four lanes wide, for example, a hypothetical "platoon" of eighty cars, 15 feet long and 45 feet apart, could cover the 1.4 miles from 1st Street to 10th Street in three minutes without hitting a single red light. And even if breakdowns, buses, mid-block stops, and slow-pokes disrupt the dance, trailing a green wave beats halting at every second or third traffic light.

Straightforward synchronization makes it easy to understand why traffic engineers love one-way streets. If only three lanes are available, for example, dedicated left- and right-turn lanes at intersections with two-way streets allow at least one dedicated lane for through traffic, which is more predictably uniform. And if the cross streets are also one-way, a second through lane encourages even greater predictability. Moreover, the coordination plan in figure 6.1 adapts readily to unevenly spaced cross streets—note that by shifting the green segments to the right or left, any of the horizontal bars may be moved up or down without affecting the 27.3 miles-per-hour speed or the 30-second bandwidth. What's more, an engineer can easily adjust the speed of the green wave as well as the length of the cycle and its constituent phases by changing the slope and width of the through bands.

Two-way traffic is more complicated. Figure 6.2 illustrates the challenge of coordinating the signals in figure 6.1 for two-way traffic. In this example, twin sets of through bands intersect at cross streets and treat both directions equally. My solution retains the 27.3 miles-per-hour speed but reduces the cycle from 60 to 40 seconds and the green phase from 30 to 20 seconds. A yellow phase of 3 seconds leaves only 37 seconds for green and red combined. Adding an all-red phase—an essential safeguard against aggressive drivers who race into the intersection when the light turns red—would further constrain the trade-off between green and red. The 40-second cycle, which reflects the 800-foot distance between intersections, might be overcome by placing signals only at every second or third intersection—or by allowing an occasional red light along one or both directions. Where cross streets are not evenly spaced, two-way synchronization is even more problematic. For unimpeded green waves in both directions the simplest, most workable strategy is one-way traffic along Main Street with a parallel street handling the other direction.

Irregularly spaced intersections are no less troublesome than the repeated retiming studies needed to synchronize cycles, phase lengths, and offsets as well as accommodate left-turn lanes, pedestrian crossings, transit vehicles, railroad crossings, and emergency vehicles. Although ongoing traffic counts can help transportation officials deal with commuter traffic, seasonal effects, special events, and bad weather, a more robust strategy is to collect flow data in real time and let a network of remote detectors, communication lines, and centralized computers adjust signals to actual conditions. Dynamic adjustment is especially important where major streets intersect.

Automated traffic management can also ease congestion on freeways by coordinating entrance-ramp signals, which regulate access, and variable-message signs, which advise motorists to change lanes, slow down, expect delays, or take an alternate route. Because it's prohibitively expensive if not politically impossible to add another expressway, Los Angeles and other sprawling metropolitan ar-

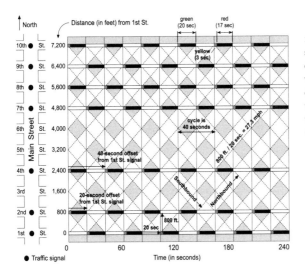

FIGURE 6.2 Time-space diagram for synchronized signals with equal accommodation of two-way traffic along the hypothetical street in figure 6.1.

eas with dim hopes for public transit look to ATMS for solutions to air pollution and other environmental consequences of rampant postwar road building.

+   +   +

Whether connected to a central computer at the traffic control center or to a microprocessor in a nearby signal cabinet, traffic-activated signals depend on electronic or electromechanical "detectors" designed to count cars, estimate speed, or merely sense the presence of vehicles waiting to cross or turn. Although the detector might be a pressure-sensitive pad, a microphone positioned to pick up engine noise, or a small radar system suspended over the roadway on a pole, most municipal traffic engineering departments rely heavily if not entirely on "inductive loop detectors" buried in the pavement. The loop is a few turns of a thin, insulated electric wire, which carries an alternating current that changes direction between ten and two hundred times a second thereby setting up a magnetic field that oscillates at the same frequency. Through a phenomenon called the ferromagnetic effect, this magnetic field induces a similar but opposite magnetic field in any nearby metallic conductor. Because the second magnetic field absorbs magnetic energy from the loop, the detector senses a vehicle whenever a large metallic object, such as an engine block, disrupts the current in the loop. A technician calibrates the loop so that when a disruption exceeds the threshold, the detector reports the presence or passage of another vehicle.

Loop detectors are easy to recognize. To embed the wire, installers cut a series of straight slots in the asphalt or concrete with a rotary saw. To avoid right-angle bends, which can stress the wire, they often bevel the corners with short, 45-degree cross cuts, as in figure 6.3. A longer cut accommodates a lead-in wire, which links the loop to a "pull box" buried in the ground at the side of the road and connected to the signal controller. Cuts are no more than a half-inch wide and about 1 to 3 inches deep. After placing the wire in the slot, the field crew fills the cut with an epoxy sealant, which encases the wire, keeps out moisture, and restores the road surface. Passing tires burnish the epoxy to a glossy gray finish, which sometimes suggests metal strips driven sideways into the pavement.

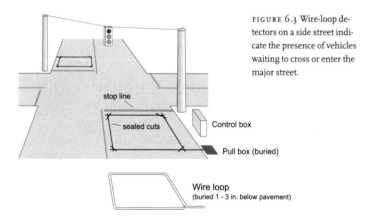

FIGURE 6.3 Wire-loop detectors on a side street indicate the presence of vehicles waiting to cross or enter the major street.

stop line

sealed cuts

Control box

Pull box (buried)

Wire loop
(buried 1 - 3 in. below pavement)

If you're curious about a signaling system's priorities, look at the placement of its loop detectors. A convenient reference point is the stop line, usually a wide white stripe perpendicular to the curb line and stretching halfway across the road just upstream from the pedestrian crossing. A loop along a minor street immediately in front of the stop line is probably intended to detect the presence of a waiting vehicle—if nothing's waiting, heavy traffic along the major street can enjoy a longer green. By contrast, a rectangular loop extending downstream from the stop line well into the intersection can sense vehicles waiting to cross or turn left—situations in which a longer yellow or left-turn (green-arrow) phase can avert gridlock or the frustration of waiting several cycles to make a left turn. At key intersections separate loops usually monitor the left-turn and through lanes.

Detector loops are especially useful along freeway ramps. Loops at both ends of an on-ramp can estimate the number of waiting vehicles, if any, whereas a detector midway down a long off-ramp can activate the stoplight ahead, which might fortuitously turn green just as your car reaches the end of the ramp. And a detector farther upstream might warn of a dangerous queue, which could back up onto the freeway unless the controller clears cars off the ramp more rapidly.

Loop detectors are usually designed for specific tasks such as counting moving vehicles or noting a stopped car or truck. The shape and size of a loop affect the extent and sensitivity of its magnetic field. For example, diamonds are deemed less likely than other designs to pick up vehicles in adjacent lanes—traffic engineers call this "splashover"—while long, narrow rectangles centered on each lane's oil line are more suitable for moving traffic. Reliable counts are especially important when transportation departments evaluate the durability of pavement or assess the need for new or wider roads. Bicycles and small motorcycles, with less inductive presence than a car or truck, are especially dicey. To detect small vehicles, loops at traffic-activated stoplights sometimes include a smaller subloop, with a few extra windings of the wire just shy of the stop line. Toronto and other cyclist-friendly cities use a series of three or four white dots to mark small bike-sensitive loops so that savvy cyclists will know where to stand when they want to cross.

A pair of closely spaced loops in the same lane can measure speed as well as traffic volume. Although traffic cops rarely use loop detectors to catch speeders—radar guns are less expensive and more portable—fear of speed traps was especially troublesome in the 1960s, when embedded loops were relatively new and some anxious truck drivers would hit the breaks at the sight of telltale lines of epoxy sealant. The worst enemies of a wire embedded in asphalt are heavy vehicles that stop suddenly and wrinkle the pavement.

Because sudden stops also cause rear-end collisions, traffic engineers are especially concerned about the signal that turns yellow when a driver is too close to the intersection for a smooth, safe stop. A motorist who cannot stop easily but is too far away to clear the intersection before the light turns red is in a "dilemma zone" where indecision and panic could precipitate a crash. An all-red phase can give the driver who doesn't stop added time to clear the intersection, but the occasionally fatal consequences of a sudden stop call for delaying the yellow phase when a vehicle is still in the dilemma zone. Although an extended green is not always practicable for steady traffic—drivers queued up to turn or cross cannot wait indefinitely —properly placed loop detectors can prudently delay the yellow phase if no one has been waiting long. Some signal controllers get by with a pair of detectors, one on each side of the zone, but more advanced systems require multiple detectors to monitor closely the number and speed of approaching vehicles. Speed is important because a fast vehicle has a long dilemma zone whereas a slow one might not need an extension.

However widespread, wire loops are not the final word in smart signaling. Some cities are supplementing or replacing their loop detectors with video cameras connected to machine-vision processors that count cars, detect queues or stopped vehicles, and differentiate inbound from outbound traffic and through vehicles from those making turns. A single camera can cover several lanes, and when positioned strategically along highways, video detectors can also monitor speed as well as spot accidents, breakdowns, and other "incidents." More expensive initially, video systems are easier to install and maintain, especially where heavy trucks tear up the pavement. In the Texas Panhandle, for instance, loop detectors often last less than eighteen months and cost as much as $15,000 to replace. As Texas Department of Transportation official David Miller told me, "Because wires embedded in asphalt can fail at any time, no one guarantees loop detectors." By contrast, contractors charge about $20,000 to install four cameras and their electronic controller, and the cameras come with a two-year warranty.

Machine vision is largely a matter of rapid, conscientious number crunching that simulates human vision by detecting edges, matching patterns, and estimating displacement. Figure 6.4 de-

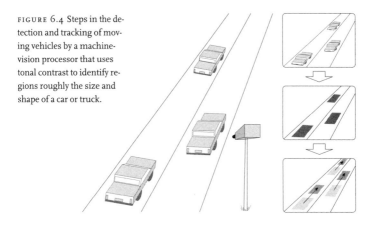

FIGURE 6.4 Steps in the detection and tracking of moving vehicles by a machine-vision processor that uses tonal contrast to identify regions roughly the size and shape of a car or truck.

scribes the steps. A computer chip in the traffic controller scans a scene, notes tonal contrast, and outlines regions that differ from the pavement and are roughly the size and shape of a car or truck. Once calibrated, the system can easily relate an object's position in the image to its location on the ground. And by tracking the object through successive scenes captured a fraction of a second apart, the processor can measure a vehicle's speed as well as detect cars making turns or changing lanes. By covering a broad area, a single camera avoids the splashover that can occur when a car occupies parts of two lanes. And if an accident occurs or a queue develops, the processor can report the incident over a telephone line or radio channel. Except during installation, the machine-vision processor does all the watching.

+   +   +

Not all traffic video cameras feed machine-vision processors. In Syracuse, New York, where I live, fiber-optic cable connects the city's traffic control center to cameras at five intersections. Officials selected these locations because of heavy traffic or a history of accidents. The control room has a huge TV screen—the kind found in sports bars and corporate boardrooms—and three smaller monitors. On the day I visited, one of the smaller monitors was cycling through the five cameras. Control room operator Harry Carlson showed me how he can call up any camera on any monitor, pan around with a joystick, and zoom in for greater detail. By entering a number, he can also rotate each camera to a carefully selected, pre-programmed "shot" showing traffic approaching or leaving the intersection in a specific direction. Mounted 30 feet above the ground, the cameras can focus on incidents more than a block away. Syracuse's closed-circuit TV cameras are part of a larger system that lets Carlson monitor and, if necessary, reprogram traffic signals at 143 of the city's 170 signal-controlled intersections. Control boxes at each intersection report in every 30 seconds, and a server stores their data for analysis by MIST (Management Information System for Traffic), a software package that optimizes offsets and extensions for through traffic in multiple directions. For hands-on analysis, a graphics workstation displays an interactive map of the area under central control. Numbers next to several dozen street segments represent volume, occupancy, or average speed, and a pull-down menu lets the operator change indicators in an instant. By clicking on an intersection, Carlson can retrieve a detailed dynamic diagram showing signal conditions in real time for each driving lane and pedestrian crosswalk. The intersection diagram also shows the presence or absence of vehicles at each loop detector and indicates whether a pedestrian has activated a "call switch." Because intersection diagrams occupy only a fraction of the screen and can be dragged about, the operator can call up several intersections at once and reposition their diagrams in the correct sequence along a synchronized route. When the maps indicate unusually sluggish traffic, the closed-circuit TV cameras might suggest a likely cause and an appropriate response.

The Syracuse Signal Interconnect Project cost over $11 million, largely to provide underground communication lines. "It's very expensive to open up the streets and bury several miles of fiber-optic cable," Carlson explained. Indeed, the cost of cabling is the primary reason why intersections well away from downtown are not linked to the central computer. Although centralized synchronization has noticeably reduced average waiting time at stoplights—by as much as 50 percent, according to one study—$11 million is a lot of money to save commuters a couple of minutes of frustration each day, especially for a medium-size city like Syracuse. The real motivation was air quality: vehicles idling at intersections threaten lungs and hearts by spewing out tons of carbon monoxide and other pollutants. That's why the federal government picked up 80 percent of the tab, and New York State subsidized another 15 percent. Synchronized stoplights are about more than saving time.

+   +   +

Bigger cities have another job for traffic surveillance: helping commuters select a route or departure time that avoids congestion. From metropolitan Washington, D.C., to Seattle, Washington, transportation departments have set up Web sites that offer continually updated maps of traffic conditions as well as live views from strategically placed video cameras. Although the effect on driver behavior is difficult to gauge, the added cost is modest because control room personnel need the data anyway to monitor flow, regulate signals, and deal with emergencies. Sharing the information helps motorists assess their options and lets the department tout its efficiency and commitment.

In Washington State's Puget Sound area, for instance, the Department of Transportation Web site (www.wsdot.wa.gov/ PugetSoundTraffic/) lets commuters choose a north-up or west-up overview. Additional maps provide greater detail for the city of Tacoma, the bridges across Lake Washington (fig. 6.5), and the northern and southern approaches to Seattle. Focused on expressways, the maps describe traffic conditions in each direction for segments roughly a mile long on the overview maps and a half-mile long on the detailed maps. Mimicking a stoplight, red, yellow, and green symbols differentiate "heavy," "moderate," and "wide open" traffic, respectively, while ominous black segments denote "stop and go" conditions, which commuters want to avoid. Gray and blue identify the network's remaining segments as "no data" (detector out of service) or "no equipment" (detectors not installed). A separate key at the top of the map shows current traffic directions along the network's reversible "express lanes"—parallel roadways that increase capacity for portions of the I-5 and I-90 corridors by changing direction with the tide of commuter traffic. Separate symbols describe conditions along the express lanes, which have no direct interchanges with cross streets and are less likely to experience back-ups near off-ramps.

Motorists curious about distinctions between "heavy" and "stop

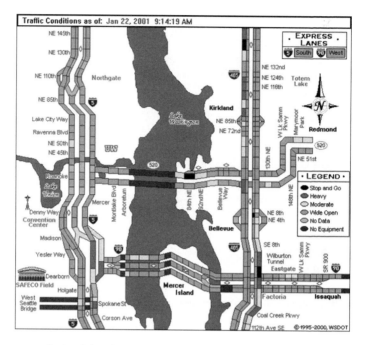

FIGURE 6.5 Detailed "Bridges" map focuses on freeways around Seattle's Lake Washington. This late-morning view shows isolated stretches of "heavy" and "stop and go" traffic. The directional key at the upper right shows the express lanes for I-5 and I-90 aligned for traffic moving to the south and west. From Washington State Department of Transportation, "Puget Sound Traffic Conditions," http://www.wsdot.wa.gov/PugetSoundTraffic/.

and go" can click on the Web site's "Cameras" button, which pulls up an index map showing locations of eighty "traffic cams" in the Seattle area. Each icon is a clickable symbol, or button, that summons a small, low-resolution video snapshot of current traffic (fig. 6.6). Viewers can quickly infer driving conditions from the average spacing of vehicles and the number of open lanes—if cars are bumper-to-bumper, that's clearly bad news. The images reload automatically every 90 seconds and are transmitted over the telephone network, which is less expensive than dedicated fiber-optic cable. Additional index maps show locations of seven traffic cams in the Tacoma area, five cameras focused on critical street intersections in Seattle, and twelve cameras covering local traffic in Bellevue, a municipality east of Lake Washington that touts itself as "the nation's most wired city."

Washington transportation officials put their traffic cams online in 1996, in response to requests from area residents who had seen the images on local television. Less than half of the state's two hundred cameras feed the Web site, which cost only $20,000 plus a bit of employee time to set up. Web traffic increased markedly in December 1999, when demonstrators at the World Trade Organization meeting disrupted Seattle traffic. Between November 29 and December 6, for instance, the number of visitors jumped from 8,000 to 18,000 per day. Severe weather also stimulates usage. Residents without Web access can monitor traffic flow on television. Tacoma's city-run information channel added the local traffic cams to its morning and evening rush hour programming in 2000, and two other cable services carry the images. Don't expect to check out serious accidents, though: because live television might disturb victims' families, TV Tacoma switches quickly to its events calendar.

Traffic cams and automated surveillance offer intriguing opportunities for collaboration among public agencies and private firms.

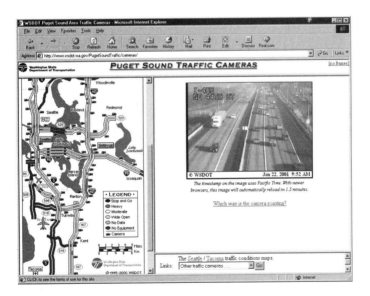

FIGURE 6.6 Clickable camera icons on the index map *(left)* summon traffic cam images *(right)*, which update every 1.5 minutes. From Washington State Department of Transportation, "Puget Sound Traffic Conditions," http://www.wsdot.wa.gov/PugetSoundTraffic/.

In metropolitan Washington, D.C., for example, SmartRoute Systems, a Cambridge, Massachusetts, firm, formed a partnership that includes the *Washington Post*, the local NBC affiliate, and transportation departments in Maryland and Virginia. Named Partners in Motion, the consortium offers free SmarTraveler bulletins on the newspaper's and television station's Web sites. Reports include verbal alerts about delays and hazardous conditions, current driving times between key points, and a clickable map showing camera locations along the Capital Beltway. Unlike Puget Sound's traffic snapshots, some of the D.C. traffic cams refresh the image several times a second. Additional buttons point to Web sites maintained by transportation agencies in Maryland and Virginia, which maintain over two hundred cameras throughout the area and supply basic data to the local SmarTraveler control center. In addition to the Web sites subsidized by advertisers or taxpayers, SmarTraveler and other traffic reporting companies are exploring a variety of fee-based services, including customized traffic reports based on the subscriber's normal commuting route and delivered automatically to a pager, cell phone, onboard navigator, or wireless handheld computer. Although timely traffic data are highly useful, wireless delivery of tiny maps to distracted drivers might have unintended consequences.

+   +   +

Photo surveillance is taking on another of the traffic cop's responsibilities—ticketing motorists who run red lights. A camera mounted above the intersection takes a snapshot of any vehicle entering after the signal turns red. These cameras typically use photographic film, which must be collected manually but provides a clearer picture than video. A clerk or image processor then reads the license plate so that a computer can find the owner's name and address in the registration database and print out a citation, complete with date, time, location, and direction of travel. The more sophisticated stoplight-camera systems photograph the windshields of approaching vehicles and embellish the ticket with a picture of the driver. Graphic evidence makes it hard for the guilty motorist to claim it's all a mistake—and easy for a parent to ground the son or daughter who ignores the rules. Video surveillance also helps localities crack down on motorists who speed through school zones or dodge around gates at railroad crossings. That said, localities willing to reduce violations (and revenue) could do so by extending the yellow phase a second or two.

Because a machine, not a police officer, generates the ticket, photo enforcement typically requires special legislation and a different set of rules. Most states do not levy points, which can increase the violator's insurance rate, and some call the mailed-out citation a "notice of liability." Although the practice might seem heavy-handed, especially when $100 fines help pay for $20,000 cameras, traffic safety experts point to an alarming increase in the number of American drivers who run red lights and cause 260,000 traffic accidents every year, about 750 of them fatal. Studies indicate that four-fifths of the population supports photo enforcement—nearly 80 percent according to a recent report by the Insurance Institute for Highway Safety—and red-light running declines markedly when motorists know they're likely to get a ticket. And because perceived risk is at least equally important, Toronto, Canada, ran an extensive advertising campaign and posted large signs with a camera logo and the warning "Red Light Camera in Operation" (fig. 6.7). Most motorists, I suspect, are unaware that the city cut costs by buying only ten cameras to rotate among forty intersections.

FIGURE 6.7 Toronto mayor Mel Lastman, a strong supporter of photo enforcement, posed next to this warning sign for a September 1998 press release. After a pilot study at this intersection revealed an average of sixty-five offenses every twenty-four hours, the Ontario government approved the use of red-light cameras. From City of Toronto, http://www.city. toronto.on.ca/ mayor/.

Photo enforcement does not sit well with libertarians, privacy advocates, and political conservatives who see the cameras as yet another encroachment of Big Brother. Inherently suspicious of video surveillance and databases, the American Civil Liberties Union is especially wary of technologies that integrate cameras and computers. As Michael Klein, an ACLU board member told the *Ventura County Star*, "What's going on right now is an increasing ability of the government to control your life. And cameras are a part of it." Resistance can be strident and effective. California legislators rejected photo enforcement after a bitter, highly partisan battle led by conservative Republicans like Assemblyman Bernie Richter, who sees red-light cameras as a form of "general surveillance [that] smacks of Nazi Germany in the 1930s." Yet many liberals and law-and-order conservatives think the end—fewer crashes, fewer deaths—justifies the means. And as Howard County, Maryland police lieutenant Glenn Hansen points out, "It's not a new law; it's a new way of enforcing the law." My hunch is that public consensus lies in selective enforcement—ignoring routine speed violations (which the police largely overlook anyway) and adjusting the size of fines to focus on persistent offenders—and camera systems that photograph only violators. Big Brother is less a threat to innocent drivers if he lacks long-term memory.

+   +   +

The story of traffic surveillance doesn't end here. Geographic technology can readily monitor our comings and goings in far greater detail than loop detectors and stoplight cameras. You know what I mean if you use E-ZPass, a clever electronic system for paying road and bridge tolls in several northeastern states. A vehicle approaching a toll barrier slows to five miles per hour and passes a detector that directs the Automatic Vehicle Identification (AVI) system to query the tiny transponder, or "tag," attached inside the windshield at the top. Sealed in a watertight case with a lithium battery that lasts ten years, the tag is a tiny transceiver, which sends back its unique serial number so that a central computer can debit the owner's account. For road tolls, which are based on mileage, the system compares entry and exit points and reports the details on your monthly statement together with the date and time of exit, down to the second. If the goal were speed enforcement, E-ZPass could easily calculate your elapsed time and—if you drive like most of us—send out a "notice of liability."

Electronic toll collection is the precursor of a transport revolution that is at once hopeful and ominous. Market-based road pricing schemes, popular among avant-garde urban planners in Europe, promise to alleviate traffic congestion and air pollution by charging drivers for using city streets during rush hour. Bolstered by GPS and E-Z Pass-like transponders, AVI technology could automatically enforce a host of traffic regulations, from speeding and red-light running to double parking, tailgating, and incomplete stopping at stop signs. A markedly different control strategy focuses on roads and cars rather than drivers. "Smart cars" with sensors that keep them safely apart and in their proper lanes could cut down on collisions as well as increase throughput along existing corridors. Where dispersed metropolitan populations and highly varied patterns of origins and destinations thwart efficient public transport, drivers using local roads could converge on grouping stations at which vehicles would be assembled into closely spaced, train-like packs for high-speed travel to downstream stations and branch points. "Drivers" would sacrifice direct control over their vehicles for much of the trip—along with the hazards of road rage and multi-car pile-ups—and could read, watch television, or talk safely on cell phones.

Although skeptics question the economic benefits of automated highways, some heavily automated, highly regimented scenario seems inevitable, at least in the long, long run. And even if exponential population growth and sprawling metropolises ultimately force urban commuters off the road onto public transit, routine surveillance of passengers and vehicles will be a key component of whatever systems transport us into the next century. Equally certain is the ability of a highly automated transportation infrastructure to monitor movement and control lives in ways few American alive today would find acceptable. Although this expanded capacity for surveillance does not make intrusive regimentation inevitable, our Brave New World's Brave New Roadways will surely challenge conventional notions of personal privacy.

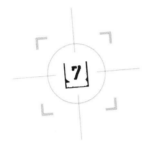

Crime Watch

Essays on privacy and law enforcement almost always bring up the Panopticon, an intriguing blend of surveillance and prison architecture designed by Jeremy Bentham (1748–1832). Bentham was a legal reformer, polemicist, and early advocate of utilitarianism, a philosophy that cedes the moral high ground to whatever works for the greatest number of people. In 1791, he published what remains his most famous work, *"Panopticon": or, the Inspection-House; containing the idea of a new principle of construction applicable to any sort of establishment, in which persons of any description are to be kept under inspection; and in particular to Penitentiary-houses, Prisons, Houses of industry, Workhouses, Poor Houses, Manufacturies, Madhouses, Lazarettos, Hospitals, and Schools; with a plan of management adopted* [sic] *to the principle.* This tortuous title is a sanitized description of the design's intent: controlling inmates of various kinds through a constant threat of random surveillance. A drawing (fig. 7.1) described the relationship between the inmate's cells, which ringed a central tower and an "inspection gallery" from which an unseen "inspector" could observe the cell's occupants at any time through visual baffles like venetian blinds. This similarity to closed-circuit television (CCTV) makes Bentham's plan an attractive metaphor for social philosophers who write expressively about the "panoptic gaze" of technologies of social control or the "panoptic power" of electronic surveillance.

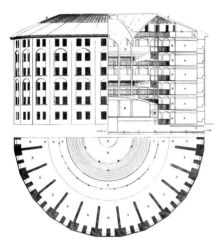

FIGURE 7.1 This drawing of Bentham's Panopticon shows the annular arrangement of cells around the inspection galleries, which are connected through a central tower to the "Inspector's Lodge" below. From Jeremy Bentham, *The Works of Jeremy Bentham, published under the superintendence of his executor, John Bowring* (Edinburgh: William Tait, 1843), vol. 6, following p. 172.

Although the metaphor seems vaguely appropriate, I am not convinced that the similarity between Bentham's model prison and video surveillance tells us anything that's not obvious about the watcher's power over the watched. My hunch is that the prison's walls and bars as well as the isolation of inmates in individual cells exert far greater control over prisoners' lives than a ready ability to spy on their actions. No doubt a voyeur-inspector would enjoy a stronger sense of power and control as well as an increased ability to make the inmates docile by rendering swift if not severe punishment for minor infractions—at least occasionally and with sufficient retribution to indicate which rules are not to be broken. What's relevant, though, is the power of surveillance to intimidate someone *already* under the watcher's control, like a prisoner (who can be beaten), an employee (who can be fired), or a motorist who runs red lights (and could be fined or lose his or her license). What the prison metaphor fails to capture is the ability of video surveillance to monitor behavior at a distance over a wide area and if response is rapid, to protect people from human predators. Remove the *con*, though, and the resulting adjective *panoptic*—*pan* means "all" and *optic* refers to seeing—seems especially appropriate when coverage is broad and thorough.

+   +   +

Video cameras are abundant if not ubiquitous. Office buildings and shopping malls have them to help security staff watch for suspicious behavior throughout the parking garage, stairwells, and obscure parts of the lobby, and banks believe that a visual record of teller and ATM transactions cuts down on armed robbery and debit card fraud. Self-service gasoline stations rely on CCTV to prosecute people who fill up and drive off without paying, while convenience store operators believe that video surveillance can deter impulsive acts like sneaking out with a jar of Cheez Whiz under your sweater. The monitors are often in plain sight: if we know we're being watched, we'll behave ourselves.

In the 1990s video surveillance came out of stores and into our streets and parks—what geographers call public space. Because public officials are skittish about being labeled Big Brother, public-space video surveillance is generally less obtrusive than the cameras used to catch motorists who run red lights. And it's used less widely in the United States than in Great Britain, which began experimenting with CCTV to combat crime and terrorism in the mid-1980s, after IRA frustrations boiled over from Northern Ireland into Central London. In the aftermath of the September 11, 2001, attacks on the World Trade Center and the Pentagon, America might decide to catch up.

For the few U.S. cities with video surveillance of pedestrian areas, coverage seems spotty, typically with less than one camera per block. A survey by the California Research Bureau, a division of the California State Library, reported a variety of video surveillance strategies in use by thirteen municipalities ranging in size from Baltimore, Maryland, and San Diego, California, to Dover, New Jersey. In general, cameras that can pan, tilt, and zoom are connected by fiber-optic cable to police headquarters or another central location, where police officers watch the monitors for part of the day. But some cities rely heavily on public funds or use volunteers, and a few systems merely record scenes passively on tape for periodic review and possible use in court.

Baltimore, for instance, installed sixteen fixed-position cameras in June 1996 in a downtown retail area with a reputation tarnished by auto break-ins, drug dealing, prostitution, and aggressive panhandling. Funded by a federal grant as well as private funds, the cameras are actively monitored by police—in two shifts, 7 A.M. to 11 P.M.—from a nearby 8-by-12-foot kiosk. The system stores its images on videotape, which is changed every twenty-four hours and retained for up to four days, after which tapes are reused or discarded unless needed as evidence in a police investigation or criminal prosecution. Because persons recorded are in plain view and have no expectation of privacy, capturing their movements on tape does not breach the Fourth Amendment ban on "unreasonable search and seizure." And as an added safeguard, only law enforcement personnel watch the monitors and screen the tapes.

Despite such safeguards, privacy advocates object vigorously to systematic monitoring by the police. In October 1996, for instance, after New York City officials vowed to jump aboard the CCTV bandwagon with twenty-four-hour video surveillance in Central Park, Norman Siegel, executive director of the New York Civil Liberties Union, warned that "if we start going in this direction, the next logical extension is to put cameras on every street corner and allow the government to monitor people engaged in innocent, lawful and confidential activities." Widespread cameras are no less a threat than the resulting tapes, according to Siegel, who charged that the video surveillance program was not only "invasive" but "raises the Orwellian specter of Big Brother government spying on its residents, and compiling a video record of the free movement of individuals as they make their way about the city." Debate quickly focused on the tapes' retention period, with Siegel arguing for erasure within seventy-two hours and the police arguing to keep the images for at least a full week because some crimes might not be reported for several days.

Intent on documenting the extent of video surveillance, NYCLU volunteers mapped the locations of all readily visible video cameras in Manhattan. Five months of fieldwork revealed 2,397 cameras, but an accompanying explanation warned that the map is "far from exhaustive" and omits "many more" cameras "tucked surreptitiously out of the line of vision or small enough to escape detection." Surprisingly, the vast majority of the cameras—2,117, or 88 percent—were privately owned, and 55 of the remaining 270 public surveillance cameras were traffic cameras operated by the transportation department, not the police. Big Brother, if he exists at all, is largely a private cop with tunnel vision and a stiff neck.

Published on the Internet to "raise awareness of the prevalence of video surveillance," the NYCLU map reveals highly uneven coverage. The excerpt in figure 7.2, for instance, shows concentrations of video cameras in front of police headquarters (toward the lower right) and around the Federal Reserve Bank (near the left edge). Elsewhere in the area camera density is comparatively low. For instance, only one camera is evident along Church Street next to the site of World Trade Center (large light-shaded block toward the upper left), which terrorists had attacked in 1993 by exploding a fertilizer bomb in the parking garage. Other parts of Manhattan have less than one camera for every four blocks. What's more, although the number of cameras probably has increased since 1998, when the map was made, video surveillance has less salience now that the United States seems unlikely to mimic Britain's eager adoption of police-operated street cameras. NYCLU leaders still follow technical developments like automatic facial recognition, but their Web site fo-

FIGURE 7.2 Excerpt from Mediaeater, "NYC Surveillance Cameras Project," http://mediaeater .com/cameras. Like many views of Manhattan, the map is oriented with north at the upper right.

cuses on more compelling issues like police brutality and reproductive rights.

Civil libertarians are not alone in considering CCTV a threat to personal privacy. In fall 2000, when my graduate seminar focused on surveillance technology, two of my seven students were highly apprehensive about denser, more intrusive coverage with sharper imagery. Fueling their fears was the British experience, which generated a wave of disapproval in the social science literature, as well as cheaper, smaller, more versatile cameras. While it's tempting to dismiss this anxiety as unfounded technological determinism, I have little doubt that our public officials could find a more dramatic and politically expedient response to a sudden increase in street crime, hooliganism, or terrorism. And venal vendors, heretofore content with the expanding private security market, would hardly object.

Whether CCTV monitoring would ever reach Orwellian proportions in either the United States or the United Kingdom is another matter. Perhaps the reason why American police have not followed their British counterparts down the panoptic path (or slippery slope, if you like) is that video surveillance of public space has proved a feeble defense against determined criminals or terrorists and only a localized inconvenience for other lawbreakers. In short, whether it works depends very much on the meaning of *works*. Evaluation studies are methodologically troublesome because cameras that reduce gang activity, drug dealing, and public urination in their immediate vicinity typically displace some of these activities to other locations, often just out of the camera's range. Proponents have oversold its effectiveness to much the same extent that opponents have overestimated its invasiveness. Whatever the technology's limitations, a majority of Britons accept CCTV as a necessary and appropriate law enforcement tool.

Given time and a huge chunk of public money, surveillance technology could, I am certain, become far more intense, powerful, and invasive. One need not be a science fiction fan to envision a future in which cameras as dense as streetlights feed images to central computers with face-recognition algorithms and biometrics software that match pedestrians to their stored profiles and track their movement through streets and parks. Whether this Orwellian enterprise would be worthwhile is another matter: accurate retina scanning requires far greater resolution than conventional street cameras, and several of the location-tracking technologies examined in the next chapter can protect citizens more reliably and less expensively. Biometrics might prove useful for screening airline passengers at the check-in desk, but the hazards of misidentification—fingering innocent pedestrians while ignoring known terrorists—seem far more daunting than the threat to personal privacy.

+   +   +

As the courts see it, whether random surveillance is constitutional usually hinges on whether citizens have a reasonable expectation of privacy. The landmark case is *Katz v. United States,* in which the Supreme Court ruled that FBI agents were wrong in putting a listening device inside a phone booth. A court order can authorize the police to tap your telephone or bug your living room, but detectives can't randomly prowl public space with a highly sensitive directional microphone in hope of uncovering a drug buy or stock swindle. Expectation of privacy is hardly an issue, though, when the sound in question is a gunshot. Residents blocks away hear the noise, and anyone alarmed by armed revelry and not afraid of the culprits might dial 911. Shooting into the air might seem a harmless way to celebrate the New Year and other festive occasions, but the laws of physics dictate the bullet's return to earth with deadly force. If you think people who complain are spoilsports, tell it to the two daughters of thirty-one-year-old Benjamin Velasco. Shortly after 1 A.M. on January 1, 2001, Velasco was headed for a party with his wife when a stray bullet struck and killed him. That morning falling bullets hit five other Los Angeles-area residents, none fatally. Velasco was not the nation's only fatality. At midnight in El Cenizo, Texas, for instance, a falling bullet struck a fourteen-year-old girl in her upper chest while she was standing with her mother in their front yard.

Instead of waiting for a complaint, police in several California cities rely on ShotSpotter, which its inventors describe as an "automatic real-time gunshot locator and display system." Their patent application, filed in August 1997 and approved in October 1999, portrays a clever marriage of seismic analysis and acoustic filtering. Landlines or wireless transmitters connect a network of pole- and

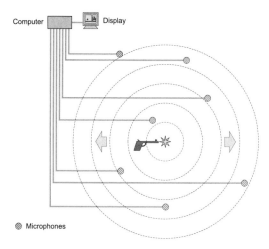

Computer | Display

Microphones

FIGURE 7.3 ShotSpotter calculates a gunshot's location from the relative arrival times of the muzzle burst at a network of microphones connected to a central computer. Adapted from figure 1 in Robert L. Showen and Jason W. Dunham, application for U.S. Patent no. 5,973,998, awarded October 26, 1999.

roof-mounted microphones, roughly 1,000 to 3,000 feet apart, to a central computer. Like an earthquake, a gunshot generates a sharply defined circular pulse, which expands outward at a constant speed. As figure 7.3 shows, ShotSpotter's microphones detect the wave at slightly different times depending on their distance from the shooter's location. The computer can use any three arrival times to calculate coordinates for a shot's origin and can use intersecting circles or spheres to triangulate a location in either two or three dimensions—especially useful in hilly terrain or for sensors at radically different heights. And when four or more microphones detect the same gunshot, ShotSpotter can choose the most reliable triangulation. The process pinpoints gunshots to within 15 yards, which can narrow the location to a particular house and perhaps one or two of its neighbors.

A key component is a sophisticated acoustic filter able to distinguish the abrupt muzzle blast from the weaker and less geometrically reliable sound of a bullet. ShotSpotter also differentiates gunshot-like explosions from background noise, including the weaker, more localized sounds of hammering, barking dogs, and slammed car doors as well as the loud, more continuous sounds of airplanes and train whistles. In determining arrival times, the system correlates acoustic waves from its various microphones, and it can use the onset and separations between multiple gunshots to calculate direction and speed for moving sources typical of "drive-by" shootings. Although able to discriminate muzzle blasts from their reverberations, ShotSpotter also triangulates fireworks, gas explosions, and backfiring vehicles. In alerting the police dispatcher to a possible gunshot, the system displays the location on a map and stores a short sound "snippet" for human confirmation.

Police use the maps as propaganda—graphic warnings telling shooters to cut it out. As the vendor's Web site asks rhetorically, "What would you do if an officer knocked at your door [with] a computer generated map that showed gunfire in your backyard? Chances are you would not do it again! If you did, you know there is a high probability that an officer will knock at your door and potentially someone will be arrested for committing this crime." However intimidating, preventive warnings are less expensive than prosecution and incarceration as well as less traumatic than the physical and emotional injuries of neighbors hit by stray or falling bullets.

Redwood City, California, a suburb of San Francisco, adopted this approach. Concerned about citizens celebrating birthdays and assorted holidays with random gunfire, city officials allocated $25,000 for a ten-week trial in 1995. Eight microphones monitored a 1-square-mile area notorious for noise and falling bullets. Thanks to "Operation Silent Night," the next New Year's was remarkably quiet, and city officials credited ShotSpotter with cutting the monthly average number of gunshot incidents from twenty-four to twelve. Although critics and the police union objected to the cost, Redwood City eventually bought the system outright—after the company reduced the price from $250,000 to $85,000.

Redwood City's success no doubt inspired the Los Angeles County Sheriff's Department to arrange a test in the densely populated Willowbrook area, the scene of gang activity and drive-by shootings as well as random gunshots. In addition to promoting prompt response by street cops, the L.A. test linked ShotSpotter with a "reverse 911" notification system called the Communicator. When a gunshot is detected, the Communicator retrieves the phone numbers of nearby homes and businesses from a geographic database, calls them up, announces that the police are aware of the gunshot, and asks anyone who can describe the culprit to press a button

and report what they know. Although the trial had yet to produce a
sale, Microsoft chairman Bill Gates nominated ShotSpotter and the
Communicator for a 2000 Computerworld Smithsonian Laureate
Award, no doubt partly because they rely on Microsoft database and
server software. The judges apparently agreed with Gates, and the
two systems became part of the national museum's collection of
"the year's most innovative applications of technology from 38
states and 21 countries." Clever indeed, but most police officials remain skeptical about either the need for a gunshot locator or its
price.

+   +   +

Computer mapping is another matter. For more than a decade, police departments throughout the country have been mapping crimes
and other "incidents" stored in their electronic databases. Although
computers expedite the process, sticking pins on wall maps is an old
strategy for guessing where a criminal might live or strike next. Law
enforcement experts still refer to detailed maps of crime locations as
"pin maps" even though mapping software marketed to police typically pinpoint crime locations with prominent dots (fig. 7.4), sometimes colored to show time of day or type of crime.

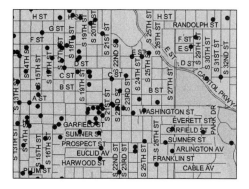

FIGURE 7.4 Portion of a pin
map showing incidents of
vandalism in Lincoln, Ne-
braska. The original color
map is from City of Lincoln/
Lancaster County, "Lincoln
Police Department 2001
Crime Data," http://
ims.ci.lincoln.ne.us/isa/
2001Crime/.

Contemporary crime mapping is rooted in a long-held belief that
law enforcement can benefit from mathematical analysis and operations research. The International Association of Chiefs of Police
has encouraged systematic collection of crime statistics since the
1930s, various task forces of the President's Crime Commission

promoted computer-aided data analysis in the 1960s, and isolated partnerships of university researchers and detectives explored applications of computer cartography in the 1970s. Although a few police departments made maps with computers in the 1980s, interest was sparse until the fortuitous convergence in the 1990s of specialized software, pedagogic propaganda, and federally funded demonstration projects.

Perhaps the greatest impetus was the Violent Crime Control and Law Enforcement Act of 1994, which promised to put 100,000 more cops on the street at a cost of $8.8 billion over six years as well as equip police agencies of all sizes with high-tech crime fighting tools, including geographic information systems. Federal grants helped many departments purchase a GIS, and the Department of Justice's Crime Mapping Research Center offered guidance in selecting and setting up a system and using its maps in daily operations. Established in 1997, the Center sponsors research on the spatial analysis of crime, maintains an information clearinghouse and online tutorial (www.ojp.usdoj.gov/cmrc/), and runs an annual conference for researchers and users. As part of its outreach mission, the Center published geographer Keith Harries's splendidly illustrated 204-page guide, *Mapping Crime: Principle and Practice,* and distributed more than 8,500 copies to targeted mailing lists that included crime analysts, police chiefs, and sheriffs.

Crime maps vary in appearance and purpose. Some mark the locations of individual crimes with point symbols like the dots in figure 7.4; some display counts by block, patrol zone, or district for a specific type of incident like auto theft or burglary; and some report counts as rates after dividing by each area's population, land area, miles of street or sidewalk, or number of households. While competent general-purpose mapping software offers all these options, only a GIS designed for crime analysis is likely to highlight hot spots. Defined as a small area with an abnormal number of crimes within a short period, a hot spot can be a street corner, a block, a schoolyard, or a neighborhood. Although many hot spots are persistent and predictable, a new hot spot might indicate a new burglar in the neighborhood, emerging conflict between street gangs, or a similar threat calling for prompt action. Mapping systems that automatically troll for similar crimes clustered in space and time can identify statisti-

FIGURE 7.5 Composite map relates homicide locations *(dots)* to hot spots for drugs *(thin ellipses)* and nonlethal violence *(thick ellipses)*. Based on 1987–90 data from the Chicago Police Department, the original color map is from Thomas F. Rich, "The Use of Computerized Mapping in Crime Control and Prevention Programs," *Research in Action* [National Institute of Justice newsletter], July 1995, 1–11; map on 4.

cally significant clusters and highlight their locations with ellipses, as in figure 7.5. The Chicago Police Department used this map to study territorial disputes between rival gangs. Note that turf violence and homicides are strongly correlated, whereas drug activity is generally less common along the perimeter of a gang's territory.

Maps can also fight crime by making precinct commanders answerable to district commanders and the chief of police. The most impressive example of map-based accountability is the ComStat (Computerized Statistics) program initiated by the New York City Police Department in 1994. Similar in principle to briefings at which battlefield commanders plan or critique a tactical assault,

ComStat also mimics the regularly scheduled meetings at which executives of large manufacturing and retailing firms review production and sales data. A similar flow of information occurs at police headquarters when precinct and district commanders gather twice a week for a three-hour early morning "crime strategy meeting." Each precinct commander makes a presentation once or twice a month using a large interactive map that displays timely crime patterns for incidents ranging from homicide to aggressive panhandling. Colleagues ask questions and offer suggestions, and higher-ups indicate their displeasure when a precinct's strategy doesn't work. In addition to underscoring effective tactics and emerging trends, the maps encourage collaboration in addressing hot spots along precinct borders as well as crime rings operating in different parts of the city.

ComStat is the brainchild of the late Jack Maple, a former New York transit policeman who demonstrated how mapping could cut down crime in subway stations. Later a private consultant, Maple helped sell ComStat to police departments in other large cities, including New Orleans and Philadelphia. Interviewed for *Government Technology,* he gave an insightful answer to the question "How does the mapping help?"

> The beauty of the mapping is that it poses the question, "Why?" What are the underlying causes of why there is a certain cluster of crime in a particular place? Is there a shopping center here? Is this why we have a lot of pickpockets and robberies? Is there a school here? Is that why we have a problem at three o'clock? Is there an abandoned house nearby? Is that why there is crack-dealing on the corner?
>
> By looking at this, you can figure out where you need to be and when. You can figure out what time the pickpockets are working. You can look at stolen cars—where they are being stolen from and where they are being recovered. If only the bones are being found, you know there is a chop shop nearby.
>
> A map can give you all this. Then you can start looking at patterns and chronic conditions.

As Maple's examples imply, ComStat maps encompass census and land-use data as well as police intelligence.

Law enforcement's ultimate accountability, of course, is to the public, which pays police salaries and elects city officials. Many departments recognize that citizens are not only their employers and clients but also potential partners in the "war on crime." And as partners, the public can benefit from timely information about when and where to be especially careful. Although police agencies typically guard their data, many have discovered Web cartography as an effective way to warn citizens about crime and recruit Neighborhood Watch volunteers. Unheard of a decade ago, police Web sites now have a key role in "community policing."

Not all police Web sites offer maps, and those that do vary widely in sophistication and flexibility. Static maps showing only beat or district boundaries are common, but a few agencies help visitors compose highly customized maps. An exemplar is the San Diego Police Department (www.sannet.gov/police/), which lets users se-

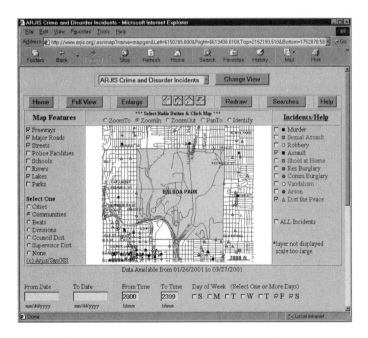

FIGURE 7.6 Among the neighborhoods surrounding San Diego's Balboa Park, the area to the southwest is especially prone to assault and rowdy behavior. The original color map is from San Diego Police Department, "Crime Statistics and Maps—Interactive Mapping Application," http://www.sannet.gov/police/stats/index.html.

lect from menus of crimes and reference features, specify starting and ending dates, and restrict the display to specific days of the week and times of day. Figure 7.6, the result of a request for a map of violent crimes reported near Balboa Park between 8 P.M. and midnight, covers a two-month period in early 2001. A visitor not satisfied with this view could zoom in or out, pan to nearby neighborhoods, or select other crimes and features.

I've heard critics charge that incident mapping ignores the underlying causes of crime. And they're right of course. Whatever the causes of crime—poverty, irresponsible parenting, inadequate education, impulsive behavior, and dysfunctional families and communities come to mind—maps will have a minor role, if any, in their abatement. But if we look instead at the causes of *victimhood*, mapping and other geographic technologies can improve the quality of life for almost everyone, and more so for the poor perhaps than for the rich. Moreover, as a *New York Times* editorial suggested in the wake of the Abner Louima lawsuit, ComStat can promote more effective law enforcement by including complaints against the police.

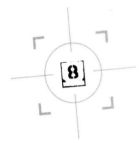

[8]

Keeping Track

Parents, do you know where your children are? What about the neighborhood pervert? In the 1980s TV spots highlighted the dangers of unsupervised teenagers out at night. Nowadays government-run Web sites spill the dirt on paroled sex offenders living in our neighborhoods. It's all there: names, addresses, offenses, and photos—a strong warning to keep our kids indoors at night and in plain sight throughout the day.

In addition to the "Megan's Law" Web sites that many states set up in the late 1990s to "out" sex offenders, GPS and radio triangulation can be used for tracking paroleed and spouse abusers as well as for reporting criminal attacks, accidents, and medical emergencies. The instantaneous calculation and transmission of an individual's location is the ultimate double-edged sword: a technology offering creative alternatives to ostracism and incarceration while threatening cell-phone users, adolescents, and ambulatory consumers with an unprecedented loss of privacy. Although many applications have clear benefits with no apparent downside, the seemingly neutral label "location-based services" includes such neo-Orwellian scenarios as a digital leash based on an implanted chip that not only reports location but can administer pain if the subject steps outside a predefined perimeter—a human version of the "electronic fence" systems for dogs.

+   +   +

Megan's Law commemorates Megan Kanka, a seven-year-old New Jersey girl abducted, raped, and murdered in 1994 by a neighbor. Neither Megan's parents nor her neighbors knew that the three men sharing the house across the street were convicted sex offenders, and that one of them, Megan's killer, had spent six years in prison for sex crimes. Had the Kankas known of the occupants' criminal histories, victims' rights advocates argued, their daughter would still be alive. Within a week fifteen hundred people had signed a petition asking that every child molester's criminal record be revealed to anyone living within 1,000 feet.

Three months later the New Jersey legislature passed the Sex Offender Registration Act of 1994. Like the Washington State statute on which it was based, the new law sorted sex felons into three categories and required them to register with the local police upon release from prison. Those in Tier One, deemed unlikely to commit further crimes, were merely reported to their victims and other police departments in the vicinity. Those in Tier Two, with a moderate risk of reoffending, were reported to the principals of nearby schools, the directors of local women's shelters and day care centers, Boy Scout leaders, and persons in charge of other potential victims. And those in Tier Three, believed to pose a high risk to the community, were subject to a thorough outing by local police, who could publicize their presence with posters, flyers, newspaper ads, and television announcements.

Motivated by sympathy for young victims and the belief that community notification protects children from pedophiles, other states adopted similar statutes. And in May 1996 President Clinton signed a bill that amended the federal Violent Crime Control and Law Enforcement Act of 1994 by renaming it Megan's Law and requiring states to "release relevant information [about sex offenders] that is necessary to protect the public." Although Congress did not specify the form of notification, states that failed to comply would lose 10 percent of their federal law enforcement allotment.

Critics questioned the constitutionality and effectiveness of community notification. Civil libertarians condemned it as a violation of ex-convicts' right to privacy as well as an unconstitutional double punishment of persons who had served their time. Psychologists noted that most child molesters were friends or family members, not strangers, and mental-health professionals scrutinized risk-assessment systems that assigned offenders points based on their crimes and behavior. Police voiced concern about vigilantism after neighbors harassed several recently released offenders and vandalized their property, while legal experts challenged the statutes' wording and warned of a slippery slope leading to less privacy for everyone. Although judges struck down Megan's Laws in several states, including New Jersey, legislatures revised and rephrased their statutes to ensure constitutionality. By the end of the decade, all states had some form of community notification, often via the Internet.

It's hard to tell exactly how many states have online sex-offender registries: although the trend is definitely rising, the number keeps changing as states set up new Web sites or change their policies on public access. Because of considerable leeway in how states can comply with the federal community notification requirement, sex-offender Web sites vary widely in the type of information provided and who may see it. For example, a May 1999 survey by the Bureau of Justice Statistics turned up fifteen states with publicly searchable online registries; ten states with Web sites providing access only to law enforcement personnel or merely describing their registry, registration requirements, and notification policy; and five states with plans to set up a Web site. A June 1999 survey by law student Jane Small found sixteen publicly searchable online registries, including four that included low-risk as well as high-risk offenders. By contrast, a May 2001 visit to the list of state sex-offender registry Web sites maintained by the National Consortium for Justice Information and Statistics found URLs for thirty states with public online searching and for another six with online program descriptions. Because the list reported incorrectly that the District of Columbia "does not maintain an online sex offender registry"—the D.C. police had set one up two months earlier—I suspect additional states might have had one as well.

Curious about whether any (s)ex-cons might be living nearby, I sent my browser to the New York State Sex Offender Registry (criminaljustice.state.ny.us/nsor/index.htm). Although the full registry includes low-, moderate-, and high-risk offenders, only the "Subdirectory of High-Risk (Level 3) Sex Offenders" is publicly accessible online. Like New Jersey, New York uses a three-level classification system, which provides a legally acceptable rationale for protecting the public by ostracizing only high-risk offenders. By contrast, Connecticut's sex-offender Web site, which published the names, addresses, and photographs of *all* sex offenders, low risk as well as high risk, was found to violate offenders' right to "due process." In his April 2001 ruling, federal judge Robert Chatigny noted that the state went well beyond the federal mandate to protect the public from dangerous individuals.

Don't expect New York's online registry to include all high-risk offenders and provide up-to-the-minute reports on their whereabouts. A 647-word disclaimer warns that the subdirectory should be used cautiously. Wary of lawsuits arising from attacks by offenders who should be in the database but aren't, the Division of Criminal Justice Services, which maintains the Web site and "updates this information regularly," notes that entries might be incorrect or out of date. What's more, some arguably dangerous offenders are missing because a federal court ordered the exclusion of "Level 3 sex offenders who committed their crime prior to January 21, 1996 [when the state's Sex Offender Registration Act took effect] and were assigned to a risk level prior to January 1, 2000," when the state revised the list of crimes requiring registration. Because protection of the public does not trump the constitutional right to due process, the state can't brand an offender as high risk without an official evaluation by its board of examiners.

Equally wary of attacks on registered offenders or persons with a close resemblance, New York warns online users that "comparisons based on appearance may . . . be misleading" and that "anyone who uses this information to injure, harass, or commit a criminal act against any person may be subject to criminal prosecution." The effectiveness of these caveats is questionable, as is the requirement that users identify themselves before searching. Although entering one's name and address might deter some harassers, a savvy vigilante could access the registry at a public library by typing in a fictitious name and address.

Resisting the temptation to conceal my identity, I advanced to a screen that invited me to search for offenders by last name, county, ZIP code, or any combination. A search for Onondaga County returned a list of seventy-seven names, each underlined to indicate a link to a detailed record that included the registrant's name, address, physical description, photo, and a concise record of sex offenses (including for some the age and sex of the victim). As a caveat at the top of the list noted, some of the names were aliases, nicknames, or alternative spellings reported by offenders. Although some matches were obvious—David was also Rockin Dave, Ron was also Ronald, and Neal was Neil—inspection of all entries revealed a number of true aliases and whittled the list down to fifty-two unique entries, a mere hundredth of a percent of the county's 2000 population.

I can see why critics object to needless fears raised by online photos. Almost all fifty-two images looked scary, even the distorted black-and-white images that resembled botched scans of police mug shots. Context might well explain this reaction: the snapshots were obviously taken under conditions of duress, and we expect people who commit sleazy crimes to look sleazy. If I replaced these felons' headshots with candid photos of my colleagues, most of whom are exceptionally nice folks, you'd probably find their pictures equally repulsive. Adding to an unwholesome impression, the typical entry described scars or tattoos.

Hardly a surprise, the group was all male. Or at least I think so: one offender, who goes by "Chris" or "Christine," could have been a cross-dresser. The color photo suggested a hint of beard, which contradicted the red lipstick and dangling hoop earrings. The entry listed his or her sex as "unknown" and reported his or her crime as attempted sodomy with a sixteen-year-old male.

Information about an offender's crimes and victims could allay or sharpen the viewer's fear. For example, felons with multiple offenses seem to prefer one sex or the other as well as a particular age group. Parents of a seven-year-old girl thus might find it reassuring that the pervert next door prefers adolescent boys. Entries also list conditions of release for parolees and include a space for describing the offense or a modus operandi. Although the "explicit nature" of the latter seems to preclude publication on the Internet in almost all cases, a message invites interested citizens to consult the local police department or call the division's "for-fee 900 # Information Line."

Rightly or wrongly, a parent's or potential victim's greatest fear is the sex offender in the immediate neighborhood or along the way to the local playground. To help users zoom in quickly, the Web site allows a ZIP code search, which can narrow the list greatly—to zero in the case of 13224, where I live. But over in 13210, closer to the university, live three high-risk offenders, one not far from the food co-op where my wife used to take our daughter when she was young. He sexually abused an eight-year-old girl five years ago, the registry reveals, and he's got wheels: a 1986 Nissan Pulsar, which parents can warn their daughters never to go near. More astute parents and grandparents will no doubt call the state's 900 number. If the guy abused the child of a woman he was living with, say, he's probably far less a threat than a predator who attacked a stranger. I'd be leery of the bastard but better aware of why "naming and shaming" (as it's called in Britain) makes rehabilitation difficult for nonrecidivist sex offenders.

Among states using the Internet for community notification, New York reflects an intermediate position between Connecticut, which until recently largely ignored relative risk, and California, which uses its Web site to advertise a sex-offender listing stored on a CD-ROM and available for searching at the county sheriff's office or, in large cities, at police headquarters. Like New York's online registry, California's public-access CD-ROM contains only high-risk offenders. Entries include the offender's name and known aliases, age and sex, a photograph (usually) and physical description, names of the crimes that resulted in registration, and the county and ZIP code of last known residence—but not his exact street address. A prospective viewer must be over eighteen years old and able to "state a distinct purpose" for searching the registry. In addition to holding a valid California driver's license or identity card, the viewer must sign a statement affirming awareness of the purpose of the data and the illegality of using the information to "harass, discriminate or commit a crime against any registrant." As an added safeguard, the viewer must also assert that he or she is not a registered sex offender—unlike legislatures in most other states, California lawmakers were wary of pedophiles using a Megan's Law registry to contact each other and exchange snapshots of their victims.

Although California prohibits unregulated online viewing of its sex-offender registry and is stingy with geographic details, local police departments can inform the public about sex offenders living in their community in a more precise way, with maps. That's the approach in Fairfield, a city of 95,000 persons midway between San Francisco and Sacramento. A reflection of increased use of GIS in law enforcement, the police department Web site (www.ci.Fairfield .ca.us/police/) serves up online pin maps centered on each of thirty-one local schools and updated every three months. A menu lists the names of the city's four high schools, five middle schools, thirteen public elementary schools, and nine church-affiliated schools. Double-clicking on a name yields a customized map (fig. 8.1) showing a portion of the local street network with the school in question at the center of a brown circle a mile in diameter. Blue stars represent schools, and red dots mark the addresses of sex registrants, labeled by street name but not house number. Even though the dots are in the middle of the street, parents familiar with the area might have no trouble narrowing a location to a handful of residences.

Variation among the states in access to their sex-offender registries could provide a rich database for studying what works, what doesn't, and why. But a meaningful evaluation requires a clear sense of what we mean by *works* and how we might tease out the consequences, intended and otherwise, of diverse approaches. A key concern is that community notification of known and convicted sex offenders addresses only part of a wider problem. Although

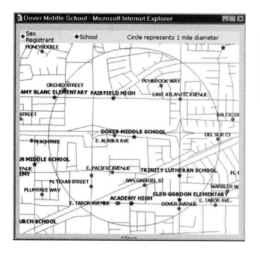

FIGURE 8.1 One of thirty-one school-centered sex-offender maps available from the Fairfield, California, Police Department Sex Offender Database, http://www.ci.fairfield.ca.us/police/map_list.asp.

Megan's Law Web sites can contribute to our children's wariness of strangers offering candy or eager to show off the new puppy in the back room, they do little to cut down on sexual abuse by Uncle Ralph, Father John, or Mom's new boyfriend. More troublesome is the need to balance our legal responsibilities to potential victims and known offenders. Although ostracism complicates an offender's return to a normal, productive life, it's clear that some individuals warrant continued surveillance once their sentences are served. Unless society and the courts are willing to incarcerate high-risk offenders for life or isolate them in "guarded villages," as social reformer Amitai Etzioni has suggested, community notification of some sort seems essential. How effective such notification is might well depend on the extent to which society accepts its responsibility for rehabilitation.

+   +   +

That community notification might be little more than a Band-Aid prompted some jurisdictions to experiment with a more proactive form of sex-offender surveillance: satellite tracking. An extension of the electronic ankle bracelets used to monitor parolees and pretrial defendants placed on home confinement, electronic tracking is a relatively inexpensive way to protect children from pedophiles and battered women from abusive husbands or boyfriends. And because vigilance is constant and discreet, the digital leash can also address the harmful effects of naming and shaming, the needs of parents who lack Internet access, and the reluctance of some offenders to report their addresses promptly and obey court-imposed restrictions.

Satellite tracking is a significant advance over older home-confinement systems based on a radio link between an ankle bracelet and a telephone set. A transmitter connected to a GPS receiver reports the offender's current position every 60 seconds to a surveillance center, where a GIS compares his location to a list of prohibited spaces such as schools, day care centers, strip clubs, bars, and the residences of the offender's victims or endangered spouse. In effect, the system establishes an "electronic fence," which can vary by time of day, for example, to let the offender go to work or return home along a prescribed route. If the subject moves outside his prescribed perimeter, the GIS can record the violation and alert authorities as well as send the offender a warning. More advanced systems designed to monitor victims as well as offenders can enforce an order of protection by repeatedly comparing a known stalker's location with that of his electronically protected prey.

The digital leash is not just for sex offenders and spouse abusers. Its steady panoptic gaze reduces the likelihood a parolee or person awaiting trial will commit a range of other crimes, petty or serious: by recording the subject's movements in both time and space, the computer produces an electronic trail, which can be correlated with crime locations to add or remove him or her, automatically, from a list of suspects. Not a substitute for a conscientious rehabilitation program, constant monitoring reduces the likelihood of missed appointments for personal counseling or drug treatment. It's no surprise, then, that cost-conscious corrections departments are experimenting with satellite tracking as an alternative to prison for a variety of offenses, especially nonviolent crimes like drug possession. Compared to incarceration, which can be more expensive than sending a son or daughter away to a good private college, the daily rental fee for a GPS-based tracking unit is cheap, typically less than fifteen dollars. What's more, taxpayers don't need to feed and clothe the gainfully employed detainee, who can then help cover the cost of monitoring or pay restitution to his or her victims. Given the option of electronic monitoring or satellite tracking, which is usually voluntary, prisoners rarely reject the chance to escape the confinement of a tiny cell.

For a "high-tech ball and chain" like the SMART (Satellite Monitoring and Remote Tracking) system, developed by Pro Tech Monitoring, the prime drawback seems to be the weight of the batteries. A 6-ounce transmitter strapped to the ankle communicates with a 3.5-pound Portable Tracking Device (PTD), which is about the size of two VHS tapes and can be strapped to the waist or carried in a knapsack or briefcase. The PTD contains a GPS receiver, a microprocessor, a radio receiver connected to the ankle bracelet, and a wireless modem linked to Pro Tech's surveillance center. The microprocessor notifies the center if the offender tries to tamper with the bracelet or violates the prescribed "inclusion" and "exclusion zones," which define where he or she should or should not be at various times and are stored on the PTD's computer. If the subject wanders out of bounds or gets too close to a victim or witness, the PTD emits a warning signal and after a few minutes reports the violation to Pro Tech, which in turn notifies the offender's "supervising agency" by pager, fax, or Internet. Zoning can also restrict a detainee to a particular state or county and declare off limits broad areas where terrain interferes with GPS or wireless reception. Because GPS does not work indoors, no-go zones might include large enclosed spaces like the Mall of America.

Although the offender must carry the PTD when traveling, it can be set down at home, work, or a friend's house. In this sense, the radio link between ankle transmitter and PTD is a programmable electronic leash. At night, when the PTD insists upon a comparatively strong signal from the transmitter, the leash is short and the offender must stay close by. At other times and locations the supervising agency can increase the allowed distance to as much as 1,000 feet so that the subject can play softball or work in a warehouse or garden. It's not a perfect arrangement because the detainee can always ditch the PTD, leaving a record of where he or she was, not where he or she is. But with smaller, lighter batteries and miniaturized components, developers can integrate the GPS, microprocessor, and modem with the ankle bracelet and reduce the chances that an offender who snaps can snap the leash.

It gets more Orwellian than Orwell's *1984*. "Third-generation" systems, talked about but yet to come, promise tamper-proof ankle bracelets that can monitor vital signs as well as location and can "shut down" a wayward offender who tries to remove the bracelet. And because of miniaturization, the units can be implanted beneath the skin like the contraceptive Norplant rather than merely strapped on. Max Winkler, a Colorado parole officer who extolled the benefits of third-generation monitoring in a July 1993 article in *The Futurist*, described a subdermal microcomputer with artificial intelligence software able to detect a dangerous pattern of vital signs and release a tranquilizer or soporific if a crime or unacceptable sexuality seems imminent. Although satellite surveillance has yet to catch up with Cyberpunk scenarios in which the "Autoinjector" and implanted "Poison Vial" offer workable solutions to twenty-third-century deviance, developers can easily add "punitive measures" to a location tracker worn as a belt or bracelet. In addition to phoning in the location of the wearer who dares turn a screw, a "monitoring and restraint system" can enforce exclusion zones by administering a mild, unobtrusive electric shock for a slight zone violation and upping the amps if the detainee fails to respond. After all, electric-shock restraints have been available for at least a decade to appearance-conscious dog owners who prefer an "invisible electronic fence" to the chain-link variety.

+   +   +

As an alternative to prison, satellite tracking seems a win-win strategy, with clear benefits for prisoners, parolees, and pretrial defendants as well as taxpayers. Assuming the technology performs perfectly and does not become a substitute for counseling and treatment, the principal threat is the ease with which society can broaden its notion of deviancy. It's a real threat, especially for an ostensibly "free" society whose history includes a willingness to experiment with Prohibition, condone restrictive covenants, and flirt with Political Correctness. Americans need not look to China and Iran for examples of well-intentioned repression.

A further risk lurks in satellite trackers designed to find lost children, wandering pets, and itinerant Alzheimer's patients—vulnerable subjects who need protection and are unlikely to resist intrusive monitoring. Parents, pet owners, and eldercare constitute a far larger market than the criminal justice system, and because peace of mind can be as valuable as protection, it's likely to prove a highly lucrative one. What's more, the spin-off potential is immense, especially for entrepreneurs who blend GPS with conventional technology or identify new uses of real-time tracking. For example, satellite systems designed to help trucking firms track equipment and manage employees can be reconfigured to help railroads avoid rear-end collisions. And the widely advertised OnStar automobile navigation system, which links GPS with a diagnostic computer and automatically summons help when a tire goes flat or an airbag deploys, might one day offer lower insurance rates to motorists willing to let an insurer monitor their driving.

Although privacy advocates are inherently leery of satellite tracking, no proposal has raised as many eyebrows as the Digital Angel under development by Applied Digital Solutions. In 1999, ADS bought rights to a patent granted two years earlier for an "apparatus for tracking and recovering humans [with] an implantable transceiver [designed] to remain implanted and functional for years without maintenance." Civil libertarians promptly warned of abuse by government snoops as well as cyber-savvy kidnappers on the lookout for lucrative prey. Critics included Susan Cutter, president of the Association of American Geographers, who condemned the "new locational e-slavery." Especially troubling to Cutter was the company's Web site (www.DigitalAngel.net), where a cartoon animation pictured an angelic winged figure swooping down to rescue Grandpa from cardiac arrest, repair motorist Jane's flat tire, and restore the bewildered Spot to his anxious owners. What loving son or daughter, loyal spouse, or concerned parent would not eagerly shell out $299 for a deal that includes a Web-delivered map (fig. 8.2) of the loved one's location, complete with street address, temperature, and pulse rate?

Offered in early 2001, the first-generation Digital Angels resembled wristwatches and belt-mounted pagers—a far cry from ADS's futuristic development plan. The firm's patent describes an "im-

Here's what the Digital Angel Delivery System looks like on a subscriber's Web-based computer:

As shown, the Digital Angel Delivery System can manage medical applications by gathering bio-readings such as pulse and temperature, and communicating the data, along with location information, to a ground station or call center.

FIGURE 8.2 The Digital Angel Corporation, an Applied Digital Solutions company, promises Web-accessible maps of the tracked person's location. Text and illustration from Digital Angel Corporation, "The Technology behind the Digital Angel," http://www.digitalangel.net/da/tech.asp.

plantable triggerable transmitting device" that conserves power by transmitting only when activated by the implantee or by a coded signal from the "tracking and locating center." Power is a key concern: although "an electromagnetic induction source . . . placed close to the body on a regular basis" can recharge the miniature storage battery, the preferred design relies on a power transducer to "derive power from physical work done by muscle fibers in the body." In times of stress "a novel sensation-feedback feature" activates the transceiver, and ground-based tracking expedites recovery. As a diagram (fig. 8.3) in the patent application shows, device D_1, implanted in the smiling, Gingerbread Man-like person P_1, can broadcast its position to antennas A_1, A_2, and A_3 or provide an electronic beacon for a recovery vehicle with mobile antennae MA and directional and mobile receivers DR and MR.

Jerry Dobson, a GIS expert at Oak Ridge National Laboratory and columnist for *GeoWorld,* objects vehemently to chip implants for tracking children who might be lost, kidnapped, or visiting a friend without permission. To dramatize the dangers of GPS-based "branding and stalking," he described a little girl's walk home from school. In an open field along the way a curious form, perhaps a rare flower or a small animal, attracts her attention. "Impulsively, she charges across the field. But suddenly, her biceps twitches. Before

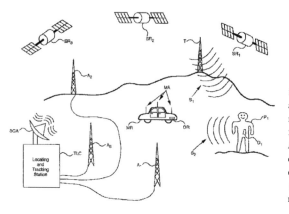

FIGURE 8.3 Figure 1 from the application for U.S. Patent no. 5,629,678, awarded May 13, 1997, and acquired by Applied Digital Solutions, describes key components of the inventor's plan for a "personal tracking and recovery system."

she can stop, her arm stings—then aches. She turns back, and her pain ceases at the sidewalk. Simultaneously, a commercial service provider reports to her parents." Although Dobson laments this lost "moment of discovery," he worries more about possessive parents reluctant to have the chip removed when the child grows up—could a "taking out" party become a new rite of passage?—as well as shrewd kidnappers not at all adverse to some ad hoc surgery.

Parental anxiety about their offspring's whereabouts is conspicuous in the growing number of teenagers with cell phones and pagers, used to keep in touch with friends but paid for by a Mom or Dad who appreciates the convenience of a wireless leash. And thanks to the Federal Communications Commission, parents will soon be able to track Junior's or Sis's location on a screen similar to the hypothetical Digital Angel Web map in figure 8.2 but for a lot less money. In 1996 the FCC, alarmed by a dramatic rise in 911 calls from cell-phone users unable to describe the location of a fire or accident, ordered wireless providers to pinpoint calls to within 125 meters (410 ft.). The original order let companies decide whether to insert a GPS chip in the handset or triangulate the caller's location with directional antennas on existing cellular towers. Removal of Selective Availability in May 2000 not only narrowed the reliability standard for handsets to 50 meters but jumpstarted a "location-based services" (LBS) industry, which is aggressively blurring the line between cell phones and PDAs. Forced to "geolocate" callers for emergency response, wireless carriers quickly discovered that the

10-meter accuracy possible with GPS could be a marketable commodity.

Loss of privacy is inevitable if the phone company can sell our coordinates to marketers and other stalkers. The wireless handheld that puts you at the center of its map or helps you locate the nearest hardware store is a marvelous invention, but who wants to stroll down Main Street and be bombarded with calls or e-mail from stores a couple doors away? Even more problematic than the commodification of location is the archive of electronic trails left by anyone talking on a cell phone or merely roaming. Bad enough that Big Brother and his mercantile siblings know where we are—without a restricted retention period and other safeguards they can easily discover where we've been.

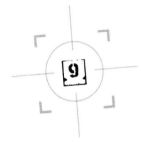

Addresses, Geocoding, and Dataveillance

For direct-mail advertisers and telemarketers, knowing where we live is nearly as useful as knowing what we might buy. Although few neighborhoods are perfectly homogeneous, most of us live near people similar in cultural conditioning, social aspirations, and spending preferences—or at least more similar than folks on the other side of town. And even demographically diverse districts can acquire an ambiance that attracts left-leaning political candidates and sellers of gourmet goodies and avant-garde clothing. Location is not a perfect predictor of consumer behavior or political preferences, but it works well enough most of the time so that people who have our addresses know—or think they know—a great deal about who we are.

How political strategists and other marketers exploit geographic proximity makes a fascinating if not frightening tale. Marketers, census takers, and locational consultants are its key characters, and software that matches addresses with neighborhoods and neighborhoods with buying habits is a recurring theme. Subplots include "neighborhood lifestyle segmentation" schemes for pigeonholing consumers by ZIP code and apportionment algorithms for integrating census information with data collected by postal code. Like much contemporary literature, the story has an ambiguous ending, inconclusive but insightful for readers who don't insist on simple solutions for complex problems.

+   +   +

What can you read into an address? Quite a bit, especially if it's on Fifth Avenue on New York's Upper East Side. Far less, though, if it's 302 Waldorf Parkway, my home in Syracuse, New York. The 302 tells you (correctly) that our next-door neighbors live at 300 and 304, while the Waldorf ambiguously suggests an expensively elegant Manhattan hotel, a popular brand of toilet paper, or a calorie-laden salad with apples and walnuts. More misleading is the appendage Parkway, which implies (incorrectly) two strips of pavement separated by a grassy median. Although planned that way, our street evolved as an ordinary town road with an oversize right-of-way. Equally confusing are the city and state parts of my address: we receive our mail through a Syracuse branch post office but pay taxes and vote in the Town of DeWitt.

If you're a catalog retailer, what really interests you is my ZIP code, 13224. According to recent estimates, our postal code includes 9,186 people living in 3,806 households. The median income of $51,125 is a cut above the national average of $41,914, but we're markedly more black (39.7 percent) and a shade less Asian (3.3 percent) than the country as a whole (at 12.4 and 3.9 percent, respectively). Not quite a melting pot but fertile territory for National Public Radio, Democratic politicians, and Lands' End outerwear. More interesting to most marketers are the area's "lifestyle clusters," which afford a concise description of not only my neighbors' consumer preferences but also their leisure pursuits, reading habits, and political inclinations.

Claritas Corporation, which pioneered clusters in the early 1970s, offers a free preview at its "You Are Where You Live" Web site (http://www.cluster2.claritas.com/YAWYL/). Two separate previews actually: one for PRIZM's "62 distinct lifestyle types, called clusters" and a second for MicroVision's "48 lifestyle types, called segments." An acronym for Potential Rating Index by Zip Markets, PRIZM evolved from a mere forty clusters in an earlier era of less diverse neighborhoods. Whereas PRIZM focuses on characterizing neighborhoods, MicroVision classifies individual households. Both approaches reflect the integration of census data with consumer and media surveys as well as diligently maintained records of catalog and online purchases. And while the ZIP code previews are free, both clustering strategies are available for a fee for much smaller neighborhoods defined by the Postal Service's nine-digit ZIP+4 codes, with between 5 and 15 houses on average, and the Census Bureau's block groups, with roughly 250 to 550 households apiece.

Although a five-digit ZIP code might contain as many as twenty different neighborhood types, the ClaritasExpress Web site reports only the top five, listed by number and name. For instance, in 13224, where I live, the most common clusters are

2	Winner's Circle
7	Money & Brains
8	Young Literati
19	New Empty Nests
30	Mid-City Mix

The numbers represent each cluster's rank on a 1-to-62 scale of affluence, while the names reflect a clever attempt to condense distinct lifestyles into glib yet meaningful labels. Although Winner's Circle might connote horse racing, not the rat race, a click on the name reveals a category of "executive suburban families" in the forty-five to sixty-four age group with professional occupations and well-above-average household incomes of $90,700. According to the Claritas databank, these households are likely to have a passport and a Keogh plan, shop at Ann Taylor, watch *NYPD Blue,* and read "epicurean" magazines like *Gourmet.* By contrast, the Mid-City Mix cluster consists of "African-American singles and families," either under eighteen or between twenty-five and thirty-four, in white-collar or service occupations and with household incomes of $35,000 and preferences for three-way calling, Pepsi Free, shopping at T.J. Maxx, watching *Nightline,* and reading *Muscle and Fitness.* These five diverse clusters and their interpretations confirm my hunch that 13224 is hardly homogeneous.

On a whim, I type in the ZIP code made famous by a TV show my daughter was addicted to back in high school, *Beverly Hills 90210.* Surprisingly, PRIZM identifies two groups prominent in 13224 as well as the country's most affluent cluster, Blue Blood Estates.

1	Blue Blood Estates
2	Winner's Circle
7	Money & Brains
10	Bohemian Mix

Only four clusters appear because the Web site doesn't include (at least not for free) clusters that account for less than 5 percent of a ZIP code's households. Fascinated by the apparent precision of these stereotypes, I key in 11104, for the Sunnyside section of Queens, New York, where my daughter lives now, on her own a year out of college. None of the five clusters is a perfect fit for Jo herself, but their names reflect the cityscape I recall from my last visit.

10	Bohemian Mix
27	Urban Achievers
29	Old Yankee Rows
45	Single City Blues
46	Hispanic Mix

Intrigued, I enter ZIP codes for the White House (20500), the Syracuse University campus (13244), Vandenberg Air Force Base, California (93737), and Pine Ridge, South Dakota (57770), an Indian reservation reputed to be the poorest place in the United States. Again, there are few surprises: the White House was "not found in the database," while the university and the air base yield single clusters aptly labeled Town and Gown and Military Quarters. And PRIZM seemed at least moderately on target for Pine Ridge, which is characterized by only two clusters, Agri-Business and Hard Scrabble, the latter typical of "families in poor, isolated areas" with household incomes of $18,100 and preferences for reading *True Story,* watching auto racing on TV, and using coupons to buy tobacco. Not a fertile market if you're hawking Godiva chocolates and Volvos.

Wholly absorbed, I looked at Claritas's other take on my Syracuse ZIP code. Despite different labels, the area's top five Micro-Vision segments are similar to their PRIZM counterparts in describing an eclectic mix of moving-up and getting-by:

8	Movers and Shakers
1	Upper Crust
24	City Ties
46	Difficult Times
45	Struggling Metro Mix

More significant is a richer array of preferences. Movers and Shakers, I learn, are "high income households containing singles and couples, age 35–49, with no children, one to two people." Yes, a few houses in my neighborhood match this description, but whether they "listen to National Public Radio [and] read *Golf Digest, Newsweek,* and *Car & Driver* magazines" is difficult to confirm. Equally puzzling is the revelation that the "low income young single adults, age 22–39, [in] one person households" in the Struggling Metro Mix segment favor "three-way custom calling" and "use [their] home PC more than 25 hours per week." Are they writers, I wonder? Or perhaps graduate students addicted to conference calls?

A competing neighborhood segmentation system named ACORN (for A Classification Of Residential Neighborhoods) presents a third but very different point of view based on forty-three clusters. Although the ACORN Web site offers a free ZIP code look-up, its reports reveal only the single most common segment—an unfortunate strategy for 13224, which the system assigns to segment 8E, Urban Working Families, summarized in four dismal sentences:

> Nearly 40 percent of this young group of single-parent families is under the age of 20. They are the working poor. They live in older, pre-war residential townhouse developments and small/multi-unit buildings. They buy take-out food, hair and skin-care products, baby products and children's clothing.

A few parts of the area might match this description, but they're hardly typical. And while my immediate neighborhood includes two single-parent families, no one would consider their middle-aged, professional moms exemplars of "the working poor." Retailers take clusters seriously, though, and ACORN's characterization might well explain the two Chinese take-out shops that opened recently in a nearby shopping strip.

Despite contradictions and ambiguities, lifestyle clusters conjured up by Claritas and other geosegmentation strategists not only choose targets for coupon promotions, fund-raising appeals, and political pitches but also help national chains locate new stores and restaurants. Marketing managers and development directors who rent or trade mailing lists consider screening by postal code or block group an effective way to increase yield. Each piece of mail is a drain on net take, after all, and a strategy that improves the response rate by just a few percentage points easily justifies the cost of screening. Political consultants are equally eager to identify swing voters, those not fully sold on their client or unlikely to vote without a reminder or a ride to the polls. Stakes are even higher for the retail or restaurant chain comparing potential sites or promoting a new location. Because the site that fails is embarrassing as well as costly, corporate planners appreciate GIS-based analyses that evaluate households within a given radius of a proposed site or send coupons only to addresses deemed receptive in both distance and lifestyle.

+   +   +

How do Claritas and its competitors identify lifestyle clusters? Although proprietary algorithms preclude an exact reconstruction, we know that neighborhood lifestyle segmentation is a marriage of two types of data: census information tabulated for block groups, census tracts, and ZIP codes and consumer data based on purchases, consumer surveys, magazine subscriptions, and credit reports. Back in the 1960s geographers and sociologists used a form of cluster analysis to explore urban structure, but marketing executives had little use for this technique until Jonathan Robbin founded Claritas in 1971. According to journalist Michael Weiss, who made a career of mapping clusters and extolling their use, Robbin was a "Harvard-educated computer whiz" who saw potential value in converting census data, typically reported for "arcane units called 'tracts,'" into ZIP codes, which marketers could understand. To make the results useable, he reduced the hundreds of census variables like average rent, median years of education, and percentage of housing units with indoor plumbing to a mere thirty-four principal factors that, in the language of statisticians, "accounted for 87 percent of the variation among U.S. neighborhoods." After scoring every ZIP code on each of the thirty-four factors, a computer partitioned ZIP codes into forty clusters with generally similar factor scores. Robbin's choice of forty clusters was largely subjective: fifty clusters would have been more homogeneous and precise, on average, but more cumbersome as well, while some members of a thirty-cluster classification would have been overly vague. Following an enthusiastic response to the census-based Claritas Cluster System, introduced in 1974, Robbin integrated his groupings with survey, consumer, and media data and released PRIZM in 1978.

PRIZM's success is apparent in the emergence of competing systems like ACORN and MicroVision (which Claritas acquired through a merger in 1999) as well as the enthusiastic adoption of clustering in Europe, Canada, and South Africa. Wide acceptance is also apparent in the gargantuan effort devoted to revising characterizations yearly if not monthly, as neighborhood change outpaces the Census Bureau's ten-year update schedule. I've witnessed massive change on Waldorf Parkway in only three years, during which two elderly neighbors died, one moved to a warmer climate, and a fourth went into long-term care. The decennial census is still important, but credit bureaus and mailing-list vendors must aggressively track movers. They accomplish this tracking partly with the help of the U.S. Postal Service, which sells its monthly NCOA (National Change of Address) updates, based on those little cards we fill out when we move. And although Claritas and its competitors rarely revise their clusters—marketers appreciate stability—their counts and characterizations for small areas require constant monitoring and perceptive forecasting. According to geographer Jon Goss, marketing executives might not understand the "'black box' mechanics of the analysis," but they accept lifestyle segmentation anyway because cluster labels "fit with their own stereotypes" of American consumers.

Part of the enigma arises from the incompatibility of census and postal geographies. With a mandate to compile redistricting data, the Census Bureau focuses on the census block. Defined more broadly as "areas bounded on all sides by visible features, such as streets, roads, streams, railroad tracks, and by invisible boundaries, such as city, town, township, and county limits, property lines, and short, imaginary extensions of streets and roads," census blocks are easily delineated in neighborhoods with curved streets and cul-de-sacs. Blocks aggregate conveniently into block groups, with between six hundred and three thousand people, and block groups combine to form tracts, intended as generally homogeneous areas with between fifteen hundred and eight thousand residents. Because reliable intercensal rates of change require a stable geography, the bureau seldom adjusts boundaries except to subdivide burgeoning tracts with more than eight thousand people.

Easy to delineate, census blocks vary considerably in size and population. In the Waldorf Parkway area, for instance, the fourteen blocks in block group 4 of tract 147 range in population from 0 to 178. As figure 9.1 reveals, a census block can be much more than a simple rectangle. For example, block 4003, where I live, is not only bounded by parts of Waldorf and three other streets but includes both sides of the 100-block of Buffington Road. Other blocks are small and uninhabited. Block 4004, for instance, contains only by a small gasoline station, and block 4006 is a tiny public park. In rural areas with few roads, census blocks as large as several square miles are not uncommon.

By contrast, postal geographies focus on the street segments that bound a block. To reap the efficiency of mail presorted by nine-digit

FIGURE 9.1 Census blocks in block group 4, tract 147, Onondaga County, New York.

ZIP code, the U.S. Postal Service routinely assigns consecutive numbers to opposite sides of the street for residential neighborhoods like mine, where the letter carrier typically walks up one side of the block and down the other. What's more, in rural areas where carriers drive their routes and all mailboxes are on one side of the road, odd and even addresses share the same ZIP+4 code even though the Census Bureau assigns them to separate blocks. And as block 4003 demonstrates in figure 9.2, census blocks occasionally include more than one ZIP code. Although precision marketing firms would prefer that the Postal Service and the Census Bureau adopt identical geocodes, what works well for delivering mail is inappropriate for electoral boundaries, and vice versa. A dirty little secret of clustering is the imperfect match between data collected by census tract and consumer statistics tabulated by ZIP code.

Not to worry. Cluster experts learned to apportion census tract counts among postal areas by assuming, for instance, that the ZIP code with 10 percent of a tract's population will contain 10 percent of the tract's foreign-born college graduates. This assumption is crucial because detailed demographic statistics based on the "long-form" questionnaires filled out by only one in six households are not available at the block and block-group levels. Apportionment begins with a block-by-block assignment of households and population. A computer calculates geographic center points for all census blocks, compares these centers with postal boundaries, and assigns each block to the ZIP code that contains its center. The software then adds the block's population and household counts to the respective totals for its dominant ZIP code (13224 in the case of block 4003 in figure 9.2). Housing and socioeconomic data available only at the tract level can then be apportioned according to population or households. If the center-point approximation assigned 10 percent of a census tract's population to ZIP code 13224, for instance, and if the tract contains two hundred foreign-born college graduates, the computer assigns twenty of them to 13224. Although proportional allocation seems reasonable, most or all of the tract's two hundred foreign-born graduates could live in the 13224 ZIP code.

The Census Bureau has its own strategy. Although the agency never discloses data for individual households, it will produce special tabulations for a fee. ZIP code aggregation began in 1972, when the bureau released a partial count by postal code. In 1981, after the Reagan Administration's budget cuts killed plans for a more complete publicly funded ZIP code tabulation, a group of ten marketing firms offered to pay $25,000 each for a detailed postal-zone count of the 1980 Census. In what one firm's president called "the sweetheart deal of the century," census officials accepted the proposal and withheld the results from other users for eighteen months. ZIP

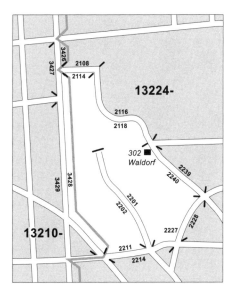

FIGURE 9.2 ZIP+4 postal codes for block 4003 and surrounding streets. The four-digit numbers are extensions of 13210 and 13224, the ZIP codes to the left and right, respectively, of the gray line.

Extending ZCTA Coverage

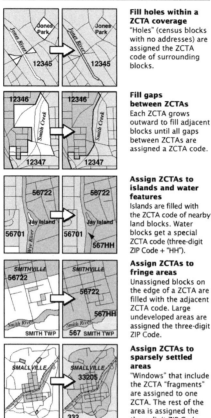

Fill holes within a ZCTA coverage
"Holes" (census blocks with no addresses) are assigned the ZCTA code of surrounding blocks.

Fill gaps between ZCTAs
Each ZCTA grows outward to fill adjacent blocks until all gaps between ZCTAs are assigned a ZCTA code.

Assign ZCTAs to islands and water features
Islands are filled with the ZCTA code of nearby land blocks. Water blocks get a special ZCTA code (three-digit ZIP Code + "HH").

Assign ZCTAs to fringe areas
Unassigned blocks on the edge of a ZCTA are filled with the adjacent ZCTA code. Large undeveloped areas are assigned the three-digit ZIP Code.

Assign ZCTAs to sparsely settled areas
"Windows" that include the ZCTA "fragments" are assigned to one ZCTA. The rest of the area is assigned the three-digit ZIP Code.

FIGURE 9.3 Because the U.S. Postal Service largely ignores areas not requiring mail delivery, the Census Bureau must fill holes and gaps in ZCTA coverage. From U.S. Census Bureau, *ZCTAs: ZIP Code Tabulation Areas for Census Data Products* (1999), 4.

code counts are now a standard census product, and in 2001, the bureau released boundary files for ZCTAs (ZIP Code Tabulation Areas), designed to help users map postal tabulations for Census 2000. By assigning each census block to the ZIP code with the most addresses and filling in gaps between ZCTAs (fig. 9.3), census officials created an expedient generalization of postal geography. It's an approximation, obviously, but so are most census products.

Although some marketing firms compile household data as well as tabulate by ZIP+4 areas, official census information summarized by five-digit postal code is useful as a reality check. What's more, geodemographics consultants can take advantage of five-digit

ZIP code tabulations by the Internal Revenue Service. Although some taxpayers might not be totally honest with the IRS, locally detailed tabulations for total income, salaries and wages, taxable interest, earned income credit, adjusted gross income, number of personal exemptions, and the numbers of taxpayers using schedules C (business income) and F (farm income) not only complement census data on income but reflect population shifts officially counted only once every ten years.

+ + +

If you think the federal government is Big Brother, guess again. Firms called "data warehouses" have gone well beyond the Census Bureau in not only collecting detailed information on individual households but also renting it to retailers, insurers, and even detective agencies. Acxiom, a data vendor with what Consumers Union calls the "largest collection of U.S. consumer, business, and telephone data available in one source," offers telemarketers and other clients a wide variety of personal information gleaned from credit reports, public records, consumer surveys, and credit card transactions. Data warehousing also includes niche firms like Moving Targets, a self-described "new resident direct marketing" firm that rents lists of "just-moved-in families" carefully selected from the Postal Service's National Change of Address (NCOA) data. And, as we have seen, Claritas clients find lifestyle clusters useful at the household level as well as for ZIP codes and census tracts.

What's scary is the ease with which data collected for one purpose, such as motor-vehicle registration, can be linked to information compiled for other purposes, such as consumer loans, voter registration, or health insurance. And it's not sufficient for government to restrict the use of our Social Security numbers. Gary Marx, a sociologist concerned with privacy issues, notes that an experienced snoop can dig up dirt or ferret out personal details by using a person's name, address, and date of birth to link records in different databases. Home telephone numbers can be especially useful as "consumer tags," and electronic credit card transactions afford nosy marketers further insights by pinpointing our shopping transactions in time as well as space. In addition, address-matching software makes it easy to find a household's census tract and block as well as estimate latitude and longitude, which are useful in plotting maps, calculating distances, and making inferences about personal indiscretions. For example, recurring room charges at motels within fifty miles of home might suggest a subject is having an extramarital affair.

Web browsing is also under surveillance thanks to software that can link our home and Internet addresses whenever we order online, fill out an electronic survey, or respond to an e-mail offer. "Geotargeting," a technology for linking Internet addresses to geographic locations, lets Web ads tout local firms. Web merchants and information vendors know a lot about our interests because of small files called cookies, which they place on viewers' hard drives, ostensibly to help them identify return visitors. Cookies let Amazon.com recommend new books, CDs, and DVDs similar to those we've purchased and help advertising firms like DoubleClick customize the banner ads that litter commercial Web pages. Thanks to cookie-based profiling, a viewer who frequently visits gardening Web sites is likely to see garden-related ads when visiting more general Web sites like *CNN.com* and weather.com. (And it might well explain the numerous offers of miniature video cameras that started popping up on my screen a few days after an intensive online search for information about web cams.) Largely benign, cookies can reveal preferences we'd rather remain hidden as well as encourage the White House Drug Office, which paid DoubleClick to track use of its Web site (www.whitehousedrugpolicy.gov), to confuse curiosity with intent. More invidious is the possibility of a "cache attack" by devious Web firms that can find out what Web sites we visited recently by scanning the cache of files our browsers store temporarily to expedite display.

Computer scientist Roger Clarke coined the term *dataveillance* to describe the "systematic use of personal data systems in the investigation or monitoring of [people's] actions or communications." Dangers include witch-hunts and illegal blacklisting as well as the harmful consequences of misidentification and erroneous data. In a capitalist milieu, in which sales and profits upstage sinister totalitarian scenarios, geodemographics firms and their clients use dataveillance to manage as well as stimulate consumption. Marketing models tell firms not only what to produce but where and how to sell it and to whom. Geographer Stephen Graham, a critic of GIS-based behavior modeling, sees this "surveillant simulation" as a force for increased segregation and polarization.

Is geographic dataveillance affecting the way society constructs places? Definitely, argues GIS scholar Michael Curry, who claims that widespread use of integrated systems fosters the impression that invasive profiling of individuals and places is both inevitable and beneficial. Conditioned to accept dataveillance as natural, most consumers consider resistance difficult if not futile. And when clusters and junk mail contribute to a sense of identity and well being, some of us even find the attention flattering. Because clusters reinforce the social status of an address, they explain the bitter complaints of people placed in a less classy ZIP code by a readjustment of Postal Service boundaries.

More serious are the dangers to personal privacy and the dilemma of too little or too much regulation. Harlan Onsrud, a legal scholar interested in the societal impacts of GIS, observed that highly local geographic data and spatial technology's prowess in integrating diverse databases foster invasions of privacy. Although he would prefer not to have information on individuals in a GIS, Onsrud recognizes competitiveness as a justification. Favoring self-regulation, accountability, and openness, he believes strongly that individuals should have the right to opt out. As a minimum, GIS managers should know the sources and reliability of their data and should be wary of the hazards of mixing data collected for different purposes or at different times. But government regulation could be stifling, Onsrud warns, especially if lawmakers use privacy protection as an excuse for restricting access to public information. Self-regulation might not be practicable either because "what is agreed to be 'smart business practices' by a large majority of practicing professionals may be considered highly unethical" by most citizens. Complex issues, conflicting mores, and evolving technology suggest that conflicts concerning data privacy might never be satisfactorily resolved.

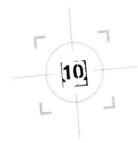

Case Clusters and Terrorist Threats

Mapping, GIS, and geographic modeling play key roles in the surveillance and control of disease. In identifying, monitoring, forecasting, and controlling epidemics, public health officials at the local, state, national, and international levels depend upon rapid and efficient collection and display of highly personal data. Health agencies also compile statistics on noninfectious diseases like cancer, many forms of which are poorly understood, and in doing so, confront conflicting requirements of confidentiality and public access. Although some disease maps are little more than descriptive propaganda or political palliatives, geographic information helps in tracking epidemics, predicting impact, distributing vaccines, spraying insecticide, administering quarantine regulations, evaluating the effectiveness of prevention and prophylactic campaigns, and communicating with medical personnel, emergency management officials, and the general public. And as I note at the end of the chapter, threats of biological warfare and bioterrorism pose new challenges for dealing with highly contagious diseases like smallpox as well as deadly pathogens manufactured in a laboratory.

+ + +

If disease mapping has a poster child, it's John Snow (1813–1858), the London anesthesiologist credited with discovering the waterborne transmission of cholera. Among geographers, Snow is best known for his 1854 map showing victims' homes clustered around Soho's infamous Broad Street Pump, which he identified as a source of contaminated water. According to epidemiological lore, the good doctor tried unsuccessfully to convince public officials to close down the pump. Undaunted, he took matters into his own hands, removed the pump's handle, and demonstrated the correctness of his theory when new cases plummeted. Truth be told, the epidemic had already run its course. What's more, Snow made his famous dot map several months later, for a revised edition of his book on cholera transmission. Even so, his pin map continues to embellish discussions of GIS and disease.

Medical geographers, GIS experts, and some epidemiologists perpetuate the Snow myth because it promotes disease mapping as a discovery tool and enhances the stature of their own disciplines. But a careful examination of Snow's writings indicates that he understood cholera's mode of transmission well before he made the map. Moreover, contemporary investigators with a different sense of the disease's origin and transmission produced more accurate maps of the Soho outbreak but misread them as evidence that foul air, not leaky cesspools, had spread the disease. Although Snow was a thoughtful observer, neither his map nor those of his rivals were of any value in generating insightful hypotheses. Snow's famous cholera map was pure propaganda—and copycat propaganda at that—but proved eminently useful later in the century, when public officials needed convincing arguments to isolate drinking water from sewage.

Belief in the power of visualization accounts for numerous atlases describing mortality variations among counties or larger units like state economic areas and hospital service areas. In 1975 the U.S. Public Health Service published its first disease atlas with an introduction that asserted "geographic patterns of cancer are useful in developing and testing etiologic hypotheses." Convinced that spatial patterns, if competently displayed, will reveal causal connections, the authors suggested that "perhaps the greatest value of the maps will be to designate high-risk communities where analytical-epidemiologic studies may detect specific carcinogenic hazards"— as if a ranked list of counties might not more efficiently point out the highest rates. A 1996 atlas praised this premier effort for revealing two "previously unnoticed clusters of high-rate counties" for which field studies "uncovered . . . the links between shipyard asbestos exposure and lung cancer and [between] snuff dipping and oral cancer." But in neither of the "field studies" cited did investigators rely on further mapping, and in neither instance were the suspected causal factors previously unknown. Although the 1975 cancer atlas might have fingered some intriguing hot spots, there is little evidence its maps ever "generat[ed] etiological hypotheses."

Still, the belief persists that maps will discover a cause, indict a polluter, or suggest a prophylaxis. And while it's easy to dismiss this cartographic scrutiny as misguided, maps produced for questionable epidemiological studies of complex, multifactor diseases no doubt promote public awareness, early detection, and lifesaving treatment. That's my assessment of the Onondaga County Breast Cancer Mapping Project, a local effort that registered an impressive 30-percent return for questionnaires included with residents' monthly mailing of Valpak coupons. The short survey, which my wife and daughter dutifully filled out in early 1998, asked for the respondent's home address, length of residence, race, date of birth, type of health insurance coverage, and the dates of most recent mammogram and breast examination by a health-care professional. Current and former breast cancer patients were asked to indicate when the tumor was discovered, the hospital at which they were treated, and where they were living at the time. Useful details, perhaps, but unlikely to reveal a normal American's exposure to carcinogens on the job or at a former residence.

Although our county executive announced that local breast cancer rates were not out of line with rates elsewhere in New York, survey participants have yet to see a summary of the data. Our only evidence of nonexceptional mortality is a ZIP code-level breast cancer map posted in April 2000 on a state health department Web site, which includes similar maps for lung cancer and colorectal cancer. Based on the state's tumor registry, which is more reliable than a mail-out survey, the Web map for Onondaga County revealed no apparent connection to race, ethnicity, income, or any other known factor for a disease especially common among affluent white women with Jewish ancestors from eastern or central Europe. Most mortality maps are equally baffling if not reassuring. Voters who don't find the absence of a clear pattern comforting might at least appreciate the concern of public officials willing to collect and map the data. Because such a map is a sign that women's health matters, breast cancer projects sometimes stimulate pleas from men for cartographic studies of prostate cancer.

Critics attacked the state's maps as not only vague but unresponsive to Long Island, which has some of the highest breast cancer rates in the nation. According to Richard Brodsky, chairman of the State Assembly's Environmental Conservation Committee, the maps "don't really identify cancer clusters, which occur at the neighborhood level, well below the ZIP Code level, and they haven't told us anything about environmental factors." Health officials, Brodsky charged, had more detailed data but weren't analyzing them. Echoing his complaint that "it's a sin to have this information and withhold it," Debbie Basile of the Babylon Breast Cancer Coalition commented, "it's a first step, but I want to see more."

While relatively detailed maps occasionally reveal suspicious clusters, careful examination typically ferrets out a nonenvironmental explanation. For example, address-level data collected by volunteers for the West Islip Breast Cancer Coalition exhibited a vague clustering of breast cancer cases in the west central portion of this affluent community on the south shore of Long Island. Especially troubling was the cluster's appearance on a map of women who had lived in the same house for at least thirty years, sufficiently long to share a common exposure. Discernible but not blatant, the cluster lies between the labels for Sunrise Highway and Union Boulevard on figure 10.1, which portrays cancers cases with large dots and other

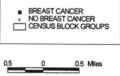

■ BREAST CANCER
• NO BREAST CANCER
☐ CENSUS BLOCK GROUPS

0.5   0   0.5 Miles

Data Source: West Islip Breast Cancer Coalition, 1993

FIGURE 10.1 Map showing
a cluster of cancer cases
among long-term residents
of West Islip, New York.
From Linda M. Timander
and Sara McLafferty, "Breast
Cancer in West Islip, NY: A
Spatial Clustering Analysis
with Covariates," *Social Science and Medicine* 46 (1998):
1623–35; map on 1630.

women in the risk pool with smaller dots. Geographers Linda Timander and Sara McLafferty, who used statistical cluster-detection
software to compare the spatial patterns of cancer cases and all longtime female residents, confirmed that the clustering of cases in this
part of West Islip was hardly random. But a closer look at the cluster
attributed most of the cases to one of two known risk factors: a family history of breast cancer and first pregnancy at age thirty or older.
Once these correlates were factored in, the cluster disappeared. As
the researchers noted, "although the finding of no spatial clustering
may be unsatisfying to local residents, it does offer a constructive response to their questions."

State officials had similarly detailed data—but more complete
and reliable data, I'm sure—and as Assemblyman Brodsky charged,
they were holding back. For a sound reason, though: confidentiality.
To gain the cooperation of patients and physicians, addresses as
well as names of cancer patients are not released as either lists or
dot maps. Nor is similar information provided for a host of ill-
nesses, principally communicable diseases like HIV infection, syph-

ilis, and gonorrhea, which physicians must report to their state or local health department. Notification, as it is called, is essential if public health officials are to monitor and control communicable diseases as well as investigate medical enigmas like breast cancer.

Grassroots groups like the West Islip Breast Cancer Coalition, which collected the data for figure 10.1, are not similarly constrained. Educated women, who do not consider cancer a stigma, lobby vigorously for detailed environmental investigations and often launch their own studies when the public health bureaucracy is slow to act. Committed to openness as well as scientifically curious, health activists readily reveal spatial details that public officials are compelled to conceal.

By contrast, health departments, which typically preserve anonymity by analyzing and reporting disease data by ZIP code or census tract, rarely release maps with the spatial specificity of figure 10.1. And if they do, they probably shouldn't: precisely positioned dots and roads are simply too revealing. A "map hacker" could register street intersections to a precise geographic framework, convert dot centers to grid coordinates, and use "reverse address matching" to recover household addresses, which could then be sold to mail-order sellers of unproven cancer cures or to enterprising lawyers recruiting plaintiffs for class-action lawsuits. Researchers can protect privacy by displacing each dot a random distance in a random direction—just enough to thwart unscrupulous snoops—and warning readers of the necessary subterfuge. Although "geographic masking" makes the maps slightly less authentic, investigators can still probe the unperturbed data for statistically significant case clusters—one less excuse for health officials to keep citizens in the dark.

+   +   +

Not all disease maps are visual placebos. Cartographic analysis contributes to eradication and remediation campaigns and, as John Snow's cholera map demonstrates, to public information efforts as well. When the health department decides to contain West Nile virus, for instance, citizens and local officials will need to know where infected birds were found and which neighborhoods require spraying. And police, highway, and health departments that request funds for traffic-accident prevention need to know where accident rates are especially high as well as related details that might indicate a need for road improvements, better signage, traffic lights, lower speed limits, or additional traffic cops. Clusters of child pedestrian accidents, for instance, can pinpoint areas requiring more vigilant enforcement of traffic laws in the late afternoon and information campaigns for parents of children attending nearby schools and playgrounds. Traffic accidents are very much a public health problem, and geographic information systems can be especially useful in developing prevention strategies and evaluating their effectiveness.

GIS can extract added value from data routinely compiled for disease surveillance. In Baltimore County, Maryland, for instance, public health professionals working with a GIS specialist identified high-risk areas for Lyme disease, a debilitating illness transmitted by deer ticks. Address-matching software converted the addresses of Lyme patients (cases) and a sample of randomly chosen households (controls) to point coordinates, which were then related to map overlays for fifty-seven separate environmental variables. Eleven of these factors proved statistically significant and provided the basis for a countywide risk map, which demonstrated the disease's strong association with steeper slopes and proximity to forested land. The researchers validated the map with data for the following year but declined to elaborate on the map's role in intervention. Medical geographer Ellen Cromley and her co-workers, who developed a GIS-based model of high-risk areas for Lyme disease in south central Connecticut, were less inhibited. Risk mapping, they argued, is useful for long-term strategies like discouraging low-density residential development in rural settings as well as for short-term tick-control measures like spraying acaricides and removing yard waste.

I found another example closer to home. My colleague Dan Griffith was the lead GIS investigator in a collaborative study of elevated blood-lead levels among children in Syracuse. The county health department, which had been screening children for lead poisoning since the early 1970s, was a rich source of data that had never been properly analyzed. Using parallel explorations of point, block, block-group, and census-tract data, Dan's team detected two parallel "swaths" with above-average blood lead, which matched patterns of older housing more closely than the configuration of heavily trafficked streets. Soil samples confirmed that lead concentration was generally higher around older dwellings, with wood siding and multiple layers of lead-based paint, than near major roads, with greater past exposure to lead additives in gasoline. Because "housing quality and maintenance practices" were more relevant than "minority status," the researchers recommended that intervention activities be focused on impoverished neighborhoods with older housing stock. Further research might recognize historical geography as important as soil-contamination data.

+ + +

On the opposite side of the confidentiality divide between health departments and other local officials is a mélange of information on technological hazards and ecological vulnerability. Environmental health units monitor air and water quality, environmental protection agencies compile annual reports on industrial releases of toxic substances, and fire departments and emergency management officials track shipments of hazardous materials as well as inventory local caches of explosive or toxic chemicals that warrant evacuation plans and other precautions. Essential to land-use planning and code enforcement, these data have been generally accessible— at least before September 11, 2001—to individuals and citizens groups as a result of "right-to-know" laws.

Making sense of the data is another matter. The U.S. Environmental Protection Agency, which collects annual reports on industrial emissions and discharges for its Toxics Release Inventory and publishes the information on the Internet (www.epa.gov/tri), makes little effort to help citizens assess impacts on lungs or livers. At a companion Web site (www.epa.gov/enviro/html/em/), the EnviroMapper pinpoints release locations and toxic-waste sites at various scales but does not integrate this information with maps of pollutants in the air, water, or soil. Arguably useful in keeping the spotlight on individual polluters and specific toxins, the Enviro-Mapper has only the weakest link to human health. A more complete picture of a contaminant's impact on drinking water, for instance, might require access to a GIS that integrates chemical and bacteriological analyses for test wells with confidential illness data and perhaps a computer model of local aquifers. But even if access were permitted, few citizens would know how to proceed.

Socially conscious GIS researchers have proposed the development of "public participation geographic information systems." Their goal is twofold: helping citizens understand the limitations and efficient use of spatial data and involving them more fully in community decision making. Although user-friendly software and broader access to data are desirable, whether PPGIS becomes an instrument of empowerment rather than marginalization depends largely on the formation of partnerships between grassroots organizations and sympathetic GIS experts. A promising example is the Community Mapping Assistance Project (CMAP) initiated by the New York Public Interest Research Group in 1997. In its first three years, CMAP staff assisted a hundred grassroots groups and other nonprofit organizations with more than 250 projects. Although most assignments addressed community planning or social services, CMAP produced a number of compelling cartographic posters like figure 10.2, in which an alarming disparity in pediatric lead levels in Brooklyn demands action.

+   +   +

For health officials charged with spotting and suppressing highly contagious diseases among people or animals, mapping is more than a propaganda tool. Geographic data systems play an important role in public health management not only by expediting the collection, organization, validation, and exchange of epidemiological data but also by promoting proactive studies of local and regional health care. Examples include tracking the spread of raccoon rabies across a region—field investigators with GPS units can easily record the coordinates and condition of infected animals—and using the maps to plan and publicize rabies clinics for household pets.

Spatial analysis helps local health agencies cope with a variety of environmental threats. A typical application is the routine monitoring of household septic tanks near municipal water wells. Because drinking water is vulnerable to contamination from malfunctioning septic systems, health officials can prioritize field inspections by defining small circular buffers around all septic tanks listed in the environmental permits database and overlaying these threat zones

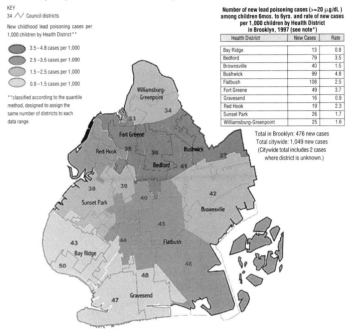

New Cases of Childhood Lead Poisoning (>=20 μg/dL) per 1,000 children 6mos.–6yrs. of age by Health District in Brooklyn, 1997* (comparative statistics showing relative rates within Brooklyn)

KEY
34 ⌒ Council districts

New childhood lead poisoning cases per 1,000 children by Health District**

- 3.5–4.8 cases per 1,000
- 2.5–3.5 cases per 1,000
- 1.5–2.5 cases per 1,000
- 0.8–1.5 cases per 1,000

**classified according to the quantile method, designed to assign the same number of districts to each data range.

Number of new lead poisoning cases (>=20 μg/dL) among children 6mos. to 6yrs. and rate of new cases per 1,000 children by Health District in Brooklyn, 1997 (see note*)

Health District	New Cases	Rate
Bay Ridge	13	0.8
Bedford	79	3.5
Brownsville	40	1.5
Bushwick	99	4.8
Flatbush	108	2.5
Fort Greene	49	3.7
Gravesend	16	0.9
Red Hook	19	2.3
Sunset Park	26	1.7
Williamsburg-Greenpoint	25	1.6

Total in Brooklyn: 476 new cases
Total citywide: 1,049 new cases
(Citywide total includes 2 cases where district is unknown.)

FIGURE 10.2 Pediatric lead poisoning in Brooklyn as mapped by the New York Public Interest Research Group's Community Mapping Assistance Project. Original color map from the CMAP map gallery, http://www.cmap.nypirg.org/map_gallery/default.asp.

on a map of primary aquifers and a map of concentric proximity zones around water-supply wells (fig. 10.3). Records of past violations as well as a hydrologic model describing the flow of ground water provide an even more precise identification of septic systems requiring more frequent inspection. Ideally the GIS would also include underground gasoline storage tanks and chemical plants as well as the locations of monitoring wells, drilled specifically for testing water quality.

Modeling can also inform cancer-screening programs, as demonstrated by government efforts to identify possible victims of thyroid cancer in eastern Washington. Between 1945 and 1951 a plutonium plant near Hanford, Washington, released substantial

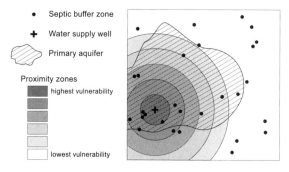

FIGURE 10.3 Schematic example of an overlay analysis for prioritizing inspections of septic systems that might threaten local drinking water.

amounts of airborne radiation, which prevailing winds dispersed eastward toward farms at which pasture-fed dairy cattle contaminated locally marketed milk with Iodine-131. Because the thyroid gland concentrates radioactive iodine from the blood, and children typically consume more milk than adults and infants, anyone who grew up in the area during the late 1940s should be evaluated for thyroid cancer. To help identify candidates for screening, researchers at the Centers for Disease Control estimated the radiation dose for average milk-drinkers in 1945 by linking a GIS and an atmospheric circulation model. Health officials then invited persons who had lived in the area to request an individual dose assessment based on their exact residential histories.

Health departments can actively combat illness by asking hospitals, health professionals, and social service agencies to collect data on infants and other vulnerable populations. In North Dakota, for example, state health officials compared birth rates with visits for prenatal care in order to identify areas requiring better health education or improved access to health services. For Hillsborough County, Florida, state officials analyzed survey data on the vaccination of two-year-olds, mapped vaccination rates by block group, and detected "immunization pockets of need," in which outbreaks of childhood diseases were especially likely. In DeKalb County, Georgia, the board of health used PRIZM lifestyle clusters to target block groups in minority neighborhoods for antismoking campaigns.

GIS also helps health officials investigate eruptions of contagious diseases. For example, when an outbreak of infectious diarrhea struck soldiers and their families on a North Carolina military base, maps of patients' quarters focused attention on a specific housing area. Field interviews of residents identified a plausible means of interfamily transmission: small wading pools set up outside for children, some of whom might have contaminated the water with fecal matter. In a replay of the Snow myth, banning the pools abruptly halted the epidemic.

In controlling malaria and similar diseases transmitted by mosquitoes or other insect vectors, health officials integrate GIS with remotely sensed imagery to detect and monitor breeding areas. As a supplement to meteorological instrumentation and field sampling, color-infrared aerial photography and high-resolution satellite imagery can describe the extent of swamps and other habitats as well as their proximity to humans and livestock. Spatial modeling, another component of vector surveillance, helps officials predict outbreaks, assess relative risk, and orchestrate carefully timed spraying of vector habitats.

Animal and plant diseases, which can infect humans and devastate agriculture, warrant use of spatial analysis for epidemiological surveillance and decision making. Whether the disease is as episodic as raccoon rabies or as sporadic as foot-and-mouth disease, GIS can be a useful instrument for early identification as well as a powerful tool for distributing vaccine and enforcing quarantine. And when an epizootic starts spreading rapidly, like the European outbreak of foot-and-mouth disease in early 2001, GIS can help officials orchestrate containment by identifying entry points, suggesting likely paths of transmission, and delineating areas in which movements of people, vehicles, and agricultural products are restricted. During the 2001 episode, for instance, Britain's Ministry of Agriculture, Fisheries, and Food used a Web site (www.maff.gov.uk) with an interactive map (fig. 10.4), updated daily, to report the epidemic's extent and provide a detailed description of restrictions. GIS also proved useful in disposing of infected carcasses and assessing damage to farms.

Britain's experience with foot-and-mouth disease demonstrates the importance of readily available spatial data and the need for timely communication among government departments. In a London *Times* article highlighting the importance of GIS in coping with the epidemic, an unnamed GIS specialist criticized the lack of information sharing among government units. "The classic case was

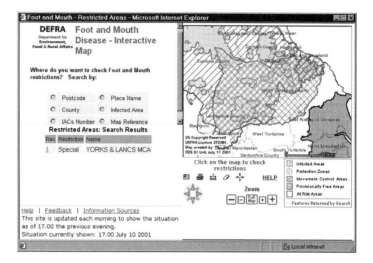

FIGURE 10.4 During the foot-and-mouth disease epidemic of 2001, an interactive map afforded Britons a detailed description of restricted areas. The original color map is from the Department for Environment, Food, and Rural Affairs, "Foot and Mouth Disease— Cases and Infected Areas," http://www.defra.org.

the burying of cattle in a site where it polluted underground wells supplying local houses and farms. That information would have been available but [was] in another department's database." This reluctance of British bureaucrats to share data is hardly unique. Information is not only a source of power but also a potential cause of embarrassment if the data aren't perfect. Adding to bureaucrats' fears is the likelihood of mistakes when databases are incompatible in currentness or level of detail. Haphazard ad hoc data sharing can be worse than no data sharing at all.

+   +   +

Advocates for fuller interagency coordination of geographic data have a new argument: the threat of bioterrorism. The ease of launching a bacterial or viral attack is as worrisome as the potential devastation. Agents range from lethally potent smallpox, which is difficult to obtain but easily cultured, to the temporarily debilitating strain of salmonella with which disciples of Bhagwan Shree Rajneesh contaminated salad bars in The Dalles, Oregon, in 1984. If the goal is disruption—the Rajneeshes wanted to stifle turnout in a local election—a terrorist group need only make its victims sick, not kill them. But if the intent is retribution, woe to anyone who inhales a deadly dose of anthrax spores. That's why the Defense Department vaccinates soldiers for anthrax, which Rear Admiral Michael Cowan, medical readiness director for the Joint Chiefs of Staff, called "the poor man's atom bomb." Also vulnerable is the nation's food supply, which can be deliberately infected with natural agents like foot-and-mouth disease.

Early detection is essential. Unlike bombings and chemical attacks, a bioterrorist assault might not be apparent for days. Smallpox, for instance, generally takes twelve to fourteen days to produce recognizable symptoms and could go unnoticed longer if public health officials lack an efficient network for collecting reports and notifying practitioners. With an incubation period of one to six days, inhalation anthrax is a bit quicker. But the two postal workers who died in the October 2001 anthrax incident did not seek medical attention for more than a week after their apparent exposure at the Brentwood, Maryland, post office. Effective detection includes far more than knowing who's infected and where they live: before health officials can start screening for exposure, administering antibiotics, and isolating likely sources of contamination, they must analyze activity patterns, consumption habits, and other clues to the disease's source and dissemination. Underscoring the need for quick, effective action is an estimate that an anthrax attack would impose a long-term economic burden as large as $26.2 billion for every 100,000 persons exposed.

On the bright side, if there is one, enhanced surveillance will also defend against potent new natural threats like hantavirus, West Nile virus, and antibiotic-resistant bacteria. According to Donald Henderson, director of the Center for Civilian Biodefense Strategies at the Johns Hopkins University, "whether the source is bioterrorism or a naturally occurring outbreak, similar resources are needed." And as Britain's battle with foot-and-mouth disease has shown, geographic data systems are a key part of this defense, particularly in managing quarantine and vaccination programs. Rapid response requires integration of data on the areal extent of exposure, the locations of treatment facilities and supplies of vaccine, and transport nodes at which quarantine is most effectively enforced. Effective response requires conscientious planning for a wide range of contingencies, including spontaneous evacuation by panicked populations. Although staying inside a well-sealed room might be the best strategy, most people's gut reaction is to get the hell out as quickly as possible.

Geographic modeling is a basic element of disaster planning. Applications include spatial models that let emergency planners simulate the spread of disease agents through a water supply system or the dispersion of airborne contaminants from chemical plants, nuclear power stations, and other attractive terrorist targets. In a similar vein, vulnerability models can help homeland security personnel identify water intakes, nuclear reactors, and other sites that threaten large populations and warrant careful surveillance. Equally valuable are models of contagious diseases with which public health officials can evaluate strategies for stockpiling vaccines as well as assess the relative efficacy of vaccination and quarantine as responses to a smallpox attack. And should terrorists attack, geospatial models can help officials forecast the near-term spread of the contaminant or disease. What's more, computer reconstruction of the incident might prevent further attacks by fingering the perpetrator.

Epilogue:

Locational Privacy

as a Basic Right

If George Orwell had not written *1984* to condemn creeping totalitarianism, Big Brother would be a heck of a brand name. A less politically anxious novelist could have told a futuristic tale of a benign state that reveres surveillance technology in much the same way liberal democrats applaud our "social safety net." Instead of "Big Brother is watching you," the mantra would be "Big Brother is watching over us." And instead of trying to manipulate minds, a warm and fuzzy Super Sibling would try to mollify any hazards it could control and warn of those it couldn't. To provide dramatic tension, the writer could add a few unscrupulous control freaks or money-hungry entrepreneurs—much like what we have today. A suitably odious villain might resemble the Acme Rent-a-Car Company, which put GPS tracking systems in its vehicles and fined unsuspecting customers for speeding. If Acme were truly interested in highway safety, it could have installed speed governors.

As a metaphor for intrusive surveillance, Big Brother is almost everywhere—thanks to Orwell, only systems that monitor weather or forest fires seem to sidestep the pejorative. Some of these fears strike me as silly. Especially ludicrous are libertarian essayists who see red-light cameras and E-ZPass as embodiments of Big Brother. Appropriately placed, widely advertised cameras make drivers more attentive, and I'm all for them, especially after an accident several years ago when I hit a driver who ran a stoplight. Equally advantageous are technologies that reduce delays at tollbooths. That said, I understand objections to systems that photograph everybody as well as the concerns voiced when San Diego and Washington, D.C., hired private firms like Lockheed-Martin to write traffic tickets and collect fines. It's always more reassuring when the folks enforcing laws are accountable to local voters rather than distant shareholders.

More akin to Orwell's Big Brother are video cameras in public places. Used to prevent theft and stifle hooliganism, surveillance cameras are the closest most cities get to 1984. Attitudes toward the cameras vary widely, perhaps because of what privacy advocates call creeping acquiescence. We see video monitors at the 7-Eleven, where they thwart thievery. We see them in office buildings, where a single guard can watch multiple entrances and every elevator. Although England adopted street cameras enthusiastically as a defense against terrorism and rising crime, video surveillance seems a bit out of place on American street corners, largely (I suspect) because local governments are not convinced it's all that useful.

Objections vary. Some people dislike being captured on film or videotape under any circumstances, others consider the cameras a poor substitute for beat cops. Civil libertarians quibble with police about the retention period—the ACLU wants the images erased within two days, the cops think a week is essential, and Chandra Levy's mysterious disappearance in May 2001 created an argument for holding the tapes for at least a month. A very different concern is whether anyone is really minding the monitor. Cities that adopt street cameras but don't watch their screens diligently can expect lawsuits from citizens mugged in places presumed safe. Posted disclaimers, the typical talisman against litigation, would only undermine the alleged power of the cameras' panoptic gaze.

Attitudes changed, momentarily at least, after the September 11, 2001, attack on the World Trade Center killed three thousand people and put tens of thousands more out of work. Realization that "it can happen here" triggered debate on trade-offs between liberty and security. One side warned of a slippery slope, the other observed that the Constitution is not a suicide pact. Although news coverage included video pictures of hijackers passing through the security checkpoint at the Portland, Maine, airport, nothing was said about street cameras, which have little to do with keeping terrorists off airplanes if not out of the country.

Facial biometrics shifts the debate. Image analysis software can reduce a person's face to a set of numbers easily compared with corresponding measurements for fugitives, known troublemakers, and anyone else on the police watch-list. If you're in the system, you can be tracked by an extensive network of cameras programmed to hand a suspect off to the next sector's video vigilantes. Privacy advocates eagerly invoke images of Big Brother while technocrats argue that face-recognition electronics is no more intrusive than a well-coordinated team of sharp-eyed cops with good memories. But what happens when the system confuses an innocent pedestrian with a terrorist bomber or deadbeat dad? I don't know about software, but the police have a poor record of admitting and apologizing for their mistakes. Unless refined facial-recognition systems can filter out known look-alikes, repeated misidentifications seem likely. The unintended consequences of flagrant false alarms might include increased public acceptance of masks and disguises in much the same way that red-light surveillance systems created a market for plastic license-plate covers designed to defeat automatic cameras.

A more cost-effective approach is the placement of retinal-scan imaging systems with high-resolution cameras at airports, where the public not only expects scrutiny but applauds the promise of shorter lines and increased security. Despite decades of libertarian warnings, passengers seem eager for a de facto national identity card with encoded biometric data. To verify a traveler's identity, the system would compare the person's retinal scan with the card's biometric profile. No match, no fly. But because most of us would want one, travel ID cards could become as commonplace and indispensable as driver's licenses, and easily linked to databases revealing far more than where we've been and what we look like.

Orwellian scenarios also encompass dataveillance. Integrated analysis of our purchases, memberships, and financial data can tell a lot about who we are and what we're thinking. Although dataveillance typically is used to sell us more of the same or something just a bit different, this form of manipulation is potentially invasive—a clear violation of Supreme Court Justice Louis Brandeis's classic definition of privacy as "the right to be let alone." Although the Gramm-Leach-Bliley Financial Services Modernization Act of 1999 gave consumers and investors limited rights to control their data, its opt-out procedures are arcane, inconsistent, and unable to guarantee the confidentiality most of us crave. More frightening to many is the heavy-handedness of health insurers who extort access to medical records and credit agencies that sell financial histories to clever private investigators. Privacy advocates face stiff resistance from well-heeled lobbyists abetted by lax legislators and complacent consumers. The controversy is certain to escalate if a de facto national identity card gives merchants a more reliable way to track consumers.

In a real war or a sustained confrontation with terrorists, the niceties of rules and regulations are easily overlooked. A classic example is the Census Bureau's insistence that no employee violate anyone's privacy through a deliberate or careless disclosure of personal data. For the most part, the policy works admirably. But a dirty little secret—if one can call a disclosure affecting thousands of innocent people "little"—is the bureau's support of the Western Defense Command's 1942 "evacuation" to internment camps of over 110,000 Japanese Americans living in the Pacific states. Although census officials refused to surrender household questionnaires, they gave the military what writer Erik Larson called "the next best thing": block-by-block counts of residents with Japanese ancestors. Ironically, because Congress broadened the Voting Rights Act in

1975 to cover Asian and Hispanic minorities, the redistricting data currently available to local politicians and anyone else include block-level counts for Asian Americans and other groups.

Although the Census Bureau ensures that its small-area data don't disclose personal information, address-matching and data-integration software help cluster consultants make vaguely reliable inferences about our neighborhoods, buying habits, and voting preferences. Marketers, fundraisers, and politicians thirsting for finer details accumulate data on purchases, investments, donations, and completed questionnaires, and trade information with other organizations. In the absence of restraints on data exchange, data warehouses construct personal profiles that help pitchmen clog our mailboxes and answering machines with unwanted solicitations. A promising solution, which data vendors dread, is an opt-in requirement whereby no one can sell or trade our records without our explicit permission. As an added safeguard, lawmakers should let us control the use of our addresses (both home and e-mail) and Social Security numbers as common links for cross-matching data collected for diverse purposes.

Lawmakers might also set guidelines for locationally precise disease and crime maps. Although data aggregated by census tract or block group generally afford suitable anonymity, maps that pinpoint cancer or crime victims could prove troubling to injured parties and other members of their households. Health advocacy groups and law enforcement agencies that make and circulate maps should be especially wary of map hackers, who can scan a pin map and convert its dot symbols to addresses. When victims want to be left alone, a detailed map could add to their pain.

Privacy rights occasionally conflict with the public access requirements of fair and open government. If you live in an area where property taxes are based on fair market value, anyone can find out how much you paid for your house, what the assessor thinks it's worth, and how many bathrooms you have. If this seems invasive, get over it—otherwise you lose a valuable tool in appealing an unfair or inaccurate assessment. Your only complaint might be with an assessment department that offers Internet access to public records that once required a tedious visit to city hall or the courthouse. However repugnant the thought of curious folks thousands of miles away browsing the local tax rolls, online access can be especially helpful to future neighbors eager to scope out the housing market. Like most forms of geospatial surveillance, online tax rolls are ethically ambiguous.

And then there's the view from above. Under the open field doctrine, whatever can be seen with commonly available technology is fair game for official or unofficial snooping. Although thermal imaging of a home's walls or roof without a warrant is now prohibited, overhead imaging of our farms or backyards is fully constitutional. Unless specifically prevented from doing so, governments can use air photos or satellite imagery to troll for illegal crops, unauthorized use of irrigation water, nonconforming land use, and a host of zoning or building-code violations, including unapproved additions, outbuildings, or swimming pools. And in much the same way that countries spy on each other, corporations can monitor competitors' loading docks, parking lots, and outdoor facilities for potentially revealing differences. Overhead spying is legal as well as practicable because an energetic commercial remote sensing industry has made high-resolution color-infrared imagery sufficiently commonplace and affordable to meet judicial standards for "commonly available"—a moving target, to say the least. What bears watching is the possibility that hyperspectral imaging will breach the limits of reasonableness and raise judicial hackles in doing so.

Although remote sensing is a few decades older than global positioning, GPS-based tracking has become far more common. In addition to pinpointing cell-phone users who push 911 as well as anyone merely walking around with a wireless device in roaming mode, satellite tracking could revolutionize criminal justice. All but the least trustworthy sex-cons could enjoy a new start unfettered by shaming, and more vigilant monitoring of parolees could cut recidivism for less abhorrent crimes. Be wary, though, of unintended consequences. Although satellite tracking might reduce prison time for minor offenders—and the likelihood of their picking up more bad habits—some electronic detainees are certain to snap their digital leashes. Equally daunting is the possibility of mainstreaming prisoners poorly prepared to reenter society—recall the mixed results in the 1960s and 1970s, when states eager to slash their mental health budgets closed psychiatric hospitals but skimped on outpatient treatment? Far scarier, a surplus of prison cells could join electronic monitoring as an incentive for expanding the list of felonies and misdemeanors. Imagine what Orwell could have done had he foreseen GPS? A real-time map of dissidents seems far more intriguing than Big Brother's ubiquitous wall screens, especially when engineers figure out a reliable, low-cost way of making GPS work indoors.

A technology to watch is the Digital Angel, which can develop in various ways, some beneficial, others frightening. GPS monitors could no doubt prove useful in tracking Alzheimer's patients, retrieving errant pets, and finding lost children in much the same manner that OnStar helps motorists who break down or crash their Cadillacs. But recall the original patent's reliance on chip implants and sensors for monitoring vital signs: a reasonable enhancement insofar as Grandpa's heart condition is at least as important as his location. Even so, it's a small step technologically if not ethically to letting parents equip their kids with a subcutaneous GPS linked to a GIS that sends a pinch or pain command when Sis or Junior steps (literally) out of bounds. Move over, Big Brother, and make room for Big Momma.

Potentially more contentious is the technological union of GPS, GIS, and everyday wireless communications. The GPS chip in your cell phone calculates your coordinates, which the wireless network forwards to a tracking center, where a GIS puts you on its map so that the police, fire service, or medics can find you in an emergency. In addition to relating a would-be victim's location to the street grid, the GIS can tell parents when a child is in the wrong place, an employer when a worker is not in the right place, and a merchant when a potential customer is nearby. Satellite tracking makes location a commodity, which the "location-based services" (LBS) industry is eager to sell to anyone concerned about where you are or where you've been. And because LBS can be enormously convenient when you need to find something, you're both a part of the product and a potential consumer.

Until recently no one spoke of "locational privacy"—before one's whereabouts was so easily determined, archived, and sold, locational nakedness was hardly an issue. This newness in no way diminishes location's status as a privacy right—all notions of privacy are social responses to innovative technologies that screen or intrude. Screening technologies that radically altered standards of personal privacy include the primitive textiles that made it easy to hide one's genitals and whatever rudimentary walls helped our distant ancestors dress in private and defecate in solitude. More recent examples are the sealed envelope and the front-door peephole. By contrast, intrusive technologies include the telephone and computerized financial records, which led to restrictions, however imperfect, on telemarketing and data exchange. And as call blocking and Caller ID illustrate, intrusive technologies often stimulate screening innovations, which in turn raise questions about cost and permeability. In this typology, wireless location tracking is an intrusive technology conveniently controlled by electronic screening.

Whether locational privacy emerges as a basic human right will depend on the inevitable battle between privacy advocates and industry lobbyists. Privacy advocates have the newness of LBS on their side as well as frightening and wholly plausible scenarios of GPS-based stalking and annoying sales pitches. Although industry lobbyists might claim otherwise, LBS is ripe for opt-in restrictions whereby wireless providers cannot sell or archive our locational data unless we let them and cannot reveal our locational history to public safety officials unless we agree or a judge signs a warrant. Without opt-in restrictions, some users, I'm sure, will assert control by leaving their cell phones at home or by removing the batteries: a strategy that erodes the effectiveness of E-911 and invites fatal consequences. For some of us, Big Business is a worse threat than Big Brother.

Notes

Chapter 1. Maps That Watch

General Sources

Insightful assessments of spatial privacy include Michael R. Curry, "The Digital Individual and the Private Realm," *Annals of the Association of American Geographers* 87 (1997): 681–99; Jerry Dobson, "Is GIS a Privacy Threat?" *GIS World* 11 (July 1998): 34–35; Jon Goss, "'We Know Who You Are and We Know Where You Live': The Instrumental Rationality of Geodemographic Systems," *Economic Geography* 71 (1995): 171–98; and Harlan J. Onsrud, Jeff P. Johnson, and Xavier Lopez, "Protecting Personal Privacy in Using Geographic Information Systems," *Photogrammetric Engineering and Remote Sensing* 60 (1994): 1083–95. Useful overviews of geographic information systems include Nicholas Chrisman, *Exploring Geographic Information Systems*, 2nd ed. (New York: John Wiley and Sons, 2001); Keith C. Clarke, *Getting Started with*

Geographic Information Systems, 3rd ed. (Upper Saddle River, N.J.: Prentice-Hall, 2001); and Paul A. Longley, Michael F. Goodchild, and David J. Maguire, eds., *Geographical Information Systems: Principles, Techniques, Applications, and Management,* 2nd ed., 2 vols. (New York: John Wiley and Sons, 1999).

Key references on remote sensing include John R. Jensen, *Remote Sensing of the Environment: An Earth Resource Perspective* (Upper Saddle River, N.J.: Prentice Hall, 2000); and Thomas M. Lillesand and Ralph W. Kiefer, *Remote Sensing and Image Interpretation,* 4th ed. (New York: John Wiley and Sons, 2000). For a history of the Landsat program, see Donald T. Lauer, Stanley A. Morain, and Vincent V. Salomonson, "The Landsat Program: Its Origins, Evolution, and Impacts," *Photogrammetric Engineering and Remote Sensing* 63 (1997): 36–38; Pamela E. Mack, *Viewing the Earth: The Social Construction of the Landsat Satellite System* (Cambridge, Mass.: MIT Press, 1990), esp. 38; and Ray A. Williamson, "The Landsat Legacy: Remote Sensing Policy and the Development of Commercial Remote Sensing," *Photogrammetric Engineering and Remote Sensing* 63 (1997): 877–85.

For general information about GPS, see Michael Ferguson, *GPS Land Navigation: A Complete Guidebook for Backcountry Users of the Navstar Satellite System* (Boise, Id.: Glassford Publishing, 1997); and Gregory T. French, *Understanding the GPS: An Introduction to the Global Positioning System* (Bethesda, Md.: GeoResearch, 1996). For the technical details of GPS, see American Society of Civil Engineers, *Navstar Global Positioning System Surveying* (Reston, Va.: ASCE Press, 2000); Elliot D. Kaplan, ed., *Understanding GPS: Principles and Applications* (Boston: Artech House, 1996); Michael Kennedy, *The Global Positioning System and GIS* (Chelsea, Mich.: Ann Arbor Press, 1996); and National Research Council, Committee on the Future of the Global Positioning System, *The Global Positioning System: A Shared National Asset* (Washington, D.C.: National Academy Press, 1995).

Notes

4   For a concise introduction to dispersion modeling, see Mark Monmonier, *Cartographies of Danger: Mapping Hazards in America* (Chicago: University of Chicago Press, 1997), 127–47, 161–67, 225–29.

4   For a concise overview of address-oriented GIS applications, see William J. Drummond, "Address Matching: GIS Technology for Mapping Human Activity Patterns," *Journal of the American Planning Association* 61 (1995): 240–51.

6   For a history of the TIGER concept, see Donald F. Cooke, "Topology and TIGER: The Census Bureau's Contribution," in *The History of Geographic Information Systems: Perspectives from the Pioneers,* ed. Timothy W. Foresman (Upper Saddle River, N.J.: Prentice Hall, 1998), 47–57.

6   For more information on the use of block data in congressional redistricting, see Mark Monmonier, *Bushmanders and Bullwinkles: How Politicians*

Manipulate Electronic Maps and Census Data to Win Elections (Chicago: University of Chicago Press, 2001), esp. 96–98.

7   For a concise summary of Census Bureau regulations on privacy and nondisclosure, see Michael R. Lavin, *Understanding the Census: A Guide for Marketers, Planners, Grant Writers, and Other Data Users* (Kenmore, N.Y.: Epoch Books, 1996), 10–11, 44–45, 363–65.

7   As its name implies, a block group is an areal unit formed by combining several contiguous blocks. A census tract has a maximum of nine block groups, each of which contains between 250 and 550 housing units and between 1,000 and 1,200 people. For a description of small geographical units used by the Census Bureau, see Lavin, *Understanding the Census,* 150–93.

7   Although fear of rapists . . . : Robert L. Jacobson, "'Megan's Laws' Reinforcing Old Patterns of Anti-Gay Police Harassment," *Georgetown Law Journal* 87 (July 1999): 2431–73, esp. 2456.

7   New York State Sex Offenders Registry, http://criminaljustice.state.ny.us/ nsor/index.htm. Before New York State opened its official online registry, a private group, Parents for Megan's Law, set up its own Web site (www .parentsformeganslaw.com) with information copied from the state registry by parent volunteers; see Sue Weibezahl, "Group's Web Site Lists Sex Convicts," *Syracuse Post-Standard,* May 2, 2000.

7   Like Web sites maintained . . . : See "Offenders Online," *Government Computer News State and Local* 6, no. 6 (March 2000): 6; and Paul Zielbauer, "Posting of Sex Offender Registries on Web Sets Off Both Praise and Criticism," *New York Times,* May 22, 2000. New Jersey's efforts to place sex-offender information on the Internet encountered substantial legal resistance; see David Kocieniewski, "Amendment Would Let State Name Sex Offenders Online," *New York Times,* March 28, 2000; and "A Court Blocks Disclosures about Sex Offenders under 'Megan's Law,'" *New York Times,* April 19, 2000.

7   For critiques of publicly accessible sex-offender registries, see Reese Dunklin, David Heath, and Julie Lucas, "About 700 Sex Offenders Do Not Appear to Live at the Addresses Listed on a St. Louis Registry," *St. Louis Post-Dispatch,* May 2, 1999; and Susan R. Paisner, "Exposed: Online Registries of Sex Offenders May Do More Harm Than Good," *Washington Post,* February 21, 1999. For a state-by-state summary of practices, see Alan R. Kabat, "Scarlet Letter Sex Offender Databases and Community Notification: Sacrificing Personal Privacy for a Symbol's Sake," *American Criminal Law Review* 35 (winter 1998): 333–70.

8   Several years ago . . . : See the State Department of Assessments and Taxation, www.dat.state.md.us/sdatweb/.

8   For further information on the Emergency Planning and Community Right-to-Know Act, see Gary D. Bass and Alair MacLean, "Enhancing the

Public's Right-to-Know about Environmental Issues," *Villanova Environmental Law Journal* 4 (1993): 287–321; and Ute J. Dymon, "Mapping: The Missing Link in Reducing Risk under SARA III (Emergency Planning and Community Right-To-Know)," *Risk: Health, Safety, and Environment* 5 (1994): 337–49.

8 The act makes . . . : William J. Craig and Sarah A. Elwood, "How and Why Community Groups Use Maps and Geographic Information," *Cartography and Geographic Information Systems* 25 (1998): 95–104.

10 For reports on the 5-foot resolution of the KH-4B imaging system, used between 1967 and 1972, see Philip J. Klass, "CIA Reveals Details of Early Spy Satellites," *Aviation Week and Space Technology* 142 (June 12, 1995): 167–68; and Kevin C. Ruffner, ed., *Corona: America's First Satellite Program* (Washington, D.C.: Central Intelligence Agency, Center for the Study of Intelligence, 1995), xv. Another authority suggests that the resolution was closer to 2 meters (6 ft.); see Robert A. McDonald, "Corona: Success for Space Reconnaissance, a Look into the Cold War, and a Revolution for Intelligence," *Photogrammetric Engineering and Remote Sensing* 61 (1995): 689–719, esp. 691.

10 For additional information on Système pour l'Observation de la Terre (SPOT), see "SPOT Earth Resources Satellite Beginning Commercial Operation," *Aviation Week and Space Technology* 124 (May 5, 1986): 101; Christopher P. Fotos, "Commercial Remote Sensing Satellites Generate Debate, Foreign Competition," *Aviation Week and Space Technology* 129 (December 19, 1988): 48; and Paul M. Treitz, Philip J. Howarth, and Peng Gong, "Application of Satellite and GIS Technologies for Land-Cover and Land-Use Mapping at the Rural-Urban Fringe: A Case Study," *Photogrammetric Engineering and Remote Sensing* 58 (1992): 439–48.

11 . . . Russia's space agency . . . : Trudy E. Bell, "Remote Sensing," *IEEE Spectrum* 32 (March 1995): 24–31.

11 According to the trade journal . . . : Craig Covault, "USAF Eyes Advanced Russian Military Reconnaissance Imagery," *Aviation Week and Space Technology* 140 (May 23, 1994): 53. For discussion of the government's mixed views on Russian efforts to sell satellite imagery, see James R. Asker, "High-Resolution Imagery Seen as Threat, Opportunity," *Aviation Week and Space Technology* 140 (May 23, 1995): 51–53.

11 America recovered . . . : Vernon Loeb, "Spy Satellite Will Take Photos for Public Sale; Launch Allows Company to Market Images of Almost Anywhere," *Washington Post*, September 25, 1999. Two other U.S. firms, Earthwatch and Orbital Imaging, were eager to share the high-resolution commercial remote sensing market; see Joseph C. Anselmo, "Competitors Chasing Ikonos into Orbit," *Aviation Week and Space Technology* 152 (January 31, 2000): 57. Earthwatch's successor company, DigitalGlobe, successfully launched its QuickBird satellite on October 18, 2001, and an-

nounced the imminent availability of 61-centimeter black-and-white and 2.44-meter color imagery. See "Colorado Company's Satellite Launched from California," Associated Press State and Local Wire, October 18, 2001. On April 27, 1999, the attempted launch of Ikonos-1 failed after a "payload fairing" (protection cover) did not separate from the rocket; see "Ikonos 1 Fails to Reach Orbit," *GeoWorld* 12 (June 1999): 12. Pronounced "eye-KOH-nos," *Ikonos* is derived from the Greek word for *image*.

11 Almost all, that is . . . : Dee Ann Divis, "Shutter Control Rattles Industry," *Geo Info Systems* 8 (September 1998): 14–16; Michael R. Gordon, "Pentagon Corners Output of Special Afghan Images," *New York Times,* October 19, 2001; and Robert Wright, "Private Eyes," *New York Times Magazine,* September 5, 1999, 50–55.

11 Intelligence satellites . . . : William E. Burrows, who no doubt relied heavily on CIA sources in writing his pioneering account of Corona, forecasts a pixel of 3 inches; see Burrows, *Deep Black: Space Espionage and National Security* (New York: Random House, 1986), 207. Arms control authority Kosta Tsipis also cites a 3-inch pixel; see Kosta Tsipis, "Arms Control Pacts Can Be Verified," *Discover* 8 (April 1987): 78–93. Journalist Howard Hough, who follows intelligence developments, reports a resolution between 3 and 6 inches; see Howard Hough, *Satellite Surveillance* (Port Townsend, Wash.: Loompanics Unlimited, 1991), esp. 16–19, 78, 180, and 186. Obsessive about secrecy, the NRO was reluctant to admit their systems' existence, much less comment on their spatial resolution; see Jeffrey Richelson, *America's Secret Eyes in Space: The U.S. Keyhole Spy Satellite Program* (New York: Harper and Row, 1990), 257–71. More recently, the Federation of American Scientists, at its Space Policy Project Web site, accords the KH-12 system, known as Improved Crystal and described as a downward-looking version of the Hubble Space Telescope, a resolution of 10 centimeters—about 3 inches; see FAS, "Improved Crystal," http://www.fas.org/spp/military/program/imint/kh-12.htm.

11 And airplanes as well . . . : Craig Covault, "Radar Flight Meets Mapping Goals," *Aviation Week and Space Technology* 152 (February 28, 2000): 43.

13 Just ask the former clients . . . : Joe Sharkey, "Most Car Rental Customers Can Relax: The Top Companies Have No Plans to Monitor Speeders," *New York Times,* July 11, 2001.

14 The twenty-four-satellite configuration in figure 1.8 does not show replacement satellites. Because satellites fail or become obsolete, the constellation also includes one or two spares, which the Air Force can reposition as required. With no air resistance in space, tiny but precisely controlled thruster rockets let the Air Force change a satellite's orbit as well as fine-tune its position within an orbit. For an example of thruster technology, see Michael A. Dornheim, "Xenon Thruster to Propel New Millennium Spacecraft," *Aviation Week and Space Technology* 150 (Septem-

ber 25, 1995): 110. Because worldwide GPS will work with fewer than twenty-four satellites, three members of the twenty-four-satellite constellation are sometimes called "active on-orbit spares." For an example, see *Navstar GPS User Equipment Introduction*, public release version (Alexandria, Va.: U.S. Coast Guard Navigation Center, September 1996), 5.

14   Because taxpayers paid . . . : Scott Pace and others, *The Global Positioning System: Assessing National Policies* (Santa Monica, Cal.: Rand Corporation, Critical Technologies Institute, 1995).

14   For additional discussion of GPS error, see *Navstar GPS User Equipment Introduction*, 16–21. According to James R. Clynch of the Naval Postgraduate School Department of Oceanography, PPS and SPS accuracy standards are not fully comparable; see Clynch, "GPS Accuracy Levels," http://www.oc.nps.navy.mil/~jclynch/gpsacc.html.

15   What's more, civilian users . . . : Even with SA, some civilian users could reduce positioning error to 1 meter through a technique called differential GPS. Users needed to link electronically to a nearby base station, the location of which having been established by a highly precise independent survey. Differences between these known coordinates and those estimated by a GPS receiver at the same spot could then be used to adjust readings for other GPS receivers in the vicinity. For a concise explanation, see Thomas A. Herring, "The Global Positioning System," *Scientific American* 274 (February 1996): 44–50; and Matt Lake, "Pentagon Lets Civilians Use the Best G.P.S. Data," *New York Times,* June 15, 2000.

15   "with SA activated . . . ": National Geodetic Survey, "Comparison of Positions with and without Selective Availability," http://www.ngs.noaa.gov/FGCS/info/sans_SA/compare/DSRC.htm. With SA turned off, differential GPS provides even more accurate coordinates.

15   Even so, the Pentagon . . . : Dee Ann Divis, "SA No More: GPS Accuracy Increases 10 Fold," *Geospatial Solutions* 10 (June 2000): 18–20; and Carla Anne Robbins, "Government Will Authorize Civilian Use of Military-Quality Positioning Signal," *Wall Street Journal,* May 1, 2000.

15   "selectively deny GPS . . . " : "Clinton Statement on Global Positioning System Accuracy," U.S. Newswire, May 1, 2000. The military may have invoked regional denial during the 2001 Afghanistan campaign; see Declan McCullagh, "U.S. Could Deny GPS to Taliban," *Wired News,* October 20, 2001, http://www.wired.com/news/conflict/0,2100,47739,00.html.

15   Although GPS surveillance . . . : Jerry Dobson, "What Are the Ethical Limits of GIS?" *GEO World* 13 (May 2000): 24–25; and Richard Stenger, "Tiny Human-Borne Monitoring Device Sparks Privacy Fears," *CNN.com,* December 20, 1999, http://www.cnn.com/1999/TECH/ptech/12/20/implant.device/.

Chapter 2. Overhead Assets

General Sources

Useful references for the early history of aerial reconnaissance and mapping include Teodor J. Blachut and Rudolf Burkhardt, *Historical Development of Photogrammetric Methods and Instruments* (Falls Church, Va.: American Society of Photogrammetry and Remote Sensing, 1989); Grover Heiman, *Aerial Photography: The Story of Aerial Mapping and Reconnaissance* (New York: Macmillan, 1972); and Harold E. Porter, *Aerial Observation: The Airplane Observer, the Balloon Observer, and the Army Corps Pilot* (New York: Harper and Brothers, 1921). For satellite remote sensing, my key source was Thomas M. Lillesand and Ralph W. Kiefer, *Remote Sensing and Image Interpretation*, 4th ed. (New York: John Wiley and Sons, 2000).

Principal references for the Corona intelligence satellite program are William E. Burrows, *Deep Black: Space Espionage and National Security* (New York: Random House, 1986); John Cloud and Keith Clarke, "To Do the Other Things: Corona and the Secret Cartography of the Cold War," *ACSM Bulletin* no. 191 (May/June 2001): 25–30; Dwayne A. Day, John M. Logsdon, and Brian Latell, eds., *Eye in the Sky: The Story of the Corona Spy Satellites* (Washington, D.C.: Smithsonian Institution Press, 1998); Kenneth E. Greer, "Corona," *Studies in Intelligence* 17, supplement (spring 1973): 1–37; Philip J. Klass, "CIA Reveals Details of Early Spy Satellites," *Aviation Week and Space Technology* 142 (June 12, 1995): 167–73; Philip Klass, *Secret Sentries in Space* (New York: Random House, 1971); Robert A. McDonald, "Corona: Success for Space Reconnaissance, a Look into the Cold War, and a Revolution for Intelligence," *Photogrammetric Engineering and Remote Sensing* 61 (1995): 689–719; Jeffrey T. Richelson, *America's Secret Eyes in Space: The U.S. Keyhole Spy Satellite Program* (New York: Harper and Row, 1990); Jeffrey Richelson, "The Keyhole Satellite Program," *Journal of Strategic Studies* 7 (1984): 121–53; Kevin C. Ruffner, ed., *Corona: America's First Satellite Program* (Washington, D.C.: Central Intelligence Agency, Center for the Study of Intelligence, 1995); and Seth Shulman, "Code Name: Corona," *Technology Review* 99 (October 1996): 22–32.

The Federation of American Scientists Web site (www.fas.org) was a rich source of information about Corona, its various successors, and current satellite intelligence. John Pike, who created content for and maintained the FAS Web site until late 2000, now pursues his interest in satellite intelligence as director of GlobalSecurity.org. For insights on contemporary satellite intelligence, I also relied on Jeffrey T. Richelson, *A Century of Spies: Intelligence in the Twentieth Century* (New York: Oxford University Press, 1995); and Jeffrey T. Richelson, *America's Space Sentinels: DSP Satellites and National Security* (Lawrence, Kans.: University of Kansas Press, 1999).

Notes

17 As a synonym for aerial or space reconnaissance, "overhead assets" is well established in the military and intelligence communities. For instance, in a March 1996 NATO press briefing on Implementation Force (IFOR) activities in the former Yugoslavia, an officer identified only as Colonel Bryan used the term twice in one paragraph in referring to satellite systems operated by the U.S. National Reconnaissance Office: "Overhead assets are available to us as I have said. IFOR does not directly control overhead assets as much as those products that come from national sources that are fed into the various forces that are under IFOR." IFOR Air Reconnaissance Brief, March 9, 1996, NATO, http://www.nato.int/ifor/trans/t960309b.htm.

18 The French army . . . : Heiman, *Aerial Photography*, 5–9.

18 The Union army . . . : Ibid., 17.

18 As long as a pilot . . . : Improved guns and shells increased the reach of antiaircraft fire from around 6,000 feet early in World War I to over 18,000 feet near the war's end. See Porter, *Aerial Observation*, 111–12, 158–62.

18 For detailed discussion of three-lens cameras used for reconnaissance mapping, see U.S. Army Air Force, "Reconnaissance Mapping with Trimetrogon Photography," in *Manual of Photogrammetry*, preliminary edition, ed. P. G. McCurdy and others (New York: Pitman Publishing Co.; Washington, D.C.: American Society of Photogrammetry, 1944), 645–712. Used heavily during World War II for photointerpretation and reconnaissance mapping, multilens cameras predated the use of aircraft; see Blachut and Burkhardt, *Historical Development of Photogrammetric Methods*, 38–40. Single-lens panoramic cameras, with a wide sweep to the left and right, were also used for photointerpretation; see Francis H. Moffitt and Edward M. Mikhail, *Photogrammetry*, 3rd ed. (New York: Harper and Row, 1980), 75–79.

19 During the mid-1940s . . . : Sidney A. Tischler, "Procedural Developments in Trimetrogon Compilation," *Photogrammetric Engineering* 14 (1948): 53–60; and "Report of Commission I—Photography, to the Sixth International Photogrammetry Congress and Exhibition," *Photogrammetric Engineering* 14 (1948): 229–79, esp. 229–30. To promote useful comparison, I have converted most post-1960 terrain measurements to metric units. For authenticity and mildly harmless inertia, earlier altitudes and areas remain in feet and square miles. Camera measurements retain the customary units of millimeters for film size and inches for focal length.

19 Commercial satellites like SPOT . . . : Because their orbits are inclined away from the poles, low-altitude satellites like Landsat, SPOT, and Ikonos typically ignore or provide less accurate coverage of polar areas.

For an overview of orbital geometry in remote sensing, see Lillesand and Kiefer, *Remote Sensing and Image Interpretation*, 379–83.

19 By contrast, Ikonos offers . . . : Flexible scanners offer different levels of resolution with somewhat different return frequencies. With a very narrow ground swath, Ikonos has a revisit time so large—and so irrelevant— that its owner, Space Imaging, does not publish a hypothetical no-tilt revisit time. For additional details on orbits, resolution, and revisit times, see the technical specifications pages at the Space Imaging Web site, http://www.spaceimaging.com.

21 During the 1930s . . . : Blachut and Burkhardt, *Historical Development of Photogrammetric Methods*, 49–136.

21 Imaging software . . . : See N. Al-Rousan and others, "Automated DEM Extraction and Orthoimage Generation from SPOT Level 1B Imagery," *Photogrammetric Engineering and Remote Sensing* 63 (1997): 965–74; and Rongxing Li, "Potential of High-Resolution Satellite Imagery for National Mapping Products," *Photogrammetric Engineering and Remote Sensing* 64 (1998): 1165–70. For discussion of general principles of orthophotography, see Lillesand and Kiefer, *Remote Sensing and Image Interpretation*, 170–74; and Kurt Novak, "Rectification of Digital Imagery," *Photogrammetric Engineering and Remote Sensing* 58 (1992): 339–44. For an early essay on the principles of satellite-enabled stereovision, see Roy Welch and Wayne Marko, "Cartographic Potential of a Spacecraft Line-Array Camera System: Stereosat," *Photogrammetric Engineering and Remote Sensing* 47 (1981): 1173–85.

22 On August 18 . . . : Klass, "CIA Reveals Details."

23 *Discoverer* was a clever . . . : According to William Burrows, although press releases stressed scientific experiments, only one Discoverer mission actually carried live animals. See Burrows, "Imaging Space Reconnaissance Operations during the Cold War: Cause, Effect, and Legacy," *Cold War Forum*, http://webster.hibo.no/asf/Cold_War/report1/williame.html.

24 The orbit was not . . . : Data are chiefly from McDonald, "Corona: Success for Space Reconnaissance," 691–95; and FAS, "KH-1 Corona," http://www.fas.org/spp/military/program/imint/kh-1.htm. Discoverer-14's elliptical orbit, similar to other Corona missions, varied from 803 kilometers (434 nautical miles) to 177 kilometers (96 naut. mi.). See *Encyclopedia Astronautica*, s.v. "KH-1," http://www.astronautix.com/craft/kh1.htm. The KH-1 camera used in early Corona missions was the optical equivalent of an electronic imaging system with a resolution of 40 feet.

24 As the satellite moved . . . : Sources do not report a ground swath, which would vary somewhat because of the elliptical orbit. For a panoramic scan of 70 degrees and a low altitude of 180 kilometers, trigonometry suggests a minimum swath of 252 kilometers.

24   The first Corona . . . : Because aircraft reconnaissance, still used outside
the Soviet Union, had been given the code name Talent, more general references to top-secret photography typically adopted the combined name
Talent-Keyhole.

25   Two stellar cameras . . . : For information on the camera system, see *The
KH-4B Camera System*, available on the Federation of American Scientists
Web site, http://www.fas.org/spp/military/program/imint/kh-4%20
camera%20system.htm. (Now declassified, this document was originally
a National Reconnaissance Office Data Book [Washington, D.C.: National
Photographic Interpretation Center, September 1967].) The KH-3, KH-4,
and KH-4A imaging systems also included one or more supplementary
cameras. Corona used two other imaging systems: between 1961 and
1964, twelve missions used a KH-5 camera, designed for small-scale geodetic positioning, and three missions carried a KH-6 camera, intended for
highly detailed intelligence monitoring. CIA records describe six of the
twelve KH-5 missions as successful, and one of the KH-6 missions as partly
successful. Intended to provide 2-foot resolution, the KH-6 system never
surpassed the KH-4B and was discontinued. For additional information,
see NASA Jet Propulsion Laboratory Mission and Spacecraft Library,
"Corona," http://samadhi.jpl.nasa.gov/msl/Programs/corona.html.

25   "scientifically or environmentally useful . . . ": William J. Clinton, "Release of Imagery Acquired by Space-Based National Reconnaissance Systems (Executive Order 12951, of February 22, 1995)," *Federal Register* 60
(1995): 10789–90. For an example of a scientific study based on declassified Corona imagery, see Robert Bindschadler and Patricia Vornberger,
"Changes in the West Antarctic Ice Sheet since 1963 from Declassified
Satellite Photography," *Science* 279 (1998): 689–92.

25   For discussion of Corona's role during the Cuban missile crisis, see Burrows, *Deep Black*, 132–37.

26   Corona not only . . . : Dwayne A. Day, "Mapping the Dark Side of the
World—Part 1: The KH-5 Argon Geodetic Satellite," *Spaceflight* 40 (1998):
264–69; Day, "Mapping the Dark Side of the World—Part 2: Secret Geodetic Programmes after Argon," *Spaceflight* 40 (1998): 303–10; and
Muneendra Kumar, "World Geodetic System 1984: A Reference Frame
for Global Mapping, Charting, and Geodetic Applications," *Surveying and
Land Information Systems* 53 (1993): 53–56.

26   Less well known . . . : Day, Logsdon, and Latell, *Eye in the Sky*, 211–14; and
Richelson, *America's Secret Eyes in Space*, 268–69.

27   "most cherished hope": Quoted in Don Oberdorfer, "SALT: The Tortuous
Path," *Washington Post*, May 11, 1979.

27   "photoreconnaissance satellites . . . ": Quoted in Edward Walsh, "Carter
Vows U.S. Will Continue Leadership in Space," *Washington Post*, October
2, 1978. Also see Richelson, "Keyhole Satellite Program," esp. 121.

27 Well-placed . . . informants . . . : Richelson describes one ostensibly inadvertent leak of satellite photos in the transcript of a congressional hearing on arms control. See Jeffrey T. Richelson, "The Future of Space Reconnaissance," *Scientific American* 264 (January 1991): 38–44, esp. 44.

27 Espionage trials . . . : For information on Kampiles, see James Ott, "Espionage Trial Highlights CIA Problems," *Aviation Week and Space Technology* 109 (November 27, 1978): 21–23; and Richelson, "Keyhole Satellite Program," 138–40. For reports on Boyce and Lee, see Robert Lindsey, "Alleged Soviet Spy Testifies He Was Blackmailed after Telling a Friend of C.I.A. 'Deception' of Australia," *New York Times*, April 27, 1977; Lindsey, "To Be Rich, Young—and a Spy," *New York Times Magazine*, May 22, 1977, 18–28, 89–94, 106–8; Ott, "Espionage Trial"; and Richelson, "Keyhole Satellite Program," 138–40.

28 Morison had sent . . . : "Satellite Pictures Show Soviet CVN Towering above Nikolaiev Shipyard," *Jane's Defence Weekly* 2 (August 11, 1984): 171–73. Also see Burrows, *Deep Black*, 329–30; George Lardner, Jr., "3 Secret Photos Called Nothing New to Soviets," *Washington Post*, October 11, 1985; Warren Richey, "Overreaction to Spy Cases Could Harm U.S. As Much As Lost Secrets," *Christian Science Monitor*, December 5, 1985; and "Spies Who Aren't," *Los Angeles Times*, May 22, 1986.

28 "just didn't really tell me . . . ": Quoted in Lardner, "3 Secret Photos."

29 One of Richelson's sources . . . : Klass, *Secret Sentries in Space*, 171–72.

29 "develop a new generation . . . ": "Industry Observer," *Aviation Week and Space Technology* 96 (February 7, 1972): 9.

29 . . . charged coupled devices (CCDs): John A. Adam, "Counting the Weapons," *IEEE Spectrum* 23 (July 1986): 46–56, esp. 47–48.

30 "greater than the KH-9 . . . ": Richelson, "Keyhole Satellite Program," 137.

30 For an overview of the KH-12 satellite, also known by the code name Improved Crystal, see FAS, "Improved Crystal," http://www.fas.org/spp/military/program/imint/kh-12.htm. For information on the space telescope imaging system, see Tim Beardsley, "Hubble's Legacy: The Space Telescope Launches a New Era in Astronomy," *Scientific American* 262 (June 1990): 18–22; and Carolyn Collins Petersen and John C. Brandt, *Hubble Vision: Astronomy with the Hubble Space Telescope* (Cambridge: Cambridge University Press, 1995), esp. 23–27.

30 "space telescope with a rocket": FAS, "Improved Crystal."

30 "an unclassified version . . . ": Quoted in Adam, "Counting the Weapons," 49.

30 For an excellent discussion of image resolution and other details of satellite reconnaissance, see FAS, "IMINT 101: Introduction to Imagery Intelligence," http://www.fas.org/irp/imint/imint_101.htm.

30 A calculation . . . : Adam, "Counting the Weapons," 49.

30 Although 4-inch resolution . . . : See, for example, D. E. Richardson, "Spy

Satellites: Someone Could Be Watching You," *Electronics and Power* 24 (1978): 573–76.

30 In fact, Pike . . . : See FAS, "Resolution Comparison: Reading Headlines and License Plates," http://www.fas.org/irp/imint/resolve5.htm.

31 Figure 2.6: Image array from FAS, "Resolution Comparison," http://www.fas.org/irp/imint/resolve4.htm.

31 For a discussion of the underlying rationale of image interpretability rating scales, see John M. Irvine and Jon C. Leachtenauer, "A Methodology for Developing Image Interpretability Rating Scales," *Technical Papers of the American Society of Photogrammetry and Remote Sensing Annual Convention,* April 1996, vol. 1, pp. 273–81; and Jon C. Leachtenauer, "National Imagery Interpretability Rating Scales: Overview and Product Description," *Technical Papers of the American Society of Photogrammetry and Remote Sensing Annual Convention,* April 1996, vol. 1, pp. 262–72.

31 Focused on usefulness . . . : Quotations from the rating levels and lists are from FAS, "National Image Interpretability Rating Scales," http://www.fas.org/irp/imint/niirs.htm.

32 "if a picture . . . ": John Pike, "Introducing the FAS Public Eye Initiative" (paper presented at Through the Keyhole: Public Policy Applications of Declassified Corona Satellite Imagery, Federation of American Scientists conference, February 16, 1999), http://www.fas.org/eye/conf9902/trans-pike.htm.

32 Look for even bigger . . . : "0.5-Meter Resolution Approved for Ikonos," *Aviation Week and Space Technology* 153 (November 27, 2000): 49.

32 For a concise explanation of SAR, see Charles Elachi, "Radar Images of the Earth from Space," *Scientific American* 247 (December 1982): 54–61; and Tony Freeman, "What Is Imaging Radar?" NASA Jet Propulsion Laboratory, http://southport.jpl.nasa.gov/desc/imagingradarv3.html. For further details, see Donald R. Wehner, *High Resolution Radar* (Norwood, Mass.: Artech House, 1987).

32 Although estimates of ground resolution . . . : The Federation of American Scientists suggests that the resolution, which might "in principle" be better than 1 meter, is rarely so in practice because of the trade-off between ground resolution and geographic scope; see FAS, "Lacrosse/Onyx," http://www.fas.org/spp/military/program/imint/lacrosse.htm.   This assessment is consistent with the estimate of "between 3 and 10 feet" reported in Richelson, "Future of Space Reconnaissance," 39.

33 For all-weather coverage . . . : My principal sources, which do not always agree, include FAS, "Lacrosse/Onyx"; Daniel Charles, "Spy Satellites: Entering a New Era," *Science* 243 (1989): 1541–43; Craig Covault, "NRO Radar, Sigint Launches Readied," *Aviation Week and Space Technology* 149 (September 1, 1997): 22–24; Paul Mann, "Congress Backs Raids, Faults

Strategy," *Aviation Week and Space Technology* 149 (December 21/28, 1998): 124–25; and Richelson, "Future of Space Reconnaissance."

33 According to John Pike . . . : For a concise overview, see Mann, "Congress Backs Raids;" and Mark Thompson, "The Pentagon's Plan," *Time* 153 (April 12, 1999): 48–49.

34 Although each . . . spy satellite . . . : See, for example, John Morrocco, "Gulf War Boosts Prospects for High-Technology Weapons," *Aviation Week and Space Technology* 134 (March 18, 1991): 45–47.

34 According to the *Los Angeles Times* . . . : James Risen and Ralph Vartabedian, "U.S. Launches Costly Overhaul of Spy Satellites," *Los Angeles Times*, September 28, 1995. Also see FAS, "8X Enhanced Imaging System," http://www.fas.org/spp/military/program/imint/8x.htm. This page includes links to assessments of 8X capability.

34 Because large image intelligence satellites can be seen by the naked eye, astronomers can easily track their orbits, as the Federation American Scientists points out with "Where are they now?" links to Heavens-Above .com and other Web sites; see John Pike, FAS, "Space Surveillance," http://www.fas.org/spp/military/program/track/. Also see Vernon Loeb, "Hobbyists Track Down Spies in the Sky," *Washington Post*, February 20, 1999.

34 Early sources of information on nonimaging intelligence satellites include John A. Adam, "Peacekeeping by Technical Means," *IEEE Spectrum* 23 (July 1986): 42–45; the Federation of American Scientists' Military Space Programs Web pages, http://www.fas.org/spp/military/program/index.html; Richelson, *America's Space Sentinels*; and Glenn Zorpette, "Monitoring the Tests," *IEEE Spectrum* 23 (July 1986): 57–66.

35 For additional information on the role of seismic networks in test-ban verification, see Paul G. Richards, "Building the Global Seismographic Network for Nuclear Test Ban Monitoring," *EARTHmatters* [Columbia Earth Institute], fall 1999, 37–40; Paul G. Richards and Won-Young Kim, "Testing the Nuclear Test-Ban Treaty," *Nature* 389 (1997): 782–83; and Kosta Tsipis, "Arms Control Pacts Can Be Verified," *Discover* 8 (April 1987): 78–93.

36 Instead of admitting . . . : Richards and Kim, "Testing the Nuclear Test-Ban Treaty;" R. Jeffrey Smith, "U.S. Officials Acted Hastily in Nuclear Test Accusation," *Washington Post*, October 20, 1997; and Lynn R. Sykes, "Small Earthquake Near Russian Test Site Leads to U.S. Charges of Cheating on Comprehensive Nuclear Test Ban Treaty," F.A.S. Public Interest Report, *Journal of the Federation of American Scientists* 50 (November/December 1997): 1–12.

36 Shortly after the incident . . . : Motivated by a firm belief in technology, my informant was not alone in questioning official claims that the attack was

an accident. In October 1999, for instance, newspapers in London and Copenhagen reported that Chinese military officers claimed the embassy had served Yugoslavian forces as a communications center, which NATO was determined to silence. See Joel Bleifuss, "A Tragic Mistake?" *In These Times* 24 (December 12, 1999): 2–3.

36 Turns out . . . : Nearly a year after the May 7, 1999, bombing, the CIA accepted responsibility. An investigation blamed the target's misidentification on a combination of haste, zeal, ignorant inference, and inadequate maps. See Steven Lee Myers, "C.I.A. Fires Officer Blamed in Bombing of China Embassy," *New York Times,* April 9, 2000; and Myers, "Chinese Embassy Bombing: A Wide Net of Blame," *New York Times,* April 17, 2000.

37 For a nontechnical introduction to antisatellite weapons, see Daniel G. Dupont, "Laser Show," *Scientific American* 278 (January 1998): 44; Dupont, "The Real Star Wars," *Scientific American* 280 (June 1999): 36; and Cynthia A. S. McKinley, "When the Enemy Has Our Eyes" (master's thesis, School of Advanced Airpower Studies, Air University, Maxwell Air Force Base, Ala., 1996).

37 For discussion of international conflict and opportunities arising from high-resolution commercial imagery, see J. Todd Black, "Commercial Satellites: Future Threats of Allies," *Naval War College Review* 52 (winter 1999): 99–114; Vipin Gupta, "New Satellite Images for Sale," *International Security* 20 (summer 1995): 94–125; and Michael J. Riezenman, "Spying for Dummies," *IEEE Spectrum* 36 (November 1999): 62–69.

37 For insights on "shutter control" and federal remote sensing policy, see Joseph C. Anselmo, "Shutter Controls: How Far Will Uncle Sam Go?" *Aviation Week and Space Technology* 152 (January 31, 2000): 55–56; Dee Ann Divis, "Remote Regs, SRTM, and Financing NSDI," *Geo Info Systems* 10 (May 2000): 18–20; House Committee on Science, Space, and Technology and the Permanent Select Committee on Intelligence, *Commercial Remote Sensing in the Post–Cold War Era,* 103rd Cong., 2nd sess., February 9, 1994; and Ray A. Williamson, "The Landsat Legacy: Remote Sensing Policy and the Development of Commercial Remote Sensing," *Photogrammetry and Remote Sensing* 63 (1997): 877–85.

37 "every bad guy . . . ": Quoted in Dan Charles, "Every Move You Make," *New Scientist* 155 (August 2, 1997): 18–19, quotation on 19.

Chapter 3. Eyes on the Farm

General Sources

Key general references on the Agricultural Adjustment Administration (AAA) include Gladys Baker, *Century of Service: The First 100 Years of the United States De-*

partment of Agriculture (Washington, D.C.: Government Printing Office, 1963), 143–78; Donald C. Blaisdell, *Government and Agriculture: The Growth of Federal Farm Aid* (New York: Farrar and Rinehart, 1940), 39–75; Edwin G. Nourse, Joseph S. David, and John D. Black, *Three Years of the Agricultural Adjustment Administration* (Washington, D.C.: Brookings Institution, 1937), esp. 60–77; and *Report of the Secretary of Agriculture, 1936* (Washington, D.C., 1936), 8–17. For information of the AAA's use of aerial photography, I relied on W. N. Brown, "Area Measurements by Use of Aerial Photography," *Photogrammetric Engineering* 2 (January-February-March 1936): 19–22; Ralph H. Moyer, "Use of Aerial Photographs in Connection with Farm Programs Administered by the Production and Marketing Administration, U.S.D.A.," *Photogrammetric Engineering* 15 (1949): 536–40; and Harry Tubis, "Aerial Photography Maps Our Farmlands: The Program of the Agricultural Adjustment Administration," *Photogrammetric Engineering* 3 (April-May-June 1937): 21–23.

General sources for my discussion of soils mapping are Mark Baldwin, Howard M. Smith, and Howard W. Whitlock, "The Use of Aerial Photographs in Soil Mapping," *Photogrammetric Engineering* 13 (1947): 532–36; Edward W. Magruder, "Aerial Photographs and the Soil Conservation Service," *Photogrammetric Engineering* 15 (1949): 517–36; Ralph J. McCracken and Douglas Helms, "Soil Surveys and Maps," in *The Literature of Soil Science,* ed. Peter McDonald (Ithaca, N.Y.: Cornell University Press, 1994), 275–311, esp. 301–4; Roy W. Simonson, "Use of Aerial Photographs in Soil Surveys," *Photogrammetric Engineering* 16 (1950): 308–15; and U.S. Department of Agriculture, Soil Conservation Service, *Aerial-Photo Interpretation in Classifying and Mapping Soils,* Agriculture Handbook no. 294 (Washington, D.C., 1966).

My principal general reference on remote sensing is Thomas M. Lillesand and Ralph W. Kiefer, *Remote Sensing and Image Interpretation,* 4th ed. (New York: John Wiley and Sons, 2000), esp. 89–93 for a discussion of spectral signatures. Useful references focused on remote sensing of soils include Maxwell B. Blanchard, Ronald Greeley, and Robert Goettelman, "Use of Visible, Near-Infrared, and Thermal Infrared Remote Sensing to Study Soil Moisture," *Proceedings of the International Symposium on Remote Sensing of Environment* 9 (1974): 693–700; L. F. Curtis, "Remote Sensing of Soil Moisture: User Requirements and Present Prospects," in *Remote Sensing of the Terrestrial Environment,* ed. R. F. Peel, L. F. Curtis, and E. C. Barrett (London: Butterworths, 1977), 143–58; Lillesand and Kiefer, *Remote Sensing and Image Interpretation,* 230–36; T. Schmugge, "Remote Sensing of Surface Soil Moisture," *Journal of Applied Meteorology* 17 (1978): 1549–57; and John R. Schott, *Remote Sensing: The Image Chain Approach* (New York: Oxford University Press, 1997), 196–211.

General references on remote sensing applications in agricultural include John E. Anderson, Robert L. Fischer, and Stephen R. Deloach, "Remote Sensing and Precision Agriculture: Ready for Harvest or Still Maturing?" *Photogrammetric Engineering and Remote Sensing* 65 (1999): 1118–23; M. S. Moran, "Landsat

TM and ETM+ Data for Resource Monitoring and Management," Basic Science and Remote Sensing Initiative, Michigan State University, http://www.bsrsi .msu.edu/~qi/landsat.html; M. S. Moran and others, "Combining Multifrequency Microwave and Optical Data for Crop Management," *Remote Sensing of Environment* 61 (1997): 96–109; M. S. Moran, Y. Inoue, and E. M. Barnes, "Opportunities and Limitations for Image-Based Remote Sensing in Precision Crop Management," *Remote Sensing of Environment* 61 (1997): 319–46; and Gail Wade, Rick Muehller, and Paul Cook, "AVHRR Map Products for Crop Condition Assessment: A Geographic Information Systems Approach," *Photogrammetric Engineering and Remote Sensing* 60 (1994): 1145–50.

General sources on precision agriculture include R. W. Gunderson and others, "The Collective: GIS and the Computer-Controlled Farm," *Geospatial Solutions* 10 (October 2000): 30–34; National Research Council, Board on Agriculture, Committee on Assessing Crop Yield: Site-Specific Farming, Information Systems, and Research Opportunities, *Precision Agriculture in the 21st Century: Geospatial and Information Technologies in Crop Management* (Washington, D.C.: National Academy Press, 1997); "Precision Agriculture: Information Technology for Improved Resource Use," *Agricultural Outlook* no. 250 (April 1998): 19–23; and J. K. Schueller, "Technology for Precision Agriculture," in *Precision Agriculture 1997*, ed. John V. Stafford (Oxford: BIOS Scientific Publishers, 1997), 33–44.

For information on agricultural applications of GPS, I relied on Thomas Bell, "Automatic Tractor Guidance Using Carrier-Phase Differential GPS," *Computers and Electronics in Agriculture* 25 (2000): 53–66; Wolfgang Lechner and Stefan Baumann, "Global Navigation Satellite Systems," *Computers and Electronics in Agriculture* 25 (2000): 67–85; and J. N. Wilson, "Guidance of Agricultural Vehicles: A Historical Perspective," *Computers and Electronics in Agriculture* 25 (2000): 3–9.

Sources concerned with the social impacts of precision agriculture include Don E. Albrecht, "The Correlates of Farm Concentration in American Agriculture," *Rural Sociology* 57 (1992): 512–20; Rick Welsh, "Vertical Coordination, Producer Response, and the Locus of Control over Agricultural Production Decisions," *Rural Sociology* 62 (1997): 491–507; Dan Whipple, "Seeds of Controversy," *Futurist* 33 (October 1998): 10–12; and Mary Zey-Ferrell and William Alex McIntosh, "Agricultural Lending Policies of Commercial Banks: Consequences of Bank Dominance and Dependency," *Rural Sociology* 52 (1987): 187–207.

Useful sources on the use of remote sensing to detect marijuana grows include C. S. T. Daughtry and C. L. Walthall, "Spectral Discrimination of *Cannabis sativa* L. Leaves and Canopies," *Remote Sensing of Environment* 64 (1998): 192–201; and appendix C of "2000 Counterdrug Research and Development Blueprint Update," Office of National Drug Control Policy, http://www.whitehousedrugpolicy.gov/ publications/scimed/blueprint00/appendixc.html.

For insights on constitutional and personal privacy issues raised by aerial imaging, see David Reed, "Thermal Surveillance: Poised at the Intersection of Technology and the Fourth Amendment," Computers and Law, University of Buffalo School of Law, http://wings.buffalo.edu/law/Complaw/ComplawPapers/ t.html; E. Terrence Slonecker, Denice M. Shaw, and Thomas M. Lillesand, "Emerging Legal and Ethical Issues in Advanced Remote Sensing Technology," *Photogrammetric Engineering and Remote Sensing* 64 (1998): 589–95; and Lisa J. Steele, "The View from on High: Satellite Remote Sensing Technology and the Fourth Amendment," *Berkeley Technology Law Journal* 6 (1991): 317–34.

Notes

39   "ever-normal granary": Baker, *Century of Service*, 158. In addition to price stabilization and conservation, New Deal farm programs included loans to farmers, drought relief, emergency marketing quotas, free food distribution to the poor, and programs to sell American farm products overseas.

39   "economic democracy": Baker, *Century of Service*, 159.

40   "Before we can . . . ": H. R. Tolley, "Aerial Photography and Agricultural Conservation," transcript, radio interview broadcast December 21, 1937, Department of Agriculture main library.

40   A planimeter is a mechanical device for measuring the area within an irregular closed curve; see D. H. Maling, *Measurements from Maps: Principles and Methods of Cartometry* (Oxford: Pergamon, 1989), 351–93.

40   "the simultaneous photographing . . . ": Tubis, "Aerial Photography," 23.

40   Coordination and training . . . : Procedures, operations, and developments discussed in this section are based on a variety of AAA documents as well as articles by USDA employees. Most noteworthy are Ralph Moyer, "Some Uses of Aerial Photographs in Connection with the Production and Marketing Programs of the U.S. Department of Agriculture," *Photogrammetric Engineering* 16 (1950): 305–7; Moyer, "Use of Aerial Photographs"; Department of Agriculture, Agricultural Adjustment Administration, North Central Region, *Procedure for Aerial Mapping in the State Office*, report NCR-State 104 (May 19, 1937); Department of Agriculture, Agricultural Adjustment Administration, Northeast Region, *County Procedure for Determination and Report of Performance (Applicable in Counties Using Aerial Photographs)*, report NER-329 (June 12, 1939); Department of Agriculture, Agricultural Adjustment Administration, Northeast Region, *Procedure for Determination and Report of Performance, Part II—Use of Aerial Photographs and Maps in Determining Performance*, report NER-219—Part II (June 20, 1938); Department of Agriculture, Agricultural Adjustment Administration, Southern Division, *Manual of Practice: Aerial Photography*, memorandum SRM-233 (November 23, 1938); Louis A. Woodward, "Aerial Photography as a Map Substitute," *Photogrammetric Engineering* 10 (1944): 68–81; and Marshall S. Wright, "The Aerial Photographic and

Photogrammetric Activities of the Federal Government," *Photogrammetric Engineering* 5 (1939): 168–76.

42 "in no event . . . ": Northeast Region, *County Procedure*, 7.

44 The relationship began . . . : Baldwin, Smith, and Whitlock, "Use of Aerial Photographs," 532–33.

44 When the United States . . . : Moyer, "Use of Aerial Photographs," 538.

44 For a concise history of military camouflage, see James F. Dunnigan and Albert A. Nofi, *Victory and Deceit: Dirty Tricks at War* (Fairfield, N.J.: William Morrow, 1995), 14–17. For an overview of infrared film, see Andrew Davidhazy, "Infrared Photography," in *The Focal Encyclopedia of Photography*, ed. Leslie Stroebel and Richard Zakia (Boston: Focal Press, 1993), 389–95.

45 "Natural grass . . . ": "Kodak Infrared Film Spots the 'Make Believe' of Enemy Camouflage" [advertisement], *United States News* 14 (March 12, 1943), 19.

46 Although most . . . : Page E. Truesdell, "Report of Unclassified Military Terrain Studies Section," *Photogrammetric Engineering* 19 (1953): 468–72.

47 For example, Landsat-7's . . . : See NASA, Earth Science Division, Ecosystem Science and Technology Branch, "Landsat 7," http://geo.arc.nasa.gov/sge/landsat/l7.html.

48 In addition to trouble-shooting . . . : Precision agriculture's unique cartographic genre includes the weed map, which recommends appropriately diverse applications of pesticide; for an example, see R. B. Brown and J.-P. G. A. Steckler, "Prescription Maps for Spatial Variable Herbicide Application in No-till Corn," *Transactions of the American Society of Agricultural Engineers* 38 (1995): 1659–66.

48 EC, which is . . . : N. R. Kitchen, K. A. Sudduth, and S. T. Drummond, "Soil Electrical Conductivity as a Crop Productivity Measure for Claypan Soils," *Journal of Production Agriculture* 12 (1999): 607–17; and E. D. Lund, C. D. Christy, and P. E. Drummond, "Applying Soil Electrical Conductivity Mapping to Improve the Economic Returns in Precision Farming" (paper presented at the 4th International Conference on Precision Agriculture, St. Paul, Minnesota, 1998).

48 "farming soils, not fields . . . ": P. M. Carr and others, "Farming Soils, Not Fields: A Strategy for Increasing Fertilizer Profitability," *Journal of Production Agriculture* 4 (1991): 57–61.

49 "It took more than . . . ": Pierre C. Robert, "Precision Agriculture: An Information Revolution in Agriculture" (paper presented at Agricultural Outlook Forum '98, Washington, D.C., February 23–24, 1999), 6.

49 For a survey of crop consultants' fees and activities, see R. J. Wright, T. A. DeVries, and S. T. Kamble, "Pest Management Practices of Crop Consultants in the Midwestern USA," *Journal of Production Agriculture* 10 (1997): 624–28.

49 For an intriguing description of one cutting crew's work and working conditions, see Shane DuBow, "Wheaties: Chasing the Ripening Harvest across America's Great Plains," *Harper's Magazine* 299 (August 1999): 33–44.

49 "the data will . . . " : Dennis Berglund, "Precision Agriculture: Past, Present, Future" (paper presented at Agricultural Outlook Forum '98, Washington, D.C., February 23–24, 1999), 2.

50 Even so, authorities . . . : "Scarecrow Points Way to Drugs for Police Officer in Helicopter," *New York Times,* June 30, 2000.

50 In the early 1990s . . . : D. S. Fung and R. Welch, "Modeling Cannabis Cultivation in North Georgia," *Technical Papers of the American Congress on Surveying and Mapping/American Society of Photogrammetry and Remote Sensing Annual Convention, 1994,* 1:217–20.

50 For concise descriptions of forward-looking infrared (FLIR) imaging, see Abe Dane, "Night Hawks," *Popular Mechanics* 171 (November 1994): 78–81; Lillesand and Kiefer, *Remote Sensing and Image Interpretation,* 361–62; and William B. Scott, "Second-Generation FLIRs Enhance Night Attack Systems," *Aviation Week and Space Technology* 138 (June 7, 1993): 143–45. For an example of FLIR detection of an indoor "grow," see Tim Bryant, "DEA Targets Indoor Pot Growers," *St. Louis Post-Dispatch,* May 9, 1993.

50 Recent postings . . . : See postings dated April 13 and 17, 2000, to the Security Forum of the Operation Overgrow bulletin board, http://www.hempcultivation.com/420/.

51 "undetected surveillance": Office of National Drug Control Policy, Counterdrug Technology Assessment Center, *Confronting Drug Crime and Abuse with Advanced Technology* (Washington, D.C., 2000), 13. The military used more sophisticated pilotless aircraft during the 2001 Afghanistan campaign; see James Dao, "U.S. Is Using More Drones, Despite Concern over Flaws," *New York Times,* November 3, 2001.

52 In rejecting Penny-Feeney's . . . : *Unites States v. Penny-Feeney,* 773 F. Supp. 220 (D. Haw. 1991) at 225–26.

52 Judges in the Seventh . . . : Douglas A. Kash, "Legal Development: Prewarrant Thermal Imaging as a Fourth Amendment Violation: A Supreme Court Question in the Making," *Albany Law Review* 60 (1997): 1295–1315; and NASA Office of Inspector General, "Remote Sensing and the Fourth Amendment: A New Law Enforcement Tool?" http://www.hq.nasa.gov/office/oig/hq/remote4.html.

53 "presumptively unreasonable": *United States v. Kyllo,* 140 F.3rd 1249 (9th Cir. 1998), quotation on 1253. Also see Bill Wallace, "Ninth Circuit Tosses Pot Conviction Case; Heat Detection Device Ruled Illegal," *San Francisco Chronicle,* April 8, 1998.

53 "Even if a thermal imager . . . ": *United States v. Kyllo,* 1254–55.

53 "measured the heat . . . ": Ibid., 1255.

53   "so revealing . . . ": *United States v. Kyllo*, 190 F.3rd 1041 (9th Cir. 1999), quotation on 1047; quotation is from the district court's original decision, which the appeals court now upheld.

53   "sense-enhancing . . . ": *Kyllo v. United States*, 150 L Ed 2d 94 (2001), quotation on 102.

53   "nothing more than . . . ": Ibid., 109.

53   "the device could not . . . ": Ibid., 112. Stevens included an appendix with examples of thermal images of Kyllo's home taken from a government exhibit presented at the trial; see ibid., 114.

53   "In the home . . . ": Ibid., 104.

53   "surprisingly broad": James J. Tomkovicz, quoted in Linda Greenhouse, "Justices Say Warrant Is Required in High-Tech Searches of Homes," *New York Times*, June 12, 2000.

54   The last time . . . : *Dow Chemical Company v. United States*, 106 S.Ct. 1819 (1986).

54   In ruling in favor . . . : Ibid., both quotations on 1823.

55   "the intimate activities . . . ": Ibid., 1826.

55   Moreover, Congress . . . : Ibid., 1827.

55   "highly sophisticated . . . ": Ibid.

55   After the *Wall Street Journal* . . . : Ross Kerber, "When Is a Satellite Photo an Unreasonable Search?" *Wall Street Journal*, January 27, 1998.

55   "high-tech military . . . ": The Libertarian Party memo "Do You Have Any Privacy Left When Big Brother Can Spy on You from Space—or through Your Walls" appeared on many Web sites, including the Canada Offshore Services, http://www.can-offshore.com/.

55   I doubt that many . . . : After the *Arizona Republic* reprinted Kerber's article, Pearson replied to his criticism in a letter to the editor; see Rita R. Pearson, "Tax-Payers Should Applaud High-Tech Enforcement of the Law," *Arizona Republic*, February 20, 1998.

56   Space Imaging no doubt . . . : Dan Leger, "Sizing Up the Competition: Earth Information Takes Commercial Intelligence to a New Level," *Imaging Notes* 15 (May/June 2000): 22–23. The courts might also need to rule on the vendor's liability when criminals, terrorists, or foreign governments use satellite imagery for illegal purposes. Would an imagery retailer be no more liable in these cases than, say, an Internet service provider or the phone company?

56   "highly sophisticated surveillance . . . ": *Dow Chemical Company v. United States*, 1827. For a review of terraserver.com, see Bill Siuru, "Spy Satellite Photography on the Internet," *Electronics Now* 70 (April 1999): 48–50.

Chapter 4. Tinder, Technology, and Tactics

General Sources

Basic references on the physics and chemistry of forest fuel and wildland fire include Margaret Fuller, *Forest Fires: An Introduction to Wildland Fire Behavior, Management, Firefighting, and Prevention* (New York: John Wiley and Sons, 1991), esp. 34–48, 69–80; and Stephen J. Pyne, Patricia L. Andrews, and Richard D. Laven, *Introduction to Wildland Fire*, 2nd ed. (New York: John Wiley and Sons, 1996), 3–168.

Sources on the use of GIS in modeling wildland fire include Vincent G. Ambrosia and others, "An Integration of Remote Sensing, GIS, and Information Distribution for Wildfire Detection and Management," *Photogrammetric Engineering and Remote Sensing* 64 (1998): 977–85; Maria J. Vasconcelos and D. Phillip Guertin, "FIREMAP—Simulation of Fire Growth with a Geographic Information System," *International Journal of Wildland Fire* 2 (1992): 87–96; and Rj Zimmer, "GIS and the Wildfires," *Professional Surveyor* 20 (December 2000): 55–59.

Principal sources on the use of satellite remote sensing in detecting wildland fire are Robert E. Burgan, Robert W. Klaver, and Jacqueline M. Klaver, "Fuel Models and Fire Potential from Satellite and Surface Observations," *International Journal of Wildland Fire* 8 (1998): 159–70; Donald R. Cahoon, Jr., and others, "Wildland Fire Detection from Space: Theory and Application," in *Biomass Burning and Its Inter-Relationships with the Climate System*, ed. John L. Innes, Martin Beniston, and Michel M. Verstraete (Dordrecht: Kluwer, 2000), 151–69; Emilio Chuvieco and M. Pilar Martin, "Global Fire Mapping and Fire Danger Estimation Using AVHRR Images," *Photogrammetric Engineering and Remote Sensing* 60 (1994): 563–70; Andrew J. L. Harris, "Towards Automated Fire Monitoring from Space: Semi-Automated Mapping of the January 1994 New South Wales Wildfires Using AVHRR Data," *International Journal of Wildland Fire* 6 (1996): 107–16; and Gary L. Hufford and others, "Use of Real-time Multisatellite and Radar Data to Support Forest Fire Management," *Weather and Forecasting* 13 (1998): 592–605.

Notes

57 For further information on the Cerro Grande Fire, see Department of the Interior, *Cerro Grande Prescribed Fire: Independent Review Board Report to the Secretary of the Interior*, May 26, 2000, http://www.doi.gov/secretary/reviewteamfinal.htm; and Michael Janofsky, "Parched U.S. Faces Worst Year for Fires since Mid-80s," *New York Times*, August 3, 2000.

58 For more information on the 1996 Mesa Verde National Park fire, see Joe Garner, "Mesa Verde Fire Tops $1.5 Million," *Denver Rocky Mountain News*, August 27, 1996; and Robert Kowalski, "Fire Damages Famed Petroglyph Stone Peeling at Mesa Verde Site," *Denver Post*, August 31, 1996.

58 Two weeks later . . . : "Colorado Fire Nears Old Indian Cliff Dwellings," *New York Times,* July 25, 2000; and Mindy Sink, "Scientists Unearth Artifacts a Step Ahead of Firefighters," *New York Times,* August 27, 2000.

59 During the 1930s, . . . : For examples, see *Fire Control Handbook, Section II: Presuppression* (n.p.: U.S. Forest Service, North Pacific Region, 1935), 7–7u; and L. G. Hornby, *Forest Fire Control Planning in the Northern Rocky Mountain Region* (n.p.: U.S. Forest Service, Rocky Mountain Forest and Range Experiment Station, 1936), 50–56.

60 Contemporary fuel maps . . . : For an example, see James K. Brown and Dennis G. Simmerman, *Appraising Fuels and Flammability in Western Aspen: A Prescribed Fire Guide,* USDA Forest Service Intermountain Research Station, General Technical Report Series, no. INT-205 (August 1986).

60 For further information on the National Fire Danger Rating System, see Pyne, Andrews, and Laven, *Introduction to Wildland Fire,* 155–59. For a description of the statistical rationale and computer program, see Patricia L. Andrews and Larry S. Bradshaw, *FIRES: Fire Information Retrieval and Evaluation System—A Program for Fire Danger Rating Analysis,* USDA Forest Service Intermountain Research Station, General Technical Report Series, no. INT-367 (August 1997).

62 "the fires literally . . . ": Quoted in Michael Paterniti, "Torched," *Outside* 20 (September 1995): 57–68, 154–56; quotation on 66.

62 For details on early fire-spread models, see Richard C. Rothermel, *How to Predict the Spread and Intensity of Forest and Range Fires,* USDA Forest Service Intermountain Forest and Range Experiment Station, General Technical Report Series, no. INT-143 (June 1983).

63 "upon the skill . . . ": Ibid., 1.

64 For a concise account of California's use of GIS in controlling wildland fire, see Tim Walsh, "In the Line of Fire," *Geospatial Solutions* 10 (June 2000): 24–29.

64 The fire burned . . . : Data are from Sarah G. Allen and others, "Interactive Application of GIS During the Vision Wildfire at Point Reyes National Seashore" (paper presented at the 1996 Arc/Info Users Conference, Palm Springs, Cal., May 20–24, 1996), National Park Service, http://www.nps .gov/gis/apps/pore/gisndx.htm.

65 "great tools for public relations": Quoted in the minutes of the National Park Service GIS Workshop, George Wright Society Meeting, Albuquerque, NM, March 20, 1997, National Park Service, http://www.nps.gov/gis/ education/gwsociety_notes.html.

65 Back in the 1980s . . . : Jay Lee, "Analyses of Visibility Sites on Topographic Surfaces," *International Journal of Geographical Information Systems* 5 (1991): 413–29.

65 For further information on POES, see Arthur P. Cracknell, *The Advanced*

Very High Resolution Radiometer (AVHRR) (London: Taylor and Francis, 1997), 5–26, 36–43.

65 For further information on GOES, see W. Paul Menzel and James F. W. Purdom, "Introducing GOES-I: The First of a New Generation of Geostationary Operational Environmental Satellites," *Bulletin of the American Meteorological Society* 75 (1994): 757–81.

66 This markedly higher orbit . . . : At 60 degrees from the equator resolution falls to approximately 5 miles (8 km). See Gary L. Hufford and others, "Detection and Growth of an Alaskan Forest Fire Using GOES-9 3.9 m Imagery," *International Journal of Wildland Fire* 9 (1999): 129–36.

66 My discussion of the Millers Reach fire is based on Hufford and others, "Use of Real-time Multisatellite Data."

68 "an ultimate detection time . . . ": "Space Imaging Techniques and Fire Management (Interim Report)," NOAA CEOS Disaster Information Server, http://www.ceos.noaa.gov/drafts/firerpt.html (site discontinued).

68 Equally intriguing . . . : Joel S. Levine and others, "FireSat and the Global Monitoring of Biomass Burning," in *Biomass Burning and Global Change*, vol. 1, *Remote Sensing, Modeling and Inventory Development, and Biomass Burning in Africa*, ed. Joel S. Levine (Cambridge, Mass.: MIT Press, 1996), 107–29; and NASA Langley Research Center, "1998 Langley Research Center Implementation Plan, Section II: Scientific Roles in Support of Earth Science Enterprise,"http://larcip.larc.nasa.gov/1998/section2.html.

68 According to research . . . : See, for example, Cahoon and others, "Wildland Fire Detection."

69 "a constellation of sixty satellites": Joel S. Levine, telephone conversation with author, October 4, 2000.

70 Another element is GOES . . . : Burgan, Klaver, and Klaver, "Fuel Models and Fire Potential"; and Dennis S. Mileti, *Disasters by Design: A Reassessment of Natural Hazards in the United States* (Washington, D.C.: Joseph Henry Press, 1999), 181. For a modified, May 2000 version of the paper by Burgan, Klaver, and Klaver, see the USDA Forest Service, http://www.fs.fed.us/land/wfas/firepot/fpipap.htm.

70 As in camouflage detection . . . : Relative greenness is based on the Normalized Difference Vegetation Index (NDVI), which compares reflectance measurements in visible red and near-infrared AVHRR bands observed for the pixel over a two-week period. Relative greenness compares the pixel's current NDVI to the maximum and minimum NDVI values observed since January 1, 1989. For formulas and a fuller explanation, see Robert E. Burgan and Roberta A. Hartford, *Monitoring Vegetation Greenness with Satellite Data,* USDA Forest Service Intermountain Research Station, General Technical Report Series, no. INT-297 (May 1993).

70 For a description of the system as well as current and archived maps, see

the Oklahoma Fire Danger Model, http://radar.metr.ou.edu/agwx/fire/. For a concise description of Mesonet and efforts to make younger residents aware of weather hazards, see Renee A. McPherson and Kenneth C. Crawford, "The Earthstorm Project: Encouraging the Use of Real-Time Data from the Oklahoma Mesonet in K-12 Classrooms," *Bulletin of the American Meteorological Society* 77 (1996): 749–61.

72 Equally inefficient . . . : Andrew C. Revkin, "Now Preventing Forest Fires: Smokey Goat," *New York Times,* June 13, 2000.

Chapter 5. Weather Eyes

General Sources

Key sources on satellite weather surveillance include W. Paul Menzel and others, "Application of GOES-8/9 Soundings to Weather Forecasting and Nowcasting," *Bulletin of the American Meteorological Society* 79 (1998): 2059–77; W. Paul Menzel and James F. W. Purdom, "Introducing GOES-I: The First of a New Generation of Geostationary Operational Environmental Satellites," *Bulletin of the American Meteorological Society* 75 (1995): 757–81; and Space Systems-Loral, *GOES I-M DataBook* (August 31, 1996), NASA Goddard Space Flight Center, http://rsd.gsfc.nasa.gov/goes/text/goes.databook.html.

Sources on the development of forecast models include Mark DeMaria, "A History of Hurricane Forecasting for the Atlantic Basin, 1920–1995," in *Historical Essays on Meteorology, 1919–1995,* ed. James Rodger Fleming (Boston: American Meteorological Society, 1996), 263–305; and Colin J. McAdie and Miles B. Lawrence, "Improvements in Tropical Cyclone Track Forecasting in the Atlantic Basin, 1970–98," *Bulletin of the American Meteorological Society* 81 (2000): 989–97.

Useful references on the development of weather radar include Elbert W. Friday, Jr., "The Modernization and Associated Restructuring of the National Weather Service: An Overview," *Bulletin of the American Meteorological Society* 75 (1994): 43–52; and Robert J. Serafin and James W. Wilson, "Operational Weather Radar in the United States: Progress and Opportunity," *Bulletin of the American Meteorological Society* 81 (2000): 501–18.

Key sources for lightning detection are Hugh J. Christian and others, "Lightning Detection from Space (A Lightning Primer)," NASA Global Hydrology and Climate Center, http://wwwghcc.msfc.nasa.gov/lisotd_old.html; K. L. Cummins and others, "A Combined TOA/MDF Technology Upgrade of the US National Lightning Detection Network," *Journal of Geophysical Research D: Atmospheres* 103 (April 27, 1998): 9035–44; NOAA National Weather Service Training Center, "Lightning Detection Systems," http://www.nwstc.noaa.gov/d.MET/Lightning/detection.htm; and Richard E. Orville, Ronald W. Henderson, and Lance F. Bosart, "An East Coast Lightning Detection Network," *Bulletin of the American Meteorological Society* 64 (1983): 1029–37.

Notes

74 In *Isaac's Storm* . . . : Erik Larson, *Isaac's Storm: A Man, a Time, and the Deadliest Hurricane in History* (New York: Random House, 1999).

74 Turn-of-the-century forecasters . . . : Mark Monmonier, *Air Apparent: How Meteorologists Learned to Map, Predict, and Dramatize Weather* (Chicago: University of Chicago Press, 1999), 10–15.

75 The antagonist . . . : Sebastian Junger, *The Perfect Storm* (New York: W. W. Norton, 1997).

75 This one, later named . . . : NOAA Marine Prediction Center, "The Marine Prediction Center and 'The Perfect Storm,'" http:www.mpc.ncep.noaa .gov/perfectstorm/mpc_ps_intro.html; and NOAA National Climatic Data Center, "The Perfect Storm," http://www.ncdc.noaa.gov/ol/satellite/ satelliteseye/cyclones/pfctstorm91/pfctstorm.html.

75 For a summary of the effects of the Halloween Storm of 1991, see Robert D. McFadden, "Report on Damage in Storm Is Grim," *New York Times*, November 3, 1991, sec. 1.

76 American and Canadian . . . : NOAA National Climatic Data Center, "Unnamed Hurricane, 1991," http://www.ncdc.noaa.gov/ol/satellite/ satelliteseye/hurricanes/unnamed91/unnamed91.html.

76 As hurricanes go . . . : Ed Rappaport, "Hurricane Andrew, 16–28 August 1992: Preliminary Report (updated 10 December 1993)," NOAA National Hurricane Center (Tropical Prediction Center), http://www.nhc.noaa .gov/1992andrew/html.

77 According to Louis Uccellini . . . : "NOAA Meteorologists Recall Drama of Forecasting 'The Perfect Storm,'" *NOAA Magazine*, June 29, 2000, http://www.noaanews.noaa.gov/stories/s451.htm.

78 "if there was a choice . . . ": Robert C. Sheets, "The National Hurricane Center—Past, Present, and Future," *Weather and Forecasting* 5 (1990): 185–232; quotation on 201.

78 Although GOES satellites . . . : U.S. General Accounting Office, *National Oceanic and Atmospheric Administration: National Weather Service Modernization and Weather Satellite Program* (statement of Joel C. Willemssen), report no. T-AIMD-00-86 (March 29, 2000).

79 Three imaging schedules . . . : See NOAA Office of Satellite Operations, "GOES Schedules and Scan Sectors," http://www.oso.noaa.gov/goes/ schd-sector/index.htm.

80 Able to scan . . . : According to Daphne S. Zaras at the National Severe Storms Laboratory (NSSL), "Super Rapid Scan is difficult to describe. The time interval between images is extremely irregular, in order to maintain

scanning of the rest of the CONUS (during each hour) and full disk (every 3 hours) while doing shorter interval scanning over a 'mesoscale' (1 km × 1 km) area. The size of the super rapid scan area is conveniently the size of the area affected by the 'Super Outbreak' of tornados April 3–4, 1974." Zaras, "GOES-IM Weather Satellites," NOAA National Severe Storms Center, http://www.nssl.noaa.gov/~zaras/Goes/delux2/scan3.html.

81 As a result, hurricane . . . : AMS Council, "Policy Statement on Hurricane Research and Forecasting," *Bulletin of the American Meteorological Society* 81 (2000): 1341–46.

81 For information on the Tropical Rainfall Measuring Mission, see NASA's TRMM Web site, http://trmm.gsfc.nasa.gov/.

82 Among the TRMM . . . : Riko Oki, Kinji Furukawa, and Shuji Shimizu, "Preliminary Results of TRMM: Part I, a Comparison of PR with Ground Observations," *Marine Technology Science Journal* 32 (winter 1998–99): 13–23.

82 This map gained . . . : William Booth and Mary Jordan, "Hurricane Rips Miami Area, Aims at Gulf States," *Washington Post,* August 25, 1992.

82 The following April . . . : Linda Martin, "National Weather Service Gets Advanced Doppler Radar," *Miami Herald,* April 15, 1993.

84 For example, a 1996 . . . : J. Madeleine Nash, "Unraveling the Mysteries of Twisters," *Time* 147 (May 20, 1996): 58–62; and National Science and Technology Council, Committee on Environment and Natural Resources, Subcommittee on Natural Disaster Reduction (SNDR), "Agency Success Stories in Natural Disaster Reduction," http://www.usgs.gov/sndr/success.html.

84 By contrast, a NOAA . . . : Curtis L. Marshall, "Strategic Planning in the National Weather Service: Case Study (June 9, 1997)," National Partnership for Reinventing Government, http://govinfo.library.unt.edu/npr/library/news/ntlwpln.html; and NOAA National Weather Service, "Reinvention Goals for 2000: Status—August 2000," http://www.nws.noaa.gov/npr5.html.

84 These and other claims . . . : Question 0200 of the WeatherQuiz, KRT Direct, April 8, 1999, http://www.krtdirect.com/weatherquiz/.

85 Because radar maps . . . : See, for example, Caren Marzban and Gregory J. Stumpf, "A Neural Network for Tornado Prediction Based on Doppler Radar-Derived Attributes," *Journal of Applied Meteorology* 35 (1996): 617–26.

85 Developed, tested . . . : "Reinvention Goals for 2000."

85 At a June 1999 hearing . . . : House Committee on Science, Subcommittee on Energy and Environment, *Tornadoes: Understanding, Modeling, and Forecasting Supercell Storms—Hearing before the Subcommittee on Energy and Environment and the Subcommittee on Basic Research,* 106th Cong., 1st sess., June 16, 1999; quotation on 37.

85 "Doppler radars . . . ": Ibid., 38.

85 Most of Oklahoma's . . . : The 180-kilometer range is a median distance reflecting the average experience of forecasters and researchers. NEXRAD Panel, National Weather Service Modernization Committee, Commission on Engineering and Technical Systems, National Research Council, *Toward a New National Weather Service: Assessment of NEXRAD Coverage and Associated Weather Services* (Washington, D.C.: National Academy Press, 1995), 12–17.

86 "a challenging event . . . ": Quoted in Jessica Gregg McNew, "Record Tornado Season Has Forecasters, Scientists Gathering for Answers," *DisasterRelief,* August 19, 1998, http://www.disasterrelief.org/Disasters/980819forum/. For additional information about the storm, see NOAA National Weather Service, Southern Region, *The Hall/White County Tornado, March 20, 1998,* National Weather Service Southern Region Service Assessment Report (May 1998), http://www.srh.noaa.gov/ftproot/msd/html/assessment/hallwhit.htm.

86 According to a 1995 . . . : NEXRAD Panel, *Toward a New National Weather Service,* 16.

86 Moreover, the 15 percent . . . : Ibid., 21–23.

87 At thirty locations . . . : Edward J. Hopkins, "Wind Profiler," University of Wisconsin Department of Meteorology, http://www.meteor.wisc.edu/~hopkins/aos100/wxi-prfl.htm; and the NOAA Profiler Network pages on the Forecast Systems Laboratory's Demonstration Division Web site, http://www.profiler.noaa.gov/jsp/index.jsp.

88 "the computer models . . . ": Quoted in Margot Ackley, Douglas W. van de Kamp, and Seth I. Gutman, "Profiling," NOAA Forecast Systems Laboratory, Demonstration Division, http://www.profiler.noaa.gov/labreview/1999/sld023.htm.

89 Although the Wind Profilers . . . : The Wind Profiler network will become officially "operational" when NOAA's research arm converts all profilers to an exclusive, authorized frequency, and the National Weather Service assumes operating responsibility. Margot Ackley, NOAA Forecast Systems Laboratory, telephone conversation with author, November 28, 2000.

90 To get a sharper picture . . . : See the NOAA National Weather Service Training Center Web site, http://www.nwstc.noaa.gov/d.MET/Lightning/Forecast_use.htm.

91 For information on NOAA's Ground-Based GPS Integrated Precipitable Water Vapor Demonstration Network, see the NOAA Forecast Systems Laboratory Web site, http://www.gpsmet.noaa.gov/jsp/index.jsp; and Steven Businger and others, "The Promise of GPS in Atmospheric Monitoring," *Bulletin of the American Meteorological Society* 77 (1996): 5–18.

91 For a sampling of the trials and triumphs of AWIPS, see U.S. General Ac-

counting Office, *Weather Forecasting: NWS Has Not Demonstrated That New Processing System Will Improve Mission Effectiveness,* report no. AIMD-96-29 (February 29, 1996); Jim Reed, "Weather's New Outlook," *Popular Science* 252 (August 1997): 56–62; and "NOAA Installs New Weather Forecasting System," *Bulletin of the American Meteorological Society* 80 (1999): 2121–22.

Chapter 6. Wire Loops and Traffic Cams

General Sources

Principal sources for traffic engineering are John E. Baerwald, ed., *Traffic Engineering Handbook,* 3rd ed. (Washington, D.C.: Institute of Traffic Engineers, 1965); John D. Edwards, Jr., ed., *Transportation Planning Handbook,* 2nd ed. (Washington, D.C.: Institute of Transportation Engineers, 1999); and William R. McShane and Roger P. Roess, *Traffic Engineering* (Englewood Cliffs, N.J.: Prentice-Hall, 1990).

Key references for video-controlled traffic signals are Carlo S. Regazzoni, Gianni Fabri, and Gianni Vernazza, eds., *Advanced Video-Based Surveillance Systems* (Boston: Kluwer Academic Publishers, 1999); Panos G. Michalopoulos, "Vehicle Detection Video Through Image Processing: The Autoscope System," *IEEE Transactions on Vehicular Technology* 40 (1991): 21–29; and Panos G. Michalopoulos and Kevin Samartin, "Recent Developments of Advanced Technology in Freeway Management Projects," *Traffic Engineering and Control* 39 (1998): 160–65.

Sources for electronic toll collection include Lazar N. Spasovic and others, "Primer on Electronic Toll Collection Technologies," *Transportation Research Record,* no. 1516 (Washington, D.C.: National Academy Press, 1995), 1–10; and ETTM On the Web, which provides detailed information on E-ZPass, including Michael Kolb's detailed and richly illustrated essay, "ETC in Focus: The Port Authority of NY and NJ," http://www.ettm.com/focus_pa/etcfocus_panynj.html.

For insights on automated driverless transportation, I relied on Steven Ashley, "Smart Cars and Automated Highways," *Mechanical Engineering* 120 (May 1998) 58–62; Glen Hiemstra, "Driving in 2020: Commuting Meets Computing," *Futurist* 34 (September/October 2000): 31–34; James H. Rillings, "Automated Highways," *Scientific American* 277 (October 1997): 80–85; and Horst Strobel, *Computer Controlled Urban Transportation* (Chichester, U.K.: John Wiley and Sons, 1982), esp. 355–411. For diverse views of the future of automated roadways, I recommend José M. del Castillo, David J. Lovell, and Carlos F. Daganzo, "Technical and Economic Viability of Automated Highway Systems: Preliminary Analysis," *Transportation Research Record,* no. 1588 (Washington, D.C.: National Academy Press, 1997), 130–36; and Steven F. Shladover, "Why We Should Develop a Truly Automated Highway System," *Transportation Research Record,* no. 1651 (Washington, D.C.: National Academy Press, 1998), 66–73.

Notes

94 For additional information about "road tubes" and other techniques for measuring traffic volume, see James H. Kell and Wolfgang S. Homburger, "Traffic Studies," in *Traffic Engineering Handbook*, 260–309, esp. 268–72. Oddly, the fifth edition of the *Handbook*, published in 2000, omits discussion of road tubes and other sensors, which are still widely used for traffic studies.

94 For guidelines used in computing splits and setting phases for isolated or nonsynchronized signals, see Herbert J. Klar, "Traffic Signalization," in *Traffic Engineering Handbook*, 382–458, esp. 404–10; and McShane and Roess, *Traffic Engineering*, 380–413.

94 For examples of time-space diagrams in traffic-signal synchronization, see Klar, "Traffic Signalization," 413–33; McShane and Roess, *Traffic Engineering*, 529–48; Peter S. Parsonson, *Signal Timing Improvement Practices*, National Cooperative Highway Research Program, Synthesis of Highway Practice report no. 172 (Washington, D.C.: Transportation Research Board, 1992), 31–45; and Jearl Walker, "How to Analyze a City Traffic-Light System from the Outside Looking In," *Scientific American* 248 (March 1983): 138–45.

96 For examples of "double-alternate" timing and other synchronization strategies for two-way traffic, see McShane and Roess, *Traffic Engineering*, 543–48.

96 For information on ramp-metering strategies for freeways, see ibid., 617–32.

97 Although the detector . . . : See Gaylon R. Claiborne, "Induction Vehicle Detectors for Traffic Actuated Signals," *Traffic Engineering* 33 (December 1962): 21–25; and Indu Sreedevi and Justin Black, "Inductive Loop Detectors," University of California, Berkeley, Partners for Advanced Transit and Highways ITS Decision Database, http://www.path.Berkeley.edu/~leap/TTM/Incident_Manage/Detection/loopdet.html.

97 For detailed information on the underlying physics, design, installation, and performance of loop detectors, see James H. Kell, Iris J. Fullerton, and Milton K. Mills, *Traffic Detector Handbook*, 2nd ed., Federal Highway Administration report no. FHWA-IP-90-002 (Washington, D.C., 1990), esp. 7–15, 105–12, and 133–34. The handbook is available at the Federal Highway Administration Safety and Operations Electronic Reading Room, http://www.fhwa.dot.gov/tfhrc/safety/pubs/Ip9000/intro.htm.

98 For discussion of the relative advantages of various shapes of loop detectors, see ibid., 73–79; and Sreedevi and Black, "Inductive Loop Detectors."

99 Reliable counts are . . . : For an overview of traffic counting in Delaware and a map of detector locations, see Ardeshir Faghri, Martin Glaubitz, and Janaki Parameswaran, "Development of Integrated Traffic Monitoring

System for Delaware," *Transportation Research Record*, no. 1536 (Washington, D.C.: National Academy Press, 1996), 40–44.

99 Toronto and other . . . : "Stop on the Dots," *Cyclometer*, no. 61 (May—June 1997), http://www.city.scarborough.on.ca/4service/cyclom61.htm (site discontinued).

100 For discussion of detector-based strategies to lower the likelihood of catching vehicles in the dilemma zone, see Kell, Fullerton, and Mills, *Traffic Detector Handbook*, 70–72, 81–88.

100 In the Texas Panhandle . . . : Beth Wilson, "Eye in the Sky: Camera Sees All, Clicks All," *Amarillo Globe-News*, March 4, 2000; and David Miller, Texas Department of Transportation, Amarillo District, telephone conversation with the author, January 16, 2001.

100 For additional information on the principles of machine vision, see Bin Ran and Henry X. Liu, "Development of Vision-Based Vehicle Detection and Recognition System for Intelligent Vehicles," *Transportation Research Record*, no. 1679 (Washington, D.C.: National Academy Press, 1999), 130–38; and Mark R. Stevens and J. Ross Beveridge, *Integrating Graphics and Vision for Object Recognition* (Boston: Kluwer Academic Publishers, 2000).

101 Not all traffic . . . : This section is based on my January 17, 2001, interview with traffic control room operator Harry Carlson and Luis Perez, "Synchronized Stopping: Computers Control Traffic Lights in Downtown Syracuse," *Syracuse Post-Standard*, May 5, 2000.

102 MIST is one of several traffic control software applications sold to state and local transportation departments. The developer, PB Farradyne, provides further information on its Web site, http://www.pbfi.com. For a general assessment of traffic control software, see Darcy Bullock and Chris Hendrickson, "Advanced Software Design and Standards for Traffic Signal Control," *Journal of Transportation Engineering* 118 (May/June 1992): 430–38.

102 For an insightful examination of the role of traffic signaling in improving air quality, see Committee for the Study of Impacts of Highway Capacity Improvements on Air Quality and Energy Consumption, *Expanding Metropolitan Highways: Implications for Air Quality and Energy Use*, Transportation Research Board Special Report 245 (Washington, D.C.: National Academy Press, 1995), esp. 38–86.

103 Motorists curious . . . : Counts are based on index maps displayed on January 24, 2001. For a fuller discussion of Internet delivery of traffic information, see Nicoline N. M. Emmer, "Web Maps and Road Traffic," in *Web Cartography: Developments and Prospects*, ed. Menno-Jan Kraak and Allan Brown (London: Taylor and Francis, 2001), 159–70; and Glenn D. Lyons and Mike McDonald, "Traveller Information and the Internet," *Traffic Engineering and Control* 39 (1998): 24–31.

104 Each icon is . . . : For further discussion of the relationship between web cams and interactive maps, see Mark Monmonier, "Webcams, Interactive Index Maps, and Our Brave New World's Brave New Globe," *Cartographic Perspectives* no. 37 (fall 2000): 12–25.

105 Washington transportation . . . : David Noack, "Puget Sound's Web Cam Traffic Network: DOT Offers Online Traffic News" (February 6, 1998), Editor and Publisher's interactive media Web site [now http://www .editorandpublisher.com], http://www.mediainfo.com/ephome/Interactive 98/stories/020698c9.htm. Also see Washington State Department of Transportation Puget Sound Traffic Conditions, "Questions and Answers," http:www.wsdot.wa.gov/PugetSoundTraffic/faq/.

105 Web traffic increased . . . : George Foster, "For Some Web Sites, a Lot of Traffic Means Lots of Online Traffic," *Seattle Post-Intelligencer,* December 19, 1999.

105 Tacoma's city-run . . . : Martha Modeen, "TV Carries Scenes from DOT Traffic Cameras," *Tacoma News Tribune,* November 2, 2000.

106 Named Partners in Motion . . . : See Marcia Myers, "Region's Road Warriors Battle-Test New Weapon," *Baltimore Sun,* January 4, 2000; and Alice Reid, "High-Tech Traffic Help Is En Route," *Washington Post,* August 10, 1998. Web sites offering the traffic reports include *NBC4.com* and *washingtonpost.com* as well as the firm's own SmarTraveler.com.

106 Unlike Puget Sound's . . . : For example, the "live video" of the Woodrow Wilson Bridge presents a mildly jerky "streaming video" image in a RealPlayer viewer, which is refreshed every two minutes with a new file encoded at 15 frames per second but displayed at a lower rate. See "Wilson Bridge Live Video," *washingtonpost.com,* http://www.washingtonpost.com/ wp-srv/local/traffic/wash1.htm.

106 The number of traffic cameras in the greater Washington area seems likely to increase. As of January 2000, Virginia's Department of Transportation planned to operate 110 cameras by June, its Maryland counterpart had 42 cameras statewide, and Montgomery County, Maryland, planned to add to its 83 cameras. See Leslie Koren, "New VDOT Website Shows Drivers the Way," *Washington Times,* January 6, 2000.

106 In addition to . . . : For examples, see Paul Bradley, "Online Road Views Aim to Ease Commute," *Richmond Times-Dispatch,* January 6, 2000; Diane Granat, "Traffic Busters," *Washingtonian* 34 (September 1999): 86– 93; Joey Ledford, "'Personalized Traffic'—How to Avoid the Rush," *Atlanta Constitution,* September 15, 1999; and Bill Steward, "High Tech Employed to Outfox Snarls," *The Oregonian,* June 19, 2000. Also see Beth Cox, "Wireless Highway Data Services Planned," *InternetNews— E-Commerce News,* May 3, 2000, http://www.internetnews.com/ec-news/ article/0,,4_353451,00.html. Microsoft introduced a similar service for Seattle drivers; see Brier Dudley, "Microsoft Offers Drivers High-Tech

Traffic Alerts," *seattletimes.com*, October 24, 2001, http://seattletimes
.nwsource.com/html/businesstechnology/134354442_msn16.html.

106 A camera mounted . . . : For examples, see Stacey Burns, "Run a Light?
Ticket's in the Mail," *Tacoma News Tribune*, August 24, 2000; and Marty
Katz, "Frown, You're on Red-Light Camera," *New York Times*, October 11,
2000.

107 Most states . . . : Jennifer Jones, "Market for Red-Light-Running Systems
Speeds Up" (June 7, 1999), *FCW.COM*, http://www.civic.com/civic/
articles/1999/CIVIC_060799_57.asp. For a concise overview of digital
license plate readers, see Catherine Greenman, "Zeroing in on the Suspicious Number above the State Motto," *New York Times*, October 25,
2001.

107 . . . an alarming increase . . . : Richard A. Retting, Robert G. Ulmer, and
Allan F. Williams, "Prevalence and Characteristics of Red Light Running
Crashes in the United States," *Accident Analysis and Prevention* 31 (1999):
687–94.

107 Studies indicate . . . : Richard A. Retting and Allan F. Williams, "Red Light
Cameras and the Perceived Risk of Being Ticketed," *Traffic Engineering
and Control* 41 (2000): 224–27.

108 "What's going on . . . ": Quoted in Aron Miller, "Use of Stoplight Cameras
Causes Swirl of Debate," *Ventura County Star*, May 30, 2000.

108 "general surveillance . . . ": Quoted in William Claiborne, "California Assembly Puts Stop to Red Light Cameras," *Washington Post*, May 10, 1998.

108 "It's not a new . . . ": Claire E. House, "Legislatures Debate Merits of Stoplight Photos" (July 1999), *Government Computer News*, http://www.gcn
.com/state/vol5_no7/news/375–1.html.

108 My hunch . . . : Portland, Oregon, for example, won legislative approval
after officials agreed to a camera that only photographs violators. See
Associated Press, "Portland Keeps Its Eye on Red Lights," *Seattle Post-
Intelligencer*, January 22, 1999.

108 A vehicle approaching . . . : For general information on this kind of
transponder, see Jian John Lu, Michael J. Rechtorik, and Shiyu Yang, "Automatic Vehicle Identification Technology Applications to Toll Collection
Services," *Transportation Research Record*, no. 1588 (Washington, D.C.: National Academy Press, 1997), 18–25.

108 Market-based . . . : For a glimpse of this pay-as-you-go future, see Richard
H. M. Emmerink, *Information and Pricing in Road Transportation* (Berlin:
Springer, 1998); and Charles Komanoff and Michael J. Smith, "It Isn't Too
Many Double-Parkers; It's Too Many Cars," *New York Times*, October 16,
1999. Another likely proving ground is Singapore, a conveniently com-
pact country that is familiar with regimentation; see A. P. Gopinath
Menon, "ERP in Singapore—a Perspective One Year On," *Traffic Engi-
neering and Control* 41 (February 2000): 40–45. Although road pricing is

unlikely to affect North America in the near future, Europe is ahead in other approaches to electronic traffic control as well. For examples, see Linda L. Brown and others, "Innovative Traffic Control: Technology and Practice in Europe—Executive Summary," *ITE Journal* 70 (2000): 45–49.

109 Bolstered by GPS . . . : For examples, see Bill McGarigle, "Full Stop," *Government Technology* 14 (May 2000): 50–54.

109 "Smart cars . . . ": For information about collision avoidance systems, see Sandy Graham, "Smart Cars Open Way for Safer, Faster Travel," *Traffic Safety* (March/April 2000): 17–19; and Peter Godwin, "The Car That Can't Crash," *New York Times Magazine*, June 11, 2000.

109 Equally certain . . . : For further insight on privacy concerns, see Sheri Alpert and Kingsley E. Haynes, "Privacy and the Intersection of Geographical Information and Intelligent Transportation Systems," in *Proceedings of the Conference on Law and Information Policy for Spatial Databases,* ed. Harlan J. Onsrud (Orono, Maine: National Center for Geographic Information and Analysis, University of Maine, 1995), 198–211.

Chapter 7. Crime Watch

General Sources

Central references on video surveillance include David Lyon, *The Electronic Eye: The Rise of Surveillance Society* (Minneapolis: University of Minnesota Press, 1994), 67; Clive Norris, Jade Moran, and Gary Armstrong, eds., *Surveillance, Closed Circuit Television, and Social Control* (Aldershot, U.K.: Ashgate, 1998); and Carlo S. Regazzoni, Gianni Fabri, and Gianni Vernazza, eds., *Advanced Video-Based Surveillance Systems* (Boston: Kluwer, 1999), 95–105.

General sources covering crime mapping include Arthur Getis and others, "Geographic Information Science and Crime Analysis," *URISA Journal* 12 (spring 2000): 7–14; Keith Harries, *Mapping Crime: Principle and Practice*, research report NCJ 178919 (Washington, D.C.: National Institute of Justice, 1999); Jack Maple and Chris Mitchell, *The Crime Fighter: Putting the Bad Guys Out of Business* (New York: Doubleday, 1999); Phillip D. Phillips, "A Prologue to the Geography of Crime," *Proceedings of the Association of American Geographers* 4 (1972): 86–91; and Arthur H. Robinson, *Early Thematic Mapping in the History of Cartography* (Chicago: University of Chicago Press, 1982), 156–70.

Notes

110 In 1791, he published . . . : Jeremy Bentham, *"Panopticon": or, the Inspection-House; containing the idea of a new principle of construction applicable to any sort of establishment, in which persons of any description are to be kept under inspection; and in particular to Penitentiary-houses, Prisons, Houses of in-*

dustry, Workhouses, Poor Houses, Manufacturies, Madhouses, Lazarettos, Hospitals, and Schools; with a plan of management adopted [sic] *to the principle; in a series of letters, written in the year 1787, from Crechoff in White Russia, to a friend in England* (London: T. Payne, 1791). Note that the drawing in figure 7.1 is from Bentham's collected writings, published posthumously by his literary executor.

111 "panoptic gaze" . . . "panoptic power": For examples, see Arturo Escobar, *Encountering Development: The Making and Unmaking of the Third World* (Princeton, N.J.: Princeton University Press, 1995), 155–56; N. Katherine Hayles, "The Materiality of Informatics," *Configurations* 1 (1993): 147–70, esp. 150–52; and Lyon, *Electronic Eye*, 67. As numerous authors point out, commercial interests as well as governments seek social control, albeit for different reasons and usually in different ways. The concept of the panoptic gaze is generally attributed to Michel Foucault; see Foucault, *Discipline and Punish: The Birth of the Prison*, trans. Alan Sheridan (New York: Pantheon, 1978; Vintage Books, 1995), 200–216.

112 For a sense of Britain's commitment to video surveillance, see Jason Ditton and Emma Short, "Evaluating Scotland's First Town Centre CCTV Scheme," in *Surveillance, Closed Circuit Television, and Social Control,* ed. Norris, Moran, and Armstrong, 155–73; and Nicholas R. Fyfe and Jon Bannister, "City Watching: Closed Circuit Television Surveillance in Public Spaces," *Area* 28 (1996): 37–46.

112 A survey by the California Research Bureau . . . : Marcus Nieto, *Public Video Surveillance: Is It an Effective Crime Prevention Tool?* report no. CRB-97-005 (Sacramento, Cal.: California Research Bureau, California State Library, 1997).

113 Baltimore, for instance . . . : A 1997 *New York Times* article labeled Baltimore's setup "one of the country's most ambitious video surveillance programs." See Michael Cooper, "With Success of Cameras, Concerns over Privacy," *New York Times,* February 5, 1997.

113 "if we start going . . .": Quoted in David Kocieniewski, "Television Cameras May Survey Public Places," *New York Times,* October 6, 1996.

113 "raises the Orwellian specter . . .": Quoted in David Kocieniewski, "Police to Press Property-Crime Fight and Install Cameras," *New York Times,* February 5, 1997.

114 Intent on documenting . . . : See New York Civil Liberties Union, "NYCLU Surveillance Camera Project," http://www.nyclu.org/surveillance.html. For the map, a more detailed explanation, and an interpretation, see Mediaeater, "NYC Surveillance Camera Project," http://www.mediaeater .com/cameras/.

115 For examples of social science critiques of CCTV, see William Bogard, *The Simulation of Surveillance: Hypercontrol in Telematic Societies* (Cambridge: Cambridge University Press, 1996); and Stephen Graham, "Spaces of

Surveillant Simulation: New Technologies, Digital Representations, and Material Geographies," *Environment and Planning D: Society and Space* 16 (1998): 483–504.

115 Evaluation studies are . . . : For insights, see David Skinns, "Crime Reduction, Diffusion, and Displacement: Evaluating the Effectiveness of CCTV," in *Surveillance, Closed Circuit Television, and Social Control,* ed. Norris, Moran, and Armstrong, 175–88; and Nick Tilley, "Evaluating the Effectiveness of CCTV Schemes," in *Surveillance, Closed Circuit Television, and Social Control,* ed. Norris, Moran, and Armstrong, 139–53.

115 . . . a majority of Britons . . . : Although how one phrases the question can have a substantial effect on the percentage of respondents with a favorable impression of CCTV, those who support the technology are a clear majority. For an examination of opinion surveys, see Jason Ditton, "Public Support for Town Centre CCTV Schemes: Myth or Reality?" in *Surveillance, Closed Circuit Television, and Social Control,* ed. Norris, Moran, and Armstrong, 221–28.

115 . . . face-recognition algorithms . . . : For a glimpse of the enabling technology, see Clive Norris, Jade Moran, and Gary Armstrong, "Algorithmic Surveillance: The Future of Automated Visual Surveillance," in *Surveillance, Closed Circuit Television, and Social Control,* ed. Norris, Moran, and Armstrong, 255–75; and P. Remagnino and others, "Automatic Visual Surveillance of Vehicles and People," in *Advanced Video-Based Surveillance Systems,* 95–105. For more detailed information on performance, see Michael Negin and others, "An Iris Biometric System for Public and Personal Use," *Computer* 33 (February 2000): 70–75; Alex Pentland and Tanzeem Choudhury, "Face Recognition for Smart Environments," *Computer* 33 (February 2000): 50–55; P. Jonathon Phillips and others, "An Introduction to Evaluating Biometric Systems," *Computer* 33 (February 2000): 56–63; and Rahul Sukthankar and Robert Stockton, "Argus: The Digital Doorman," *IEEE Intelligent Systems* 16 (March/April 2001): 14–19.

116 The landmark case is . . . : *Katz v. United States,* 389 U.S. 347 (1967). A right to privacy exists in a situation when a citizen expects privacy and society at large considers that expectation reasonable.

116 If you think people who complain . . . : Erin Texeira, "Man Killed by Stray Bullet on New Year's," *Los Angeles Times,* January 2, 2001.

116 At midnight . . . : "Reveler's Gunfire Likely Cause of Girl's Death," *Houston Chronicle,* January 3, 2001.

116 Their patent application . . . : The U.S. Patent and Trademark Office awarded patent no. 5,973,998 ("Automatic Real-Time Gunshot Locator and Display System") to Robert L. Showen and Jason W. Dunham on October 26, 1999.

117 The process pinpoints gunshots . . . : Police in Redwood City, California, tested ShotSpotter by firing blank rounds at known locations throughout

a test area. According to police captain Jim Granucci, 80 percent of all the test shots were located within 15 yards of the known locations. Marshall Wilson, "Redwood City Gunshot Locator Passes Tests—Gets Trial Run," *San Francisco Chronicle*, July 11, 1996.

118   "What would you do if an officer . . . ": Trilon Technology, "Frequently Asked Questions," *ShotSpotter: The 9-1-1 Gunfire Alert System*, http://www .shotspotter.com/g-faq.html. The quotation is part of the answer to the question "Is ShotSpotter intended to prevent gunfire or to assist police in arresting those who shoot their firearms?"

118   . . . a ten-week trial in 1995: For details, see Marshall Wilson, "Redwood City Endorses Gunshot Locator System," *San Francisco Chronicle*, March 18, 1997; and Wilson, "Redwood City Gunshot Locator Passes Tests."

118   When a gunshot is detected . . . : Bobby Cuza, "Gadgets on Patrol against Crime," *Los Angeles Times,* June 9, 2000; and Willoughby Mariano, "Way to Locate Sources of Gunfire Shown," *Los Angeles Times,* December 30, 1999.

119   "the year's most innovative . . . ": "Using Technology in the Fight against Random Gunfire," *Microsoft PressPass,* April 3, 2000, http://www.microsoft .com/presspass/features/2000/04-03shotspotter.asp.

119   Although computers expedite . . . : For a concise discussion of early maps of crime data, see Phillips, "Geography of Crime;" and Robinson, *Early Thematic Mapping*, 156–70. Both authors examine maps of area data, but neither mentions "pin maps." For an overview of research and educational issues in contemporary GIS-based crime analysis, see Arthur Getis and others, "Geographic Information Science and Crime Analysis," *URISA Journal* 12 (spring 2000): 7–14.

119   The International Association of Chiefs of Police . . . : Michael D. Maltz, "From Poisson to the Present: Applying Operations Research to Problems of Crime and Justice," *Journal of Quantitative Criminology* 12 (1996): 3–61.

120   Perhaps the greatest impetus . . . : Robert K. Bratt, Joseph R. Lake, Jr., and Theresa Whistler, "Implementation of GIS at Local Law Enforcement Agencies," *Proceedings of the 1995 Arc/Info Users Conference*, http://www .esri.com/library/userconf/proc95/to200/p185.html.

120   As part of its outreach . . . : Harries, *Mapping Crime*. Distribution data from Jolene Hernon, National Institute of Justice, e-mail communication with the author, March 23, 2001.

121   The Chicago Police Department used . . . : Keith Harries warns that hot-spot ellipses should always be compared with the underlying point pattern. He also warns that hot-spot mapping, which focuses largely on street crime, might distract from white-collar crime. See Harries, *Mapping Crime*, 113–18.

121   For further information on ComStat, see Harries, *Mapping Crime*, 78–80; and Philip G. McGuire, "The New York Police Department ComStat

Process," in *Analyzing Crime Patterns: Frontiers of Practice*, ed. Victor Goldsmith and others (Thousand Oaks, Calif.: Sage Publications, 2000), 11–22.

122 . . . he gave an insightful answer . . . : Raymond Dussault, "Jack Maple: Betting on Intelligence," *Government Technology* 12 (April 1999): 26–28; quotation on 27. Also see Jack Maple and Chris Mitchell, *The Crime Fighter: Putting the Bad Guys Out of Business* (New York: Doubleday, 1999).

124 . . . complaints against the police: "Compensating Abner Louima," *New York Times*, March 24, 2001. Louima, a Haitian immigrant, was the victim of a vicious attack by a police officer who shoved a broom handle up his rectum. Respect for police plummeted, several officers went to prison, and the city and the police union agreed to pay over $8 million in damages to settle Louima's lawsuit, thereby avoiding another embarrassing trial.

Chapter 8. Keeping Track

General Sources

Key sources for legal and administrative information on Megan's Law and sex-offender databases are Paul Koenig, "Does Congress Abuse Its Spending Clause Power by Attaching Conditions on the Receipt of Federal Law Enforcement Funds to a State's Compliance with 'Megan's Law'?" *Journal of Criminal Law and Criminology* 88 (1998): 721–65; and Bonnie Steinbock, "A Policy Perspective: Megan's Law—Community Notification of the Release of Sex Offenders," *Criminal Justice Ethics* 14 (summer-fall 1995): 4–9.

Critiques of the constitutionality and effectiveness of Megan's Laws include James Bickley and Anthony R. Beech, "Classifying Child Abusers: Its Relevance to Theory and Clinical Practice," *International Journal of Offender Therapy and Comparative Criminology* 45 (2001): 51–69; Alexander D. Brooks, "The Legal Issues: Megan's Law—Community Notification of the Release of Sex Offenders," *Criminal Justice Ethics* 14 (summer-fall 1995): 12–16; Charles J. Dlabik, "Convicted Sex Offenders: Where Do You Live? Are We Entitled to Know? A Year's Retrospective of Ex Post Facto Challenges to Sex Offender Community Notification Laws," *Nova Law Review* 22 (1998): 585–644; R. Karl Hanson, "What Do We Know about Sex Offender Risk Assessment?" *Psychology, Public Policy, and Law* 4 (1998): 50–72; and Philip H. Witt and others, "Sex Offender Risk Assessment and the Law," *Journal of Psychiatry and Law* 24 (1996): 343–77.

Sources of information on satellite tracking of offenders include Joseph Hoshen, Jim Sennott, and Max Winkler, "Keeping Tabs on Criminals," *IEEE Spectrum* 32 (February 1995): 26–32; Linda Johansson, "Invisible Chains," *UNESCO Courier* 51 (June 1998): 13–14; Dee Reid, "High-tech House Arrest: Electronic Ankle Bracelets Used to Monitor Prisoners under Home Detention," *Technology Review* 89 (July 1986): 12–14; and Robert E. Sullivan, Jr., "Reach Out and Guard

Someone: Using Phones and Bracelets to Reduce Prison Overcrowding," *Rolling Stone*, November 29, 1990, 51.

Notes

126 Within a week fifteen hundred people . . . : James Barron, "Vigil for Slain Girl, 7, Backs a Law on Offenders," *New York Times*, August 3, 1994. Actually a collection of laws regulating sex offenders, New Jersey's Megan's Law included a community notification statute based on a 1990 Washington State law. For an overview, see Joseph F. Sullivan, "Whitman Approves Stringent Restrictions on Sex Criminals," *New York Times*, November 1, 1994.

126 And those in Tier Three . . . : The law required the attorney general to draw up notification guidelines, which were published in late December; see Michael Booth, "Who Must Register and Who Should Know?" *New Jersey Law Journal*, December 26, 1994, 16.

127 "release relevant information . . . ": "Megan's Law," *Congressional Record* 142 (daily ed.; May 7, 1996): H4451–52; quotation on H4451.

127 For example, a May 1999 survey . . . : Devon B. Adams, "Summary of State Sex Offender Registry Dissemination Procedures," *Bureau of Justice Statistics Fact Sheet* publication no. NCJ 177620 (August 1999).

127 A June 1999 survey . . . : Jane A. Small, "Who Are the People in Your Neighborhood? Due Process, Public Protection, and Sex Offender Notification Laws," *New York University Law Review* 74 (1999): 1451–93.

127 By contrast, a May 2001 visit . . . : National Consortium for Justice Information and Statistics, "State Sex Offender Registry Websites," http://www.search.org/policy/nsor/state_webs.asp.

128 "does not maintain . . . ": "In Brief: The District," *Washington Post*, March 11, 2001.

128 In his April 2001 ruling . . . : Connecticut's attorney general asserted his intent to appeal the ruling, and as of May 8, 2001, the state's online sex-offender registry (www.state.ct.us/dps/Sor.htm) was still operating without any apparent recognition of risk level. But under increased court pressure, the state took its registry offline on May 18; see Paul Zielbauer, "Hartford's Sex-Offender Registry Shut Down after Judge's Order," *New York Times*, May 19, 2001. Meanwhile, state officials were deliberating a change in policy; see Stacey Stowe, "Talks Set to Begin on Sex Offender Site," *New York Times*, April 8, 2001, Connecticut Weekly section; and "Mend Megan's Law" [editorial], *Hartford Courant*, April 18, 2001.

128 "updates this information . . . ": Quotations in this and the following paragraph are from New York State Division of Criminal Justice Services, "Sex Offender Registry," http://criminaljustice.state.ny.us/nsor/index.htm, which also includes an explanation of New York's Sex Offender Registration Act. For information on the court ruling, see David W. Chen, "Federal

Judge Bars New York's Method of Classifying Sex Offenders," *New York Times*, May 8, 1998.

130 "naming and shaming": For an example, see "'Website Plan to Name Sex Offenders," *Herald* (Glasgow), November 15, 2000.

131 A prospective viewer . . . : See Office of the Attorney General, State of California Department of Justice, "Registered Sex Offenders (Megan's Law)," http://caag.state.ca.us/megan/index.htm.

131 For a description of the Fairfield, California, maps and restrictions on their use, see City of Fairfield, Police Department Sex Offender Database, http://www.ci.fairfield.ca.us/police/disclaimer.asp; and the Fairfield Police Department News Media Release "Megan's Law/Sex Registrant Maps on Police Website," December 11, 2000, http://www.ci.fairfield.ca.us/announcements/files/PressRelease/PoliceDepartment/381568636/PR0000.htm. For the map infigure 8.1, see specifically http://www.ci.fairfield.ca.us/police/map.asp?school_id=5.

132 More troublesome is the need . . . : For an overview of legal and ethical issues surrounding community notification, see Scott Matson, "Community Notification and Education," Center for Sex Offender Management, April 2001, http://www.csom.org/pubs/notedu.html.

132 "guarded villages": Etzioni suggests allowing offenders to live comparatively normal lives, hold steady jobs, and share social responsibilities within the guarded perimeter and "protective custody" of a community offering freedom from intrusion and shaming as long as they did not leave. See Amitai Etzioni, *The Limits of Privacy* (New York: Basic Books, 1999), 73–74.

132 For discussion of satellite tracking as a remedy for domestic violence as well as an alternative to parole for sex offenders, see David R. Kazak, "Home Monitoring Doesn't Stop Crime in Homes," *Chicago Daily Herald*, February 5, 2001; and Lori Montgomery and Daniel LeDuc, "Killing of Frederick Boy Stirs Debate about Freeing Molesters," *Washington Post*, January 21, 2001.

133 Satellite tracking is a significant advance . . . : Perhaps the earliest proposal for a location-tracking system required a network of pole-mounted receivers similar to the ShotSpotter system discussed in chapter 7; see Joseph A. Meyer, "Crime Deterrent Transponder System," *IEEE Transactions on Aerospace and Electronic Systems* 7 (1971): 2–22.

133 More advanced systems . . . : George Lane, "State to Test Satellite-based Tracking of Parolees," *Denver Post*, August 28, 1999. For discussion of distance restrictions, see Bill McGarigle, "The Walls Have Come Down," *Government Technology*, May 1997, http://www.govtech.net/publications/gt/1997/may/may1997-geoinfo/may1997-geoinfo.phtml.

133 Compared to incarceration . . . : Tracking systems are usually leased, at a daily cost per detainee ranging from $7.50 to $18.00, according to various

sources; see Lane, "State to Test Satellite-based Tracking"; McGarigle, "The Walls Have Come Down"; Montgomery and LeDuc, "Killing of Frederick Boy Stirs Debate"; and Graham Rayman, "Monitoring Domestic Violence," *New York Newsday,* July 23, 1999, Queens edition.

134 "high-tech ball and chain": Heather Hayes, "The Long Arm of the Law," *FCW.com (Federal Computer Week),* December 6, 1999, http://www.fcw.com/civic/articles/1999/CIVIC_120699_43.asp. Information about SMART is from Pro Tech's Web site (www.ptm.com).

134 Zoning can also restrict . . . : McGarigle, "The Walls Have Come Down." Building interiors are occasionally dead zones for wireless telephony; see Robert K. Morrow, Jr., and Theodore S. Rappaport, "Getting In," *Wireless Review* 17 (March 1, 2000): 42–44.

135 "Third-generation" systems . . . : Max Winkler, "Walking Prisons: The Developing Technology of Electronic Controls," *The Futurist* 27 (July/August 1993): 34–36.

135 For a description of the "Autoinjector," "Poison Vial," and similarly sinister implants, see Michael LaBossiere, "New Cyber Equipment for 2300 ad and Cyberpunk," *One Man's Views of 2300 ad,* http://www.crosswinds.net/~anch_stevec/newcyber.htm. For more contemporary approaches, see Hoshen, Sennott, and Winkler, "Keeping Tabs on Criminals"; and Ed Grabowski, "Electronic Monitoring of Prisoners" (November 1996), Computers and Law, University of Buffalo School of Law, http://wings.buffalo.edu/law/Complaw/CompLawPapers/grabowsk.html (site discontinued).

135 "invisible electronic fence": Canine systems typically use an electric shock to reinforce an audible warning; see Pati Simon Gelfman, "Invisible Fence for Dogs," *Family Handiman* 38 (January 1988): 44–45.

136 . . . to help railroads avoid rear-end collisions: Christine White, "On-Road, On-Time, and On-Line," *Byte* 20 (April 1995): 60–66; and Tom Sullivan, "PTC: Is FRA Pushing Too Hard?" *Railway Age* 200 (August 1999): 49–57.

136 . . . let an insurer monitor their driving: William Siuru, "OnStar to the Rescue," *Electronics Now* 69 (September 1998): 61–62. In 1998 the Progressive Insurance Company started to explore a role for GPS-based monitoring in setting auto insurance rates; see Greg Hassell, "Cheap Insurance Comes at a Price," *Houston Chronicle,* November 3, 1999, business section.

136 "apparatus for tracking . . . ": The U.S. Patent and Trademark Office issued patent no. 5,629,678 ("Personal Tracking and Recovery System") to Paul A. Gargano and others on May 13, 1997. The quotation is from the abstract of the patent. Also see Mark Harrington, "Alliance Boosts Monitoring System," *Newsday,* September 20, 2000; and Chris Trumble, "GPS Tracking Is Only Skin Deep," *Smart Computing* 11 (April 2000): 6.

136 Civil libertarians promptly warned . . . : Kurt Kleiner, "They Can Find You: GPS Implants Will Make It Easy to Pinpoint People," *New Scientist* 165 (January 8, 2000): 7. Also see Richard Stenger, "Tiny Human-Borne Monitoring Device Sparks Privacy Fears," *CNN.com,* December 20, 1999, http://www.cnn.com/1999/TECH/ptech/12/20/implant.device/index .html.

136 "new locational e-slavery": Susan L. Cutter, "President's Column—Big Brother's New Handheld," *AAG Newsletter* 36 (May 2001): 3–4; quotation on 3.

136 What loving son or daughter . . . : The preorder price of $299 did not include tax and shipping; see Digital Angel, "Preorder and Reserve," http:// www.digitalangel.net/contact/preorder.htm.

136 Offered in early 2001 . . . : Based on ADS press releases, a November 1, 2000, news story on *WorldNetDaily.com* described "a miniature sensor device designed to be implanted just under the skin" as well as the firm's plans to produce a "more sophisticated version . . . powered electro-mechanically through muscle movement." See "Digital Angel Unveiled: Human-Tracking Subdermal Implant Technology Makes Debut," archived at Direct Source Radio, http://www.directsourceradio.com/links/11012000/ 110120004.html.

136 "implantable triggerable transmitting device": Quotations and figure 8.3 are from the application for U.S. Patent no. 5,629,678, granted May 13, 1997.

137 "branding and stalking": Quotations are from Jerome E. Dobson, "What Are the Ethical Limits of GIS?" *GeoWorld* 13 (May 2000): 24–25.

138 In 1996 the FCC . . . : Under the original mandate, carriers had to be able to estimate location to within 125 meters for 67 percent of callers by October 2001, and for all callers by the end of 2002. See Dee Ann Divis, "Privacy Matters: Data, Mobile Commerce, GIS," *Geospatial Solutions* 10 (October 2000): 18–20. Extended 911 wireless regulations are more complex than most writers suggest, and the FCC has revised them several times since 1996. When carriers failed to meet an October 2001 deadline, the FCC granted a generous extension but imposed various intermediate milestones intended to encourage nearly complete compliance by the end of 2005. See Suzanne King and David Hayes, "Deadline Extended for 911 Technology," *Kansas City Star,* October 9, 2001; and "FCC Acts on Wireless Carrier and Public Safety Requests Regarding Enhanced Wireless 911 Services." *FCC News,* October 5, 2001, http://www.fcc.gov/Bureaus/Wireless/ News_Releases/2001/ nrwl0127.html.

138 The original order let . . . : Kevin McLaughlin, "Wireless Carriers Announce Location Tech Plans," *Business 2.0,* November 10, 2000, http:// www.business2.com/content/channels/technology/2/11/10/22478 .htm.

138 For examples of location-based services, see Jay Benson, "LBS Technology Delivers Information Where and When It's Needed," *Business Geographics* 9 (February 2001): 20–22; and Jonathan W. Lowe, "The Power of Babble: Congregating around LBS," *Geospatial Solutions* 11 (February 2001): 46–51.

139 Loss of privacy is inevitable . . . : For hypothetical examples of privacy issues raised by wireless tracking based on GPS, see Mike France and Dennis K. Berman, "Big Brother Calling: Location Technology in Devices Such as Cell Phones," *Business Week* no. 3700 (September 25, 2000): 92–98; and Robert Poe, "Location Disorder," *Business 2.0*, March 26, 2001, http://www.business2.com/technology/2001/03/28411.htm. For wider insights on the effects of GPS and mobile telephony on personal privacy, see Roger Clarke, "Person-Location and Person-Tracking: Technologies, Risks, and Policy Implications," *Roger Clarke's Dataveillance and Information Privacy Pages* (hosted by Australian National University), http://www.anu.edu.au/people/Roger.Clarke/DV/PLT.html.

Chapter 9. Addresses, Geocoding, and Dataveillance

General Sources

Sources on the use and social implications of clustering include Jon Goss, " 'We Know Who You Are and We Know Where You Live': The Instrumental Rationality of Geodemographic Systems," *Economic Geography* 71 (1995): 171–98; Erik Larson, *The Naked Consumer: How Our Private Lives Become Public Commodities* (New York: Henry Holt and Company, 1992); Michael J. Weiss, *The Clustered World: How We Live, What We Buy, and What It All Means about Who We Are* (Boston: Little, Brown, 2000); and Michael J. Weiss, *The Clustering of America* (New York: Harper and Row, 1988).

Key sources on data privacy include Roger A. Clarke, "Information Technology and Dataveillance," *Communications of the Association for Computing Machinery* 31 (1988): 498–512; Michael R. Curry, "The Digital Individual and the Private Realm," *Annals of the Association of American Geographers* 87 (1997): 681–99; Jon Goss, "Marketing the New Marketing," in *Ground Truth: The Social Implications of Geographic Information Systems*, ed. John Pickles (New York: Guilford Press, 1995), 130–70; Gary T. Marx, *Undercover: Police Surveillance in America* (Berkeley: University of California Press, 1988); Harlan J. Onsrud, Jeff P. Johnson, and Xavier R. Lopez, "Protecting Personal Privacy in Using Geographic Information Systems," *Photogrammetric Engineering and Remote Sensing* 60 (1994): 1083–95; and Harlan J. Onsrud, "The Tragedy of the Information Commons," in *Policy Issues in Modern Cartography*, ed. D. R. Fraser Taylor (New York: Pergamon, 1998), 141–58.

Notes

141   According to recent estimates . . . : Tabulations are from ESRI Business Information Solutions, "Free Zip Code Report" (based on 2000 projections),http://infods.com/freedata. In early 2002, ESRI Business Information Solutions acquired the marketing services division of CACI, which had developed ACORN.

142   Two separate previews actually . . . : Cluster descriptions and quotations are from ClaritasExpress, "You Are Where You Live," http://www.cluster2.claritas.com/YAWYL.

142   . . . reports only the top five . . . : A list might include fewer than five clusters because the Web site does not list lifestyle types that characterize less than 5 percent of an area's population.

142   Although "Winner's Circle" might connote . . . : Advertising consultant Robin Page crafted names for PRIZM's clusters; see Philip H. Dougherty, "ZIP Area: Key to Markets," *New York Times,* July 17, 1980.

144   . . . named ACORN . . . : Clusters and quotations from CACI, "IDS On the Web," http://www.infods.com.

145   Each piece of mail . . . : For insights on the advantages of custom-screened mailing lists, see Christopher Carey, "More and More Companies Are Reaching Their Customers through Direct Mail," *St. Louis Post-Dispatch,* December 7, 1998; and Amy Merrick, "New Population Data Will Help Marketers Pitch Their Products," *Wall Street Journal,* February 14, 2001. According to Merrick, Hyundai pays $200,000 annually for customized mailing lists that maximize its response rate for test-drive promotions.

145   Political consultants are equally eager . . . : For discussion of targeted mailing in political campaigns, see David Beiler, "Precision Politics," *Campaigns & Elections* 10 (February/March 1990): 33–36, 38; Ron Faucheux, "Hitting the Bull's Eye," *Campaigns & Elections* 20 (July 1999): 20–25; and Leslie Wayne, "Voter Profiles Selling Briskly as Privacy Issues Are Raised," *New York Times,* September 9, 2000.

146   "Harvard-educated computer whiz": Weiss, *Clustering of America,* 10.

146   "accounted for 87 percent . . . ": Ibid., 11. For a concise introduction to the use of factor analysis in detecting and describing lifestyle clusters, see David J. Curry, *The New Marketing Research Systems: How to Use Strategic Database Information for Better Marketing Decisions* (New York: John Wiley and Sons, 1993), 203–6.

146   PRIZM's success is apparent . . . : National Decision Systems introduced MicroVision in 1990. VNU, the Dutch company that acquired Claritas in 1986 and National Decision Systems in 1997, merged NDS into Claritas in 1999. For further information on Claritas, see "Company Info—Claritas History," http://www.claritas.com/index.html. For a discussion of clustering outside North America, see Weiss, *Clustered World.*

147 For additional information on the U.S. Postal Service's marketing of National Change of Address (NCOA) data to private-sector mailing-list companies, see "Move Update: Keeping Up with Your Moving Customers," U.S. Postal Service booklet (August 2000); and "Panel: USPS Violates Privacy and Law by Making Public Change-of-Address Orders," *Direct Marketing* 55 (February 1993): 10–11.

147 "'black box' mechanics . . .": Goss, "'We Know Who You Are," 187.

147 Defined more broadly . . . : Definitions and populations are from U.S. Census Bureau, "Geographic Terms and Concepts," http://www.census.gov/geo/www/tiger/glossry2.html.

147 Blocks aggregate conveniently . . . : The "optimum" populations of block groups and census tracts are fifteen hundred and four thousand, respectively. Ibid.

148 This assumption is crucial . . . : For a concise overview of the inverse relationship between the geographic precision of small-area data and the demographic precision of detailed cross-tabulations, see John Kavaliunas, "Get Ready to Use Census 2000 Data," *Marketing Research* 12 (fall 2000): 42–43.

148 A computer calculates geographic . . . : See, for example, ESRI BIS, "Demographic Update Methodology," http://www.infods.com/methodology/.

149 Although the agency never discloses . . . : As part of the "Fifth Count" round of tabulations for the 1970 census, the Census Bureau released estimated counts based on the long-form questionnaires filled out by 5-, 15-, and 20-percent samples of households. Estimates focused on race, age, sex, marital status, income, education, and condition of housing and were distributed on magnetic tape. Fifth Count File 5A contained estimates for three-digit ZIP Codes for the entire country, and Fifth Count File 5B contained estimates for approximately 12,500 five-digit ZIP codes within metropolitan areas. See National Archives and Records Administration, Center for Electronic Records, Reference Report no. 11, http://www.nara.gov/nara/electronic/cen1970.html.

149 "the sweetheart deal of the century": Edward Spar, president of Market Statistics, quoted in Larson, *Naked Consumer,* 45.

151 The Internal Revenue Service's SOI Products & Services directory is available online: http://www.irs.gov/tax_stats/.

151 "largest collection of U.S. consumer . . . ": "Selling Is Getting Personal," *Consumer Reports* 65 (November 2000): 16–20; quotation on 18. Also see Robert O'Harrow, Jr., "Eye at the Keyhole: Privacy in the Digital Age," *Washington Post,* March 8, 1998.

151 "new resident direct marketing": Quotations are from Moving Targets, "How We Target Mailings to the Latest and Best New Movers," http://www.movingtargets.com/moreinfo2.html.

151 . . . Claritas clients find . . . : Susan Mitchell, "Birds of a Feather," *Ameri-*

can Demographics 17 (February 1995): 40–48; and Tom Spencer and
David Tedrow, "Capture Customers for Life," *Business Geographics* 8 (September 2000): 28–30.

151　. . . an experienced snoop can dig up dirt . . . : Marx, *Undercover*, 210–11.

151　Home telephone numbers . . . : Robert O'Harrow, Jr., "A Hidden Toll on
Free Calls: Lost Privacy," *Washington Post*, December 19, 1999; and Gary
Angel and Joel Hadary, "Using Card Transaction Data," *American Demographics* 20 (August 1998): 38–41.

151　For an overview of address-matching technology and applications, see
William J. Drummond, "Address Matching: GIS Technology for Mapping
Human Activity Patterns," *Journal of the American Planning Association* 61
(1995): 240–51.

152　Web browsing is also under surveillance . . . : For examples, see Amy Harmon, "Software to Track E-Mail Raises Privacy Concerns," *New York
Times*, November 22, 2000.

152　"Geotargeting": Stefanie Olsen, "Yahoo Ads Close in on Visitors' Locale,"
CNET News.com, June 27, 2001, http://news.com.com/2100-1023-269155
.html.

152　For a concise explanation of cookies, see Glenn Fleishman, "Fresh from
Your Browser's Oven," *New York Times*, July 15, 1999.

152　. . . customize the banner ads . . . : Bob Tedeschi, "Critics Press Legal Assault on Tracking of Web Users," *New York Times*, February 7, 2000.

152　Largely benign, cookies can reveal . . . : Lance Gay, "Drug Czar Asks Congress to Reopen the 'Cookie' Jar," *Syracuse Post-Standard*, July 16, 2000.

152　"cache attack": Ian Austen, "Study Finds That Caching by Browsers Creates a Threat to Surfers' Privacy," *New York Times*, December 14, 2000.

152　"systematic use of personal data . . . ": Clarke, "Information Technology
and Dataveillance," 499.

152　In a capitalist milieu . . . : Goss, "We Know Who You Are," 192–93.

153　. . . critic of GIS-based behavioral modeling . . . : For example, Stephen
Graham, "Surveillant Simulation and the City: GIS and Urban Panopticism" (paper presented at the National Center for Geographic Information and Analysis Conference on Spatial Technologies, Geographic
Information, and the City, Baltimore, Md., September 9–11, 1996,
http://www.ncgia.ucsb.edu/conf/BALTIMORE/authors/graham/paper
.html).

153　. . . widespread use of integrated systems . . . : See Curry, "The Digital Individual and the Private Realm."

153　For examples of clusters that reinforce an address's prestige, see Beth Daley, "Residents Ride Latest Wave of New Numbers," *Boston Globe*, February 2, 1998; and Emily Wax, "Mail, the Great Equalizer," *New York Times*,
July 12, 1998, Queens edition.

153 ... integrating diverse databases fosters . . . : See Onsrud, "Information Commons."

153 "what is agreed to be 'smart business practices' . . . ": Harlan J. Onsrud, "Ethical Issues in the Use and Development of GIS," *Proceedings of GIS/LIS '97*, 400–401; quotation on 401.

Chapter 10. Case Clusters and Terrorist Threats

General Sources

Sources addressing environmental "right-to-know" laws include Bradley C. Karkkainen, "Information as Environmental Regulation: TRI and Performance Benchmarking, Precursor to a New Paradigm," *Georgetown Law Journal* 89 (2001): 257–370; and Sidney M. Wolf, "Fear and Loathing about the Public Right to Know: The Surprising Success of the Emergency Planning and Community Right-to-Know Act," *Journal of Land Use and Environmental Law* 11 (1996): 217–324.

Basic works on disease mapping are Andrew B. Lawson and Fiona L. R. Williams, *An Introductory Guide to Disease Mapping* (New York: John Wiley, 2001); and Steven M. Teutsch and R. Elliott Churchill, eds., *Principles and Practice of Public Health Surveillance* (New York: Oxford University Press, 2000).

Useful references on the use of GIS in public health include Keith C. Clarke, Sara L. McLafferty, and Barbara J. Tempalski, "On Epidemiology and Geographic Information Systems: A Review and Discussion of Future Directions," *Emerging Infectious Diseases* 2 (1996): 85–92; P. E. R. Dale and others, "An Overview of Remote Sensing and GIS for Surveillance of Mosquito Vector Habitats and Risk Assessment," *Journal of Vector Ecology* 23 (1998): 54–61; Andrew Lovett and others, "Improving Health Needs Assessment Using Patient Register Information in a GIS," in *GIS and Health,* ed. Anthony G. Gatrell and Markku Löytönen (London: Taylor and Francis, 1998), 191–203; Thomas J. McGinn, 3rd, Peter Cowen, and David W. Wray, "Geographic Information Systems for Animal Health Management and Disease Control," *Journal of the American Veterinary Medicine Association* 209 (1996): 1917–21; Thomas B. Richards, Charles M. Croner, and Lloyd F. Novick, "Atlas of State and Local Geographic Information Systems (GIS) Maps to Improve Community Health," *Journal of Public Health Management and Practice* 5 (March 1999): 2–8; Gerard Rushton, Gregory Elmes, and Robert McMaster, "Considerations for Improving Geographic Information System Research in Public Health," *URISA Journal* 12 (spring 2000): 31–49; Robert K. Washino and Byron L. Wood, "Application of Remote Sensing to Arthropod Vector Surveillance and Control," *American Journal of Tropical Medicine and Hygiene* 50, supplement (1994): 134–44; and Paul Wilkinson and others, "GIS in Public Health," in *GIS and Health,* ed. Anthony G. Gatrell and Markku Löytönen (London: Taylor and Francis, 1998), 179–89.

Notes

155 . . . Snow made his famous dot map . . . : Howard Brody and others, "Map-Making and Myth-Making in Broad Street: The London Cholera Epidemic, 1954," *Lancet* 356 (2000): 64–68. Also see John Snow, *On the Mode of Communication of Cholera*, 2nd ed. (London: Churchill, 1855).

155 Even so, his pin map . . . : For an example, see Laura Lang, *GIS for Health Organizations* (Redlands, Calif.: ESRI Press, 2000), 13–15. In addition to a picture of Snow and a facsimile of his original map, Lang includes a map of Snow's 1854 data as plotted with a contemporary GIS. For a much earlier disease map, see Frank A. Barrett, "Finke's 1792 Map of Human Diseases: The First World Disease Map?" *Social Science and Medicine* 50 (2000): 915–21.

155 Moreover, contemporary investigators . . . : Kari S. McLeod, "Our Sense of Snow: The Myth of John Snow in Medical Geography," *Social Science and Medicine* 50 (2000): 923–35.

156 "geographic patterns of cancer . . . ": Thomas J. Mason and others, *Atlas of Cancer Mortality for U.S. Counties, 1950–1969*, Department of Health, Education and Welfare publication no. (NIH) 75–780 (Washington, D.C., 1975), v.

156 "perhaps the greatest value of the maps . . . ": Ibid.

156 "previously unnoticed clusters . . . ": Linda Williams Pickle and others, *Atlas of United States Mortality*, Department of Health and Human Services publication no. (PHS) 97–1015 (Hyattsville, Md., 1996), 1.

156 the "field studies" cited . . . : William J. Blot and others, "Lung Cancer after Employment in Shipyards during World War II," *New England Journal of Medicine* 299 (1978): 620–24; and Deborah M. Winn and others, "Snuff Dipping and Oral Cancer among Women in the Southern United States," *New England Journal of Medicine* 304 (1981): 745–49.

156 "generate[ed] etiological hypotheses": Pickle and others, *Atlas of United States Mortality*, 1.

156 Sources of information on the Onondaga County Breast Cancer Mapping Project include Sue Weibezahl, "Cancer Survey Will Be Largest in Nation," *Syracuse Herald Journal*, February 19, 1999; and Nicholas J. Pirro, Memorandum to members of the Onondaga County Legislature Onondaga County, New York, Press Releases, September 15, 1999, http://www3.co.onondaga.ny.us/Press/press.releases/budmess.html.

156 Although our county executive . . . : Nicholas J. Pirro, "County Executive Pirro Delivers His 2000 State of the County Message," Onondaga County, New York, Press Releases, March 6, 2000, http://www3.co.onondaga.ny.us/Press/press.releases/2000306.html.

157 . . . ZIP code-level breast cancer map . . . : See Richard Perez-Pina, "Breast Cancer Is Pinpointed by ZIP Code," *New York Times*, April 12, 2000; and New York State Department of Health, New York State Cancer Surveil-

lance Improvement Initiative, http://www.health.state.ny.us/nysdoh/
cancer/csii/main.htm.

157 . . . a disease especially common . . . : Martin Kulldorff and others, "Breast
Cancer Clusters in the Northeast United States: A Geographic Analysis,"
American Journal of Epidemiology 146 (1997): 161–70.

157 "don't really identify cancer clusters . . . ": Quoted in Perez-Pina, "Breast
Cancer Is Pinpointed."

157 "it's a sin to have . . . " and "it's a first step . . . ": Quoted in Dan Fagin,
"Reading the Maps: State Tracks Breast Cancer but Warns Causes Still
Elusive," *New York Newsday*, April 12, 2000.

157 While relatively detailed maps . . . : See, for example, Steven D. Stellman
and others, "Breast Cancer Risk in Relation to Adipose Concentrations of
Organochlorine Pesticides and Polychlorinated Biphenyls in Long Island,
New York," *Cancer Epidemiology, Biomarkers, and Prevention* 9 (2000):
1241–50. For reactions of breast cancer activists to the Stellman study, see
John Rather, "Breast Cancer Groups Question New Study," *New York
Times*, December 3, 2000, Long Island edition.

158 "although the finding of no spatial clustering . . . ": Linda M. Timander
and Sara McLafferty, "Breast Cancer in West Islip, NY: A Spatial Clustering Analysis with Covariates," *Social Science and Medicine* 46 (1998):
1623–35; quotation on 1634.

159 A "map hacker" could . . . : Marc P. Armstrong and Amy J. Ruggles, "Map
Hacking: On the Use of Inverse Address-Matching to Discover Individual
Identities from Point-Mapped Information Sources" (paper presented at
the Geographic Information and Society Conference, University of Minnesota—Twin Cities, June 20–22, 1999, sponsored by the National Center for Geographic Information and Analysis), http://www.socsci.umn
.edu/~bongman/gisoc99/new/armstrong.htm.

159 Researchers can protect privacy . . . : Marc P. Armstrong, Gerard Rushton,
and Dale L. Zimmerman, "Geographically Masking Health Data to Preserve Confidentiality," *Statistics in Medicine* 18 (1999): 497–525.

159 For an overview of West Nile virus and its spread in the northeastern
United States, see Martin Enserink, "The Enigma of West Nile," *Science*
290 (2000): 1482–84. Also see "Guidelines for the Surveillance, Prevention, and Control of West Nile Virus Infection—United States," *Morbidity
and Mortality Weekly Report* 49 (January 21, 2000): 25–28.

160 Clusters of child pedestrian accidents . . . : Mary Braddock and others,
"Using a Geographic Information System to Understand Child Pedestrian Injury," *American Journal of Public Health* 84 (1994): 1158–61.

160 The researchers validated the map . . . : Gregory E. Glass and others, "Environmental Risk Factors for Lyme Disease Identified with Geographic Information Systems," *American Journal of Public Health* 85 (1995): 944–48.

160 . . . a GIS-based model for high-risk areas . . . : Ellen K. Cromley and oth-

ers, "Residential Setting as a Risk Factor for Lyme Disease in a Hyperendemic Region," *American Journal of Epidemiology* 147 (1998): 472–77.

161 "housing quality and maintenance practices": Daniel A. Griffith and others, "A Tale of Two Swaths: Urban Childhood Blood-Lead Levels across Syracuse, New York," *Annals of the Association of American Geographers* 88 (1998): 640–65; quotations on 661.

161 ... "right-to-know" laws: Despite the legislated openness, for some data you might need to file a Freedom of Information Act (FOIA) request or join a volunteer fire department.

162 ... a computer model of local aquifers: For examples, see Mark Monmonier, *Cartographies of Danger: Mapping Hazards in America* (Chicago: University of Chicago Press, 1997), 127–47.

162 For a concise overview of public participation GIS, see Nancy J. Obermeyer, "The Evolution of Public Participation GIS," *Cartography and Geographic Information Systems* 25 (1998): 65–66.

162 For an examination of the need for partnerships in PPGIS, see Trevor Harris and Daniel Weiner, "Empowerment, Marginalization, and 'Community-integrated' GIS," *Cartography and Geographic Information Systems* 25 (1998): 67–76.

162 Community Mapping Assistance Project: See the project's Web site (www.cmap.nypirg.org); and Melissa P. McNamara, "Project Gives Small Nonprofit Groups a Big-Time Mapping Tool," *New York Times,* July 20, 2000.

163 ... thyroid cancer in eastern Washington: William D. Henriques and Robert F. Spengler, "Locations around the Hanford Nuclear Facility Where Average Milk Consumption by Children in 1945 Would Have Resulted in an Estimated Median Iodine-131 Dose to the Thyroid of 10 Rad or Higher, Washington," *Journal of Public Health Management and Practice* 5 (March 1999): 35–36. Also see Washington Department of Health Individual Dose Assessment, "Hanford IDA Questions and Answers" http://www.doh.wa.gov/ida/q&a.htm.

164 In North Dakota, for example . . . : Leona Kuntz and Alana Knudson-Buresh, "Adequate Prenatal Care Rates in North Dakota, 1991–1995," *Journal of Public Health Management and Practice* 5 (March 1999): 23–24.

164 For Hillsborough County, Florida . . . : Jason Devine, William K. Gallo, and Henry T. Janowski, "Identifying Predicted Immunization 'Pockets of Need,' Hillsborough County, Florida, 1996–1997," *Journal of Public Health Management and Practice* 5 (March 1999): 15–16.

164 In DeKalb County, Georgia . . . : Michael Y. Rogers, "Using Marketing Information to Focus Smoking Cessation Programs on Specific Census Block Groups along the Buford Highway Corridor, DeKalb County, Georgia, 1996," *Journal of Public Health Management and Practice* 5 (March 1999): 55–57.

164 ... on a North Carolina military base . . . : Kelly T. McKee, Jr., "Application

of a Geographic Information System to the Tracking and Control of an Outbreak of Shigellosis," *Clinical Infectious Diseases* 31 (2000): 728–33.

165 And when an epizootic starts spreading rapidly . . . : For an example of a GIS designed to combat epidemics in animals, see Robert L. Sanson, Roger S. Morris, and Mark W. Stern, "EpiMAN-FMD: A Decision Support System for Managing Epidemics of Vesicular Disease," *Revu scientifique et technique* (International Office of Epizootics) 18 (1999): 593–605.

165 "The classic case was the burying . . . ": Quoted in Chris Partridge, "How Computers Can Help to Beat Foot-and-Mouth," *Times* (London), June 21, 2001.

166 For a concise overview of the Rajneeshee salmonella attack, see Steven M. Block, "The Growing Threat of Biological Weapons," *American Scientist* 89 (2001): 28–37. Also see Charles Marwick, "Scary Scenarios Spark Action at Bioterrorism Symposium," *Journal of the American Medical Association* 281 (1999): 1071–73.

167 "the poor man's atom bomb": Quoted in an Associated Press story published in New York's *Newsday,* August 15, 1998.

167 Also vulnerable is the nation's food supply . . . : Cheryl Pellerin, "The Next Target of Bioterrorism: Your Food," *Environmental Health Perspectives* 108 (2000): A126–29.

167 Average incubation periods for smallpox and anthrax are from Johns Hopkins Center for Civilian Biodefense Strategies agent fact sheets, http://www.hopkins-biodefense.org/pages/agents/agent.html.

167 But the two postal workers . . . : Johns Hopkins Bloomberg School of Public Health, "Researchers Examine Deaths of Two Postal Workers from Inhalational Anthrax," http://www.jhsph.edu/pubaffairs/press/postal_workers.htm.

167 . . . a long-term economic burden . . . : Arnold F. Kaufmann, Martin I. Meltzer, and George P. Schmid, "The Economic Impact of a Bioterrorist Attack: Are Prevention and Postattack Intervention Programs Justifiable?" *Emerging Infectious Diseases* 3 (April—June 1997): 83–94.

167 "whether the source is bioterrorism . . . ": Donald A. Henderson, "A New Strategy for Fighting Biological Terrorism," *The National Academies in Focus* 1 (spring 2001): 20–21.

Epilogue. Locational Privacy as a Basic Right

Notes

170 A suitably odious villain . . . : See Catherine Greenman, "The Car Snitched. He Sued," *New York Times,* June 28, 2001; and Paul Zielbauer, "Agency Protests Company's Fines on Speeders," *New York Times,* July 5, 2001.

170   . . . hired private firms like Lockheed-Martin . . . : Molly Ball, "Police Tout Success of Red-Light Cameras," *Washington Post,* August 9, 2001, Howard extra; and Dana Wilkie, "Red-Light Cameras Debated," *San Diego Union-Tribune,* August 1, 2001.

171   Image analysis software . . . : Andy Newman, "Those Dimples May Be Digits," *New York Times,* May 3, 2001. The first serious controversy in the United States arose in Tampa, Florida. See Dana Canedy, "Tampa Scans the Faces in Its Crowds for Criminals," *New York Times,* July 4, 2001; and Miki Meek, "You Can't Hide Those Lying Eyes in Tampa," *U.S. News and World Report* 131 (August 6, 2001): 20.

171   For an example of unintended consequences of red-light cameras, see the Protector antiphoto license plate cover offered by Jammers Store.com, http://www.jammersstore.com/anti_photo.htm.

172   "the right to be let alone": The phrase appears on the first page of a seminal article by Brandeis and a coauthor, who later repeat the wording inside quotation marks and attribute the last four words to a "Judge Cooley," cited as "*Cooley on Torts,* 2d ed., p. 29." See Samuel Warren and Louis D. Brandeis, "The Right to Privacy," *Harvard Law Review* 4 (1890): 193–220; quotation on 193 and 195.

172   For an assessment of the Gramm-Leach-Bliley Financial Services Modernization Act of 1999, see John Schwartz, "Privacy Policy Notices Are Called Too Common and Too Confusing," *New York Times,* May 7, 2001.

172   For discussion of cavalier disclosure of credit reports and medical records, see Simpson Garfinkle, *Database Nation: The Death of Privacy in the 21st Century* (Sebastopol, Cal.: O'Reilly, 2000), 21–29, 125–53.

172   "the next best thing": Erik Larson, *The Naked Consumer: How Our Private Lives Become Public Commodities* (New York: Henry Holt, 1992), 53–54; quotation on 53.

173   For a promising example of guidelines addressing maps and locational privacy, see Julie Wartell and J. Thomas McEwen, *Privacy in the Information Age: A Guide for Sharing Crime Maps and Spatial Data,* report no. NCJ-188739 (Washington, D.C.: National Institute of Justice, 2001).

Index

in, 74; lead time, 77–78, 81, 83–88; reliability, 81; storm size as a factor in, 73–75, 81, 86; by storm track, 74–75
Web sites: address mapping, 4–5; community notification of sex offenders, 7, 125–32; community policing, 123–24; health and mortality data, 157, 165; lifestyle segmentation, 142; New York Civil Liberties Union, 114–15; property assessment, 7–8, 173–74; satellite position, 34; traffic flow, 103–5; of vendors, 118, 136; wildland fire support, 70–71
Welch, Roy, 50
West Islip Breast Cancer Coalition, 157–59
West Nile Virus, geographic analysis of, 159–60, 167
Wildland fire: firebrands, 62, 70; fuel maps, 60; fuel models, 60–63, 70; fire-spread models, 61–64; ignition

by lightning, 59; prescribed, 57, 63–64, 72; retrospective models, 65; risk maps, 59–60, 70–71; suppression as a national policy, 71–72; terrain effects, 62–63
Wind Profilers, 87–90, 203
Wire loop detectors, 97
Wireless telephony: dead zones, 216; integration with GPS, 15–16, 174–75; 911 service, 138–39, 176
World Trade Center, 2, 112, 114, 171
World War I, use of aerial reconnaissance during, 18

ZCTAs (ZIP Code Tabulation Areas), 150
ZIP codes: relation to census data, 147–51, 220; in marketing, 142–51; in medical geography, 157; and self-identity, 153; for searching sex-offender databases, 130